Disc
B.C. 48 230

Body of Christ—The Secret of the Essenes And Other Marvelous Tales

232.9
Ricc

Body of Christ—The Secret of the Essenes And Other Marvelous Tales

Dominick Ricca

Copyright © 2010 by Dominick Ricca.

Library of Congress Control Number: 2010908532
ISBN: Hardcover   978-1-4535-1981-3
               Softcover   978-1-4535-1980-6
               Ebook   978-1-4535-1982-0

All rights reserved. No part of this book may be reproduced or transmitted in any form or by any means, electronic or mechanical, including photocopying, recording, or by any information storage and retrieval system, without permission in writing from the copyright owner.

This is a work of fiction. Names, characters, places and incidents either are the product of the author's imagination or are used fictitiously, and any resemblance to any actual persons, living or dead, events, or locales is entirely coincidental.

This book was printed in the United States of America.

To order additional copies of this book, contact:
Xlibris Corporation
1-888-795-4274
www.Xlibris.com
Orders@Xlibris.com
81909

Dedication:

For Frank and Connie Capodicasa with affection

Body Of Christ—The Secret Of The Essenes

1

Professor Julian Apply stood at the lectern on the platform in front of a large assembly of scholars in the lecture hall of Wrightwell, a Christian fundamentalist college in South Carolina. The young professor had been surprised and mystified when he received the invitation to lecture at this conservative institution. He knew that he would be in the enemy camp and that he would be facing a hostile audience. So why the invitation? Julian wondered. Could it be that the professors at Wrightwell wanted to know what their enemies at Voltaire College were thinking?

They surely had good reason to be wary of that college. Voltaire College was founded by Angus Renshaw, a wealthy industrialist, some seventy-five years ago. Mr. Renshaw himself had written the charter of the college. It began with the words "The primary reason for the existence of this college and its mission will be to turn out men and women who are freethinkers, who have no affiliation with any religion, who are skeptical of all so-called religious truths, and above all will be sworn enemies of all and any kind of religious cult. Organized religion is the bane of civilization. As that great thinker and compassionate man Voltaire said repeatedly in letters to his friends, 'Crush the infamy!' His goal in life was to liberate humanity from the cruel oppression and deluding thralldom of religion and priestcraft. We must continue that noble man's crusade against the foulest tyranny this world has ever seen. Crush the infamy!"

Julian had come to this symposium on religion prepared to give a two-hour lecture. And he was going to speak frankly. He was not going to let this audience of conservative religious scholars disconcert or faze him. He was strongly fortified by the strong anti-religious zeal he had absorbed at Voltaire College.

Julian had been at that college eleven years, seven as an assistant professor and four years as a fully tenured professor. Only a year ago he had been appointed head of the Bibilical Studies department. Julian was fluent in Latin, Greek (ancient) Hebrew, Italian, French and German. He was thirty-six years old and unmarried.

In the last eight years Julian had published five books, all displaying impeccable scholarship. The last two books were sensational best-sellers and highly controversial. The title of the first one was "There Is No Such Thing as Divine Revelation." The sequel and companion volume was "All Religious Beliefs Are the Inventions of Man's Brain Cells."

Even before Julian began to deliver his lecture, the title of it alone caused a restless stirring in his audience.

"Ladies and Gentlemen," he began, "the title of my lecture is 'Christ the Jew Died and Stayed Dead.'"

All during the long lecture Julian was fully aware of the hundreds of glowering faces staring up at him. In many of those faces he saw positive ferocious hatred. One woman hissed venomously, "You damned atheist! You should be hanged!" A few times there were shouts of "Anti-Christian bigot!"

But Julian went bravely on in spite of the distractions. He was finishing his lecture with the words "Jesus never walked out of that tomb and he never—" when he was interrupted by a man in the front row who jumped up from his seat and shouted angrily at Julian, "Jesus Christ, our Lord and Savior, rose from the dead and ascended up to heaven!"

"I respectfully disagree," Julian said, smiling.

"Okay, Mr. godless, irreligious smarty-pants, if Jesus didn't rise from and dead and ascended up to heaven—where is his body? What happened to it? Let's see you answer that question!"

Julian was stunned into silence by the taunting question. The smile vanished from his face. It froze in shock and consternation. He stared dumbly at the man, seeming to see him for the first time.

He was tall, heavyset, with a long white beard. When he got up from his seat with his angry outburst, he had shot daggers at Julian with his eyes. And he was bursting with a furious rage, his beard seeming to quiver.

Now, looking at Julian, who remained speechless, his mouth open, thoroughly discomfited, the man was relaxed, calm, smiling, complacently brushing down his beard, enjoying his triumph.

"Well, you intellectual heir of Voltaire, aren't you going to answer me?" the man said. "Cat got your tongue? Once again I ask you, if Jesus did not rise from the dead and went up to heaven, what became of his body?"

Julian had no answer.

The men and women in the hall suddenly got to their feet clapping, cheering and chanting together, "What became of the body? What became of the body? What became of the body?"

Julian walked glumbly off the platform, feeling embarrassed, humiliated. He was thinking of all the books on the life of Jesus he had read, most of them casting doubt on his resurrection. And he agreed with them.

But . . . what did become of his body, if he didn't . . . ?

In a small room at the back of the platform Susan Monroe, Julian's research assistant was waiting for him. He was annoyed by the pitying expression on her face.

"Julian, don't let those Christian fanatics get you down. They are all gullible fools."

"But, Susan, what did become of his body?"

"It rotted away, like all dead bodies."

"No, that's not answer enough."

"What other answer is there? Or do you want the Christian answer? Is that what you want?"

"No, of course not. Dead men don't walk out of their tombs."

"So, where are we?"

"We unbelievers are nowhere, in limbo, intellectually speaking. The believers have an answer. But what do unbelievers have?"

"How about some lunch?"

"I suppose," Julian said indifferently.

"Do you want to go to a restaurant in town, or to the one in our hotel?"

A bright sparkle appeared in Julian's eyes. "Let's make it the hotel," he said eagerly.

Susan knew what to expect. After lunch they would go up to Julian's room and make love. They had been having intimate relations for three years now, only a few months after Susan came to work at Voltaire as a research specialist in biblical studies.

Twice a week Susan would have dinner in Julian's cottage on campus, and she would sleep over. Julian considered Susan his sex partner, someone with whom he could get rid of his sexual tension quick and fast. With Julian there were no ardent, affectionate preliminaries. He was in and out in a hurry, and was asleep in five minutes. And then one more time before breakfast and then on to his teaching and studies.

It was not the same with Susan, in spite of Julian's hurry-up lovemaking, if you could call it that. Susan did not think of Julian simply as her sex partner. She thought of him as her lover, because she loved Julian.

She was pretty in a plain sort of way, had a pretty good body, which she kept in shape by working out in a health club four times a week.

Two hours later, as they lay in bed, Julian said, "Susan, I'm going to quit working on my book."

"Oh, no, Julian, no," Susan cried in dismay. "You said it was going to be your magnum opus. I can't count how many hours we've spent taking notes on the Higher Criticism of the nineteenth-century German scholars—David Strauss, Bruno Bauer, and all the others."

"I know, I know, we've both worked hard, put in a lot of time."

"You can't drop your major project now. We're already four hundred pages into the book, which you said was going to run to more than a thousand pages. When we started on it you vowed that you would utterly and completely destroy the very foundation of the Christian religion—the resurrection of Jesus."

"Susan, that's just it! I'm a scholar, a scholar! But I couldn't answer that man's question!"

"What became of the body of Christ if . . . ."

"Precisely. I have to have the answer to that question! As a scholar, I can't turn my back on it, walk away from it!"

Susan leaned over and kissed Julian passionately on the lips. They tongued each other for a few minutes. Then, when Susan looked down at Julian and saw no reaction between his legs, she dropped her head back down on the pillow with a sigh.

"Julian, what can you do about it—the question, I mean?" How can you answer it? After all . . . two thousand years ago."

"I'm a scholar, damnit, Susan, a scholar! I can't ignore it!"

"Are you serious?"

"Yes, I am."

"Well, okay, pull yourself together and start acting like a scholar. Find the answer to that question! As you said in your lecture, Jesus stayed dead. But what became of his body? That is, at the time. Julian, find out what happened to the body of Jesus from the time it was placed in that tomb up until the time those women, Mary Magdalene and the rest, came on that sabbath morning to anoint it with spices."

"And how do I do that? Hire private investigators to hunt up clues? It all seems to hopeless and yet . . . ."

"Julian, don't get discouraged. Maybe we can find out what happened to Jesus' body after it disappeared from the tomb. We can't find the body itself, after all this time, but it's possible we can find out how it got out of the tomb. We know it didn't walk out, that's for sure."

"Susan, how I wish, how I wish we could—God, that question is like a drill on my brain! But where do we start, tell me where do we start?"

Suddenly Sudan jumped up and sat on Julian's hairless chest. She was bursting with excitement. She took Julian's face in both her hands and said, "I have it, I have it!"

"And what is it you have?"

"The Jews, Julian, the Jews!"

"What can the Jews do?" he asked, taking Susan's hands away from his face. "How can the Jews help me?"

"Us, Julian, us. I'm in this with you all the way!"

"Okay, tell me how the Jews can help us solve the mystery of the ages for us unbelievers?"

"They were there when Jesus was placed in that sepulcher, don't you see? They were witnesses!"

"Those witnesses are all dead."

"But maybe they passed on something to other Jews, to their descendants, you know. They must know something, the Jews. They were the only ones on the spot when Jesus was crucified, except for the Romans, and they don't count, because the ancient Romans no longer exist, that is they didn't leave any direct descendants, like the Jews."

"Susan, I always thought of you as a levelheaded person, but now I think you've gone off the deep end."

"Julian, didn't you once tell me that thinkers had to think daringly? So, why don't you follow your own advice?"

"Okay, okay, maybe you have a point. Let's look at this problem cooly and objectively."

"Right!"

"But before we go into this further, would you please get off my chest." After Susan did so and sat down cross-legged beside Julian, he continued. "You and I firmly believe that Jesus stayed dead and that his body never left this planet."

"The book that you were working on was going to prove just that positively and indisputably, thereby probably demolishing the Christian religion."

"True, but this way—finding out what became of Jesus' body—will be quicker, and will more certainly finish off the Christian creed. By doing that we will prove that the core belief of the Christians is based on a lie—false history."

"That's it in a nutshell."

"But where do we start?"

"I've already told you—the Jews!"

"Will you please tell me how the Jews are going to help us?"

"Julian, you aren't forgetting the small community of Jews who lived in Jerusalem after Jesus' crucifixion and believed that he was the Messiah who would one day return, liberate the Jews from Roman oppression and set up his heavenly kingdom."

"Of course I haven't forgotten them. The community was led by James, the brother of Jesus. They worshiped in the Temple like all the other Jews, but differed from their fellow Jews only in the belief that Jesus was the Messiah. It's all in Acts, which I have read a dozen times. I suppose you could call those Jews the first Christians. So what about them?"

"The Jews revolted against the Romans thirty years or so after Jesus was executed, didn't they?"

"It was a futile revolt against the powerful Roman legions, ending in bloody disaster for the Jews. What about it?"

"Over the centuries a story has lingered that during the siege of Jerusalem by the Romans under the leadership of Titus, the Jewish Christian community somehow managed to escape from the city and make it to Pella, a village east of the Jordan River. If we could find the descendants of those Jewish Christians, maybe they could tell us something."

Julian laughed in Susan's face and told her that that was all it was, a story, a pious legend. There was absolutely no proof that anyone escaped through the tight Roman siege. And those who did try and were caught were crucified in plain sight for all the Jews behind the walls of Jerusalem to see as a warning.

"So you see, nobody got through the Roman lines and lived," Julian said emphatically.

"Didn't one rabbi sneak out in a coffin?"

"Okay, I forgot about him. One man and his two or three pallbearers, I can believe. But a whole community of men, woman and children? Come on, Susan, get real."

Susan was stumped and showed it on her face.

"Yes," she conceded slowly, "that does seem a bit farfetched. But maybe there was some way . . . ."

"What way, Susan, what way? No, face it, we are up against a stone wall, and we can't get through it. Deadlocked, that's what we are."

Susan frowned, shaking her head, thinking. After a few moments her face brightened hopefully. She smiled and clapped her hands.

"What is it, a brainstorm?"

"Sort of! Let's go to Professor Zorn! He might be able to shed some light on our mystery!"

"Hiram Zorn?" Julian snorted contemptuously. "You can't be serious. That addle-brained old crackpot help us? You got to be joking!"

"Yes, I admit he does act a bit odd at times."

"A bit odd! The absurd, cockamamie books he's written! I don't know how he gets them published."

"But they sell," Susan remarked.

"Sure, the public likes sensationalism. For thirty years now, in six or seven books, he has predicted the imminent, the imminent, mind you, return of Jesus to set up his heavenly kingdom here on this strife-torn earth."

"He's a professor here at Wrightwell," Susan pointed out.

"Of course he teaches at this nutty Christian fundamentalist college. What other college would have a loony like him on its faculty?"

"But you have to admit that Professor Zorn is a learned man."

"Yes, I'll give him that. The man's a walking encyclopedia. I met him once, at a conference of historians. In his presence I felt like an undergraduate."

"He is certainly a man of massive erudition. He has deciphered the cuneiform writings of the Sumerians, Assyrians and Babylonians from thousands of clay tablets. He has written a dozen books on the ancient religions, and on the Jewish and Christian religions. And he has his own translation of the New Testament. It was published last year, and it sold very well."

"But with all his impressive learning he is still just another oddball character who thinks that Jesus will set up his kingdom any day now. But first he has to fly down from heaven, says this mad professor!"

"No, Julian, you have it all wrong," Susan said. "A few years ago I had tea with the professor, and he said something that stunned me."

"And what was it he said that stunned you?"

"I happened to say that I didn't believe that Jesus had come back to life and had ascended up to heaven.

"He smiled owlishly at me in that knowing way he has and said, 'Our Lord and Savior does not have to return to this planet. He is already here, here on this earth. He never left it.' Well, Julian, what have you got to say to that?"

"That's typical Professor Zorn wackiness. The old coot was just sounding off in his usual eccentric way."

"I still think it's worth our time to see him. He lives on campus here at Wrightwell. I wonder why he wasn't at the symposium."

"I know why. I asked one of the professors at Wrightwell about Zorn. He had a stroke a week ago. He spent four days in the hospital and he's back in his house."

"Julian, let's go see him."

"It would be a waste of time."

"Don't you want to find out the answer to the empty tomb?"

"Sure I do, but I don't think Zorn can help us in anyway."

"But there has to be an explanation for that empty tomb!"

"Maybe you're learning toward the Gospel resurrection stories?"

"No, no, Julian. I don't believe anymore than you do that Jesus strolled out of his final resting place. But what do you say to Mary Magdalene's claim that she saw Jesus alive, talked to him?"

"That woman had a twisted, deranged mind. Remember the story about Jesus driving devils out of her? Devil-possession, my foot! Mary was an emotionally disturbed woman, probably a nympho who had a red-hot, frustrated sexual-craving for Jesus, who in his kindness showed great affection for Mary, but being a devout Jew, would not go all the way with her."

"You think Mary imagined meeting Jesus on that sabbath morning?"

"Yes."

"But she must have seen something, somebody."

"Sure she did, in her sex-crazed mind. Her mad sexual desire for Jesus made it impossible to accept his death. And in her unbalanced mind she saw him in the flesh."

"And had a conversation with him too, didn't she?"

"But it was all in her mind! Mary had a sex-inspired vision. If you had been standing beside her on that most famous of all mornings, you would not have seen Jesus because you didn't have Mary's mad love for Jesus. Jesus was alive and in the flesh only in her skull, between her two ears. There's your explanation for Jesus' supposed resurrection."

"And the empty tomb? How about explaining that, Professor Julian Apply."

"You've got me there, Susan. That blasted empty tomb! Where do we go to find the answer to that question?"

"To Professor Hiram Zorn."

"Him again!"

"Why are you afraid to go to him?"

"I'm not afraid. I just don't think that crack-brain can help us, that's all."

"Julian, please, as a personal favor to me, let's go see him."

"But . . . what do we say to him?"

"Ask him that one question that is burning a hole in your head and mine—what became of the body of Jesus Christ?"

"Where does he live on campus?"

"We'll find out from the administration office."

2

A male nurse in a white coat opened the door to Zorn's cottage. "I'm sorry, you can't see the professor," he told Julian and Susan in a firm voice as they stood on the porch.

"Why not?" Julian asked.

"We have to see Professor Zorn on a very important matter," Susan added.

"Impossible. The professor is near death. Two days ago he had a second massive stroke. He was taken to the hospital, but this morning he insisted on being brought home. He wants to die in the same bed where his wife died."

"Uh . . . how is his mind?" Julian said.

"Well, sometimes it wanders, and a few minutes later, it's clear as a bell. Twice he called out to his wife, Jessica. When I left him just now to answer the doorbell, he was in one of his lucid moments. But they don't last long. The doctor left an hour ago. He was amazed that the professor was still alive after those two bad strokes. His physical condition is hopeless. I don't know how much longer he can hang on. Sometimes, when he seems comatose, he murmurs fitfully and with great urgency in his voice, 'I must tell someone about HIM! I must tell someone about HIM! I refuse to die until I have revealed the secret of the ages! Stay away, Death, stay away! I will not go with you until I have spoken to a person who can understand the Secret!' To me it all sounded like a lot of raving gibberish."

"Secret of the ages," Susan said slowly, pondering.

"We have to see Professor Zorn, no matter what his condition!" Julian said, very much excited. "He has a message for us!"

"He cannot see you. He is a dying man."

"We are not budging from here until we have seen Professor Zorn!" Julian shouted at the top of his voice."

"Take us to his bedroom!" Susan demanded.

"I tell you the man is at death's door!"

"We have to see him before he dies!" Julian said.

"You are not entering this house."

"Get out of the way and let us in!" Susan said.

"Yes, Elmo, show them in," a feeble voice said behind the nurse.

He turned around and saw to his amazement Professor Zorn standing with his hand on a side table to give him support. He was wearing striped pyjamas, a rumpled bathrobe, a high cowboy hat and shiny cowboy boots. He was very pale and his hands shook. He could barely stand on his legs.

"For God's sake, professor, what are you doing out of bed!" Elmo said. "Doctor Ellison said that you were not to get out of bed!

Ignoring the nurse, Professor Zorn smiled wanly and said graciously to Julian and Susan, "Enter, my friends, enter. Yes . . . though my brains are a bit scrambled, I do recall meeting both of you, but . . . your names . . . ."

Julian and Susan brushed passed the nurse and gave their names. They stood on each side of the professor, anxiously staring at him, afraid that he might fall down at any minute.

"I'll help you back to your bed," the nurse said.

"You will leave us!" Professor Zorn commanded.

With a disapproving grunt the nurse disappeared down a hall. Professor Zorn led his guests into a small library, just off the living room. It had books from floor to ceiling, a rolltop desk in a corner and in the center of the room a small round table and chairs.

"Sit down, sit down," the professor said.

Julian took a good look at him. How he had aged, he thought. He had to be close to eighty. The last time he saw him was at least ten years ago. He wondered why he had not retired.

Professor Zorn got a bottle and glasses from a shelf, sat down at the table and poured out the liquid.

"You have to drink this brandy very slowly. It's very old brandy. I got it in France many years ago, the last time my wife and I visited that country. We had a marvelous time, how Jessica enjoyed herself. She . . . yes, she was a wonderful wife, wonderful . . . ."

To lighten the mood in the room Julian said, "I like your hat, professor."

"And your boots," Susan said.

"I got them a long time when I spent a summer on a ranch in Montana, about twenty miles from Helena. I . . . remember now . . . we went there on our honeymoon, Jessica and I. Beautiful country, beautiful country. This was no dude rance. It was a working rance. Jessica wanted to get material for a Western she was writing, her first book. She was a novelist, you know. Oh, she was such a loving wife, such a good companion. I had a very happy marriage. But I'm sure you two have not come here to listen to me reminisce about my happy marriage."

"Professor Zorn, I'll get right to the point of our visit," Julian said. He told him about the taunting question hurled at him by the Christian fundamentalist and reminded him about the puzzling remark he had made to Susan about Jesus.

"Yes, Professor, don't you remember? You told me that Jesus had never left this earth, didn't you?"

The old man stiffened and glanced nervously around the room. "Would one of you please close the door. I don't want Elmo to hear what I have to say."

Susan quickly got up and closed the door. Returning to her chair she said eagerly, "So you can help us, professor?"

"I can. But you will have to listen to a long story."

"We have all the time in the world," Julian assured him, just as long as you can help us solve that mystery: What became of the body of Jesus?"

"I'm sure that you two scholars have read Josephus' description of that monastic Jewish sect, the Essenes, in his book 'The Jewish War!"

"Yes, we have," Julian said.

"Those holy men lived celibate lives in their monastic communities far off in the desert, long distances from any town or villages. They followed a very strict regimen, living self-denying, devout lives. I admire them, but as a Jew I must say that those Essenes, with their vow of celibacy, not marrying and raising a family as God commanded us to do, were not acting like true Jews and were not following the traditional Jewish way of life. We have rabbis who combine holiness with marriage and raising a family. There is no conflict with living a holy life and having lawful sexual relations. Sex and marriage can go hand in hand with a deeply religious life. Thus have our wisest Jewish sages taught down through the ages. Sexual pleasure is God's gift to married men and woman. The celibate life is an unnatural life. Such foolish thinking came from the Greeks and from the East with its pessimistic outlook on life. We Jews celebrate life and rejoice in—"

"Pardon me, professor," Julian interrupted, "but what have the Essenes and the Jewish celebration of sex got to do with answering the question—what became of Jesus' body?"

"Patience, patience, I'm coming to that. Hear me out."

"Tell us what made you say that Jesus never left this earth," Susan urged."

"You young people . . . well, I shall try to be as brief as possible."

"Please, professor!" Julian said impatiently.

"Very well. There is a tradition among some Jews that Jesus, before starting on his ministry, spent some months with an Essene community that lived in the desert, fifteen or twenty miles from Jerusalem. Even after he left them, Jesus remained heart and soul an Essene. Occasionally, after he began his preaching career, he returned to this community for a little peace and quiet as a break from the wrangling and disputes in the towns and villages. I don't blame him. How Jews love to disagree among themselves! You might call it the Jewish relious sport! But that's neither here nor there. The important thing is that Jesus was an Essene in spirit!"

Naturally, Julian and Susan were astounded to hear this. Jesus an Essene? they both thought to themselves. There was no hint in the four Gospels that Jesus ever lived with the Essenes. They are not even mentioned in those books. That was what Julian and Susan both were thinking.

"Professor, are you sure about what you are saying?" Julian asked skeptically. "I have written three books on Jesus, and Susan did the research on them, but never have we come across anything about Jesus living with the Essenes."

"Nevertheless I am telling you that he did!" Professor Zorn said with deep conviction.

"What was the exact location of this Essene community where Jesus stayed for some time?" Susan asked.

"Not was—is. The Essene community where Jesus stayed for some months is still there, with those holy men working their farm and waiting for the Glorious Day!"

"What are you talking about?" Julian and Susan asked in amazement.

"They are waiting for the Glorious Day, I tell you!"

"What glorious day?" Julian said.

"Before I answer that question, I want to answer Susan's question. Susan, you asked me for the location of the Essene community where Jesus stayed.

"Where is it?"

"I think I have to correct myself. The community where Jesus spent some time, and which is still thriving, is located some thirty miles southeast of Jerusalem, and seven or eight miles down the western side of the Dead Sea."

Julian and Susan were staring at the old man with bulging eyes. Without thinking, Julian poured himself out some brandy and drank it in one gulp.

"Professor, is this all really true? This is unbelievable!" Susan said.

"There is more to come that you will think is even more unbelievable, I assure you."

"This is all very breathtaking," Julian said, "but I don't see where it's getting us. The body of Jesus, professor, the body of Jesus!"

"I'm now coming to the heart of this Jewish tradition. When the Essenes heard that the Romans had arrested Jesus—"

"How could they?" Susan said. They were living miles away from Jerusalem."

"Once a week they came to Jerusalem to sell their fruits and vegetables and purchase pots and certain farm implements they could not make themselves."

"How did they travel?" Julian said. "On foot?"

"No, they kept a few donkeys for plowing and they used them when they went to Jerusalem with their produce, and to buy the things they needed."

"Okay," Julian said, "Essenes were in the city when Jesus was arrested."

"Any idea how many?" Susan asked.

"That I can't tell you. Who knows? Perhaps three or four."

"What comes next?" Julian said.

"These Essenes were present at the trial of Jesus and they witnessed his death on the cross, a Roman method of execution, I wish to remind you. The four Gospels are grossly unfair to the Jews in their description of the trial of Jesus, and the reason for so much anti-Semitism in the world. The Messiah was tried by the Romans and brutally crucified by them."

"Yes, yes, professor, I agree with you there. But what about the Essenes? Where do they fit in?" Julian said.

"Yes," Susan said, "what do they have to do with explaining about the body of Jesus?"

"The Essenes knew all about Jesus' prediction, or prophecy that even if he was killed he would rise from the dead . . . given time."

"And so?" Julian asked, staring hard at Professor Zorn.

"And so when the body of Jesus was placed in that tomb, the Essenes were watching all the time. Late that night they returned with wineskins. The wine had been doped up. In a very short time they had the tomb guards drunk and out cold on that drugged wine. With the help of the donkeys and strong ropes, they were able to roll back the heavy rock from the entrance to the tomb. Once inside they quickly picked up Jesus' body and placed it reverently on one of the donkeys and carried it back to their community by the Dead Sea. They have maintained a vigil over it for almost two thousand years."

"How could they?" Susan objected. "The body must have rotted and turned to dust by now."

"By some secret formula they concocted from the plants they grow, they have been able to preserve the body, prevent any decay at all."

"Are you telling us that? . . ." Julian could not finish the sentence, so astonished he was.

"Yes, the body of Jesus, the Jewish Messiah, as the Essenes believe him to be, and not the Savior and Redeemer, as the Christians believe, is in a state of perfect preservation. He looks as alive and fresh as when he worked as a carpenter in Nazareth, as when he preached his message up and down the length and breath of old Palestine, and when he had that last supper of the paschal lamb with his disciples in the upper room."

Julian had recovered from his momentary astonishment. Reality had returned to him. "Professor, how do you know all this is true, and isn't a lot of holy rubbish?"

"Because I saw it."

"You saw the body of Jesus?" Julian and Susan asked together.

"Yes, I saw it, I saw it! With these two eyes! They are old, but I still see pretty clearly with them!"

"When did you see the body?" Susan asked. "How long ago?"

"Three years ago, I took a sabbatical to do research on a book I was writing on modern Israel. So I gave as my reason to Wrightwell. But that was not my real purpose. I went to Israel to find out if there was any truth to the story, tradition, whatever you want to call it, about the Essenes spiriting away the body of Jesus and what had become of it. Three days after I got to Israel I rented a car and set out to find the Essene community. When I got to the farm, after having some difficulty in finding it, I told their superior or leader that I had come there to join their community. I had to. They were very suspicious of me. They hate any kind of publicity like the plague. They must have taken me for some snoopy reporter. I told them that I was fed up with the modern world and would remain with them until I died."

"And did the Essenes believe this yarn?" Julian asked.

"For the first couple of months they were not so sure about my sincerity. They kept a close watch on me. But when I was with them for about six or seven months, working hard on the farm, doing all the jobs assigned to me to their satisfaction, even to cleaning the latrines, they relaxed their vigilance over me and accepted me as a person who truly wanted to live the life of an Essene. I went through a ritual ceremony of baptism in a small pool in their house of worship. After this initiation ritual I was taught the central doctrines of their creed—that the Kingdom of Heaven would be established on this earth when Jesus returned to life. With Jesus as the royal ruler of the world, and the Essenes as his ministers, the long-hoped for heaven on earth would be finally set up on this planet, with Jerusalem as the capital.

"Didn't you point out, professor, that the Christian belief is that Jesus came back to life and flew up to heaven?" Susan said.

"Yes, but they informed me that the Gospel writers, Matthew, Mark, Luke and John, fabricated that story, that it was false history. It was just a lot of pious hooey, hokum! That's when they confirmed the story from tradition how they had taken the body of Jesus out of that tomb after stupefying the guards with the drugged wine. Jesus never came back to life!"

"You are telling us that Jesus is still here, on this earth?" Julian said.

"And still dead?" Susan said.

"Yes, to both questions."

"Tell us about the time you actually saw the body of Jesus."

"One night, when I was with the Essenes almost a year, the leader of the Essenes, along with two other Essenes, took me down to the small crypt under their house of worship through a trapdoor over which was a carpet."

"This was it?" Julian asked excitedly. "They were going to show you the body of—"

"Julian, please don't interrupt me."

"Go on, professor, go on!" Susan said eagerly.

"With the two Essenes carrying flaming torches and the superior leading the way, we descended a long flight of stairs. We walked down a tunnel that was at least a hundred yards long. The rough walls were of solid stone, the ground underfoot was soft earth. With our shadows moving weirdly along beside us on the walls, and the three men maintaining a grim silence, let me tell you I began to worry and sweat. A chill ran up and down my spine. Were they going to murder me? I wondered, with my blood running cold.

"But these were holy men," Julian said. "How could you think they would kill you?"

"So-called holy men have burned thousands of men and women at the stake for the love of God," Professor Zorn said sadly.

"What happened when you came to the end of the tunnel?" Susan asked.

"We entered a chamber. In the ceiling an oil lamp was burning over a plain wooden box. It was less than six feet long and three feet wide. It rested on a low platform. The three Essenes went up to the box, bowed their heads and began to chant softly in Hebrew."

"With your knowledge of Hebrew you understood what they were saying, of course," Julian commented.

"Yes... but with a great deal of difficulty. You see, they were chanting and praying in ancient Hebrew, not in modern Hebrew."

"But you did grasp what they were saying." Susan said.

"Yes.... They kept repeating 'We await your glorious resurrection, Messiah. We know that you will establish your heavenly kingdom on earth, with your capital in Jerusalem and we Essenes as your counselors and chief ministers. Make it soon, Rabboni, make it soon!'"

"Those were the words they chanted?" Julian said.

"Yes, as well as I could understand them."

"And then what happened?" Susan said.

"Then the superior whispered something to the two other Essenes, and they very slowly and carefully removed the lid from the box. And then the superior motioned for me to step up to the platform.

"I did so and gazed down into the box and saw a man who was between thirty and thirty-five years old."

"Wh—what did he look like?" Susan asked, her voice hushed.

"He was not tall, say five feet six, seven. He had a sheet over him, but his feet were showing. He was wearing worn leather sandals. His clasped hands rested on his belly. They were the callused hands of a workman. And I saw marks on his wrists."

"His face," Julian said, "his face!"

"His hair was long down to his shoulders. The skin color was good, natural. The nose was slightly beaked, the lips full and his short beard had a reddish tint."

Behold the Messiah! the superior declared solemnly.

"I turned to look at the Essenes. They had come close up to me and were staring down at the dead man with serene, smiling, loving expressions."

"Did you ask who the dead man was?" Julian said.

"Yes, and when I did one of them said, 'He is Jesus who died on the cross and will one day come back to life!' Looking down at Jesus I almost began to believe those words. He seemed to be sleeping, just sleeping. I think at that moment that if he had opened his eyes and sat up, I would not have been in the least shocked.

"I know what you are thinking," the superior said. "Yes, it will all happen. One day he will come to life and transform the world. There is so much that is bad and wrong in it. We Essenes have never wavered in that belief."

Julian shook his head and grinned. "No, no, professor, all this is crazy. You must have thought that you were in a community of loonies."

"Julian, how can you talk like that? I believe the professor, and I believe those Essenes," Susan said.

"Yes, they impressed me as being supremely sane."

"Professor, tell me what you think. I want a straight answer. Do you believe that the man in that box is Jesus?"

"My answer is that the man in that box is the Jew that was condemned to death by Pontius Pilate."

"And what about the Essenes' belief that Jesus will come back to life and set up his righteous kingdom to replace this world of injustice, war, hate, disease and death?" Julian demanded.

"I am no prophet . . . but the Jew in me says . . . maybe . . . ."

"And the ex-Catholic in me says it's all a lot of bunk!"

"You are wrong, Julian!" shouted Zorn with great passion. "It could happen! God could make it happen—" Suddenly, the old man pressed his hand to his heart and stared at Julian, open-mouthed, gasping for air. His head dropped to the table.

"Nurse, nurse!" Susan said, running to the door and opening it.

Elmo ran into the room, picked up the professor and laid him on the table. He felt his pulse.

"It looks like he's had a heart attack," Julian said.

"Should we call for an ambulance?" Susan said.

Elmo let go of the professor's hand. "It's too late for an ambulance. Professor Zorn is dead."

3

A week later, Julian and Susan were back in Voltaire College. They were having martinis in Julian's cottage before going out to dinner.

"Julian, you've been wool-gathering since I got here a half hour ago. What's on your mind?"

"Susan, I've been thinking."

"About Professor Zorn's story, of course."

"You know what a stickler I am for research."

"I should, I'm the one that does most of it for you."

"Yes, that's true."

"Julian, what're you getting at?"

"Susan, you and I are going to Israel!"

"We are?"

"Yes! We are going to get into the Essene community and somehow swipe that body! I'm going to bring it here to Voltaire, hold a TV press conference and reveal to the Christians all over the world that they have been worshiping as the son of God a cadaver! I'm going to put to an end once and for all to this Christian nonsense that has lasted two thousand years!"

"But what about our jobs here at Voltaire?"

"I've got some influence with the president. My best-selling books got this college a lot of publicity, which meant more students coming here, which meant more money for Voltaire. I'm sure I can get a month's leave of absence for us."

"But, Julian, how are we going to get into the Essene community. And how are we going to sneak off with that wooden box?"

"All this week I've been thinking of nothing else. I have it all figured out. I'll fill you in when we get to Jerusalem."

"This is beginning to look like a very exciting adventure!"

"If we can pull this off, my life's work will be complete—proving that Christianity is a sham religion. And I'll be able to answer that Christian fundamentalist's question: What became of the body of Jesus? Jesus never came back to life! He's still dead, and he's going to stay dead!"

"Uh . . . Julian, after dinner are we coming back here?"

"Yes! I feel like I'm going to explode! Susan, be prepared for a long, sleepless night of sex!"

"How about love?"

"I'll call a travel agent first thing tomorrow morning!"

4

Julian revealed his plan to Susan the evening they arrived in Jerusalem and checked into the Atlas Hotel. It was over dinner he told her how they were going to get into the Essene community.

"First, we have to rent a pickup truck."

"And just drive up to where the Essenes live?"

"No, the truck is to get us close to the community and to transport the box back here to Jerusalem."

"But, Julian, how do we get the Essenes to take us in and give us the opportunity to get at the box?"

"Stop your fretting. The Essenes are good men. They will not drive away two men who are dizzy with the heat, lost, exhausted and dying of thirst. We will be dressed in shorts, sleeveless shirts, and we will be carrying backpacks and canteens, empty canteens."

"Uh, Julian, you said two men . . . ."

"Right. Tomorrow you have to get a crewcut."

"A crewcut, me?"

"Yes," Julian said, looking her over. "For once I'm glad that you don't have big breasts.

"Okay, I get my hair close cropped. But what do we do with the truck?"

"Susan, it's all very simple. We drive down to within a few hundred yards of the Essenes community and leave the truck among some rocks. Then we walking around under that blazing sun and in that scorching heat for about an hour. And then we stagger up to the Essenes."

It was getting on toward twilight. A bright moon shone in the star-filled sky. An elderly Essene in a light-colored robe was watering a row of cabbages with a bucket. When it was empty, he walked down to the end of the row to the long trough to refill it.

A movement a few hundred feet away caught his eye. Placing the bucket on the edge of the trough, he peered out into the semidarkness of the desert. He saw two figures moving slowly toward him.

The Essene did not move. When the figures were a hundred feet from him one of them shouted in a weak, desperate voice, "Help us! For God's sake, help us! Water, water!"

Both of them were holding on to each other. They staggered forward fifty more feet and then collapsed. The old man ran over to them. They were soaked with sweat. Their lips were caked with sand, their eyes bulged out of their sockets.

"Water, water!" one of them cried.

The Essene ran back to the trough, filled the bucket and brought it to them. He watched as they drank thirstily. The water revived them.

"Where are we?" Julian said, getting up and helping Susan to her feet.

"This is an Essene community. You must waiting here. I have to inform the reverend superior."

A half hour later, after a quick wash-up, Julian and Susan were eating a meal of lentil soup, vegetables and dates. Five Essenes stood behind them. Sitting at the table across from them was a gray-haired man of about fifty. He had a gaunt face and a short beard, like the other Essenes. He was watching these two strangers intently.

When he saw that they were finished eating he said, "My name is Baruch. I am the leader of this community. Now, you say you got lost in the desert wilderness?"

"Yes, I'm a geologist. I teach at a college in America. My . . . research assistant and I started from Jerusalem three days ago. We had enough food for a couple of days, but foolishly didn't bring enough water. We had not counted on this heat. When we ran out of water we became disoriented and got lost. No food, no water. We were giving up all hope when we saw your buildings."

"You were very lucky that you did. We have found in the desert the bones of a few tourists who got lost and . . . ."

"I think we should introduce ourselves. My name is Julian Smith."

"And I'm Mike Jones," Susan said, in a husky voice.

Baruch nodded but said nothing.

"Uh . . . is this a Christian community of monks?" Julian asked.

"Why do you think that?"

"Well . . . aren't you men monks?"

"No, we are not Christians!" Baruch said, offended by the question. We are Jews! Essenes!"

"There are still Essenes in Palestine . . . Israel? I read in a book that the Romans killed them all in the Jewish revolt," Julian said.

"Those murderous pagans didn't find this community. Too remote. We survived and have survived these two thousand years. We are waiting for the Messiah to replace this sinful world with a much better one."

"Two thousand years is a long time to waiting," Susan said.

"We have good reason to be patient. And we have faith. But let us get on to something else. You can stay the night, but early tomorrow morning, after breakfast, you must leave. We will give you food and water. And if you feel the need, I will have two men accompany you until you are north of the Dead Sea and on the road to Jerusalem."

"I thank you for your very gracious hospitality and offer of help," Julian said.

"Fine," Baruch said, rising from the table. "And now if you will excuse us, at this time we have an evening service. I'll have you taken to our sick room. It has several beds. You can sleep there.

"Reverend Superior," Julian said, "may we join you in this religious service, or at least attend it?"

"If you wish, certainly," Baruch said, a pleased expression on his face. "Oh, one thing. Do not talking to the men. They would not understand you. I am the only one who speaks English."

Julian and Susan glanced over their shoulders at the silent, bearded men standing behind them in their light-colored robes. Their complexion was swarthy, the skin lined and the eyes blank.

As they went through the main building, with Baruch leading the way, and the Essenes behind them, Julian and Susan carefully studied the layout of their surroundings. After walking down a short corridor, they entered the place of worship. Already in the room there were about thirty Essenes sitting on low stools. They all rose as Baruch entered, followed by Julian, Susan and the other Essenes.

Turning to Julian and Susan Barch said, "Please stay here in the back." Then he went to stand beside a small table on which lay a Bible and which faced the congregation. He read from the Bible in Hebrew for a few minutes, and then preached a short homily, also in Hebrew.

Julian did not understand the ancient Hebrew. But he was too excited to concentrate on what Baruch was saying, anyway. He was staring at the center of the room. It was covered with a thinking, faded carpet.

His voice trembling with emotion he whispered to Susan, "The carpet, see it! The carpet! Just where Professor Zorn said it would be!"

"Let's hope the trapdoor is under it," Susan whispered back.

When the service was over, Baruch came over to his guests and said, "One of the men will show you to your sleeping quarters. Good night."

All the Essenes filed out of the room but one. He beckoned Julian and Susan to follow him. He led them down a long hall, turned a corner, opened a door, and left them.

They entered a room that had five pallets and pillows on the floor. On a small side table a burning oil lamp illuminated the room. The walls were bare. One of them had a narrow window.

Sitting down on one of the pallets Susan said, "Now what do we do?"

Going over to the window, Julian looked out. By the light of the moon he saw long, barren stretches of desert, with here and there big boulders.

He came back and stood over Susan, thinking.

"Well, Julian, what now? We made it into this community—now what?"

"We go for that box!"

"Right away?"

Julian looked down at his wristwatch, holding it toward the oil lamp. "It's now ten forty-five. These guys are farmers, probably getting up at dawn. They should be all asleep in a little while. But just to make sure, we'll waiting until after midnight before we go to work."

"Julian, this crazy adventure has stimulated my libido, excited me!" Susan said, taking off her clothes. When she was naked, she lay down on the pallet, squirming, throwing out her arms to Julian and breathing heavily.

"Boy, if I ever saw a dame that wanted it real bad!"

"Hurry, darling, hurry! Get undressed!"

"Okay, but only once. We have to save our energy for the job ahead. And then we'll take a short nap."

"Whatever you say! Get those clothes off!"

5

Julian raised his head from between Susan's breasts and held his wristwatch up to the oil lamp. It was twenty minutes after three. Susan was sleeping soundly, her breathing regular.

"Wake up, Susan, wake up."

Opening her eyes Susan said sleepily, " . . . Uh . . . you want to make love again?"

"No! The box, Susan, the box! We have work to do! Come on, get up, get your clothes on!"

In two minutes they were creeping silently down the long hall and entered the pitch-dark room where the religious service had been held.

Julian took out of his shorts pocket a small flashlight. Flicking it on, he moved down the center of the room, Susan following him. He pulled the carpet aside.

"The trapdoor!" Susan said.

"Quiet!" Julian hissed.

He lifted the trapdoor, which was on rope hinges, and led the way down the steep stairs, holding his flashlight in front of him, with Susan's hand on his shoulder. They descended about fifty feet.

When they got to the bottom, Julian played his flashlight on the stone walls and the dirt floor of the tunnel. The air was damp.

Still holding his light in front of him, Julian led the way down the dark tunnel. After they had walked a few minutes they saw a light in the distance.

"The oil lamp over the box!" Julian exclaimed, speeding up his pace, Susan hurrying along beside him.

In another minute they were in the small chapel-like room, staring in silent awe and wonder at the box that contained the body of the Jewish

Messiah to the Essenes, and to the Christians, Jesus Christ, the Lord and Savior of the world who had died on the cross to save humanity.

Shaking off the stark emotion that had gripped him, in spite of himself, Julian said, "Susan is it true, really true?"

"That in that box is the body of Jesus of Nazareth?"

"Yes. Or have we gone on a bizarre, wild goose chase?"

Susan moved closer and looked down at the lid on the box. For answer, she pointed to it and said, "Read those words. Your knowledge of Hebrew should help you."

Looking down Julian read out loud, very slowly, "Jesus, son of Joseph and Mary, the Messiah who was crucified by the Romans and who will one day overcome death and establish God's Kingdom on earth. Rise, Messiah, rise! We await your glorious resurrection!"

"Well, are you still skeptical?" Susan asked. "Do you think that Professor Zorn was out of his skull?"

"I . . . don't know what to think, Susan. It could be the body of Jesus, but . . . . But the story he said about the Essenes taking Jesus' corpse out of that tomb and bringing it here . . . . I don't know. In America the fantastic story seemed possible. But standing here, now . . . ."

"Julian, we can at least verify one thing Zorn said about the Essenes."

"By viewing the body and seeing if it is perfectly preserved?"

"Exactly. Seeing is believing."

Moving to each end of the box, Julian and Susan lifted the lid and placed it on the ground. And then they returned to the front of the box and looked down into it.

They both grasped, shocked at what they saw. The face had living color in it, no deathly pallor of the dead as they had seen in many coffins. The rough hands, with the red marks in the wrists, rested on the belly, as Professor Zorn had said. The beard was short but scraggly, not trimmed. Julian and Susan were thinking the same thing: Jews wore beards as a sign of piety, not for reasons of vanity. Various scents emanated from the body.

"Those odors must be the drugs that keep the body looking so lifelike, so well preserved," Julian said.

"Professor Zorn was certainly speaking the truth when he said that the man seemed not dead but asleep and about to wake up."

"Yes, it's uncanny how the Essenes have preserved this body."

"Julian, I . . . want to touch the face. Do you think it would be all right?"

"Go ahead."

The instant Susan's fingers touched the check she cried out, "Julian, it's soft! It doesn't feel hard and cold! A long time ago, when my aunt Dorothy died, I kissed her on the forehead before they closed the coffin. It was like kissing a cold stone. Do you think that maybe Jesus will come back to life, as the Essenes believe?"

"Susan, get a grip on yourself. You are Susan, my very capable and very professional research assistant. This corpse is not coming back to life. Like all things that die, it is going to stay dead. That is the immutable law of life and nature."

"Yes," Susan remarked sadly, looking down at the body of Jesus, "he's not ever going to get up from that box."

"Spoken like a true non-believer."

"Okay, what do we do next?"

"What we came here to do. We carry the body and the box to the pickup truck."

"The box too! It must be very heavy."

"No, I don't think so. Look how thinking the sides are, worn down after two thousand years. We have to take the box to show the world the words written on the lid. Experts can confirm its antiquity—all very important when I make my case. God, I can't waiting to hold that press conference, with a dozen TV cameras and a hundred reporters! At last, at last, my dream of destroying Christianity will come true! I have here absolute proof that the Christian religion is phony! All those Catholic priests and Protestant ministers will be out of a job and will have to do a day's work like everyone else."

"Julian, you shouldn't be so brutally gleeful."

"Oh, and the Pope and all those cardinals and bishops!" Julian said, ignoring Susan. "They can burn all those gorgeous vestments they wear when they are putting on their razzle-dazzle religious performances. They can all live out their days in a retirement home. Who needs them! Susan, I have succeeded in my life's work! Only months after my press conference with the body of the Jesus for all the world to see, the antiquated, savage, goofy Christian creed will disappear from the face of the earth. And I say good riddance! Now, let's hop to it."

"Julian, we can't carry both the box and the body at the same time. No way."

"I realize that. We will carry them one at a time. First the body and then the box. You take the feet."

It took great effort and a lot of straining and sweat, but in twenty minutes they had the body a hundred yards from the Essene community. They stopped to rest.

"Only a hundred yards to go," Julian said, panting.

Susan had dropped to her knees, also panting and wiping the sweat from her face.

After a couple of minutes Julian said, "Okay, let's get on with it."

They reached the rocks where the pickup was hidden and carefully slid the body in the back of the truck.

"Susan, I think I can carry the box by myself. You don't mind staying here alone with this stiff, do you?"

"No . . . I'll be all right . . . ."

"Are you sure? You never know, Jesus might take just this time to come back to life and set up his wacky heavenly kingdom!"

"Can't you at least show some respect for the dead?"

"What did I say that was so bad?"

"Calling Jesus a stiff."

"That's what all dead persons are—stiffs. Well, I'm off."

Even in the warm desert air Susan felt a sudden chill as she watched Julian disappear into the darkness. They had placed the body feet forward in the truck. By the light of the bright moon, and moving to one side, Susan had a clear view of Jesus' face.

She bent closer, gazing intently at it. There was no doubt in her mind that this cadaver was to Christians the man-God who had come down from heaven to die that atoning, redeeming death on the cross to bring salvation to the human race. More than a billion human beings believed just that. That belief sustained them through their sometimes troubled life, and adversity, and gave them the strength to face death bravely because they knew that Jesus had won a better life for them.

Staring down at the serene face of Jesus, Susan began to experience doubts, qualms, about this enterprise. A force she could not explain tugged at her conscience.

With conflicting emotions, Susan turned away from the body and looked out at the desert, quiet, still, as it had been for thousands and thousands of years.

She loved Julian, but . . . would it be right for him to put on display the body of Jesus for all the world to see and shatter the beliefs and hopes of so many millions of people? No! she answered herself. It would be brutally, viciously cruel! A wicked crime! It would be a crushing blow to Christians, who believed in Jesus as their Lord and Savior. The cemetery would become for them simply a dumping ground where their bodies would rot, and not a place from which their immortal souls would rise to heaven.

Grunting, panting sounds broke in on her thoughts. A few hundred feet away she saw Julian struggling with the box, which he carried on his shoulders. She ran to help him.

By the time she got to him, Julian had dropped to the ground, the box as his side, his mouth open, gasping.

"Julian, are you okay?" Susan asked anxiously."

"I'm . . . okay, okay," Julian said, panting. "Help me get this box on the truck. We have to get out of here. It's after four o'clock . . . those Essenes will be up soon."

6

Twenty minutes later they were on the main highway to Jerusalem. Julian was feeling very good about himself. He was smiling and humming a tune. Susan had not spoken since they got in the truck.

"Why so quiet, Susan? We did it! We did it! I can see the headlines in the paper: BODY OF JESUS DISCOVERED BY NOTED HIStorian! Won't that be something!"

"Yes, it will be," Susan said sadly.

"Say, what's the matter with you? Why are you so down in the dumps? We pull off the biggest find of all time, and you look like you're at a wake."

"I was thinking of those good, pious, gentle Essenes from whom we stole the body of Jesus."

"So what? Didn't they do the same thing two thousand years ago?"

"Julian, try to show some sympathy for them. They were so nice to us, feeding us, giving us shelter, so . . . trusting . . . ."

"Susan, don't be so softhearted. Those men will get over it."

"Get over it! Julian, don't you realize what we have done? We stole more than a body! We stole their belief in their Messiah who would one day come back to life and set up his kingdom of heaven here on this grubby, suffering planet! Julian, we have committed a hateful, heinous crime! We have taken that dream away from them!"

"And that's all is—a dream, a fantasy. I am not ashamed of what we did. We did it in a noble cause—for the sake of historical truth!"

"No matter how many lives it hurts."

"Right! Truth marches on!"

"Like a steamroller over those good men in that community back there in the desert."

"Yes, and that damned dopey Christian religion based on a colossal piece of fiction."

"You are obsessed about destroying that religion."

"No, I want the truth to prevail. It's a creed founded on an eventually that never took place—the resurrection of Jesus. And I have the irrefutable proof, the incontrovertible evidence, in the back of this truck. Christianity—poof!"

"Julian, how can you be so heartless, so cruel to Christians? You will be taking away their reason for living, their hope that there is a life beyond the grave."

"That can't be helped. Nothing must stand in the way of truth, no sappy compassion—nothing! Those Christians must face reality. There is no life after death. We are on a planet revolving in boundless space. Why are we here? For what purpose? Is there a loving god that has some master plan for the universe, for us? Is there life after death? All these so-called profound questions are irrelevant and pointless because they can never be answered. Philosophers have racked their brains over them for centuries, and they all come up with different cockeyed answers. Men and women should be grateful for this great, mysterious gift called life. They should enjoy all the good things it has to offer, like good food, fine wine, the pleasure of reading and doing the kind of work that suits you, and entertainment, regular bowel movements and a good night's sleep."

"Didn't you forget something?"

"Oh, yes, sex!"

"How about love? Like I love you and you love me."

"Oh, that. Susan . . . I've been thinking about it, yes, thinking about that thing . . . ."

"I'm so happy to hear it. You can make me even happier by turning this truck around and returning that body . . . Jesus to the Essenes."

"Not a chance. Truth, like this truck, rolls on. How I'm looking forward to the press conference in Jerusalem! Look, you Christians, look at the rotting, stinking body of your Lord and Savior, Jesus Christ!"

As they got nearer and nearer to Jerusalem, Susan kept pleading with Julian to change his mind. But he would not listen to her. He stepped on the gas pedal and kept repeating "No, no, no!"

7

As they drove through the suburbs some of the lights were on in the houses and apartment buildings. When they were inside the city the cafeterias and small eateries were putting chairs and table outside, getting ready for the morning's business.

"How about stopping to get breakfast?" Julian said briskly. "We haven't had anything to eat since that skimpy meal the Essenes gave us last night. After the work we did, I think I could put away four or five eggs. How about you?"

"I'm . . . not hungry," Susan said glumly.

After going a half mile more into Jerusalem, Julian braked the truck in front of a cafeteria and turned off the ignition.

"Julian, you aren't going to leave the truck here on this main street with—with that body back there, are you?"

"Yes . . . I think you're right. We'll park it on a side street and walk back here, or find some other place to eat. My stomach is beginning to rumble."

A quarter of a mile away they found a short side street and parked the truck. When they came out of it they saw a number of men and women going into a church.

Julian stopped, watched them, thinking.

"Julian, what's the matter?" Susan asked.

For answer, he said abruptly, "I'm going in."

It was a Catholic church. The familiar sights and smells of his childhood and teenage years greeted Julian as he and Susan walked down the main aisle.

They entered a pew and sat down. Julian stared across at the white marble altar. He looked around him. The candles at the feet of the statues

41

of the saints. The Stations of the Cross on the walls. The scent of wax and incense. The stained-glass windows . . . .

The priest came out of the vestry, followed by an altar boy. Everybody got up. Julian glanced at the men and women. They believed the miracle the priest was about to perform—the miracle of the Catholic Mass. He was going to change bread and wine into the body and blood of a Jew who had died two thousand years ago.

And he had the body of the man these Catholics believed was their savior in his truck, not more than a few hundred feet away. For some reason he could not explain to himself, that fact filled him with bitter disappointment.

All during the service old thoughts came back to him, things he thought he had long forgotten. He saw himself, very proud, in his first long pants when he made his first communion. He had a white silk bow on his arm, symbol of purity and innocence.

This mental image was followed by a second one. He saw himself in a photographer's studio on that day of his first communion. He was kneeling on a prie-dieu, his head bowed as if in prayer, looking so serious, so . . . religious. His godfather, Uncle Christ, was standing behind him. On the wall beside him was a painting of Saint Anthony holding the Infant Jesus.

Julian was filled with sorrowful regret. When had he stopped believing as that boy did? Was it when he was in high school? After a few years in college? He could not remember. All he knew with a great longing was that he could once again be that boy kneeling in that studio.

But he realized with sorrow in his heart that he could never be that little boy again. He was a grown man, with the convictions of a grown man. But Julian could not help wishing . . . if only . . . .

Coming to himself from out of his past he saw with a shock that he was kneeling and his hands were clasped. Susan was also kneeling, with her palms pressed together.

Julian saw the priest, a tall, slender man, holding the host high up in front of him. All the men and women had their heads bowed. He unclasped his hands.

Inwardly shaking off these feelings in him that he thought were long dead, Julian wanted to get up and shout, "You blind, ignorant fools! Your mass is just another form of pagan worship! This is not the only religion that taught people that they could eat their god! Come to your senses! Act like civilized human beings, and not like stupid savages! The man you worship as God did not walking out of that tomb! His body was stolen! Yes, the body was carried away by the Essenes! And I can prove it! Just up the block I have the corpse that you worship as the Son of God! He was no god, just a deluded, demented fool who went around Palestine prattling about his cockeyed kingdom of heaven! He is dead and will never come back to life!"

But the words died on his lips, and the raging anger died away from him as he saw the men and women going up to receive communion. He watched them intently as they returned to their pews, knelt down and pressed their hands to their faces.

Turning to Susan he saw that her head was bowed. Was she praying? No, he could not believe that of her. But a question occurred to him.

"Susan, Susan, I want to ask you something," he said, shaking her by the shoulder.

Her eyes seemed bleary, as if she had come out of a deep sleep.

"Wh—what is it, Julian?"

A little embarrassed he asked, "Uh . . . Susan, what . . . religion were you brought up in?"

"Catholic."

"You were a Catholic?"

"Yes."

"And when did you stop believing, lose your faith?"

"I don't remember. It just fell away from me, piece by piece, over the years. And you?"

"The same thing. The world works on you like water on a rock. If only we didn't grow up, damnit!"

The service was almost over. The people were making responses to the priest's words of praise to the Lord's blessings.

"Julian, tell me honestly and frankly, don't you envy these men and women?"

Reluctantly, Julian said, "I hate to admit it, but, damnit, I sure as hell do! They have something to look forward to! We got nothing, nothing!"

The people were getting up to leave the church. Julian and Susan went out with them. When they were outside Julian took Susan's hand and said with pain showing in his face, tears in his eyes and his voice trembling, "I can't do it, Susan, I can't do it! I can't take away from those men and women their faith! I can't rob them of it! It would be a cruel and monstrous thing to do, and I'm not going to do it!"

"Julian, I'm so glad, so glad!"

"If I did such a terrible thing I'd feel like a criminal for the rest of my life! No, I'm not going to do it!"

"Julian, I just thought of something. What do we do with the body in the truck?"

"There's only one thing to do. We'll drive back to the Essene community late tonight and leave the box outside the main building. They'll be sure to see it when they get up in the morning."

Two nights later, after a good dinner in an outdoor restaurant, Julian and Susan were strolling through Old Jerusalem. The weather was pleasantly mild, and thousands of stars glittered in a clear, deep blue sky that had a three-quarters moon.

Hand-in-hand they walked down the dark streets, stopping now and them to gaze up at an old building, or to enjoy a long kiss.

"Julian, what are your plans now?" Susan asked. "Do you have any project in mind when we get back to Voltaire College?"

"You know, Susan, I haven't thought about that."

"What about that book you were writing?"

"I am going to chuck it. I had in mind a book incisively analyzing the resurrection chapters in the four Gospels that was going to prove positively that they are all pure baloney. That was before I came to Jerusalem. In the last few days I have acquired a soft heart for Christians, if not for Christianity."

"Julian, you've become a different person, a better one."

"Yes, I suppose I have. If people want to believe that the Creator of this great big universe sent a message, a revelation to certain persons—to Moses, Jesus, Mahomet—what right do I have to take away that comforting belief?"

"But, Julian, what kind of books will you write when we get back?"

"I was thinking about that. Maybe I'll turn away from writing all those thick tomes that require so much research and try my hand at writing fiction."

"You mean novel-writing?"

"Sure. In that racket, all you have to do is let your imagination fly."

"And what about you and me?" Susan asked, stopping and standing in front of Julian.

"Susan, here in this ancient land I have experienced a romantic awakening. I love you and want to go on making love to you for the rest of my life."

"Julian, is this a proposal of marriage?"

"Sweetheart, let's go to that church we were in yesterday and arrange to be married there."

"Darling!" Susan said, throwing her arms around Julian's neck. "I love you!"

Professor Alfred Malbrim's Vibrating Replicator

1

Alfred Malbrim had been professor of physics at Bantwell State College for eleven years, since he was twenty-six years old. He was divorced, with no children. Amy, his wife of ten years, divorced Alfred months ago. The reason given for the breakfast-up of the marriage was incompatibility. But there was more to it than that.

When the professor was thirty-two years old, he found in a second-hand book store a dusty old book in German. Alfred had spent two years in a university in Berlin studying physics.

The books fascinated Alfred. It was written by a professor of videology, a science he had never heard of. The professor specialized in inventions. One of the inventions he thought could be built gripped Alfred's mind powerfully.

Alfred read the chapter of that invention many times. Was the German professor insane? Was it actually possible to build such an invention? Was the whole concept wildly and outrageously irrational? Was it science? Or science fiction?

Day and night Alfred thought about it. He became obsessed by the German's idea for that invention. He lost his appetite for food, and fifteen pounds. Several times in the classroom Alfred's mind would drift off from the subject of physics and focus on that bizarre concept. And when his mind returned to the classroom, he would see his students staring at him in openmouthed bewilderment.

Sometimes the professor would become upset and angry over the very queerness of such an invention. It simply did not make sense. But its oddness not only made him angry, it frightened and yet intrigued him. If he did not have that rigidly scientific mind he would have thought the whole idea of such an invention was mad, or that it had something of the supernatural to it.

But the problem was that Alfred did believe that such an invention was possible, was feasible. But how did one go about producing such a fabulous machine?

After thinking about it for many months he declared to himself that he would do it! Yes, he would produce that invention!

But he had to admit that he was intellectually limited by being only a physics professor. He realized that he would be required to take a long course in higher mathematics and definitely a course in videology, and possibly in electrical engineering for good measure.

In a college reference book he found that Clark University, twenty miles away, gave courses in all the branches of learning he needed.

And so for the next two years, after his classes, Alfred drove to Clark University four nights a week. To round out his advanced education he also took classes in astrodynamics.

Alfred was confident that with all that knowledge he would succeed in solving that gigantic problem which for months had been boiling and brimming over in his busy mind.

All that activity, those nightly drives to the university, took their toll on his marriage, socially and sexually. Amy was a very outgoing, sociable woman. She loved to give and to go to parties. She enjoyed very much dining out in restaurants. And Amy was also a hot-blooded woman, with a voracious sexual appetite.

Amy's jolly life suffered dearly when Alfred began his education program. He returned very late and was asleep a minute after his head hit the pillow, leaving his wife staring down at him with fury in her heart.

And even when Alfred finished his courses at the university, he would go straight into his study to work on the idea for his invention. But things did not go smoothly. Sometimes he would think he had solved the problem, but the right answer, the correct equations, proved to be wrong. At such times he felt like a man in a desert seeing a mirage. But that was all it was, and he would have to start all over again, attacking the baffling problem with fierce, maniacal energy.

A number of times Amy barged in on him and angrily demanded that Alfred come to bed. And she would bitterly complain to her husband that they had not had sexual intercourse in many weeks.

His response at these interruptions when he was engaged on his mighty project was to tell Amy to go to the devil, that he was doing very important scientific research, and to get out and leave him to his work.

However there were a few times when Amy was able to persuade Alfred to stopped working and get in bed with her. But his wife did not have sleep on her mind. The sex diet her husband had imposed on her because of his negligence gave Amy a mad craving for lovemaking.

But Alfred was of no use to her in that regard. All the strain, the mental agitation, left him impotent. No matter what Amy did to stimulate him sexually, Alfred could not perform his marital duty. At such times Amy would rush out of the bedroom howling in frustrated sexual rage. Alfred, exhausted from his research work, would drop off into a deep sleep.

After months of this agonizing celibate marriage, Amy made a frank confession to her husband. They were having dinner when she calmly announced to Alfred that she had taken a lover.

Sipping his Chablis (they were having baked lemon sole) he politely asked, "Who is it?"

"It's Lester Wehrmann."

"Oh, that young chap. Professor of archeology, isn't he?"

Her eyes blazing, her face crimson, infuriated at her husband's cool indifference, Amy shouted across the table, "Alfred, is that all you have to say!"

"No, I do have a comment to make."

"And what is that?"

"I hope the archeologist enjoys himself exploring deep inside you. He might discover something. I never did."

"Alfred, you beastly bastard, I'm going to divorce you!"

"While you are at it, maybe you could induce your lover to marry you. That way I won't have to pay you alimony."

"I don't know why I ever married you!"

"I think I know why. I have a strong suspicion it was because of my wealthy, unmarried and sickly brother. He made a fortune in real estate early in life. He has been retired for years with a serious illness, that's supposed to be life-threatening, but apparently not life-ending. He might outlive us all."

"When we got married you never told me that you and your brother were estranged and had not spoken to each other for years. What happened between you two?"

"A very private family matter that had something to do with my father's will. For years he's been living in the family mansion, servants to look after him, and sitting on a huge pile of stocks and bonds. And you dreamed of getting your greedy hands of some of that money, didn't you?"

"I'll be leaving in the morning!"

"You'll have to call a livery service. Remember, the car is in my name. Oh, and please don't invite me to the wedding."

"I'd invite a boa constrictor first!" Amy yelled, getting up from the table. "Goodby! I'll be gone before you wake up tomorrow morning!"

Reaching for a piece of lemon sole with his fork Alfred said, "Don't slam the door on your way out. Tomorrow is Saturday and I like to sleep late."

2

When Alfred got up the next morning he went around the house. All of Amy's things were gone from the closets and drawers. He was glad. Now he could do some real work without that woman nagging him about that infernal sex.

He made himself a breakfast of scrambled eggs and bacon. While he was eating Alfred thought of the preceding night. He regretted his coldhearted response to Amy's declaration that she had taken on a lover. He knew that he had no right to blame her. From the years of their married life he was keenly aware of her strong passionate temperament. In bed she was a hellcat, always demanding more. And Alfred had to admit to himself that he had not been doing his duty to Amy as a husband. She had every right to find what she wanted in the arms of another man.

Alfred was sorry about those remarks he made at the dinner table. He was not a mean person. But his mind was so on edge, so obsessively preoccupied with that machine he was trying to invent, and not getting anywhere, that he took out his frustration on Amy. This morning, with his brain cells rested and relaxed after a good night's sleep, he was very remorseful over those snide, hurtful words. He sincerely wished Amy all the happiness in the world.

Alfred idly wondered where Amy had gone when she left the house. To her widowed mother in Fairfield, about forty-five miles away? Or did she move right in with Wehrmann in his bachelor cottage on the campus?

He would leave the divorce business up to Amy. She would be sure to take the initiative. Soon he would be receiving papers from her lawyer. Alfred told himself that he would not contest the action.

All that was of no consequence. He had to concentrate on the Herculean task he had taken on. And thinking about it Alfred realized why he was making little headway in his massive project. He needed to know more about computers, more about how the magic of television worked, and he needed to know something about electrical engineering.

So, he would have to take courses in those fields. Back to school! But it was how television worked that gripped his mind with great force. How was it possible to transmit images from thousands of miles away? The winter Olympic sports from Japan could be seen instantly in New York, more than ten thousand miles away. He was a physicist, Alfred told himself, but he did not understand any of it!

But that was party the key to the invention he was going to build! It was those images that could be sent through the air! But there was something else Alfred had in mind. Was it possible that the atmosphere, the air itself, could <u>forever</u> retain those images? That was the question he had to, he must, answer!

3

It was four months since Amy walked out on Alfred. He was now a free man. The divorce had gone smoothly, and only days after, Amy and Wehrmann were married. Alfred sent a good luck card, to which his ex-wife did not respond.

In those months Alfred had built a small workshop-laboratory behind his house. From his unmarried sister, who was the sole owner of eight women's health clubs, Alfred borrowed forty thousand dollars. Most of the money went to buy a large TV screen (ten feet high and five feet wide), an intricate computer which he designed, and a powerful generator.

Alfred spent all his time in that shed when he was not teaching. He ate there, and he slept there. In a corner was a desk where did his paper work. He got only a few hours of sleep, going to be usually at about three or four o'clock in the morning, stumbling over to a cot half asleep, with the alarm clock set to go off at seven o'clock so he could get to his class on time.

Almost a year after his divorce Alfred began slowly to realize that the generator he had was not powerful enough to do the job for which it was intended. On paper he was fairly certain that his theory was sound. But he had to test it. And to do that he was confronted with a seemingly insuperable problem. He needed a huge amount of money to buy a more expensive and bigger generator. It would cost at least a million dollars. And, Alfred, calculated, the machine itself, the invention, with all its valuable jewel-like parts, would cost millions more.

All work on his project had to be halted for lack of funds. And what was more maddening for Alfred was that over time he was positively convinced that his invention would work! Yes, he told himself, it was possible to produce such a machine. But he needed the money to carry out at least one experiment that would prove he was a true scientist and not some crackpot visionary.

Not having the money, all Alfred could do was mark time, continue with his work on paper and hope that something would turn up. He could not turn to his sister. She did not have that kind of money.

And while hoping for some miracle, he went on working on his mathematical equations, especially the ones dealing with the science of vibrations—those enduring vibrations that did not expire but were retained in the atmosphere, but invisibly. And with the help of a very powerful generator he was certain he could make them visible!

Once again, while working at his calculations late at night, Alfred reviewed his theory. All past events remained in the atmosphere could not be seen by the human eye. The colossal scientific problem for him was simply to replicate those past events. But it was not that simple! All because of a lack of money!

4

One Saturday morning, sitting in his study, almost on the verge of a nervous breakdown, Alfred heard the doorbell ring. He glanced at his wristwatch. He did not have to get up to answer the door. It was the mailman.

After about a half hour he dragged himself out of the deep leather armchair and walked listlessly out of the room. He opened the door to his house and checked the mailbox. It had one long envelope.

The letter was from a lawyer by the name of Eric Spardell. The lawyer informed Alfred that his brother, Judson, had finally succumbed to his long illness and that he was the sole beneficiary of his brother's estate, which was valued at thirty millions dollars.

It took over a month to get his hands on those millions. Within two months Alfred had his powerful generator, the machine of his own making and design, and an even larger screen.

On the day he completed his work and was ready to test his invention he gazed fondly at it, with a broad, proud smile. What should he call it? Why not call it what it was? Yes! He would call it the Vibrating Replicator!

"I have invented a machine that can replicate every event that has taken place in the past, no matter whether it took place last year, or centuries ago!"

But would the Vibrating Replicator really work? It did seem so on paper and in theory. But would it actually work?

"It has to work!" Alfred said with passionate conviction. "Science doesn't lie! I'm going to try it right now!"

But, he asked himself, what event in the past should he attempt to replicate? The beheading of Marie Antoinette!

With his head throbbing, his mouth dry, his heart pounding, Professor Alfred Malbrim turned on the switch of his invention. Immediately there was a low humming sound that got louder and louder. The screen lighted up with a hazy glow. But it stayed blank.

To Alfred this was not unexpected. He knew that he had to make some adjustments. Slowly he walked up close to the machine and gazed down at the rows of keys. He picked up a clipboard from a table. It had several sheets of papers on it. He flipped over the pages, studying the charts. When he was sure he had the correct equations, Alfred carefully, gingerly tapped out fourteen numbers on the keys.

Stepping back a few paces he saw the screen go suddenly very black. And them, amazingly, stunning Alfred with its clearness and vividness in rich color, he saw a woman sitting in a wagon. She had a doleful, resigned expression on her face. Lining the street as she moved along it were thousands of men and women. Their faces were filled with a demonic hatred and they were yelling at the woman in the wagon as she went by, and making threatening gestures.

"It's her!" Alfred shouted with rapturous joy. "It's Marie Antoinette sitting in the tumbrel, the cart that was taking her to her doom, to be guillotined!"

Alfred had read it all in Carlyle's history of the French Revolution. He kept his eyes glued to the screen as the cart carrying the Queen of France wound its way through the streets of Paris, the Paris of more than two hundred years ago! Alfred told himself.

He watched as the cart reached the scaffold. And now Alfred saw that Marie Antoinette was truly a queen. With regal bearing, head held high, she mounted the steps and without hesitating a moment, gracefully knelt down, and in a moment, the blade slid down and neatly severed her head from her shoulders.

Now Alfred saw the executioner pick up the bleeding head of the Queen of France and hold it up to the gleefully yelling mob.

Sickened by the sight, Alfred shut off the machine. He dropped into a chair. His feelings of revulsion were succeeded by a different kind of emotion—a kind of exultant sensation. His mind seemed to be soaring high up in the sky.

Wiping the sweat from his face he cried out in wonder and pride, "I have achieved my goal! I can bring back the living past! I'll go down in history as the greatest scientist of all time! Greater than Galileo, Newton, and even Einstein!"

But had it been a lucky fluke? Alfred asked himself. One successful experiment did not positively prove anything. He had to be certain that he had truly invented a marvelous machine.

Once again he turned on his invention. He knew the scene he wanted to witness on the screen. He consulted the charts on the clipboard, made his calculations, and tapped twenty-two keys.

In one minute he was seeing Giordano Bruno being burnt at the stake in Rome in the year 1600. How he howled in agony as the hot flames from the burning fagots licked at his body. To one side of the suffering man Alfred saw the smirking Jesuits and the grinning monks.

Alfred could not stand to see anymore. He tapped on the keys thirty-two times. Now he was seeing the Renaissance pope Alexander, father of the notorious Lucrezia Borgia and Cesare Borgia. His Holiness was in bed with his favorite mistress. What disgusting things he had her perform on his gross corpulent body! What revolting porn stuff!

After tapping on forty-one keys Alfred was witnessing the killing of Julius Caesar, men stabbing him repeatedly with long knives. God, the blood, Alfred thought, full of pity for the man who would be emperor.

He moved on. This time he tapped down on thirty-nine keys. And now he was seeing Cleopatra commit suicide by pressing the asp to her chest.

Once again he shut off the machine. No, this was no fluky invention. This was pure science. He had the power to recapture the past! There was no doubt about that.

That night, sitting in his living room after his supper, Alfred confronted himself. Why had he worked so hard to invent this machine. Was it a purely scientific endeavor? To prove that such an invention could actually be produced?

No, he had to be honest with himself. That was not the reason. Yes, he considered himself a man of science, a physicist. Science had become his religious creed. But that was a contradiction. Science could never replace religion. Science could answer questions about the world around us, the plants, the animals, the stars. But it could not explain the reason for the existence of the universe. Why were we here? Did we have a soul? An immortal soul that survived the death of the body?

Science could not answer those questions. It could not give meaning and purpose to our lives. Is there salvation? Is there damnation?

Alfred had been brought up a Lutheran Christian. But with his keen interest in science he began to lose his faith in the last year in high school.

The years in college, under the influence of the materialist professors, completed the wreckage of the faith of his fathers.

For a time Alfred was content with a materialist creed. But as the years went by he began to sense a great emptiness deep inside him, a kind of loneliness, an aridness. Some nights he was gripped with such chilling despair that he would cry out in desperation, "You, you, if you exist, help me! Help me find my way back to . . . ."

To what? he would ask himself a dozen times a day, even when he was giving his class. Just what was it he wanted to find his way back to?

And then one day, when he was having lunch in the college cafeteria, it hit him like a punch to the head. He wanted to regain his Lutheran faith, that was what he wanted! And what did that mean? It meant believing in Jesus Christ as his Lord and Savior!

Now he had to admit to himself that that was the reason why he wanted to invent his Vibrating Replicator. It had been the religious undercurrent in his mind all the time.

Yes, he did want to believe in Jesus as his Redeemer. But that would mean believing in his resurrection. But his skepticism and belief in science had eroded his religious mentality too much for him simply to have the conventional faith that Jesus had risen from the dead, that he had truly walked out of that sepulcher, and also that he had ascended up to heaven.

I must see those events for me to become once again a sincere Christian, Alfred told himself. See them, witness them. And now he finally acknowledged to himself why he had invented his wonder machine.

He must see Jesus emerge from that tomb. He must see Jesus rise up, up to the sky. Then, and only then would he believe that Jesus Christ had died for the sins of the world.

The time had to come for him to find out. That night he went into his shed with dread and hope in his heart. Would he be disappointed and see nothing? Or would he see and witness all he was so desperately longing and yearning to see—the Risen Christ!

With his hands clammy and his face sweaty, he switched on the Vibrating Replicator. When the humming was good and loud, he reckoned on his chart the number of keys he had to tap out. The number came to twenty-seven.

And then he stepped back and unconsciously he pressed his palms together, and in spite of himself murmured a short prayer.

And suddenly there appeared on the screen a sight that almost made Alfred's eyes pop out of their sockets! To his horror he was seeing the crucifixion of Jesus! But it was not at all as he had seen it in movies and paintings. It was so much more brutally cruel, vicious, revolting and, yes, even disgusting.

What agony Jesus was suffering nailed to that cross between the two thieves. How he twisted and turned. How much pain he endured with every breath he took, when he raised himself and the nailed flesh caused more agony, more suffering.

The soldiers near the cross were ignoring the victims on the cross. They had to stay and to pass the time they placed at some game.

Alfred observed the crowd of Jesus standing by the cross. He could see that a few them, in priestly garments, were smiling and making mocking remarks, Alfred assumed. Now he was sorry that his invention was limited in that he got only a kind of moving pictures, but without sound. His invention was only a video invention, without the audio. It was like looking at a silent-screen movie of the 1920s.

Seeing those Temple priests taunting the suffering Jesus on the cross infuriated Alfred. But he noticed that all the other Jews had sorrowful, grieving expressions on their faces. Many of the Jewish women were on their knees, crying bitterly, and beating the ground in their despair to see one of their own die such a ghastly death at the hands of their oppressors, the hated Romans. Alfred imagined that he could hear those women shrieking out their sorrow at the dying Jews on the cross.

Soon as Alfred saw a soldier drive his spear into the side of Jesus, he turned off the machine. He could not help himself. He dropped to his knees and cried like a baby.

But when he returned to his house, had calmed down and was in a sober state of mind, Alfred was still saddened by what he had witnessed on the screen. And yet, he was also thrilled and exhilarated by what he had achieved so far. His invention was able to bring back the past because of the two scientific facts he had discovered: events in the past continued to vibrate invisibly in the atmosphere, and the Vibrating Replicator was capable of producing them on that screen.

Alfred was satisfied with himself, with his marvelous scientific achievement, but not completely. He reminded himself that he had worked so hard to build his invention for one reason, and one reason only: Did the risen Jesus walking out of that tomb? He had to know! Only seeing that event would make a Christian believer of him. He was not capable of blind religious faith! He was too much the scientist. He had to see, he had to see Jesus alive, walking out of that tomb!

Late that night he returned to the shed. And without hesitating, he switched on the machine. He picked up the clipboard and studied the charts. He came up with the number twenty-eight.

And then he waited for the screen to light up. It did light up, but it remained blank. For a half hour Alfred waited for something to show on the screen. Nothing, nothing.

He checked and rechecked the charts. Always he came up with the number twenty-eight. Five times he hit the keys twenty-eight times, but each time he met with failure. The screen stayed maddeningly blank.

That night Alfred got very little sleep. Several times he got out of bed and paced the bedroom. What was wrong? he kept asking himself. Why wasn't he getting the desired results?

When he lay back down on the bed, Alfred found that he could not get to sleep not because of his failure with the machine. It was something else that was keeping him awake. He was experiencing a sensation he had not felt in a long time—carnal desire! How he desperately wished that he could have a woman in bed with him!

What had caused this awakening of his libido? Was it his great success with his invention? That could be it. All that strain on his brain had damped down his sexual desire.

So what was he going to do about it? No, Alfred told himself, he was not going to start a casual affair with one of the readily available female professors. He had to feel a deep emotional attachment, a personal liking for the woman to get in bed with her.

With one half of Alfred bursting with lust, and the other half in anguish over his failure with his invention to show him what he spiritually craved to see, he dropped off to sleep.

5

The next day, Sunday, Alfred worked on the machine for hours, stopping only to rush into the house for a sandwich, and then getting back to work.

All afternoon and late into the night, he worked but he saw nothing but shadowy figures moving across the blurred screen. He made adjustments, tried different combinations of numbers, and in his anger kicked the machine. Nothing worked.

It was almost two o'clock in the morning when he dragged himself back to the house, undressed and dropped into bed. But it took him a long time to fall asleep. He kept seeing moving tantalizingly across the snowy screen a beautifully shaped naked woman. Alfred groaned in his agony

"What is the answer to that problem!" he cried out bitterly. And added, "God, I need a woman!"

The next morning he had to be at the college by 9 A.M. Alfred was thankful that the class would not be too difficult. His mind was groggy from lack of sleep. He had to give a test. Once he handed out the test papers he would have an associate professor to stay in the classroom while he had a walk around the campus.

He sat down in a small wooded area that had a few wooden benches and immediately he began to think of his invention. Why was it able to show him all those other past events so clearly, but not the one vital event for which he had invented his machine?

He had a long, worried expression on his face when Gail Hansen came up the dirt path. She had joined the faculty five months ago. She gave a course in statistical analysis. Though this science had great possibilities for business and commerce, not many students attended her class.

Gail was thirty-four years old, recently divorced like Alfred. She had auburn hair, striking blue eyes, and a nicely shaped face. Her trim figure, with the tight skirts Gail wore, had professors and students turning around to observe her swaying hips and the up-and-down motion of well-rounded buttocks. Alfred had spoken to Gail casually a few times.

"Why so glum, Alfred?" she asked, sitting down on the bench.

"Oh, hello, Gail," he said, putting on a weak smile. "No class?"

"Not for another hour. What're you doing here?"

"I'm giving a test and I have Jenkins watching to see the students don't cheat."

"Uh . . . you were looking kind of down in the dumps, Alfred. Any particular reason?"

Alfred sat up and turned to face Gail directly. He was thinking about her, that is not exactly about her but about the class she gave. A faint glimmer of hope surged in him.

Could Gail help him with his problem? After all, her subject dealt with numbers. And Alfred had a hunch that that was, or had something to do with his problem.

But something else immediately occurred to Alfred. Could he trust Gail with his secret, his invention? And would she think him crazy? Well, if she did, he would show her Marie Antoinette getting her head chopped off, Giordano Bruno being burnt at the stake, and Julius Caesar getting knifed to death!

And so for the next forty minutes Alfred told Gail everything about his invention. And also about his successes, and his one big failure to witness the resurrection of Jesus Christ. He told Gail he was stumped and maybe, just maybe, she could help him.

Of course when he was finished, she stared at Alfred with eyes opened wide. She was flabbergasted, speechless, awed by what Alfred had told her. She turned away from him and looked out across the broad grassy campus.

"Gail, you don't believe me, do you? You don't believe that I have manufactured, invented, such a machine, do you?"

Turning to Alfred she said, "But it's too . . . fantastic, unscientific. What you have told me is crazier, nuttier, than all the wonders in Alice's Adventures in Wonderland, The Wizard of Oz, and Pinocchio. Alfred, are you in some kind of whimsical mood? Or is this your idea of a weird joke? Come on, let's have it. Have you taken to writing science fiction in your spare time?"

"No joke. And I have not taken to writing that stuff."

So what's the punch line?" Gail asked, smiling."

For answer, Alfred said very seriously, "Gail, are you free to have dinner with me at my place?"

"Yes, I'm free," she said, the smile disappearing from her face. "What time?"

6

Immediately after eating, without even serving coffee, Alfred led Gail into the shed. The light was already on. He went straight to the machine and said, "There it is. That's it."

Gail looked over the machine, studying it, moving her hands on the keys but not pressing down on them. Then she stepped back and turned to Alfred.

"You aren't serious, are you? Are you telling me that this—this thing can bring back the past?"

Switching on the machine he said, "Gail, keep your eyes on the screen."

In quick succession Alfred showed Gail the deaths of the Queen of France, Giordano Bruno, and Julius Caesar. Then he shut off the machine and gazed at Gail. She seemed stunned, hypnotized, as she continued to stare at the screen.

"Well, now do you believe me?" Alfred said.

"I have to!" Gail said, finding her voice. "But how . . . ?"

He slowly and minutely explained the science that made it possible for him to invent the marvelous machine. Gail listened and nodded, understanding everything Alfred was telling her. One of her majors in college was electrodynamics.

When Alfred was done Gail said, "I can see by the troubled look on your face that there is something else you want to tell me. What is it?"

"Gail, I need your help, and I am certain you can solve a problem I have. I want to go back to that Sunday morning when Jesus is supposed to have come back to life and walked out of his tomb. If you think me crazy, go on and say so.

"No, Alfred, I don't think you're nuts. I too would like to get back my lost faith."

"You too?" Alfred said.

"I'm what is commonly called a fallen-away Catholic."

"And we both are in the same fix. Too much infused with the scientific spirit to believe on faith. We must have seeing proof, for seeing is believing!"

"Alfred, you mentioned something about needing my help. I can surmise what you problem is. You can get those other events in the past, but you can't get the one you passionately want."

"Yes, the resurrection of Jesus Christ, if it really happened."

"What do you want from me?"

"I want to put to work your expertise in numbers, statistical analysis. Gail, I'm going to show you something that will horrify and stagger you. Brace yourself. You are going to witness the suffering and death of Jesus Christ on the cross."

After Gail had seen that cruel, bloody death, she had to sit down and get herself together. Alfred shut off the machine. He waited a few minutes and then he asked her, "Gail, are you okay? Do you want to go back to the house for a drink?"

Getting up and shaking her head she said, "Alfred, we have to go forward approximately forty-two hours after Jesus died on the cross."

"Gail, how did you come up with that figure of forty-two hours?"

"The Gospels tell us that Jesus died on the ninth hour. The Jews reckoned the start of the day at six A.M. That means Jesus gave up the ghost at three o'clock in the afternoon. At three in the afternoon the next day, Jesus was dead twenty-four hours. The Gospels mention dawn or early in the morning when the women came to the tomb to anoint Jesus' body. So we add . . . let's say eighteen hours at the time the resurrection is supposed to have happened, which means Jesus was dead for forty-two hours before he . . . that is if he actually did . . . ."

"Gail, you do have a way with numbers. I doubt that many Christians know that Jesus was dead for only forty-two hours . . . that is if he . . . ."

"That is all the time it was . . . if . . . ."

"Gail, here is my problem in a nutshell. I tapped on the various keys twenty-seven times to get the crucifixion scene. I figured if I moved the number up to twenty-eight keys, I would get the resurrection scene, that is if it actually happened. But I keep getting only a blank or blurred screen. What do you make of it, my expert in statistical analysis?"

"Alfred, show me your papers, your notes," Gail said.

They went over to the desk and Alfred brought out from the drawers three hefty stacks of sheets tied with a cord. He dropped them on the desk and untied the cords.

And then they both sat down and went to work. But it was really Gail who did all the brain-work. Alfred watched her, and was amazed at her deftness with numbers. Over and over, Gail made calculations in a notebook, and over and over she kept tearing out the page with an angry curse and kept plugging away at her figures. Every once in a while Gail asked Alfred a question about his Vibrating Replicator. After she got the answer, she would think for a while and then go back to writing down her numbers and doing her calculations.

When it was almost midnight Gail announced, "Alfred, you have to tap out twenty-seven and two eights, and I am certain that you will replicate on your screen that historic morning, that is if history was made that morning."

"But my invention does not do fractions! Gail, I'm sunk! I have failed! All that work for nothing!"

Alfred got up from the desk, his hands jammed in his pants pockets, despondent, disgusted with himself. He stood in front of his invention shaking his head in despair.

Gail went up to him and said, "Alfred, I don't want you to talking and think like a quieter! Things aren't that bleak or hopeless."

"But what can I do? My machine does only whole numbers."

"My good friend, who built this machine, who invented it?"

"Gail, why are you asking me that question? You know I did."

"And so you did! And so you can add keys that do fractions!"

"Do fractions?"

"Yes, get to work, Alfred! Get out your tool kit! Maybe I can help you. In the high school I attended, my father was the custodian, and sometimes I helped him fix a lot of things in the school that broke down. He taught me a lot. Come on, let's get to work on this crazy invention of yours!"

But it was not that easy or that simple. At two o'clock in the morning Alfred had the keys in place. But when he turned on the machine and tapped out the requisite keys with the fraction added, the screen remained disappointingly blank, sometimes turning a hazy gray.

"Alfred, don't get discouraged. Maybe my numbers were wrong. Let's go back to the desk and do the numbers again."

"Gail, it's two o'clock in the morning, and we have to be in our classrooms in eight or nine hours. We are both tired, and our minds are fagged out. Let's hit the sack."

"Together?" Gail said, smiling. "Or separately?"

"Perhaps sexual relaxation might do us a lot of good."

"Alfred, I may give the appearance of a refined lady, but I want you to know that when I engage in sex it is more savage violence than relaxation with me."

"Is that why your marriage didn't succeed? You were too demanding on your husband?"

"Yes, Lionel said I was a menace to his health, that I was wearing him down to a frazzle. But what can you expect from a psychology professor!"

"And you think a physics professor will be more . . . physical?"

"Well, I'm hoping . . . ."

"Gail, because I've been so obsessed with my Vibrating Replicator, I've been sexually inactive for a very long time, even before I broke up with Amy."

"She left you because you weren't giving her enough?"

"I was giving her nothing, zero. Working so hard on my invention stalled my sex drive. But lately it's perked up a good bit. In fact, it's gone into overdrive, but only mentally."

"Meaning that you will be coming at me like a charging bull, Alfred?"

"Gail, all I can say is I've stored up plenty of sex energy. Make that a famished, charging bull!"

"Darling, let's stopped this idle chatter and get to your bedroom!"

7

For the next few days Alfred and Gail followed the same routine. After their classes they went to Alfred's house for dinner and then got to work in the shed.

A number of times, when Gail gave Alfred a new set of figures, he made adjustments on his machine. But each time they met with failure.

Finally, on the sixth night Gail made a whooping shout of joyous victory. She was positive that she had the numbers right.

"Alfred, the absolutely correct number is twenty-seven and one sixteenth! I'm positively certain that I have it right this time! Get to work on the keys!"

Wearily, Alfred picked up his tool kit and walked slowly over to the machine. He looked worried and unsure of himself. But not Gail. Following behind him, she was smilingly confident, even relaxed. She knew her numbers would not fail her this time.

"Alfred, will you please wipe that distraught look off your face. It's going to work this time. Statistics don't lie. I live by them, I believe in them—and damnit, your invention is going to work! I guarantee it!"

An hour later, when Alfred had finished making the painstaking and precise adjustments he stepped back from the machine and said, "Gail, you deserve the honor of switching it on. If this thing works this time, most of the credit has to go to you."

"Alfred, you are being too modest. The astounding concept is all yours!"

"Gail, I want you to turn it on. Go ahead!"

"Alfred, do you really want to know?"

"I must know the truth!"

"The truth! Alfred, you are hoping that you see Jesus walk away from that tomb, aren't you, aren't you?"

"Yes, yes! I admit it! I want to get back my old Christian faith! Science is good, but it doesn't warm the heart!"

"But what if that heavy stone remains still across the entrance to the sepulcher?" Gail asked gravely. "You will never recapture your Christian faith. Alfred, there is a lot to be said for religious faith. Believers have to rely on it for the things they believe but have not witnessed. Alfred, are you sure you want to know the truth, even if the truth causes you bitter sorrow and crushing disappointment?"

"Gail, I'm willing to take that chance! No matter how much suffering it causes me! My Christian belief must be based on fact and not on faith!"

"Alfred, think of what you are saying," Gail said, pleading with him. She could see how desperate he was to believe in the resurrection of Jesus. But if he did not see it, how miserable, how unhappy he would be. She was afraid he would have a nervous breakdown. Anything could happen. Alfred could lose his mind. Somehow, she had to sway him temporarily from making his momentous and fateful decision.

"Go on, Gail, what're you waiting for?"

"Alfred, I want you to think about this. You may not like what you will see on the screen. It could be what you don't want to see."

"Then I must accept historical truth, no matter how hard and painful it is."

"And go on living with your soulless science creed, Alfred? Is that what you want? Perhaps . . . who knows . . . God one day may give you the grace to believe on faith."

"Gail, now you are not talking like a college professor, but more like some Bible Belt preacher."

But the words "soulless science creed" chilled Alfred's blood. His heart seemed to stand still. He thought about what Gail had said. Maybe it might not be a bad idea to put off for three or four days before he found out the truth. Give him time to think about it. Fact versus faith. Faith versus fact. Which would he eventually have to embrace?

"Alfred, I can see the doubt in your eyes."

"You are very perceptive, Gail."

"Does that mean? . . ."

"I'm going to take your advice. I want to think about it."

"For three or four days?"

"Yes, for that much time. It's late. Let's go to bed."

"But not to sleep!" Gail said, throwing her arms around Alfred. "Not right away!"

"Certainly not! God, all this intellectual activity makes me horny as hell!"

"Me too, me too!"

It took Alfred five days to get up the courage to want to see for sure if Jesus did truly rise from the dead. Or if that belief was pure fantasy. He appreciated the risk that he was taking. If the greatest of all miracles did not occur, he would have to go on being simply a physicist who believed only that the universe existed through accident or necessity, or that it had a loving Father who sent his Son to bring salvation to the human race by dying that terrible death on the cross.

What would his invention tell him? That the universe was indifferent to the fate of humans? That it did not care whether they lived or died? That there was no life after death?

Or would the machine show Alfred the risen Christ? And prove to him that the universe was infused with the love of the heavenly Father, whose beloved Son gave up his life that we humans may have and enjoy everlasting bliss.

He would find out that night.

It was almost eight o'clock when Alfred and Gail were standing in front of the machine. He had hardly touched his food at supper.

Now, standing by his invention, gazing up at the screen, his nerves taut as violin strings, his mouth dry as if he had dust in it, his hands sweating and his head pounding, he turned to Gail and nodded.

"Alfred, are you sure this is what you want?" she asked.

"This is what I want," he answered after swallowing hard and barely able to get out the words. "I must know—one way or the other! Even if I'll be wretched for the rest of my life!"

Gail stepped two paces forward. Soon as she turned on the machine, she stepped back, taking Alfred's hand, smiling at him. He smiled weakly back at her.

And then they waited and stared up at the screen.

Minutes after the humming started it got louder and louder, and then subsided so that it could barely be heard.

And then suddenly, vividly, amazingly, there appeared on the screen the outside of the tomb where the crucified body of Jesus had been placed. The huge stone blocking the entrance to the tomb had been pushed back.

And then, in rapid succession, Gail and Alfred saw the four scenes as depicted in the Gospels of Matthew, Mark, Luke and John, proving beyond any doubt that Jesus had walked out of his sepulcher. Alfred was keenly and poignantly impressed by the meeting between Jesus and Mary Magdalene. And when Jesus spoke to Mary, how Alfred wished that he had the audio along with the video!

But he knew the words by heart, for in the last few days he had read and reread the resurrection chapters in the Gospels dozens of times.

And so Alfred could lip-read the words spoken on the silent screen. In answer to the question the two angels asked Mary, Alfre felt he could actually heard what she said.

She was weeping because, "They have taken away my Lord, and I know not where they have laid him."

And immediately Jesus appeared, standing beside Mary.

"Woman, why weepest thou?" Jesus said. "Whom sleekest thou?"

Alfred could see that she thought Jesus was the gardener.

"Sir," she said, "if thou have borne him hence, tell me where thou hast laid him, and I will take him away."

And Jesus said to her, "Mary."

She turned around and recognizing Jesus said (and Gail and Alfred could see the exultant joy in her face) "Rabboni, Master!"

Jesus said, "Touch me not, for I am not yet ascended to my Father. But go to my brethren, and say unto them, I ascend unto my Father, and your Father. And to my God, and your God."

Alfred was so overcome with emotion that when he shut off his invention he thought he was in a dream. But he was still holding on to Gail's hand tightly and almost crushing it when he shouted joyfully, "It is true, it is true! He is risen! Jesus did come back from the dead! My Savior lives! Gail, I have regained my lost faith! Praise the Lord! Hallelujah, whoopee and hooray!"

"Alfred, you're breaking my hand!" Gail cried, wincing in pain. "For Christ's sake, let go of my hand!"

"Yes, yes, for Christ's sake!" not really knowing what he was saying, so deliriously happy he was. But he did let go of her hand, and came to his senses. "Oh, I'm so sorry, darling! Forgive me. Did I hurt you?"

"Oh, what's a few broken fingers!" she laughed.

"I didn't, did I?"

"Just joking. But what we just saw was . . . stupendously fantastic, wasn't it?"

"No, Gail, it was astoundingly factual. No fantasy to it. It was real, living history, brought before our eyes by my marvelous Vibrating Replicator! I am once again a sincerely believing Christian. But I want to complete my happiness by seeing one more thing."

"And what's that?"

"The glorious ascension of my Savior up to heaven!"

"Where did that event take place?"

"Gail, I'm disappointed in you! You don't know?"

"Alfred, I frankly admit my ignorance of the New Testament, even though I went to a parochial school and to a Catholic high school. I suppose I forgot all the religious stuff during those four years at Princeton."

"I see I shall have to job your memory."

"I'm listening."

"Of all the Gospel writers, only Luke gives a description of Our Lord's flight up to heaven and the location."

"And where did all that take place?"

"Gail, before I answer that question I have a very important question I want to ask you. Do you believe that Jesus Christ rose from the dead?"

"Alfred, how can you ask me such a thing? Not too many minutes ago I saw him do just that thing! How can I deny the testimony of my own two eyes?"

"Fine. Now tell me something, do you once again, as you did in your parochial and high school years, accept Jesus Christ as your Lord and Savior?"

"With all my heart and soul! How good it feels to be once again a Catholic! How I missed the Church!"

"My exact sentiments, my darling! How good it feels to be once again a Lutheran! And, Gail, our churches aren't too far apart!"

"Just a few doctrines separate us!"

"And the Catholic and Lutheran theologians are trying to work out some kind of doctrinal rapprochement."

"And in time they will succeed, Alfred! Now, tell me about Luke and Jesus' ascension up to heaven."

"Jesus took off for heaven from the small village of Bethany."

"Where is Bethany?"

"A few miles outside Jerusalem."

"Go on. What does Luke tell us?"

"Well . . . let's see. Jesus lead led his disciples out of Jerusalem as far as Bethany, and he raised his hands and blessed them."

"Go on," Gail urged. "What happened next?"

"I'm not sure I can remember Luke's exact words. He said that as Jesus was blessing the disciples he was parted from them and carried up into heaven."

"And they watched him go higher and higher?"

"Yes."

"And what did the disciples do when Jesus disappeared from sight?"

"What else could they do? Luke tells us that they returned to Jerusalem with great joy, and they were always in the Temple, praising and blessing God. Amen."

"Alfred, how I wish I could have seen that spectacular sight of Jesus going up, up and away," Gail said dreamily. "Doesn't one of the Gospel writers say that now Jesus is sitting at the right hand of God?"

"Yes, that's Mark."

"God has hands? I always thought of him as a great big Spirit, sort of spread out all over the universe."

"That's only a figure of speech on Mark's part. Gail, I want to see my Savior go up to heaven. Would you please make the necessary calculations and tap out numbers on the keys."

In less than five minutes Alfred was gratified and pleased to see Jesus at the head of his disciples walking along a dusty road until they stopped a short distance from the village of Bethany, whose houses could be plainly seen rising on a hill.

Alfred watched with eye-popping happiness as he saw Jesus begin to rise from the ground as he blessed the disciples. Slowly, Jesus rose higher and higher, as the men, grouped together, looked up with awe-stricken faces.

"Damnit, I wish we had sound!" Alfred said in angry frustration. "I sure as hell would like to hear what Jesus was saying!"

"But you wouldn't understand what he was saying to his friends. You don't speak Aramaic."

"So what! I just wish I could hear his blessed voice!"

"Calm down and watch the screen, and be thankful for what you are witnessing."

"Oh, I am, Gail, I'm devoutly thankful."

They watched as Jesus continued to bless the disciples as he rose high up in the sky until he was only a speck, and finally disappeared behind a cloud bank.

And then the screen went blank.

Alfred, thrilled and exhilarated, cried out in his happiness, "Gail, wasn't that wonderful, wonderful! I'm so glad I got back my Christian faith! Why did I ever give it up for mere cold science!"

"Well," Gail said, "we grow up and . . . ."

"Yes, but many men and women grow down, as I did. But now I'm back on the right track!"

"And I'm happy to be back in the Catholic fold. But I do have a secular curiosity about some past events. One of my majors in college was history."

"Gail, what're you getting at?"

"In my college years and even after, I devoured books on the American Civil war. I read Bruce Catton, Shelby Foote, and biographies of Lincoln, Grant, Lee, Davis, and others of that time. For a while I considered myself something of a Civil war buff."

"Okay, tell me what you would like to see replicated on the screen from that war."

"For years I've always wanted to see the bloodiest and most decisive battle of the American Civil war. I've made three trips to Gettysburg, and I've walked over the battlefield any number of times, trying to imagine what it was like when on the third day Lee made his last desperate attempt to break through the Union lines and gain the victory."

"Go right ahead and work out the numbers, Gail. I'll tap them out on the keys."

In a few minutes Alfred and Gail were seeing it all. They saw Pickett's charge. Thousands of Confederate soldiers in row after row came slowly and steadily toward the Union entrenchment on Cemetery Rige, with the Union soldiers firing their rifles directly at their Rebel foes, killing them by the hundreds. And the Union artillery blasting gaping holes in the ranks of the enemy. Some of the Rebels made it to the ridge, but they were quickly cut down by the Union soldiers. The attack had been thwarted. The Confederate soldiers, those who had survived, drifted back to their own lines.

"Oh, how magnificent, and how terrible!" Gail wailed. "All those brave young men! I—I wish I had never seen it! How different it all is from the books!"

"Is there anything else you want to see? Some other battle?" Alfred asked.

"I . . . thought I wanted to see some of the other big battles . . . Bull Run, Shilo, Chancellorsville, Fredericksburg . . . Antietam. But . . . I think I've seen enough bloodshed to last me a lifetime. Now, I don't want to anymore of that. But there is one more thing from the Civil War I'd like to see. But it came after the war was over."

"I think I can guess what it is. You want to see John Wilkes Booth assassinate Abraham Lincoln. Go on, work out the numbers."

But, again, like with the Gettysburg battle, Gail was pensively regretful and sorrowful. Immediately after the assassin booth limped off the stage of the Ford Theater, she quickly switched off the machine. She turned to Alfred with brooding eyes.

Concerned, he asked, "Gail, you okay?"

"I'm . . . okay . . . but wasn't it horrible to see that great man shot to death like an animal? Oh, Alfred, I want to blot it out of my mind! Make love to me tonight like a fiend, an animal, a barbarian! Help me to escape from this brutal world, even if only for a short time."

8

That night, even after making love five times, Alfred and Gail could not fall asleep. Their bodies were tired, ached, but their minds were wide awake.

Both were thinking different thoughts.

Gail expressed herself first. "Alfred, are you going public with your invention? You could make make millions, millions, you know."

Alfred leaned over, kissed one of Gail's large pink nipples and said, "More likely billions, billions."

"Do you intend to raise capital, form your own company?"

"I am not going to do any of those things. I did not invent my Vibrating Replicator to make money."

"I know. You wanted to find out the truth about Jesus."

"And now I have it, the divine truth. And I want the whole world to know it. Yes, I am going to show the truth about Jesus to every man, woman and child."

"Alfred, what are you saying?"

"I'm saying that if they want to achieve salvation, they must accept Jesus Christ as their Lord and Savior, who died on the cross for our sins, and rose from the dead in a glorious resurrection! Those who believe will be saved, and those who reject Jesus as their Savior will be damned to everlasting torment!"

"Alfred, you are being heartless, cruel, intolerant!" Gail cried out in horror. "Those people have had their own religions for centuries. Hindus, Muslims, Jews, Buddhists and others have been content with their creeds. Don't take that belief away from them."

"But don't you see, my dear Gail, those billions of non-believers—"

"They are not non-believers! They believe in their own religion! Don't rob them of it, I beg you!"

"Gail, how can you be so stupidly blind! Those people don't have the right to go on believing in their false religion! With my invention I can show the unbelieving world the indisputable, irrefutable proof that Jesus Christ rose from the dead like the Son of God that he is, and flew off to heaven! You saw it yourself! Tell me, Gail, did Moses, Buddha, Mahomet rise from the dead and take off for heaven? They most certainly did not! Their bodies rotted and turned to dust! But not my Savior's body! It is up in heaven with his Father, the Father of the whole human race, who wants to see everyone saved! And I am going to give them that chance. It is my moral duty."

"And how do you plan to do that?" Gail asked.

"I'll tell you how I am going to do it. I'm going to show my invention in every major city of the world. And after viewing the scenes that prove that the Christian religion is the absolutely only true path to salvation, and they still adhere to their heathenish beliefs, their souls will be carted off to the nether regions, where the fires of hell await them!"

"Alfred, how can you talk like that?" Gail said reproachfully. "You are beginning to sound like a medieval religious fanatic, an intolerant bigot. I hate to say it, but you have turned into a hateful Torquemada! You have converted Christ's teaching of love, charity and compassion into one of inhuman cruelty! I have to say, I liked you better when you were an unbelieving scientist."

"Gail, please spare me your maudlin sentiment. Can't you see I'm trying to save billions of souls? What you call my cruelty is really love!"

Gail could see how hopeless it was to get Alfred to change his mind on the religious question. She thought she would try a different tack. If reason would not persuade him to change course, perhaps money would.

"Alfred haven't you considered something else?" she asked.

"What?"

"The commercial value of your invention. You could make a fortune, a dozen fortunes. Why, you could be the richest man in the world!"

"Gail, I am not going to put my Vibrating Replicator to commercial use. God gave me the intellectual resources to produce this machine for the salvation of souls! All human beings must embrace Jesus Christ as their Redeemer and Savior! With my invention, they will have one last chance to gain salvation. And if they turn their backs on that opportunity, they must suffer the consequences—damnation!"

9

That night, Alfred was vastly disappointed with his lover. Gail did not make love with her usual gusto, vigor and wild abandon. Alfred had to do all the work. She lay under him like a rug, thinking of his harsh religious intolerance.

After his third orgasm, with very little cooperation from Gail, Alfred rolled off her in disgust, and soon was fast asleep.

But not Gail. She lay awake for hours. She was agitated, worried and distressed. She did not at all like the plans that Alfred had for the world's religions: Extinction. Except for the Christian religion. It was wrong, cruelly wrong. Those Buddhists, Hindus, Muslims, Jews, and people of other creeds cherished their religious beliefs. They had held to them for centuries.

But what can I do? Gail asked herself, to stop Alfred from carrying out his brutal plan. He believes he has a mandate from heaven, and heaven help us from humans who think like that. It dehumanizes them.

Only with the approach of dawn was Gail finally able to drop off to sleep. She had a dream. In the dream she saw Alfred as some kind of mad prophet with a crazed gleam in his eyes. He was enormous, more than a hundred feet tall. And he carried a long, huge sledgehammer, and with it he was gleefully smashing to smithereens all the houses of worship in the world. except the Christian churches.

In her anguished sleep Gail murmured, "He mustn't . . . he must not do that. Alfred . . . Alfred . . . come to your senses . . . ."

10

Gail was sitting in the college cafeteria glumly poking at her meatloaf with her fork. She had no appetite at all. That morning, on their way to their classrooms, Gail had tried every argument she could think of to turn Alfred away from his planned religious revolution.

But she had failed. Alfred remained hard as a rock. He told Gail he was going to start his campaign during Christmas week, one month away.

"Why the long face?" Professor Muqdad Al-Zulhadid said as he sat down at Gail's table with his tray of lamb chops, rice and mixed vegetables. With his meal he was having bottled water.

Gail had been hunched over the table with her head bowed. Now she sat up, managed a wan smile and said, "Oh, hello, Muqdad. I was just . . . thinking . . . ."

"I hope it wasn't an unpleasant thought," Muqdad remarked, smiling genially and cutting into a lamb chop.

"No . . . only . . . serious . . . ."

Professor Muqdad Al-Zulhadid had the chair of Islamic studies at Bantwell State College. He had been at the college for three years. In outward appearance he showed the world an easy-going, agreeable, likable persona. But that was only a pose.

Behind the smiling face was a fanatical Muslim Fundamentalist of the most dangerous and deadly kind. He maintained close ties with all the Muslim terrorist groups in the Middle East-Hamas, Hezebellah, Islamic Jihad, and the most powerful one of them all, al Qaeda. He raised money for these organizations, and contributed generously himself.

Muqdad hated Western secular democracy with a ferocious, violent, murderous hatred. He long ago dedicated his life to destroying it. And he pursued his goal with relentless fanaticism. In his youth he had participated in several bombing missions in Israel and Lebanon, resulting in death for scores of men, women and children. And after each bloody mission, he would enter a mosque, drop to his knees and pray to Allah, the Compassionate, the Merciful. At night he would experience in a brothel with the help of hashish and two or three whores a foretaste of the paradise awaiting all Muslim men promised to them by the Prophet.

Muqdad strongly believed that one day Islam must rule the world, and that all laws must be based on the teachings of the Koran. There is no God but Allah and Mahomet was his prophet. One day everyone on this earth would accept those words as divine truth. So the professor believed.

He also truly and devoutly believed that all unbelievers were doomed to everlasting hell. One other belief that gave Muqdad great comfort was that all male Muslims would have seventy-two virgins waiting for them in the Muslim paradise.

Once in a debate a Christian professor had asked Muqdad Al-Zulhadid, "Will there also be seventy-two studs in your Muslim heaven for women?"

Three days later two men burst into that professor's house and cut out his tongue. This incident happened in a European university, and it was known about in America.

This was the kind of man who was sitting opposite Gail. He was disarming with his light chatter, his sports talk, that no one would ever suspect the kind of man he really was.

And when the professor once again asked Gail why the long face, she felt compelled to unburden herself of her anxieties, her worries. Muqdad Al-Zulhadid seemed such a friendly person, and she just had to tell someone about Alfred's invention.

And Gail did. For a half hour she talked. Muqdad listened intently, his food forgotten. Gail told him all about the Vibrating Replicator, and what Alfred intended to use it for—to see all the religions of the world disappear, except the Christian religion. It would reign supreme. All the Hindu gods and goddesses would be forgotten, along with the Jews' Jehovah, and of course the God of the Muslims—Allah.

Muqdad had a very difficult time listening to Gail tell her story and hiding his furious anger. But he did succeed. He kept up a smiling, amused expression, but his mind was ablaze with wonder, astonishment, and even skepticism.

Was such an invention possible? the Muslim thought to himself? He was not too strong on science, but in these days of technological marvels, who knows? Muqdad mused. Or was Gail ribbing him, pulling his leg? He had to find out if she was serious about this crazy invention.

And so while one half of his mind was boiling mad, and the other half was in a state of bafflement, Muqdad jokingly asked, "Come on, Gail, do you really expect me to believe that such a stupendous machine could be invented, that it actually exists?"

"I'm telling you it does exist!" Gail said irritably, annoyed by the professor's joking manner and skepticism.

Swallowing a spoonful of rice without even knowing it, Muqdad said evenly, "Gail, I consider myself a rational person, a levelheaded person. I demand proof."

"Very well, you shall have your proof! I'll show you the machine tonight, and give you a demonstration! That should convince you that I am not out of my skull!"

"But won't Professor Malbrim object?"

"He doesn't have to know about it."

"And how do you intend to keep him from knowing that you are going to show me his invention?"

"Alfred . . . uh, Professor Malbrim, is lecturing to a group of visiting physicists in town tonight at the Traymore Hotel."

"So the coast will be clear."

"Yes. Professor Malbrim will not get home until after ten o'clock."

"Gail, why have you told me all this, and why do you want to show me the invention?"

"I . . . have my reasons. I believe in freedom of religion. Whether true or false, people have the right to remain in the religion in which they were born. It gives them hope, it gives them comfort, it sustains them through the troubles and worries of life. This horrible invention will only upset and demoralize men and women all over the world. I say leave well enough alone. This newfangled invention is just . . . just too much! It's almost as bad as television!"

"You think television has been bad for humanity?"

"I do, I do! Men, women and children spend too much of their lives staring at the TV screen, like it was some kind of idol. It is an idol that is sucking the souls out of human beings, turning them into humoids."

"Yes, Gail, there is some truth in what you say. What time do we meet, and where?"

"Meet me behind Hathaway Hall at eight o'clock."

"I'll be there."

11

Gail and Muqdad were in the shed and standing in front of the Vibrating Replicator. The Muslim did not know what to make of it from its appearance. It was about six feet long, with a row of keys and a large screen.

The first thing Gail asked the professor was what event in the past he wished to see. When he told her, she sat down at the desk and made the calculations.

Now she was ready. She took two steps forward and tapped out the key numbers. Then she stepped back and turned to the Muslim.

"Keep your eyes on the screen," Gail said.

Muqdad nodded without speaking. His staring eyes were glued to the screen. He heard the humming from the machine rising higher and higher in intensity.

The Muslim felt as if two hands were gripping his throat, as if he were being strangled. He waited with fervent impatience, his heart beating rapidly. Was it true? Muqdad asked himself? Would this invention actually make him see an event that had happened in Arabia about fourteen hundred years ago?

Suddenly the screen lit up in a blaze of light, and then it darkened. And now the Muslim saw inside a cave a man kneeling in prayer.

"It's the cave outside Mecca where the Prophet received his first message from Allah!" Muqdad shouted exultingly, his heart filled with joyful wonderment. "The Prophet is in the cave praying to Allah! It's true, it's true! This is a real invention! It does have the power to bring back the past!"

"You are convinced this is no trick?" Gail asked.

"I am indeed! This is a genuine, marvelous invention!"

"You know, now that I have shown it to someone, I feel a little better, strangely enough. Why, I don't know, but I do. I think I need a drink to celebrate, maybe more than one drink, professor. What do you say we go down in town to the Flamingo Bar and down a few drinks? How about it?"

Though a fanatical Muslim, Muqdad, since his time in the States, had acquired a fondness for vodka on the rocks.

"Yes, I think that's just what I need, Gail! Let's go!"

When he left Gail that night, a bit tipsy but still clear headed enough to know what he must do, he hurried to his small cottage on the college grounds and made an overseas phone call.

He talked rapidly and excitedly to the man on the other end of the line in Saudi Arabia. It took the professor a half hour to convince the man that what he was telling him was the absolute truth, and finally he did succeed.

"I'm sure you appreciate the necessity for prompt action!" Muqdad urged.

"Yes, I do," the man said.

"Good. Get your team ready to come to America!"

"Do you want us to kill this Alfred Malbrim?"

"No, I don't want the police investigating his death."

"So what do you want my team to do?"

"Here's what I want you to do," Muqdad said.

And he told him.

Three nights later, when Alfred and Gail entered the shed, they found the Vibrating Replicator totally demolished, smashed into an unrecognizable wreck.

Stunned and shocked, Alfred turned to Gail. He saw something in her eyes that made him suspicious. He could plainly see by the guilty, abashed expression on her face that she knew something. She turned her back to him.

Roughly turning Gail around he said, "You know anything about this?"

"I . . . ."

Grabbing her by the shoulders and shaking her he yelled like a madman, "Damnit, talk, talk! What do you know! Tell me!"

"Alfred, let go of me! You're hurting me!"

After a few moments he said, "Okay, Gail, I've let you go. Now let's hear what you know about the destruction of my invention!"

"Well . . . you see . . . ."

"No beating around the bush! I can see you had something to do with this outrage! I want to know everything, everything! Talk!"

And so Gail did.

When she was done, Alfred paced up and down in short, jerky strides, running his hand through his hair. His eyes blazing with furious anger.

"So you brought that religion-crazy Muqdad here and gave him a demonstration of my invention! I saw through his phony, cheerful, pleasant manner long ago. He never fooled me, but he certainly fooled you!"

"But Alfred, he seems such a nice—"

"All an act! And you fell for it! He's responsible for wrecking the Vibrating Replicator! Who else? He had men come here and do the job!"

And Alfred was right. The phone call Muqdad made was to the notorious Zutu al-Kahlid, the leader of one of the most ruthless Muslim killer organizations, called Allah's Avengers. Al-Kahlid and his murderous gang were responsible for numerous car bombings, suicide bombings and assassinations, resulting in death for thousands of men, women and children.

After accomplishing their mission of destroying Alfred's invention, Muqdad ordered the four-man team to remain in the United States. He thought he might have further work for them.

12

"How nice of you to call on me, both of you," Muqdad said with a smiling face to Alfred and Gail when he opened the door to his cottage. "Come in, come in. You are most cordially welcome."

Gail was silent and Alfred was stony-faced and tight-lipped as they followed the professor down a short hall and into the living room. It was furnished in the Middle Eastern style.

"May I offer you a drink?" Muqdad said genially. "I have Scotch, bourbon, rye, vodka—"

"Cut out the nice-guy Westerner act, Muqdad!" Alfred shouted angrily. "I know you for what you are, a wacky religious bigot and sicko fanatic! I know you had my invention destroyed!"

"Why did you do it?" Gail demanded. "So much hard work went into it! I thought I could trust you. It was a terrible crime!"

The Muslim abruptly dropped his friendly manner. It was as if he had taken off a mask. The smiling face was no longer smiling. It had taken on a hard, bitter expression. In the shining eyes was mingled triumphant joy and malignant hatred

"No, it was not a crime!" he said proudly, "it was a religious obligation. Malbrim, the world will never know of wicked machine! I did my duty as a faithful Muslim. Islam will triumph over all the other creeds of the world! The crescent banner will be raised in every city, town and village! Listen well you two unbelievers! There is no God but Allah, and Mahomet, may he be forever praised, is his prophet!"

"Your ravings are the words of a demented, mentally deranged creature!" Alfred shouted back at Muqdad. "Fool, you destroyed metal, wires, plastic, chips! That is all you destroyed! But you did not and cannot destroy the ideas that went into the making of my invention! They are still in my head, and in Gail's head!"

"So you and your Muslim thugs have accomplished nothing, nothing!" Gail laughed gleefully. "Alfred and I will rebuild the machine and one day Islam will be blown away like the desert sands from which it came. Nothing true and rich and nourishing can grow in the desert. And that is why in Muslim lands there is poverty, misery, stagnation and tyranny! Muslims come to Western countries by the millions to improve their standard of living, their quality of life. They want to escape the dry rot that Islam creates. How many people in the West choose to live in Muslim countries?"

Muqdad's face paled the color of chalk. He was astonished, shocked, that anyone would dare to speak so insultingly about his dearly held religion. He stared, speechless, at Alfred and Gail as they laughed mockingly in his face.

Alfred and Gail were laughing all the way to the door. Soon as he heard it slam, Muqdad was on the phone to Zutu al-Kahlid. He and his team of terrorists were staying at a hotel sixty miles away.

"Those two must die!" Muqdad told him. "Get to work right away! We must stop them from building another one of those devilish machines! I don't care how they die, but die they must! Allah be praised!"

After their classes the next day, Alfred and Gail went to his house. In a safe in the living room, behind a painting of Thomas Edison, Alfred had stored all his notebooks and papers relating to the Vibrating Replicator.

They went to work in the kitchen because it had more bright lights. They were sitting at the kitchen table only a half hour when a terrific explosion ripped away the living room and most of the dining room. Alfred and Gail suffered only minor injuries from flying pieces of wood. But of course they were a good deal shaken up.

The police were on the scene in a matter of minutes, as well as three fire trucks. Except for the kitchen and toilet, the house was in a shambles. The firemen left after making sure there was no threat of a fire starting.

Three police officers and a captain remained, sifting through the debris for evidence. The police captain left his men to their work and went into the kitchen. Gail and Alfred were having a drink at the kitchen table.

The captain said bluntly, "Professor, this was a deliberate attempt to kill you. We are pretty certain that a bomb was tossed into your living room, probably through an open window. Do you have any enemies? Would anyone want to see you dead?"

"Captain, I teach physics," Alfred said. "It is a non-controversial and apolitical subject. I can think of no one who wants me dead. It must have been a lunatic who did this."

The captain gave him a hard skeptical look and walked out.

After the police were gone Alfred said, "Gail, we have to disappear—and fast! Muqdad was behind this attempt to kill us! We have to go someplace where we can rebuild my invention. We have to get away from that mad professor's terrorists! They failed this time, but I'm sure they will try again."

"Where can we go?" Gail asked.

"Do you have a passport?"

"Yes."

"Go home and start packing!"

"Where are we going? Do you have a place in mind?"

"Yes, the beautiful island of St. Lucia in the Caribbean. Muqdad's killers will never find us there. We can continue our work there. I'll rent a house. We'll be able to work in peace, and in six or seven weeks we'll have a Vibrating Replicator number two! Whatever equipment we need we can get down there, and if not, I'll have it shipped to us. Gail, nothing can stop us! In two months I will show the world that the Christian religion is the only true religion, and the others are all manmade."

But Professor Alfred Malbrim was wrong. Halfway to that lovely island the plane blew up, and all two hundred and eighty-seven passengers on board perished.

And that is why the world never heard of Professor's Malbrim's marvelous invention. But whether Christianity or Islam will one day be the only religion on this planet, only time will tell.

The Lady and the Coconut Boy

By

Dominick Ricca

They came to the top of the hill along the coast road and Mal Kravitiz stopped the car. The panoramic view was breathtakingly beautiful. From this high up they could see almost a third of this Caribbean island of Bonada. On the oceanside to their right, below the rugged cliffs, stretched miles and miles of golden sandy beaches. Whitecapped waves splashed soundlessly ashore. The tops of the palm trees swayed slowly in the mild breeze. The light sparkled in the dazzling sun.

"Pretty, isn't it?" Mal said to the woman sitting beside him.

Evelyn Damant smiled wanly.

"Yes, it's pretty," she said indifferently. "So what."

"That bump on the horizon is Martinique, about twenty miles from this island."

"Twenty miles . . . I'll have to write that down so I don't forget it."

"I've been on a dozen of these islands. Bonada sure has them beat for beauty and beaches." He took a nip from the pint bottle of Scotch whisky he held in his hand.

"That's so important for me to know," Evelyn said. "Now will you stop drinking. You've been hitting the bottle since breakfast."

"I can handle it," Mal said, setting the car in motion.

After they drove for ten minutes without speaking Evelyn burst out, "Mal, can't we get off this road! I'm sick of looking at all that goddamn water!"

"What've you got against the Atlantic Ocean?"

"There's too much of it! And with your boozing and this lousy narrow road with all those potholes, we could skid over these cliffs! You want to get us both killed?"

"Okay, okay," Mal said, turning into a side road.

In a matter of minutes they were inland and driving through lush green hills and a dense forest. Here the air was much cooler. Even in the late afternoon a heavy mist hung like gray veils among the hills.

Just as Mal was about to take a sip from the bottle, Evelyn snatched it out of his hand and flung it out the window.

"Hey, what the hell you do that for?"

"How many times have I told you not to drink and drive?"

"Evelyn, you been cranky since we arrived on this island five days ago, a real grouch. Lighten up, will you? We came here to have a good time."

"You came to Bonada to have a good time. I came to forget."

"What're you beefing about? So your last movie bombed. You still made three million out of that turkey."

"I used to be able to demand fifteen million, and get it—and with a percentage of the profits! But it isn't the money, damnit, it never was only the money with me. The goddamn movie fans have turned their backs on me, me, Evelyn Damant! Four movies in a row, and all stinkers! I was once the top female star in Hollywood, and now look at me! I'm not talked about, I'm not mentioned in the gossip columns! A has-been, all washed up at thirty-seven!"

Mal braked the car and turned to Evelyn, shaking his head, a pitying smile on his face.

"Evelyn, this is me, Mal, you're talking to, not some movie magazine reporter."

"What do you mean?"

"You were thirty-seven ten years ago. Why don't you face reality?"

"What reality?"

"The reality that you are no longer a young woman."

"I'm still a very attractive woman, goddamn you, Mal!"

"Sure you are, sure you are—and still plenty desirable. But you can't go on insisting that you play that young beauty who starred in all those big hit movies."

Evelyn's face softened as she stared through the windshield in happy recollection, her eyes a little misty.

"Yes, oh, yes, yes," she said, smiling. "What wonderful, outstanding movies, and those exciting, memorable roles I played . . . . "Woman of New Orleans" . . . "Death and Desire" . . . "A Woman with a Past" . . . "Her Demon Lover" . . . "The Wife and the Mistress" . . . "Fire in the Blood" . . . and so many others, so many others . . . ."

"Yes, and all box-office smashes. You left everybody in the dust. You made a more powerful impact on the screen than Garbo. You had a sultry, torrid sex appeal, and you could act. When you played a role, you were that woman. You always performed with convincing sincerity."

"Evelyn turned sharply around and faced Mal.

"Why are you talking about me in the past tense? Why can't those marvelous times come back, Mal, why, why? Tell me why."

"You won't like my answer."

"Tell me, Mal, tell me!"

"Okay, you want it—here it is. I'll tell you why. Because movie stars are like empires."

"What the hell you talking about?"

"Empires rise and fall, and so do movie stars."

"No, no, Mal! Not to me! Not to Evelyn Damant!"

"Why should you be any different? It happened to Bette Davis, Doris Day, Joan Crawford, Claudette Colbert—I could go on and on."

"But why, Mal, why?"

"Age, Evelyn, age. It gets them all eventually, except Jean Harlow and she died young. But your movie career hasn't come to an end just because of all those flops."

"What are you getting at? You think I should go to one of those beauty resorts, or get a facelift?"

"Evelyn, face facts. You have to stop living in your glorious past. You have grown older, but you haven't grown up. You have to start accepting the parts of older, mature woman—you know, the wise aunt, the self-sacrificing mother, the woman of experience who helps the young heroine with her big problem. Get what I mean? You have to move on."

"To supporting roles?'

"Well, yes, to supporting roles."

"Never, never! I'm Evelyn Damant! A star! Forever and always! I will never play lowly character roles!"

"Evelyn, I'll tell it to you straight. That last movie of yours failed because you were too old for the role—a middle-aged woman falling in love with a young man of twenty-five."

"But I wasn't supposed to be a middle-aged woman!"

'That's my whole point. That's how the movie audience saw you, and all the makeup people in Hollywood couldn't give you a youthful appearance and hide your real age. It's no wonder people in the theaters across the country laughed at the movie."

"No, now! You have it all wrong, Mal, all wrong! It wasn't me! "A Woman in Love" could have succeeded! The idea was good! I was right for the part! The movie stunk because of that crappy script and the moronic lines I had to speak! You should've written the script! I don't want you for my agent. I want you to write screenplays for me. You were once Hollywood's top screen writer. Why don't you go back to doing what you do best?"

"I—I lost the knack. The fire for writing has . . . burned out in me. It's all . . . gone . . . gone . . . ."

"Mal, that's not true. You still have that talent in you. If only you could get off the booze, you would get that old fire back."

"Evelyn, I tell you it's gone—gone forever."
"Don't talk like that. You can get back that writing drive again, I know you can."
"I don't know, I . . . ."
"Okay, Mal, maybe you're right, maybe that guy in the movie was too young for me. He should have been a mature man. But I just know I can make a come-back if you'd only write me a good script."
"Evelyn, believe me, I'm dead inside. Sometimes I think my libido is extinct. Even sex . . . doesn't . . . you know what I mean."
"I was wondering about that. You haven't come to my bedroom since we arrived on this island."
"It's not you, it's me. My sex desire comes and it goes. Right now I don't feel anything."
Evelyn stared at Mal. He turned his eyes away from.
"Mal, when were married you were such a passionate lover. You could never get enough of me."
He looked back at her and smiled.
"When I was your hubby number three I was much younger."
"You were a good husband to me."
"But you still divorced me for husband number four, and then went on to husband number five."
"I fall in love so easily."
"And fall out of love just as easily."
"Let's get back to my career and forget about my love life."
"You mean your sex life. Evelyn, have you ever really loved a man?"
She ignored the question. After staring up at the hills for several moments she looked back at Mal.

"Damnit, Mal, it's up to you! You hold the fate of my career! You, you!"
"How me?"
"I was thinking . . . if you could write me a terrific script—"
"Back to that again!"
"But if you could get back to work."
"A big if."

"Oh, Mal, if only you could write me a sensational script, I'm sure we could get Todd Andrews to put up the money."

"I'm not so sure. He took an awful bath in that ridiculous "A Woman in Love." But then what the hell is twelve million dollars to Andrews. Ten years ago, at the age of thirty, he inherited billions—an international conglomerate. And so he took up a hobby, playing at being a big-shot movie producer. He did it to get close to the movie stars. God, what lavish parties he could throw.

"Mal, I know he still has a great deal of admiration for me, in spite of the fact that the movie was a dud."

'Yes, I remember the first time he met you at one of his parties. How he drooled over you. He even asked you for your autograph."

"How he gushed over me, telling me that he'd seen all my movies, that he'd been a great fan of mine for years, and what an honor it was for him to meet me in person."

"And as I watched him looking at you like some dopey starry-eyed kid, I suddenly had this brilliant idea. I got him alone and asked him if he'd like to produce your next movie. He nearly fell off the chair. Of course he would produce Evelyn Damant's next movie! What a an honor to be the producer Evelyn Damant picture! What a thrill for him to see his name on the screen with the name of a Hollywood living legend! And right then and there he took out his checkbook and asked me how much I needed."

"So that's how easy it was?"

"That's all there was to it."

"Mal, he's crazy about me, but not as a woman. More as an icon, an idol."

"Yes, you're right. He sure as hell worships you. He would no more think of getting in bed with you than a Catholic would think of sleeping with the Virgin Mary."

"You think he'd produce my next movie?"

"Probably."

"So the problem of the money is solved. Now all you have to do is write me that script. Mal, you can do it! I have confidence in you! I know you can go back to being the great creative screen writer you once were! Yes, yes, with Todd Andrews' money and you your old self, I'll be once again the queen of Hollywood—a star is reborn!

"Dream on, dream on."

"Mal, damnit, I'm not dreaming! Goddamn you, write me a crackerjack script, like the one you wrote when we were married. What was it? The title?"

"That was . . . "The Girl of Your Dreams.""

"Yes, that was it! How the critics raved over my performance! And those torrid love scenes! Oh, Mal, I want so desperately to go back to those beautiful times!"

Mal stared thoughtfully at Evelyn's excited face and said, "I think we should be getting back to the villa," and he started the car.

After driving a few miles they saw women along the side of the road. Piles of coconuts were at their feet. In one hand they held out a coconut, and in the other hand they held a machete.

Mal slowed down the car and stopped beside one of the women.

"I'm thirsty," he said. "I'm going to have a coconut. You want one?"

"I'm not thirsty."

"One," Mal said to the woman.

With a swift stroke of the machete she cut off the top of the coconut and handed it to Mal.

"One dollar American money, please," she said, smiling.

Mal gave her the dollar and drove off. After drinking all the juice in the coconut, he tossed it out the window.

"Ah, that was good, very refreshing. You should have tried one."

"I'll have a drink when we get home," Evelyn said.

"So will I, and more than one."

"You just can't satisfy that unquenchable thirst, can you?"

"I'll be reaching for a drink when I'm dying."

Suddenly Evelyn leaned eagerly forward and said excitedly, "Look, look!"

"I'm looking. All I see is a boy selling coconuts."

"Stop the car."

"What for?"

"I'm—I'm thirsty!"

As mal slowed to stop beside the boy, Evelyn stared him with wide-open eyes. Her lips were parted, and she began to take deep breaths.

The boy was selling his coconuts on Evelyn's side of the road. He was bare from the waist up. He wore ragged shorts that had originally been long pants, and worn canvas shoes with his toes sticking out of them.

He had a very unusual appearance. He seemed to be more white than black, and yet he was black, but with a lot of white blood in him.

The explanation was in the history of Bonada. The British and French had fought over the island and it had changed hands half a dozen times, until the British won out in the early nineteenth century. The official language was English, but many of the people spoke a French patois. Bonada got its independence more than twenty years ago.

And so this young seller of coconuts had in him the blood of Norman and English aristocrats and princes of Africa. He showed it clearly in his looks. His hair was slightly kinky, but a shining blond. His eyes were blue. His nose was straight and long, the cheek bones not too high, and the thin lips were the lips of his blue-blooded ancestors. His body was slender and wiry, and in the late afternoon sunlight shone with a bronze glow.

"You like coconut, lady?" he said smiling and showing perfectly even white teeth. His soft voice had a singsong quality to it.

Evelyn was entranced by the exquisiteness of his youthful male beauty. She had never seen anyone like him. She was tempted to reach out and touch his shining bronze-colored skin. And how handsome he was! She was so fascinated by him that, though she heard his voice, the words did not register.

"Evelyn," Mal said roughly, "he's asked you twice already if you want a coconut . . . . Well, do you?"

"Oh, yes, yes, please."

The boy cut off the top of the coconut and handed it to Evelyn with a broad smile.

"Thank you," she said.

"One dollar, please."

'Give him five dollars, Mal," Evelyn said, tipping her head back and putting the coconut to her mouth.

"Five bucks! For a coconut?"

"No, make it ten dollars."

"This is your lucky day, kid," Mal said, giving the young man the money.

"Thank you very kindly," he said, looking at Evelyn with his big smile.

"Okay, sonny. Well, Evelyn, let's get going."

"Wait, Mal. I want to finish this here."

Mal watched her impatiently as she drank all the juice in the coconut. When she was done she handed it back to the young man.

"Thank you, that was delicious."

"So glad you enjoy it, lady," he said, tossing the coconut over his shoulder into the woods behind him.

"Can we go now, Evelyn?" Mal said.

"Uh . . . what's your name?" Evelyn said.

"Me?"

"Yes, you. What are you called?"

"I am Emile."

"That's French. Do you parlez francais?"

"Oui, madame. Je parle francais. Vous aussi, you too?"

"My second husband was French and he taught me a few words."

"Come on, let's get back to the villa," Mal grumbled. "I need a dip in the pool. I'm roasting in this car."

"Every day from ten to five o'clock, except on Sunday."

'Goodby, Emile. My name is Evelyn."

"And my name is Mal, if you want to know, kid!" Mal said, driving off.

"Goodby, Miss Evelyn," Emile shouted. "Goodby and come again!"

Evelyn stuck her head out the window, looking back at Emile, who was waving his hand. She waved back at him. Only when they made a turn in the road and she could no longer see him did she lean back on the seat, smiling and for some reason feeling very good.

"What a good-looking young man," she said. "I can't make Emile out. He's black and yet he isn't black."

'You got a lot of those half-breeds on these islands. Remember, these blacks were slaves on these Caribbean islands for centuries. Whenever the white masters took a fancy to a pretty slave girl, hell, they just did what they pleased and her father and brothers couldn't say a damn thing. And the wives of the white men knew better than to complain. They had to bear their shame in slice. So that's why there are all these people of mixed blood."

"Yes," Evelyn said slowly, "but Emile is different . . . unique. That blond hair, those blue eyes . . . those regular features . . . . And that superb, lightly tanned, golden body. Mal, he is different."

"Well, yes, I have to admit he is a different kind of half-breed. "I've never seen one quite like him. He sure is one of a kind."

In a half hour they were going up the long driveway to the villa. It was a fourteen-room house in a three-acre park with palm trees and nicely trimmed bushes and hedgerows all around it. The house was on a bluff a few hundred feet above a mile-long beach. It came with a maid, a cook and a butler who doubled as a gardener.

Evelyn had rented it for two months to get away from the States and the scathing, ridiculing criticism of the movie, "A Woman in Love," that she had so desperately hoped would revive her career.

For weeks after the disaster she brooded in her Bel Air mansion, deeply depressed, too embarrassed, refusing to give interviews to newspaper reporters and on television.

The dismal failure of her last movie and all the others had shattered her. She could not sleep. She would wake up the middle of the night, pick up the container with her sleeping pills and wonder how many it would take to end her life.

She lay in bed for days, going without a bath, eating alone in her bedroom, and going out only late at night to wander the grounds, bitterly cursing her fate. Even the stars twinkling in the night sky caused her anguish and were hateful to her.

Once her, Evelyn Damant, had been a brightly shining star in the public eye. Now the star had dimmed, burnt out.

But no, no, she told herself, walking up and down on the grass and wringing her hands. Her star had not gone out! It would never go out! It was hidden behind a cloud. That cloud would pass and once again Evelyn Damant would be a star! Yes, the biggest and the brightest star!

The only people living in the house with her were Mal, a cook, a maid and a chauffeur who had not done any driving for days.

One day Mal was able to persuade Evelyn to leave her room and sit with him by the pool. He got her to eat some breakfast. After she ate he talked to her for a long time, trying to cheer her up, break her out of her apathy. She listened glumly, but said nothing.

After talking for over an hour to Evelyn without getting a response from her, Mal leaned back and said, "Goddamnit, Evelyn, come on, snap out of it! You can't go on being a zombie for the rest of your life! So all those movies laid a big fat egg! That's not the end of the world!"

"It's worse than that," Evelyn said, suddenly sitting up and shaking off her apathy in fiery anger. "It's the end of my career!" My career is more important to me than my life! I have no life without my career—as a star, a star! I'll always be a star! This is only a temporary setback! Evelyn Damant will shine in the sky forever, forever! Do you hear that, Mal? Forever and ever!"

"All right, okay, I won't argue with you. I've been on the phone talking to a number of movie producers, but nobody is interested in you. One of them told me he thought you were box-office poison."

"Me? Evelyn Damant, box-office poison! The goddamn nerve of the bastard! Not too many years ago they were begging me to work for them!"

"Evelyn, maybe what you need is a rest, I mean a change of scenery. Southern California—bah! Let's lose ourselves for a couple of months on one of those small Caribbean islands. What do you say?"

"Anything to get away from this lousy, fickle Hollywood, and those nosy, hounding reporters. What island do you have in mind?"

"Bonada. You'll like it. Peaceful, quiet. It doesn't get mobs of tourists. I was there years ago."

And so they came to Bonada. Laborie was the capital. It was a town of about forty thousand people, half the population of the island.

Evelyn never visited Laborie. She saw it once, when they drove through it on their way to the villa, and she did not like what she saw. It seemed to her a shabby, jerry-built, over-crowded town with dirty streets, dilapidated buildings and wooden shacks that had corrugated, rusty metal roofs.

She spent all her time and near the villa. Every few days Mal took the rented car and drove to Laborie to shop for groceries with Hortense, the maid.

Mornings Evelyn sat moping by the pool with a book in her hands she hardly looked at, or she went down the long flight of stone steps to the beach and swam out for a half mile. She prided herself on being a strong, skilled swimmer.

After she came out of the water she would lie in the shade of a palm tree, trying to keep her mind blank, but sometimes recalling with bittersweet happiness the years when she was Hollywood's top star and America's most popular actress.

Yes, when she entered a room, all eyes were on her. Producers, director, and all the big move stars rushed to greet her. The premieres of her movies were gala events, with thousands waiting outside the theater to catch a glimpse of her when she arrived. And when the queen of Hollywood stepped out of her limousine, how wildly they cheered! And as she walked toward the theater, a dozen flashbulbs popped all around her.

When she found herself brooding sadly over her change of fortune, she would quickly get up, stare far out to sea, gritting her teeth and vow that she would once again be the great star she had been.

She was sure her luck would change. Something would happen, something great and wonderful, a tremendously successful movie! That was all she needed, she told herself. And she was certain that only Mal could do it, write her a magnificent screenplay! He had done it before, and he could do it again, if only he would get off the liquor! If only he had the willpower! She needed a break—a smash movie! And once again she would be the one and only, Evelyn Damant—star of stars! The reigning queen of Hollywood! The winner of three Academy Awards for Best Actress!

Nights she and Mal watched on the VCR tapes of her old movies, her "great triumphs," Evelyn called them. She had brought a dozen of them to Bonada.

On the fourth night they were on the island, Mal wanted to see "Beyond Love and Life." He had written the screenplay, and it was the one tape he himself had brought with him to Bonada.

The movie was not one of Evelyn's favorites, and she did not enjoy watching it. The character of the woman she played had no appeal for her. The part when she was a woman of the world, embracing life and all it had to offer with great gusto, Evelyn loved playing. But when she had that religious conversion—that part of the movie she felt uncomfortable playing.

The story was about a woman who becomes disillusioned with the way she was living, the life of pleasure, luxury and many husbands and lovers. One night, driving alone on a country road, she is caught in a storm and has to seek shelter in a convent. She spends a week in that convent, living closely with the nuns, observing them and thinking . . . thinking of her own aimless, shallow life.

When she leaves the convent, she is a completely changed woman. At the end of the movie, she returns to the faith of her fathers. She uses her great wealth to build a hospital and clinic in West Africa, and spends the rest of her life in a leper colony.

Evelyn always liked to watch a film completely in the dark so that she could concentrate on it without any visible distractions. When the movie was over, she switched on the light in the living room and saw that Mal was not in the armchair where he had been sitting.

She went out to the terrace. Mal was acing up and down.

"Mal, what're you doing out here? Why did you walk out on the movie? I thought you liked it."

"That's just it, I like it too much. I think it was my best work."

"I disagree. You produced better stuff."

"Evelyn, I wanted to write something serious, not provide moviegoers with just mere entertainment."

"Mere entertainment! That's what they put down good money for—to be entertained. They don't want a sermon, they don't want to be preached at."

'Evelyn, didn't the film influence you in any way, make you think of the way you live?"

"The way I live?"

"Yes. In the first part of the movie I had you in mind—the woman who lives only for herself, who thinks only of enjoying herself, of pleasure, of men."

"And what the hell is wrong with that? That's what real life is all about. How I loathed and despised that woman in your story that gave up everything, her life of luxury and wealth, to work in a leper colony! What a dope she was, what a sappy ending you gave the film. Why would any sane person want to live among lepers—those hideously deformed creatures, no mouths, no noses, stumps where their hands were? Tell me why. It's abnormal, unnatural."

"She acquired ideals, Evelyn, ideals."

Ideals are for fools. I love the life I'm living. I would not give it up for anything. And another thing, "Beyond Love and Life" was not a big money-maker. In these prosperous times people don't care for that maudlin religious crap. That's why it didn't make money, Mal, it didn't make much money."

"Money, money!" Mal said disgustedly. "And let me tell you something. That woman in my story wasn't abnormal. There are many men and women right now doing the same thing with lepers and Aids victims."

"That's their morbid vocation in life."

"And what's your lofty vocation?" Mal asked.
"My . . . vocation?"
"Yes, tell me what it is. I'd like to know."
"It's . . . why, it's—it's being a star!"
"You are no longer a star, Evelyn."
"Damn you, Mal, that's not true! I am Evelyn Damant! She will always be a star!"

The sun was beginning to go down when Emile sold his last coconuts to a group of hiking German tourists. It was an hour since Mal and Evelyn had driven off. He counted his money and was satisfied. The ten dollars the Americans gave him made it and extra good day.

Emile started for home. Sometimes he was lucky and hitched a ride on a truck and did not have to walk the five miles to the small fishing village where he lived with Elise in a three-room house.

Today he was picked up by a truck carrying bananas. Emile sat with the driver looking out at field after field of banana trees. The bananas were wrapped in plastic bags to protect them against insects. The fruit was shipped to England. That was half of Bonada's economy. The other half was tourism. Much of the fish that was brought in from the sea was sold to the scores of hotels on the island, but most of it went to feed the native population.

In less than an hour Emile was walking through the fishing village. The truck had dropped him off less than a mile away. A number of boats were lying on their sides on the beach. Men and women were sitting on the sand mending the fishing nets.

They all gave Emile a cheerful greeting as he approached them. But when he was the men and women, many of them shook their heads sadly, thinking of the double tragedy.

The small house Emile lived in with Elise was at the end of the village. He dropped the machete on the porch and entered the house. Elise was standing over the stove, stirring a steaming pot. She turned around when she heard him come in.

"Emile," she said, smiling brightly, "you are early. You sold all the coconuts?"

"Every one. Today I didn't have to carry any back. And I had good luck today!"

"What good luck?"

"Look," he said, taking out the money and holding out the ten-dollar bill.

Elise took in both hands and stared at it in wonder.

"Ten dollars! How did you get it?"

"Americans, a man and a woman, they gave it to me. Now I can buy you that dress I promised you."

"No, no, Emile. That can wait. I want you to buy yourself a good pair of shorts."

"Elise, I promised you that new dress and you will get it! No arguments!"

"All right. Get washed. Supper is almost ready."

Emile and Elise had had a terrible tragedy in their lives. A year ago their parents went out in their fishing boat as they had done for years. They were caught in a violent storm and were lost at sea. The boat was found overturned days later, but the bodies were never recovered.

Father Lebreton brought them the tragic news. The heartbroken children cried for hours. The old priest tried to give what comfort he could, but he cried too. The parents of Emile and Elise had been very dear friends of his. He had come from France thirty years ago, and for fifteen years he had been the village priest.

But the immediate problem was where they were going to live. Several families had offered to take them into their homes.

Father Lebreton asked Emile and Elise which family they wanted to live with. But they shocked him by saying that they had decided to live together in the house where Emile had lived all his life with his parents.

After they had been living together for six months the old priest went to see them and suggested that they should get married. It did not look good, he told them, a boy and a girl living together all by themselves. The people in the village thought it a great scandal, two youngsters living together as if they were man and wife.

When Father Lebreton left Emile said, "Elise, what do you think? Do you want me for your husband?"

"Emile, you know how much I love you. We have been sleeping in the same bed for many months now, and I consider myself already your wife."

"And I feel the same way."

"Oui, oui! Emile, vous savez come je t'aime!"

"Et moi, je ne t'aime pas!"

"Mais . . . je crois . . . I thought you loved me . . . ."

"No, I do not love you! Je t'adore, je t'adore, ma belle cherie! I adore you, adore you, my darling! My darling wife!"

When Emile came out for supper after washing up, he placed the ten-dollar bill on the table. He liked to look at it. And after the supper, as they did every night, Emile and Elise walked down to the other end of the village to the old stone church.

At the back of the church, behind the pews, was an ebony carving of the crucified Christ. The work was so realistically done that the body seemed to be writhing in agony.

Emile and Elise knelt down on the prie-dieu in front of the carving, looking up intently at the figure on the cross and praying.

"How he must have suffered," Elise said when they got up.

"Yes," Emile said, "he did it out of love for all us weak sinners."

Then, as was their nightly practice, they walked down a side aisle and into a chapel near the main altar. Above the small altar in the chapel was another ebony carving, this one of the Holy Family, the Virgin Mother holding the Christ Child in her arms and St. Joseph standing beside them.

After glancing briefly at the carving, Emile and Elise stood holding hands in front of a stained-glass window. In the wall below the window were two marble plaques inscribed with the names of their parents. They remained there in silent meditation for several minutes.

As they were walking back to the house, Emile suddenly stopped in the deserted, dark village square and took Elise in his arms.

"Elise, I want to do . . . this in a formal way."

"What, Emile? What are you talking about, formal way?"

"Elise, I love you. Will you be my wife?"

"Yes, yes! I will be your wife with all my heart!"

"We will be married in May. What a lovely May bride you will make, my darling."

That afternoon when Evelyn brought the coconut from Emile and they returned to the villa, they both got into their bathing suits and had a dip in the pool. While Evelyn stayed in the pool swimming back and forth, Mal sat under an umbrella at a table drinking a tall Scotch on the rocks and gazing out at the sea.

When Evelyn got in bed that night, and even after taking two sleeping pills, she could not sleep. She felt restless, nervous, tossing and turning in bed. Some vague though was gnawing at her, but what, what? she kept asking herself.

Was she troubled because of the film they had watch that night? It was "The Secret World of Naomi Kendell," the movie that had catapulted her to fame. And it was followed by a second enormous success—"The Hellcat." And then more and more successes and Hollywood was at her feet.

But it was not her lost popularity that was troubling her tonight. It was something else. But she could not grasp what exactly it was.

For the third time Evelyn got out of bed and walked around the dark room. She picked up things and put them down. She looked closely at the clock on the night table. It was ten minutes after five o'clock. She turned on the lamp, and quickly turned it off.

She opened the French doors and looked out. There was half a moon shining in a dark sky with a few puffy white clouds. There was no breeze. Everything was still and silent.

And then she heard a voice, a drunken voice.

It was Mal. He was staggering down the terrace, holding a quart bottle of whisky by the neck.

"The hell with writing!" he mumbled to himself. "The hell with it! Been writing for too many damn years! All written out! The hell with it! I'll take Scotch!"

Evelyn watched Mal. He stopped, swaying a little. He put the bottle to his mouth and took a long drink.

"Ah, that was good," he said, wiping his mouth, "better than beating my brains out on a typewriter!"

And then he saw Evelyn.

"Evelyn, you're just what I need! This stuff has waked up my libido!"
"You are filthy drunk!"

"Evelyn," he said, coming closer to her, "Evelyn, let me in. I need you tonight, God, how I need you!"

"Get away from me, you drunken sot!"

"Goddamnit, I was once your husband!"

"Yes, and you were once a man. Act like a man again, and I'll treat you like a man."

"What do you want from me?"

"First you have to stop the drinking."

"Sure, Evelyn, anything you say," Mal said, hurling the bottle against the side of the house and shattering it to bits, and making a long black stain on the wall.

"See, Evelyn, I stopped drinking," he said, trying to put his arms around her. "Now let me come in."

She pushed him away from her. He staggered backward.

"What the hell's the matter with you? I did what you said."

"All you did was break a bottle. Now prove to me you are the man you once were."

"How do I do that?"

"Write me a screenplay, help me get back my career."

"Evelyn . . . have a heart . . . I can't. It isn't in me anymore."

"Write me a smash screenplay, something like "The Defiant Miss Pritchard," and—and we'll get married again."

"I can't, I can't do it."

"So why did you bring your typewriter to Bonada?"

"I've had that machine for twenty years. I never go anywhere without it. Don't you remember, I took it with me when we went on our honeymoon to Morocco?"

"Yes, and I think you spent more time with it than you spent with me in bed."

"When my head is swimming with a story, I have to get it down when it's red hot. "The Sins of Marie Rose" was one of my best screenplays. And your performance in it got you your second Oscar."

"So why can't you do it again?" Evelyn asked. "Try, try! Get back to writing!"

"I have tried, damnit, how I've tried in California. And even here on Bonada. The first morning after we arrived on this island I swore to myself I was going to get back to doing my real work. I was bursting with determination. Right after breakfast I went to my room, sat down at my typewriter, put a sheet in it and . . . ."

"And what?"

"Nothing," Mal said. "Nothing came to me. I sat staring at that blank paper for an hour. It was maddening, frustrating, the worst kind of fiendish torture . . . worse than anything that a writer can experience. I tried again the next day, and again—nothing. No ideas came to me. My mind remained a blank, a total blank."

'Mal, it's just writer's block."

"No, no, it isn't just that. Writer's block doesn't last for years. I've lost it . . . for good."

'No, you haven't, Mal, you haven't."

"I have no ideas, Evelyn, no ideas. Give me an idea, a story-line, something."

"What idea, what storyline, can I give you? You're the writer."

"I was the writer. I'm sorry, Evelyn, I'm sorry. I hope you understand. Now . . . will you please let me come in. I really need it. I need it real bad. Please, Evelyn, please . . . please."

"No, you have to earn it!" Evelyn said harshly.

"You won't let me in?"

"Not until you show me you're the man you once were."

"I'm not! I never can be! My brains are all dried up!"

"Your brains aren't dried up, they are soaked in alcohol."

"Okay, okay, the hell with you! I know where I can get it. There's plenty of meat available in Laborie. I've seen lots of women walking the streets in town. I can get all I want there. Now I'm going back to my room, and I'm going to get good and drunk!"

"You are already drunk."

"I said good and drunk!" Mal said, and staggered away.

After he was gone Evelyn remained standing in the doorway a long time. That nagging thought came back to her. She tried hard to think what it was. It was something that happened yesterday. But what had happened yesterday? she asked herself.

After a while she noticed an orange glow spreading across the sky, followed by a rosy light. Dawn was breaking. Her eyes began to feel very heavy. She felt so sleepy, so very sleepy. She went back to the bed, fell down on it and in a minute was asleep.

When she woke up it was broad daylight. Bright sunshine came in through the windows of the French doors. She turned over and looked at the clock. It was ten to twelve.

After a quick shower Evelyn went out to the terrace. Hortense was picking something out of the pool with a long-handled scooper.

"Hortense, have you seen Mr. Kravitz?"

"No, madam. I have not seen him all morning."

Sleeping off his drunk, Evelyn thought.

"Would madam like some breakfast?"

"I'm not hungry. Just toast and coffee, please."

"Yes, madam."

After the light breakfast Evelyn sat at the table, musing, thinking of Mal, herself and wondering about that vague thought that went round and round in her head.

Suddenly she got up. A restless, nervous excitement gripped her. She went quickly into her room, slipped into a one-piece bathing suit, stepped into her sandals and went out.

She almost ran down the stone steps, hurried across the sand and dived into the water. She swam almost a mile out with hard, vigorous strokes as if she were in a race. When she came out of the water she was exhausted, dropping down with her back to a palm tree, her head bowed, panting.

When she got her breath back she stared far out to sea. The nervous excitement had left her, but her mind was still grappling with that troubling thought.

The waves pounding on the beach had a hypnotic effort on her. She began to nod. She tried to keep her eyes open, but she could not. A peaceful, restful drowsiness came over her, and then she dropped off to sleep.

When she woke up she saw that the sun was more than halfway across the sky. Her mind was clear, and it came to her, the answer to the question her mind had been seeking, the answer to that vague, persistent thought. Yes, that was it! That was it! She had to see that coconut boy! She had to see Emile, talk to him!

She went up the steps two at a time, and when she got to the top she saw Hortense sweeping the terrace.

"Hortense, what time is it?"

The maid glanced at her wristwatch.

"It is twenty minutes past four o'clock, madam."
"Have you seen Mr. Kravitz?"

"He left the villa about an hour ago, madam.
"Did he say where he was going?"
"I heard him tell the livery driver to take him to Laborie."
"Oh, so he didn't take our rented car?"
"No, madam. He phoned to town for a livery car."

To find himself a woman, Evelyn thought. Well . . . let him. He was such an unhappy man, maybe a little fun would do him some good. And anyway, she had something more important on her mind.

"Hortense," she said, "I'm going for a drive. I should be back in a little while."

"Very good, madam."

In her room she changed into a light summer dress and went out to the car. She drove down the driveway, up a hill and then on to the road.

But where was she going? Where had they seen Emile? On which road? By now if was after four-thirty, and Emile said he stopped working at five o'clock.

She went up and down roads, passing only women coconut sellers, and then, finally, she saw him a hundred yards away, on her right.

When she came up beside him she stopped the car and leaned over on the passenger side. She was so happy to see him.

"Oh, Miss Evelyn, you like another one of my coconuts?"

She stared silently at Emile in simple wonder and admiration. She had seen many beautiful male bodies in her life, but never one like Emile's. He was standing in the fading sunlight, and his bronze, lithe body shone with a golden, shining luster. She could not take her eyes off him, all of him, his blue eyes, his blond hair, his pearly white teeth and his fine lips.

She was so absorbed in looking at Emile that she did not hear his question, and he said, once again, "Miss, Evelyn, you like another one of my coconuts?"

Evelyn's throat suddenly felt very dry. There seemed to be a lump in it. She swallowed hard.

"Yes, yes, Emile, I'm very thirsty."

He cut off the top of the coconut with his machete and gave it to her. She drank greedily, not stopping until she emptied the juice in the coconut. She gave it back to Emile, and he tossed it in the woods behind him. He stood there, with the machete in his hand, smiling at her. Evelyn smiled back at him.

"You were very thirsty, Miss Evelyn. Maybe you would like to drink more?"

"No . . . no thank you, Emile."

"One dollar, please."

Evelyn opened her handbag and took out a roll of bills.

"Emile, here, take this . . . all of it."

After counting the money he looked at Evelyn in surprise.

"This is two hundred dollars. You give this all to me?"

"Yes, all for you. Emile, I want you to get in the car—come with me."

"Go with you, to your home?"

"Yes, yes."

"You want me, Emile, to get in the car with you?"

"Yes, Emile. I—I want you to have dinner with me in my place."

Emile took a step back and stared curiously at Evelyn, wrinkling his forehead, as if seeing her for the first time.

"I have seen your face before, in the movies, yes in the movies! You are Evelyn . . . Damant, the Hollywood star!"

"So, you finally recognized me."

"Miss Evelyn, you are so much more beautiful in person than you are on the big screen."

"Thank you, Emile. That's the nicest thing anyone has ever said about me. You really think I'm very beautiful?"

"Yes, Miss Evelyn, the most beautiful woman I have ever seen."

"Emile, you certainly know how to compliment a lady."

"It's true," he said with a serious face. "Miss Evelyn, you are so—so—"

"Emile, call me Evelyn. I want us to be friends."

"Miss . . . uh . . . Evelyn, you want me to be your friend?"

"Yes, we're going to be very good friends. Come, get in, I want to show you my place, where I live. We'll have a nice dinner, have a good talk, and get to know each other better."

Emile hesitated, thinking of Elise. If he accepted this invitation from Evelyn, she would worry about him. He always came straight home after his work was done for the day. Then he remembered that Father Lebreton had a phone, the only one in the village. Yes, he would call the old priest when he got to Evelyn's house, and he would tell Elise that he would be late getting home.

"Okay, yes, Evelyn, I come with you," he said, stepping into the car after throwing into the woods the four coconuts he had not sold.

"Emile, would you please put down that big knife," Evelyn said, turning on the ignition.

"Oh, I'm sorry, yes," he said, placing the machete between his feet on the car floor.

During the drive Emile told Evelyn about the phone call he had to make.

"Oh, of course, you want your parents to know where you are."

Emile did not say anything.

When they got to the villa, Evelyn took Emile out to the terrace. She could see he was deeply impressed by the large, luxurious house and the spectacular view of the sea.

"You can use that phone on the table by the pool," Evelyn said to Emile.

While he was making the call, Hortense came out of the house. Evelyn told her that she was having a guest for dinner.

"Yes, madam," Hortense said, looking briefly at the light-skinned boy talking into the phone twenty feet from her. She saw that he was shirtless and wearing only a ragged pair of shorts. She wondered where madam had picked up this plaything and how much she would be paying him for his services.

"Hortense, has Mr. Kravitz returned from Laborie?"

"He phoned a half h our ago to say he was spending the night in town."

Good, Evelyn thought to herself, Mal's got a whore to shack up with. I'll have Emile all to myself. How wonderfully intimate it will be, just the two of us.

"Hortense" she said, "tell cook to give us an especially delicious dinner. I want a big platter of plenty of rice with shrimp, chicken, and beef. Also a nice big lobster salad. And with the appetizers I want some beluga caviar. We'll eat out here."

"Yes, madam. What will you have to drink?"

"Champagne, of course. And make it four bottles."

"Yes, madam," Hortense said, and went into the house.

Emile put down the receiver and came over to Evelyn.

"Everything is all right," he said.

"Fine. Dinner should be ready in about an hour. Let's go down to the beach."

They walked a few feet from the waves that came splashing on the sand. The sun, an orange ball, cast crimson rays across the sea as it hovered just above the horizon.

"Emile, tell me about yourself," Evelyn said. "How old are you?"

"Well . . . this is October . . . in April I'll be eighteen."

"Eighteen years old. You have your whole life ahead of you. What do you intend to do with it?"

"With my life?" Emile asked.

"Yes. What do you want to do?"

"I don't know what you mean. Go on selling coconuts, I suppose."

"Do you make a good living at it?"

"Enough to get by."

"Can't you do anything else? I saw a number of fishing villages up and down the coast."

Emile told Evelyn how his parents died. He said he swore he would never have anything to do with fishing.

After expressing her sympathy, Evelyn asked, "Who do you live with? An aunt, an uncle?"

"I live with Elise."

"Who is Elise?" Evelyn said.

Emile told her that Elise's parents had died with his mother and father at sea, and that since the tragedy they had been living together.

"As brother and sister?"

"We love each other."

"So you are lovers."

"Yes, I love Elise and she loves me. Yes, we are lovers."

"How old is Elise?"

"Three months younger than me."

Emile thought of telling Evelyn that they planned to get married in the spring. But for some reason he could not explain to himself, he did not want her to know.

"Emile, where do you live? In Laborie?"

"No, in a small fishing village. I have lived there all my life. It is called Praslin. Elise and me live in the house my father built when he married my mother."

"Are you happy with your life?"

"I don't know about happy. I am satisfied."

They continued walking up and down the length of the long beach, talking and occasionally stopping to gaze at the setting sun. Dusk began descending over the island. The sun seemed to be sinking in the yellow, shimmering sea.

"Isn't that a lovely sunset?" Evelyn said.

"Yes, very lovely," Emile said.

"Come, our dinner must be ready by now."

When they reached the terrace Hortense was lighting the candles on the table, which had on it several platters covered with silver lids. On a stand beside it was an ice bucket with four bottles of champagne.

"How romantic!" Evelyn said. "Dinner by candlelight! And everything smells so good!"

"Shall I serve, madam?" Hortense asked.

"No, Hortense, thank you, that will be all."

The maid went into the house.

"Sit down, Emile, sit down."

"Like this," Emile said, with his hands to his bare chest.

"Yes, of course! I love to look at you—all of you!"

They sat down at the table.

"Emile, do you like champagne?"

"I have never tasted it. Plain wine, yes, but not champagne."

"How perfectly charming! Reach over to the bucket and open a bottle."

Emile picked up a bottle out of the ice bucket. He held it in both hands and looked at Evelyn.

"Well, what're you waiting for?" Evelyn said. "Open it."

"How do I get the cork off?"

"You are inexperienced. How refreshing. Push up on the cork with your thumb."

The cork came out with a pop and Emile poured the gushing champagne into the glasses. Evelyn picked up her glass.

"Emile, let's drink a toast—to you and me, and to a wonderful friendship!"

They clinked glasses. Evelyn tossed off her wine in one quick gulp. Emile took a short sip and put down his glass.

"No, no, Emile. You must drink it all! Tonight I will show you how to drink champagne!"

Emile emptied his glass. He smiled at Evelyn.

"Fine! Now pour out more wine," Evelyn said as she removed the lids from the platters.

An hour later the slender candles had melted down to small stumps. Thousands of stars glittered in the sky. A soft breeze came in from the sea.

"Come, Emile, you must have more lobster salad."

"Oh, no," he said, "I couldn't eat another bite. I never had some much to eat in all my life."

"At least we can finish this last bottle. There's just enough in it for two glasses."

Emile filled the glasses. He looked at the bottle it was empty.

"How do you like bubbly wine?"

Emile blinked his eyes and smiled sleepily.

"I like the taste, but it goes to the head so fast."

"That's what it's supposed to do, you sweet, innocent boy!" Evelyn said, standing up. "It makes everything so nice and cheerful."

"Yes, it does that," Emile said, trying to keep his eyes open.

"Now I'm going to give you dessert, Emile. I'm sure you will like and enjoy it."

"What dessert?"

"Me! All of me! I'll be back in two minutes. Don't move. Stay just where you are."

Evelyn went into her moonlit, semidark bedroom and took off all her clothes. After perfuming her body all over, she gazed at her naked reflection in the full-length mirror. She smiled proudly, pleased at what she saw. Her belly was flat, her broad, curved hips as sexually enticing as when she was a young woman. And her breasts, because they were not too large, but ample enough, were still firm and did not sag.

"Evelyn," she said to her reflection, "you are still one luscious piece!"

She opened a drawer in the dresser and of the half-dozen bikinis she took out she slipped into the skimpiest one. The top part barely covered her nipples and the lower one was only a few inches wide and was held up by thin straps that went around her thighs.

Before she went out she took one last look at herself in the mirror, from the front, from the back and from the side.

"Evelyn Damant," she said proudly, "the greatest of all movie stars and the most desirable woman in the world! There is no other woman like you!"

She hurried out to the terrace in eager anticipation to see how Emile would respond to her almost naked appearance in the briefest of bikinis. How many times in the past men had stared in open-mouthed awe and wonder at her perfectly shaped, exquisitely beautiful nude body! And how she gloried at their thunderstruck admiration! And when they came to their senses, how they reached out for her, mad with desire.

She came back to Emile from behind him. He was sitting quietly, not moving, his head bent forward, his hands in his lap.

"Emile," Evelyn said softly, smiling.

He did not move.

She made a whirling motion several times, finally stopping in front of him, smiling, her arms raised high.

"Emile, look at me!"

And then she saw that he was sleeping.

"Emile, wake up!" she shouted louder.

His head moved forward until it rested on the table.

Evelyn dropped her hands to her hips and looked at Emile, frowning. Then, shaking her head, she burst out laughing.

"I understand, Emile. It's my fault. I filled you up with too much wine. So instead of a night of passionate love-making, we'll both have a good night's sleep. I'm beginning to feel sleepy myself. Well, okay, Emile, good night."

Evelyn walked slowly back to the bedroom. After taking off the bikini she looked at herself in the mirror.

"That damn champagne! I thought I was going to have that beautiful young creature make love to me! He could have had Evelyn Damant, the movie queen! And what does he do! He falls asleep on me!"

With a deep sigh she turned around and fell down on the bed.

Evelyn was awakened by the sound of a voice. Someone had called her several times. The voice had a hollow sound, and as if it came from a long distance away. How long had she been sleeping? she wondered.

Again she heard her name called. This time she heard it more distinctly, as if it was very close. She was lying on her stomach. She raised her heard and turned over.

"Evelyn."

"Emile, is that you?"

"Yes."

He stood silhouetted in the moonlight between the open French doors. She could see by the smooth shape of his shining body that he was naked.

"Evelyn, I want you. Do you want me?"

"Oh, yes, yes!" God, how I want you, Emile!"

With a wild cry he rushed into the room and leaped on her like a panther. Evelyn threw her arms around him.

"You darling boy, since the first day I saw I wanted you!"

"I am not a boy!"

"No, no! You are not a boy! Oh, what a great big man you are, my darling Emile! Never have I felt any man so deep inside me! Emile, you give me marvelous pain and beautiful pleasure!"

Emile was making grunting, almost angry sounds as he pumped up and down on her with savage frenzy. They rolled over and over on the bed. One moment he was on top of Evelyn, and suddenly she was bouncing joyously up and down on him, shouting with mad delight.

Never in all her life had Evelyn experienced such sweet melting pleasure. She panted frantically, gasping for air. Her breathing became labored. Sweat poured down her face, her body. She made low, gurgling moaning sounds. Wave after wave of rapturous ecstasy swept over her. She felt she was soaring in space. The pleasure became unbearable, too much for her, and after begging Emile not to stop, she began to plead with him to stop.

But Emile went on and on, with more vigorous, maddened fury. It was all too much for Evelyn. She went into a swoon, and fainted.

When she became conscious again and opened her eyes she was looking up at stars in the dark-blue sky. She was being carried. Evelyn turned her head and gazed at Emile's face. He was holding her in his arms, staring straight ahead. They were on the beach. She heard the waves splashing on the sand.

Emile walked into the water and when he was hip deep, he let go of Evelyn and dived in after her, taking her once again in his arms.

"Are you all right?" he asked.

"Yes, yes, I'm all right.

He carried her out of the water and up the beach to the palm trees. He placed her gently on the sand, and when he saw her looking up at him with yearning eyes he fell on top of her.

"Emile, oh, my darling Emile, you wonderful and best of lovers!

They spent the whole night on the beach, making love, sleeping, making love. When they woke up for the fourth time it was bright daylight.

"What time is it, Emile?" Evelyn said, sitting up and brushing sand out of her hair.

He glanced up at the sky.

"It's about eight o'clock."

"We'll have breakfast, and then I'll drive you home."

"Evelyn, you have no regrets?"

"Why should I have any regrets?"

"Well . . . you are such a famous movie star and I am only . . . ."

"Don't talk like that, Emile. You have given me the best night of love I have ever had, and believe me I have had many nights of love. Do you have any regrets, I mean because of your friend? What did you say her name was?"

"Elise."

"Well, are you sorry?"

Emile thought for a moment about Elise.

"No," he lied, "I am not sorry."

An hour later they were driving through the fishing village. Emile pointed to the house at the end of it, and Evelyn stopped the car. They looked into each other's eyes. Emile was thinking of Elise and how he would explain staying away all night. Evelyn was thinking of something else, an idea that thrilled her.

"Would you like to see Elise?" he asked.

But she was not listening to him. The idea had become clearer in her mind. She had to get back to the villa right away and tell Mal about it, see what he thought of it.

"Emile," she said, very excited, "I have just had a wonderful idea! I must see you again! You must come to my house again, spend a few days with me! I'll come back and pick you up tomorrow. Please, please, Emile, say yes!"

"I don't know . . ." Emile said, thinking of Elise.

"I'll pay you three hundred dollars if you stay at my house, and it's not because of what we did last night. It's something entirely different."

"Only two days?"

"Yes, just two days."

"All right, I'll come," he said, getting out of the car.

"Thank you, Emile."

"Would you like to meet Elise? I'll call her out."

"Another time. I'm in a hurry to get back to my place."

"Goodby, Evelyn."

"Until tomorrow," she said, and drove off.

Driving at breakneck speed to get back to the villa, Evelyn nearly collided with a panel truck on the narrow, bumpy road. She was hoping that Mal had returned from Laborie. She was eager to tell him about her inspired idea for a movie.

After parking the car outside the villa, she walked hurriedly through it and went out to the terrace. Mal was having breakfast by the pool.

"Mal, I'm so glad you're here," Evelyn said, sitting down at the table.

He put down his knife and fork.

"What's up? What're you so excited about?"

"Mal, I—"

"Oh, by the way," he said, interrupting her, "I'm sorry I didn't get back last night. I had too much to drink and I thought I'd sleep it off in town."

Evelyn told him about her night with Emile, and that she had just returned from driving him home.

"Well, since you're being so frank with me, I might as well be likewise with you. I didn't sleep off my drunk alone. I got in a conversation with this lonely English tourist in a bar and I spent the night with her. But, Evelyn, why are you so happy, excited and brimming over with enthusiasm? Was Emile's sexual performance that great?"

"It was stupendous, but that's not why I'm so excited. I have something very important to tell you."

"Go ahead, I'm listening," Mal said, picking up his tall whisky drink.

Evelyn took the glass out of his hand and placed it on the table.

"Hey, what's the matter with you! That's only my third drink this morning! You want me to die of thirst?"

"You won't die of thirst. I want you to have a clear head to hear what I have to say."

"And then can I have a drink?"

"Mal, I don't want you to touch another drop until you do a job for me."

"You are asking the impossible!"

"I know from the past that when you are working on a story, you stay cold sober."

"That was a long time ago. And besides, I don't have a story in my head."

"You don't, but I do."

"Evelyn, you have a story, for a movie?"

"Not exactly a story for a movie, but an idea for a story."

Mal leaned back and folded his arms. He was skeptical about this story Evelyn had. A number of times actors had come to him with the outline of story that they thought would make a great movie. But what they showed him always turned out to be worthless.

"Okay, let's hear it," he said. "What's this brilliant idea for a movie?"

"A wealthy middle-aged woman goes to live for a few weeks on a Caribbean island. She was recently divorced her . . . let's say her third husband. She is very unhappy, depressed, even having thoughts of suicide. She meets a handsome young native and has an affair with him. He—he resembles Emile, you know, black, but with a lot of white in him. The affair turns to love for this woman. Yes, for the first time in her life she truly and deeply loves someone. Yes, she loves this young man passionately, with a strong, abiding love, and—"

"And what?"

"Well . . . I don't know. You fill in the rest."

"I don't know . . . . It's a lean idea for a movie."

"But it is something to work on, isn't it?"

"Maybe, maybe. Who is going to play this handsome native?"

"Emile, of course. With his good looks, mixed blood, he'd be perfect for the role."

"I'm not sure. He's never done any acting."

"He won't have to act, just play himself, a shy innocent young man. Mal, I'm certain he's a natural for the part."

"But, Evelyn, you haven't given me much to work on. The story has to be developed further. There has to be conflict . . . . something more than just this woman falling madly in love with a half-breed.

"Mal, you can do it, you can flesh out the story—give it bite!"

"Assuming I am able to work up a scrip, where do we find the money to bankroll this movie?"

"Todd Andrews."

"After the ten of dough he lost on your last movie?"

"Mal, the last time I saw Todd was at that party in Vegas, about two months ago. Do you know what he told to me?"

"What?"

"He said, 'Evelyn darling, I don't give a hoot that I dropped a bundle on that movie. Just being the producer of a film starring Evelyn Damant made it all worthwhile. You are my favorite actress, and nothing can make me change my mind. I am your most loyal fan.'"

"He told you that?"

"His exact words."

Mal got up abruptly and walked up and down, thinking. Evelyn looked at him anxiously. Once he stopped his pacing and gazed at Evelyn for several moments, and then resumed his pacing. A few times he nodded his head approvingly, and once he shook his head angrily. Finally he stood in front of Evelyn and punched the palm of his hand.

"Evelyn, I think you have it on a great idea! As a movie, I'm sure it will be a fabulous success. A real money-maker! Yes, by playing up the race angle the film will be a whopper at the box office! But today a lot of blacks and whites are intermarrying. It's becoming too common, accepted. There's something in a white woman marrying a black guy today. We have to have conflict in our movie."

"So how do we inject conflict in it?"

"Simple. I'll turn the clock back, back to the 1950s. I'll give your wealthy middle-aged woman a Southern, aristocratic background. Her family tree goes back to antebellum times. Her ancestors were slave-holders with thousands of acres. Yes, the time is the '50s, when the South was still the Solid South, the openly racist, bigoted South. She marries this half-breed on this island, and when she brings him home to her estate in . . . Alabama, she is confronted by shock, disgust from all her relatives and friends."

"Sounds terrific!" Evelyn said. "We have the conflict!"

"All those race bigots demand that she give up her black husband or face ostracism. Yes, they will shun her, treat her like an outcast if she refuses to do as they say."

"Does she, does she give up her husband?"

"Wait, wait. We have to have some violence. The Ku Klux Klan gets involved. Remember, this is the '50s, when the Klan was riding high. That sweet outfit threatens the woman with death, burns fiery crosses outside her home, fires shots through her windows and—"

"Mal, tell me how it ends!" Evelyn asked impatiently. "Does she give up her man?"

"I don't know, I haven't thought that far ahead."

"Mal, I want to her to be a strong-will woman! A woman of character who is prepared to stand up to those vicious bigots! I want to play the role of a woman who is willing to sacrifice all, to fight for the man she loves! I'll give the greatest performance of my career! It's sure to get me a fourth Oscar!"

"Slow down, Evelyn, slow down. I'm the one who will be writing the script, and I'll be the one to decide what kind of ending the film has. You understand that?"

"Yes, Mal, whatever you say."

"Fine," Mal said, picking up his drink, walking to the pool and pouring it out. "Evelyn, I swear I won't touch a drop until I finish the script."

Evelyn rose from her chair and threw her arms around Mal.

"Darling, you're my old Mal again! Quick, use the phone here by the pool and call up Todd. I hope that playboy isn't on one of his globe-trotting trips. If he is, he'll be hard to contact."

"No need to worry. I saw in the paper the other day that he was in his Wall Street office piling millions on top of his millions with a couple of merger deals."

"Good," Evelyn said, "call New York right now."

"I'll call him from my room," Mal said, walking toward the house. "I want to get this story down on paper. And then I'll read it off to him and see what he thinks."

"I'm sure he'll like it," Evelyn said. "Tell Todd I think it will make a great film."

A half hour later Mal returned to the terrace. He was beaming.

"Todd loves the story," he said. "He's so crazy about it he's flying down here in his private jet, and he's bringing a bunch of his friends with him."

"How many friends?" Evelyn, frowning.

"He said about fifteen or twenty."

"Mal, I don't have room for all those people!"

"It's okay, they'll be staying at the Hotel Excelsior, ten miles up the road." Todd owns the place."

"Well, that's a relief."

"Evelyn, there's something on another matter I'd like to ask you, if you don't mind."

"What is it?"

"Is Emile really as good in bed as you said?"

"He's the most passionate lover I have ever had, like a bull."

"Good, good! Let's hope the electricity between you and Emile comes across on the silver screen!"

Ten days later a noisy party was going on around Evelyn's pool.

A steel band was providing music at one end of the pool, and seven or eight men and women were swimming in it in the nude. Buffet tables and a bar had been set up. Todd Andrews had brought over from the Hotel Excelsior waiters and a bartender. The women lounging by the pool or sitting beside it at the tables were barebreasted. There was the pungent smell of marijuana in the air. This party had been going on for three days. The men and women would come to the villa around one o'clock in the afternoon and leave three or four o'clock in the morning.

Emile had been living at the villa for ten days.

Now he stood at one end of the pool, disgusted with himself, and disgusted at what he saw all around him. He was dressed in a white suit, yellow silk shirt and sporty white alligator shoes.

A little while ago a man offered him a marijuana, lit it and slapped him on the back. After one puffed he flicked it away in anger. A few moments later, three men and two women ran past him, giggling and laughing, and disappeared behind a hedgerow.

Emile turned away and looked out to sea. It was about five o'clock in the afternoon and he knew that the party would go on for many hours more.

He thought of the life he was living here in the villa. Every night he slept with Evelyn. He was ashamed of himself, ashamed of his obsession with her body. He seemed to be chained to that supple, perfectly shaped body. He had to break that chain that bound him to that body! He had to! He could not go on living this sinful life.

He thought of Elise, and felt even more shame. When he left her he promised her that he would be back in two days. Now he was too embarrassed to phone Father Lebreton to let Elise know why he had not returned. But what could he tell her? The truth? That he had become enslaved by Evelyn's body?

Two bikini-clad girls, a blonde and a redhead, staggered up to him. Emile tried to turn away, but they each took an arm and spun him around.

"Emile, why aren't you joining the party?" the blonde giggled drunkenly."

"Why don't we have our own private party?" the redhead suggested. She too was drunk.

"Sure, Emile, let's go up to one of the rooms and get better acquainted with you."

"Please leave me alone," he said, pulling his arms out of their grasp.

"Emile, what's wrong with you? Don't you like girls?"

"Yes, I do. I like ladies.":

"Oh, Emile, you beautiful creature, I want to eat you alive! God, you look so—so yummy!"

"You handsome creature! Let me show you the many ways I can make you happy!"

Evelyn came out on the terrace. She was wearing shorts and a jersey. She was looking for Emile. When she saw him with the two girls, she walked quickly over to them.

"You girls leave my co-star alone! He's not for you two! Go find yourselves another playmate!"

"But we were just trying to be sociable," the blonde said.

"Go and be sociable with someone else. I have an important matter to discuss with Emile. Now scat, go away."

The girls left and Evelyn turned to Emile with a bright smile.

"I hope those girls weren't annoying you, darling," she said.

"They wanted me to go to a room with them."

"Those dirty little sluts!" Evelyn laughed. "But they didn't mean any harm. It's just their way of being friendly. Let's forget them and talk about the movie we're going to make. Todd Andrews is flying down a film crew in a few days. Mal is just about done with the script."

"I have seen very little of Mr. Kravitz."

"Yes, he's been working like a man possessed, like a demon. What a changed man he is. He's been in his room at his desk twelve hours a day, writing and rewriting. He stops working only to eat and get four or five hours of sleep."

"Evelyn," Emile said slowly, "I'm not so sure about doing this movie. What do I know about acting?"

"Darling, don't let that worry you. Today there is no acting talent in Hollywood, just a lot of attractive men and pretty women. The last good actors and actresses died years ago. Of course I'm excluding myself."

"But, Evelyn. I don't know . . . to act in front of a camera . . . ."

"Emile, listen to me. All you have to do is memorize your lines and do what the director tells you. It's simple as that. Your good looks and marvelous body will do all the rest. I know you are going to be a sensation."

Just then Todd Andrews came out of the house and hurried over to them. He was dressed in a black blazer and blue pants. Andrews was a short, fat man with a thick neck, and a red, chubby face.

"Hello, Emile." he said. "Evelyn, I just came from Mal and—"

"Todd, we are facing a crisis," Evelyn said, interrupting him.

"Crisis, what crisis?"

"My maid Hortense told me a half hour ago that we are running out of food, beer and liquor. I didn't think you'd bring this army down here with you. Do you realize this party had been going on for three days?"

"Three days? Is that all? I once gave a party in my Tuscan palazzo, outside Florence, that lasted a week. And I had more than fifty guests. I do so love a party. Life should be one long, endless party, don't you think?"

"But what about the food and drink? I'm almost out."

"Don't fret yourself over that. I'll think of something."

"Well, if you want this party to go on, you'd better think of something soon."

"I will, I will. But that's not what I came to see you about. Mal has hit a snag in the script. He wants to see you."

"Well, that is a pleasant surprise. The last two times I went to his room to get him to join the party, he growled at me and told me to get out. Why does he want to see me now?"

"Mal is uncertain as to just what kind of ending he should give our picture. He says you've helped him out in the past."

"What does he have in mind?"

"Two endings," Andrews said, "but he's not sure which one to use. In one of them the Klan shoots dead the woman and hangs her black husband from a tree."

"And the other one?" Evelyn asked.

"They return to that Caribbean island where they met and live happily ever after."

"Yes, yes, I see."

"Which one do you prefer?" Andrews asked.

"Let's go and talk it over with Mal."

"If you ask me, I think we should give the movie audience a happy ending. I don't like moviegoers leaving the theater feeling bitter and unhappy. I like to have them walk out feeling good."

"Yes," Evelyn said, "I think you have a point there."

"Emile," Andrews said, "this film is going to make you a star. I'm planning to give you a big publicity build-up."

"Thanks, Mr. Andrews, but I . . . ."

"You just leave everything to me. Everything will work out fine. My lawyers in New York are drawing up your contract."

"Emile, I'll be back in ten minutes, and then you and I will have a good heart-to-heart talk," Evelyn said. "And don't worry about your acting ability. I'll help you out."

"It isn't only that, it's all this . . . ."

"Emile, stop looking so glum," Andrews said. "It's a swell party! Enjoy it!"

Emile shook his head as he watched Evelyn and Andrews go into the house. Once again he looked down the length of the pool and was sick at the things he saw. A girl was vomiting into the pool. Two girls and a drunken, potbellied old man disappeared behind a clump of bushes.

No, he told himself, this was not the life for him. He turned away in disgust, and as he walked down the stone stops to the beach, he thought of Elise. How he missed her, taking her in his arms, kissing her. How he missed coming home and smelling the aroma of the dinner Elise was cooking. And how he missed going to the church at night and standing in the chapel with Elise, holding her hand and thinking of his mother and father . . . and so many, many other things he missed . . . .

Just as Emile was about to walk down to the water, he saw Elise. She was standing behind a palm tree, a sad look on her face.

"Elise!" he shouted, so happy to see her.

He rushed up to embrace her, but she put up her hands to stop him.

"What's the matter?" he said, smiling. "What's wrong?"

Elise did not smile back. She stood in front of him, sad-faced, silent, gazing at him.

"How—how did you find out where I was staying?"

"I asked at some of the big hotels. They told me where the rich American woman had her house. And they told me things, things about you and this woman. You are not staying in her house. You are living with her."

"Elsie, I want you to understand that, well, I . . . . Tell me how you got here. Did someone drive you?"

"A car drove me part of the way. I had to see you about something."

"What?"

"First I want to know the answer to a question."

"What is the question?" Emile said.

"Emile, are you happy . . . living with this woman?"

"Elise, I don't know how to answer you. I though . . . but now I begin to see things in a different way. Her life is so different from the life I have known, the life we have."

"Do you love . . . her?"

"Elise, Elise . . . ."

"Do you want to go away with her?"

"She wants me to be in a movie with her."

"And so you will go away with her and become rich and famous."

"Elise, you said you had something to tell me. What is it?"

"Do you still love me? If you no longer love me and want to go away with the American, I will not tell you."

"Elise, I love you! Oui, je t'adore!"

She smiled and kissed him on the lips.

"Emile, I am pregnant."

Taking her joyfully in his arms he said, "A baby! Are you sure? Are you really sure you are pregnant?"

"Yes, I thought so three weeks ago, but I was not certain. That was why I didn't tell you. I was afraid I might disappoint you."

"And how do you know for sure now?"

"Yesterday I went to see a doctor in Laborie. He told me I was pregnant. Yes, Emile, I am going to have a baby."

"No, Elise, we are going to have a baby!"

"Emile, are you truly happy?"

"Truly and very, very happy! You are going to be a mother, and I am going to be a father! Elise, we will be a family, a real family!"

"But what about her?"

"The American woman?"

"Yes. What will you do about her?"

"Leave her, that is what I will do!"

"Emile, you will be giving up so much . . . the kind of life she can give you. With me you will have . . . ."

"Happiness, happiness, Elise! I was thinking of leaving her, and now, after what you have told me, I have made up my mind."

"Emile, are you sure this is what you want?"

"Yes, yes!"

"You want to come home with me?"

"Home! That word sounds so good!"

Looking up at the house Elise said, "You want to leave all that, Emile? I don't want you to have any regrets later."

"I won't have any regrets. You can't know how glad I am to be leaving here. I feel like a man who is walking out of a swamp. Come, Elise, let's go home. I don't belong here."

As they started walking down the beach and away from the house, Evelyn came quickly down the steps. She was startled to see Emile with a young girl.

"Emile, Emile," she called, "where are you going?"

"Away."

"Away? What are you talking about? And who is this girl?"

"This is Elise."

"Oh, yes, the girl you were living with. She's very pretty. How do you do, Elise."

"Hello," Elise said quietly.

"She's very charming, Emile, very charming indeed. I've been taking with Mal. He's got two more scenes to write. I was discussing the scrip with him, the kind of ending the movie should have. We just can't decide how the picture should end. That's so important. Should it have a happy ending, or a tragic ending? What do you think?"

Emile hesitated a moment before speaking. He knew he was going to hurt Evelyn, but he had to be frank with her.

"Evelyn, it will end right here and now. I'm not going to be in this picture with you."

"What has come over you? Stop this foolish talk. Of course you will be in the movie. Mal has written a great script. And he has a title for the film—"The Lady and the Coconut Boy." What do you think of it?"

"Evelyn, don't you understand what is said? I am leaving you. I'm going back where I came from. I don't belong in your world."

"Emile, you don't realize what you're saying! I must have you in this movie! You're so . . . different! It will be a big hit! It will make a star again—the biggest name in Hollywood! It will make you a star! Now come on back up to the house like a good boy!"

"I am not your boy! I am a man, and I am leaving you!"

"Emile, I offer you a whole new, rich life. This house I have here is nothing. My home in California is three times as big. And you can live in it with me. And you'll have more money than you ever dreamed of."

"Goodby, Evelyn."

"After all I did for you, is this my thanks?"

"What did you do for me?"

"I found you wearing a piece of rag on a roadside, and now look at you, look at you! A thousand-dollar suit, a silk shirt and decent shoes!"

Emile quickly pulled off his coat, shirt and shoes and threw them on the ground. He was about to take off his pants but stopped.

"I'll send the pants back to you."

Throwing her arms around his neck Evelyn said, "Emile, I'm sorry for what I said. Please forgive me! You can keep these things!"

"I don't want anything of yours!"

"Emile, don't leave me!" she pleaded. I want you, I need you!"

Pulling her arms off him he said, "Come, Elise, let's go."

And when Evelyn tried to throw her arms around him, he shoved her away, knocking her to the ground. As she lay on the sand she watched as Emile and Elise walked down the beach. She continued watching them as their figures got smaller and smaller until they disappeared.

For a long time she lay there, numb with shock, too paralyzed to move. She could not believe that Emile had left her, walked out of her life. And then she turned over on her stomach and cried uncontrollably.

When she stopped crying, she did not want to move, she did not want to think. For a long time she lay on her stomach.

Finally she got up slowly and gazed out at the sea. The sun was just above the horizon. Twilight was approaching. There was a chill in the air.

Like a sleepwalker she walked down to the water, her eyes far out to sea. She was thinking, Yes, why not do it, why not drown myself? I will not be a star reborn. I will go on living just as another has-been, getting older and older. People will be asking, "Whatever became of Evelyn Damant? Is she still alive?"

"No, no," she shouted up at the sky. "That isn't going to happen to Evelyn Damant!"

She looked down and was astonished to see that the water was halfway up her legs. She quickly stepped back up on the beach, frightened. What was she thinking? Did she really intend to kill herself? No, she told herself, this isn't the end of Evelyn Damant! I'm a movie star, the greatest and most popular of all the stars of Hollywood! The others are dead, lying in their graves! But I'm alive!

As she walked up the steps she noticed how quiet it was. When she reached the terrace she saw that all the guests were gone. The waiters were cleaning up. Hortense was stacking dishes on a table.

"Hortense, where have they all gone?"

"Well, after we ran out of everything Mr. Andrews suggested that they continue the party at the Hotel Excelsior."

"Did Mr. Kravatiz go with them?"

"Yes, and he said to tell you that he finished the script and to join him at the hotel."

"Thank you, Hortense."

Evelyn hurried into the house and down the hall to Mal's room. On the desk beside the typewriter she saw the script. She sat down and began to read it, slowly, carefully.

When she was done, she stood up, looking down at the script, deeply impressed. It was Mal's best work. What a story he had written, and what a character he had created for her to play. Yes, this role would do it, it would make her a star again. But Emile had to be in the movie! He had to be!

"I'll make him change his mind!" she said, full of renewed determination. "I must go to him, talk to him, convince him that he is throwing away a great movie career! And there is something else I'll tell him that will bring him back to me! I'll tell him I love him, and I do, yes, I do!"

She went to her room and changed into a skirt and blouse. In the bathroom she washed her tear-streaked face and applied makeup. Before she left the room she looked at herself in the mirror and was pleased at what she saw—a beautiful, glamorous woman.

"Emile won't be able to resist me!" she said confidently.

Twice when she was driving to the village she had to swerve on the bumpy, narrow road to avoid hitting the car. But she still drove with her foot hard on the accelerator.

She was still driving very fast when she went down the village and came to a skidding stop in front of the house.

"Emile, Emile!" she called as she stepped out of the car.

He came out immediately, carrying the white pants in one hand. He was wearing his shorts. Elise appeared in the doorway watching, an anxious expression on her face.

"Here's the pants," Emile said, holding them out to her.

Evelyn came up on the porch and pulled the pants out of his hand, flinging them aside.

"I didn't come here for a pair of pants."

"Why have you come here?"

"To talk some sense into you. I know I said the wrong things on the beach—talking about fame and money and a big, beautiful house. There is something else I want to tell you."

"And what is that?"

"Emile, Emile darling, I love you. Yes, Emile, I love you. And—and I want to marry you. I want you for my husband, Emile. I love you, Emile, yes, I love you!"

"Evelyn, you do not love me."

"Emile, I love you!"

"A woman like you cannot love. You are too much in love with yourself to love another. You can only desire, desire a man's body. And when you have satisfied your lust on that body, you divorce the man. You have told me of your marriages. I will not be your husband. I will be a number, number six. Evelyn, I do feel sorry for you. All you know is desire. Love you will never know."

"That's not true! Emile, I Love you deeply, passionately, as a woman loves a man—forever!"

Emile called to Elise. She came and stood beside him. He put his arm around her waist. Evelyn stared at her with hate in her eyes, her lips compressed.

"This is the woman I love," Emile said calmly. "This is my woman."

"Woman! That chit! She's now woman! She's now woman! I'm a woman—all woman, and I've shown you the kind of woman, all those nights we slept together! How can you love that child?"

"Evelyn, I love Elise and she loves me. We desire each other, yes, but when we are old and the desire is gone, we still love each other. Yes, in old age our love will be as strong as it is now. You can never understand that kind of love, a love that never dies. You think you are rich, Evelyn, but you are not. You are poor. I will stay here with Elise for always."

"Stay here, in this crummy, miserable village and live in that dump you call your home, that shack, that shanty?"

"Yes."

"And what will you do?"

"Sell coconuts."

"Emile, you are crazy, crazy! I offer you my love and a life of fame and wealth, and you choose to live the life of a coconut seller!"

"We will have a good life. Evelyn, it is useless for you to try to change my mind. In one month we will be married. We have already arranged everything with the village priest."

"Married? Emile, you can't marry that—that girl!"

"In one month we will be man and wife."

"I hope you have a rotten life!"

"I know we will be very happy in our love."

"Fool, don't you know what you are sacrificing to marry her?"

"Elise will make me the happiest man on this island—in the whole world."

"Emile, one day you will regret this decision! You'll see, you'll see! When you think of the kind of life you could have had with me, me, Evelyn Damant!"

"I think you'd better leave. Goodby . . . Evelyn."

She watched in shocked, silent dismay as Emile and Elise entered the house and closed the door. This could not really be happening, she told herself. Emile had not left her for good. He couldn't do that to her, he couldn't. She needed him, she absolutely needed Emile in the movie. He was just perfect for the role. The film would not be a success without him. And she had to have a spectacular success to be once again the queen of Hollywood.

"Emile," she called out, rushing across the porch and banging on the door with clenched fists, "Emile, come out, come out! I want to talk to you! Come out alone, you hear, alone! I have so much more to tell you, darling! Believe me, Emile, I do so much love you! Yes, I love you, love you! Yes, I admit it, I have only craved a man's body for the pleasure it could give me. I have never loved those other men! But it isn't the same with you, I swear it! I love you, Emile, love you forever and forever. I love you with every beat of my heart! Please, please, Emile, open the door, come out!"

But Emile did not come out. The door remained shut.

When Evelyn realized he was not coming out, she turned around slowly, walked across the porch and sat down on the step, looking quietly down at the ground.

After a few minutes she got up and started walking past the houses in the village. She seemed to be in a daze. She did not see the few people she passed who looked at her curiously.

Without even knowing what she was doing, Evelyn went into the church. The first thing she saw was the ebony carving of the crucified Christ. Looking up at the twisted figure on the cross, she knelt down and began to mumble some words. After a few moments she stopped.

"No, no!" Evelyn said scornfully, getting up and stepping back in revulsion. "Why have I come to you? You can't help me! You are dead, dead! They killed you! What good is praying to a dead piece of wood going to do for me? Give me back my brilliant career? Make me a star again? You can't do anything for me, you dead thing! You couldn't help yourself—so how can you help me? Evelyn Damant doesn't need you!"

She fled from the church as if she feared that the figure on the cross would run after her. By now it was fully dark. The moon was hidden behind thick clouds. She hurried down to her car and drove out of the village.

She headed north, along the coast road. But she really did not know where she was going. All Evelyn knew was that she wanted to drive fast, fast, get away from everything.

A cold, panic-stricken fear had taken hold of Evelyn. Dimly she began to realize that her dream of making a great, smashing come-back was not going to happen. But she tried desperately to block the horror of that thought out of her mind. She refused to believe it.

An oncoming car swerved to avoid hitting her, the man in it honking his horn. But Evelyn did not see or hear anything. Scenes from her films flashed across her mind. And she smiled in proud, happy triumph.

"Those days will come again, yes, they will!" she screamed in a mad frenzy, gripping the wheel more tightly and pressing down harder on the accelerator. "They can't keep Evelyn Damant from being what she is—the greatest star that ever lived! She will rise up, greater, more wonderful, more popular than ever!"

By now Evelyn was speeding alongside of the cliffs, on her right side. But she did not see them. She was staring straight ahead, head headlights piercing the pitch-black night.

As her car sped down the road her mind swung wildly from arrogant exaltation to angry frustration, and she cried out in despair, "Emile, Emile, why did you desert me? What exciting, tempestuous screen lovers we would have made! The lovely white woman and the beautiful half-breed! What passionate love scenes! How the movie audiences would have been shocked and thrilled! We would have made movie history! We would have become the great screen lovers of the world! And I would be once again the star or stars. Emile, you robbed me of my glorious resurrection! Yes, being a has-been is like death to me! If this is the way it has to be, I don't want to go on living! Better to be dead! I must be Evelyn Damant, First Lady of the Screen—or nothing! Yes, yes, Evelyn Damant, movie queen of the world—always and forever!"

And she turned the wheel to her right. The car skidded across the road, toppled over the cliffs and plunged into the ocean.

The Short Presidency Of Harriet Clayton

By

Dominick Ricca

The First Lady lay awake in bed beside her sleeping lover, national security adviser Thurston Howard. It was a Saturday morning, and she saw by the bedside clock that the time was twenty minutes after six.

Harriet Clayton stretched her legs and thought of the wonderful night of love. Thurston was a marvelously vigorous lover. An intellectual, but a man who knew how to satisfy woman. He was a beast in bed, a man who made love savagely and yet tenderly. The first time he had brought her to this house, his lovemaking had been a shattering experience, a revelation. This was what man and woman were created for—to make this kind of love.

She wondered how she had ever been satisfied by the college boyfriends she had had. That made her think of her husband. Yes, Wendell was all right. Adequate. But they had stopped having sexual relations over two years ago because of his condition.

Harriet was happy and proud to be the mistress of a man who was not only a great lover and handsome, but intelligent as well. He had come to the White House from Harvard, where he had taught history and political science. He had written a number of books, not best-sellers but highly acclaimed for their learning and penetrating insights.

And there was something else about Thurston that appealed to Harriet. His family background was as aristocratic as you could get in America. He came from an old Tidewater family in Virginia that had owned thousands of acres and hundreds of slaves. That was important to Harriet. Her people had been dirt farmers for six generations.

Harriet glanced up at the chintz curtains on the bed that was probably as old as the house. Thurston had told her the first time he had brought her to the old antebellum house that it was over a hundred and seventy-five years old.

Thurston had inherited the small mansion from a widowed, childless aunt, along with seven million dollar. It was located two miles outside the charming old southern town of Charlottesville, which was in central Virginia, about a hundred miles from Washington, D.C.

Thurston had told Harriet of the dark, bloody tragedy that took place in the house in 1838. It was about a great-great-uncle of his, a doctor. One night he had to go out late to visit a sick patient. He told his wife that he would probably have to spend the night with the man.

But his patient was not as seriously ill as he had thought, and he returned home at three o'clock in the morning. He found his wife in bed with a man, the very bed Harriet was lying in. The wife and the man were sleeping.

The doctor got an axe and killed his wife and her lover. He dumped their bodies in a well and sealed it. The story he told his neighbors was that his wife had run off with a man. He said that she had left a note, but he didn't show the note to anyone.

Only when his diary was found in his desk years after he was killed in the Civil War did the truth come out that he had committed a double murder.

Harriet was thrilled and impressed by the doctor's ferocious ruthlessness when Thurston told her the story.

Now as she lay bed she though, Yes, that was the way to act. If something had to be done, do it! And what was it that she strongly felt had to be done? The answer was in her mind, but she looked at it only sideways.

Then, taking a deep breath, she looked at it squarely in the face. Yes, it would be the best thing for the country.

Harriet reviewed the first three and a half years of President Wendell Clayton's presidency. After the first three months of euphoric high hopes, everything went from bad to worse. Downhill all the way.

The tax bill had not stimulated the economy. Unemployment continued to rise. And with no abatement in the spending programs over which her husband had no control (damn those spending maniacs in Congress!), inflation and interest rates skyrocketed, and were now even higher than they had been in the bad days of Jimmy Carter.

And her husband's foreign policies had made a hash of things. He had alienated England, France, and Russian. The Japanese went on smiling sweetly while getting the better of America. And as usual, the Arab states were dissatisfied, making all kinds of demands and causing a lot of trouble.

The daunting domestic and foreign problems could not be solved by a weak-willed, indecisive president. And that was what her husband was—weak, indecisive. A loser.

America desperately needed new vigorous leadership. It needed a radical solution to the ills plaguing it. The men of the country had made a mess of things.

The country needed—yes—yes, she would face it, admit it to herself, damnit! It needed Harriet Clayton as president of the United States!

President Harriet Clayton.

Yes, she would become president, but first the thing that had to be done, must be done. She would be the savior of America.

There was one last great service Wendell Clayton could do for his country—die for it.

With the country in such bad shape, Harriet wondered how her husband ever got the Party's nomination to run for a second term. One young senator had challenged him, but when a news story came out revealing that he was secretly supporting his illegitimate child by an eighteen-year-old girl, he quickly dropped out of the race.

Outside the convention hall in Chicago, Harriet had seen many "Dump Clayton" signs. A few had even appeared on the convention floor. The Party was stuck with President Clayton, but he had to endure the humiliation of getting the nomination only on the third roll-call.

The revolt had been put down, but the delegates left Chicago divided, dissatisfied, and with a feeling of impending doom. And to make matters worse, thought Harriet, Wendell was sticking with his vice president, that nitwit Pete Fennelly, a fool if there ever was one.

That was a week ago, the third week in July. In two days President Clayton would kick off his campaign with a nine-day swing through five southern states, and them eleven days campaigning in six northern states, climaxing with a big rally in New York City in Madison Square Garden.

Harriet knew that her husband was in deep political trouble. His own party was not solidly behind him. The regular members were not happy with him. And the independents, who came out strongly for Wendell Clayton when he ran for president the first time, were now deserting him in droves.

Already the first polls showed the president trailing his challenger, Marshall Edwards. The polls had it forty-two percent for Edwards, thirty-eight percent for Clayton, fifteen percent for the no-party candidate, multibillionaire Horace Giddings, and the rest undecided.

It was a mystery to Harriet what anybody saw in the simpleminded Giddings with his sappy smile and his easy solutions to the really tough problems facing the country.

No, Harriet told herself, there was no way Wendell was going to turn things around. He was not a fighter, not a political brawler. He was too much the gentleman.

At the three debates that were scheduled, Edwards, smooth, confident, articulate, would make mincemeat of her husband, who could not think fast on his feet, as he had amply demonstrated by the number of goofs at his press conferences.

No, Wendell was a sore loser. Edwards was going to win the election. There was no doubt about that . . . unless . . . .

Harriet turned her mind away from her husband's dismal political prospects and looked at Thurston, still sleeping. She smiled, a smile full of love and pride. She didn't feel that she was an adulterous wife. She had no pangs of guild, no feelings of remorse. There had been no love between her and Wendell for over two years. No love, and no sex.

But she did feel guilty and foolish over the brief affair with her husband's press secretary, Teddy Wilton. There she had been stupidly reckless.

Wilton was only twenty-six years old when her husband chose him as his press secretary. He had been a reporter for a small Midwestern newspaper, and had made a name for himself with a series of articles exposing corruption and waste in the state capital. He had come to work early in Wendell Clayton's bid for the presidency, and had been very helpful. After he won the election, he rewarded the young man by giving him the job of press secretary.

At the time Harriet had thought it was a bad choice. She had wanted someone who knew his way around Washington, a veteran reporter who was on good terms with the White House press corps.

When things started going badly for President Clayton, he was moody and silent when he and Harriet were alone together, burying himself in the biographies he loved to read of kings and statesmen long dead. In bed he would turn his back on Harriet and quickly drop off to sleep with the help of sleeping pills.

One night, after they had not had sexual relations for three months, Harriet tried to initiate the lovemaking by caressing his chest and licking his ear. Wendell moved abruptly away from her and said that he was tired.

"But . . . Wendell, it's been months since we . . . ."

"Harriet," he said irritably, "I have things on my mind, more important than that,"

Harriet was indignant and hurt. "What do you mean by that remark? Isn't 'that' important to you anymore?"

"Harriet, I'm the president now, and I have serious responsibilities."

"Wendell, you are my husband first, and then the president. You talk about responsibilities. What about your responsibilities to your wife?"

Wendell sighed. "Okay, if you want me to be frank."

"Yes, please be frank. Tell me why you haven't made love to me all this time."

"The . . . desire is gone . . . ."

"Are you saying you don't have sexual desire for me?"

"I don't have any sexual desire at all. None at all."

"Wendell, what are you saying?"

"I'm saying my sex drive, my sex urge, is gone."

"But where . . . how? . . ."

"Harriet . . . ."

"Wendell, how did you lose it?"

"I don't know," he said wearily. "I guess my job swallowed it up. All I can tell you is that I don't . . . desire anymore."

Harriet thought or her three pregnancies, each one ending in a miscarriage. The third time the gynecologist advised her not to risk another pregnancy. It might be dangerous for her. She wondered why she thought of that now.

"Darling," she said, "why don't you see a doctor?"

"I don't want to see a doctor."

"But your condition might be curable. Why don't you see a specialist?"

"What kind of specialist could do me any good?"

"Ah . . . you know, a urologist. Sure, a urologist might be able to help you. Why don't you give it a try?"

"No, definitely not! If word got out that I was getting treatment for my impotence, a man my age, only fifty-three, the whole country would laugh at me. I'd be the butt of every sleazy comic on TV and in night clubs. No, I am not seeing a urologist!"

"Wendell, it could be done very discreetly."

"I said no!"

"Okay, no urologist. How about letting me try to bring it up? There were times in the past when you worked too hard or were tried, and I gave you an erection when I—"

"No, Harriet. Please don't embarrass me any further by continuing this discussion. Ever since I was a young man, I always woke up with an erection. And now—nothing. It's just a dead piece of meat only good for urinating. Harriet, my sex life is over."

"And that's supposed to go for me too?"

Out of shame, President Clayton had been talking with his back to Harriet. Now he turned around and looked at her in the dark.

"Harriet, remember, you are the First Lady," he said earnestly.

"I'm a woman, with a woman's natural desires."

"Please don't embarrass me or my administration. I've got enough troubles. I don't need a White House scandal."

"You want me to live like a nun?"

He didn't answer her. He turned his back on her. In a few minutes she heard his regular breathing. She lay on her back with her eyes open.

No, she told herself, his sex life was over, but not heirs!

For the next few weeks Harriet studied the single men who worked in the White House. She wanted a man in his twenties or early thirties, someone with a weak character, someone she could control, dominate. She didn't want any emotional complications. All she desired was a sexually potent man to satisfy her craving for sexual pleasure.

She finally decided on Teddy Wilton, the President's press secretary. He had boyish good looks. He was shallow and dull. Teddy was a grown man, but there was still something of the college kid, even of the preppie, in him. Yes, Harriet thought, he was lacking in maturity. But that didn't matter so long as he was strong in bed.

Harriet waited until she could get him alone in his office. One night at about eleven o'clock she walked into his office. He was alone, sitting at his desk and typing furiously.

"Getting in some overtime?" she said, smiling.

"I want to get this report on the president's desk by tomorrow morning, Mrs. Clayton."

"Harriet," she said, looking him in the eye.

Teddy was startled, and he showed it by blushing. He was about to continue typing, but he thought it would be rude.

"Uh . . . is there something you wanted . . . Harriet?"

"Teddy, you know you are a good-looking man."

"Thank you."

"You must have a lot of girl friends."

"A few."

"No steady?"

"No, I don't have a steady girl friend."

"Any particular reason?"

"You really want to know?" he said in a serious voice.

"Yes."

"Today's females are fickle and frivolous. No depth to them, no womanliness. They are so uptight and aggressively female that they have stopped being women. There are plenty of yapping females around today, but few women. That's why I like to see the movies of the '30s and '40s. Bette Davis, Joan Crawford, Marlene Dietrich—those were women, real women!"

Harriet was astonished. She didn't expect so much feeling from Teddy. Maybe there was more to the man than she thought.

"What do you think of me, Teddy? Am I in the same class with those movie stars?""

"Oh, yes, yes, Harriet. You aren't a girl, you are a woman!"

This was all very interesting, thought Harriet, but it was getting her nowhere. She had to be bold. Go right ahead and get Teddy to do what she wanted him to do.

"Teddy, I have something to say to you, but I can't say it here. Tell me, do you ever sleep here in your office?"

"Sometimes when I work so late I sleep on a cot I have in the closet. Why do you ask?"

She ignored his question. "Teddy, I want you to come to the Lincoln Room at one o'clock. That's about two hours from now. Will you come?"

"Why, yes, of course, but I don't see why you can't tell me what you want right here."

"Because we might be disturbed. There are always people working late or going about. No one goes into the Lincoln Room."

"Okay, Harriet, I'll be there at one."

At one o'clock she slipped out of bed. The president was sleeping. When she entered the Lincoln Room she had on her silk dressing gown. She didn't see anyone.

"Teddy, where are you?" she whispered nervously in the dark room.

He emerged out of the darkness from a corner and came close to her. Before he could speak, she threw her arm around Teddy and kissed him passionately, hungrily, on the lips. It was a long kiss.

"I—I, Harriet," he stammered, "I—I don't think we should . . . ."

"Teddy, I want you! I want you to make love to me! Now take off your clothes, right away!"

"Are you sure this is what you want?"

"Yes, damnit, yes! Some nights the president is too tired and—"

"Okay, Harriet, I understand."

"So start undressing!" she said, taking off her dressing gown and tossing it on a chair. She was naked. When Teddy had all his clothes off, she drew him quickly to the bed.

For over two hours they made love without stopping. Harriet was amazed at the physical intensity of his lovemaking. Every time he had an orgasm he cried like a baby, lying with his head between her breasts and telling her he had never had a woman like her. She was his goddess, his life, his joy. He adored her, worshiped her. He never wanted to make love to another woman.

On and on he prattled about how much he loved her. The first night Harriet didn't mind the way Teddy expressed himself. It was all very flattering to her. But she thought it was all boyish nonsense. Calling her his goddess, the great love of his life, silly boy. He would get over it in time.

The affair was brief. For two months they met in the Lincoln Room two or three times a week. Then once a week, and finally, when Harriet got sick and tired of Teddy's cloying, clinging, slobbering love, she told him that it was all over. She pretended that she realized that what she was doing was sinful, wicked. After all, she was a married woman, and the wife of the president of the United States.

"No, no, my darling, my goddess, it can't be over!" he cried. "It can never be over, never!"

They were lying in the bed. His head was resting between her breasts. She knew it would come to this with this over-emotional boy. She should never have started this affair with this overgrown boy. How could she explain to him that there had never been any love on her part? All she had wanted from him was raw sexual pleasure, that was all. Yes, it had been a mistake getting involved with Teddy. She had acted foolishly, impulsively. She needed a real man, someone more her own age.

"Teddy, I'm sorry, but it's over. I've committed a great sin. I can't go on being unfaithful to my husband."

"Darling, I love you," he sobbed. "Life without you would be death to me. I couldn't go on living without your love."

"I never gave you my love. All I wanted from you was sex, sex, the temporary use of your penis. I've had my fling with you and now I must go back to being a faithful wife."

"No, no, my goddess! I'm crazy in love with you!"

Harriet was disgusted with him. He was just a school boy with a crush on his teacher. But she was a little worried. Was she going to have trouble getting rid of him? She tried to rise from the bed, but he held her down with one hand on her shoulder and the other hand holding her breast.

"Teddy, let me get up!"

"Say you love me," he said squeezing her breast hard.

"You're hurting me!"

"Tell me you love me."

Harriet remained silent.

"Say you love me!"

"I certainly do not love you, Teddy. I love my husband. Now, Teddy, you must be brave. Act like a man. It is all over between us. If you don't take your hands away from me I swear I'll scream. I don't care what happens."

"All right," he said quietly. "But it isn't over for me. Never, you hear, never. I'll always love you, always."

Harriet got out of the bed and put on her dressing gown. She stepped into her slippers. She looked at Teddy. He was lying on his stomach, his face buried in the pillows.

"Teddy, before you leave, make up the bed."

He was sobbing uncontrollably when she walked out of the Lincoln Room.

For weeks after that night Teddy tried to talk to Harriet when he could catch her alone, making an annoying pest of himself. She always rebuffed him coldly as if there had never been anything between them. When was he going to stop mooning over her?

One day when he was telling her with tears in his eyes how much he loved her, Harriet threatened to have him fired. That terrified him.

Teddy had at least to go on seeing the woman he passionately loved, his goddess. He had to remain in the White House.

After that threat, he was frigidly polite with Harriet. But she saw in his eyes the burning love for her. My God, she thought uneasily, would he ever get over it?

Harriet deeply regretted the affair with Teddy. It had been a foolish and dangerous escapade. Sex with a silly boy in the Lincoln Room! It was crazy!

Months went by. Months of sleeping with a man who ignored her in bed. But this time it wasn't simply her body aching for sex. This time it had to be a man who truly loved her. Yes, she wanted to see desire for her in a man's eyes, but she also wanted to hear that man say, "Harriet, I love you."

But where was that man? Would he ever come into her life?

Harriet didn't realize that the kind of man she wanted was working in the White House as President Clayton's national security adviser. She had been introduced to him casually and had seen him only several times after that.

Three months after Harriet had broken with Teddy, she was standing at her husband's side during a welcoming ceremony on the White House lawn for the president of Ecuador.

As the president was making his brief speech, Harriet noticed the great physical change that had come over her husband in the last year and a half. A year and a half as president had aged him a good deal. He had lost weight, and his suit hung loosely on him.

In the harsh, glaring sunlight, Harriet saw for the first time how deeply lined, craggy and pale his face was. Only a year ago his hair was gray. Now it was turning white. He was only five years older than she was, but she felt that he could pass for her father. Why, she thought with dismay, I'm married to an old man, a tired old man.

She bowed her head, afraid that someone might notice something in her face. And when she looked up she saw across from her the national security adviser, Thurston Howard, staring at her with eyes what seemed to bore right through her. His black eyes, staring at her with such intensity, had an almost hypnotic effect on her.

Harriet tried to avert her eyes, but for the life of her she could not. Thurston was trying to send a message to her. She no longer heard the president speaking as she tried to fathom what those black eyes were saying to her.

Finally, with great effort, she was able to close her eyes for several moments. When she opened them again and looked at the national security adviser, she saw that he was listening attentively to the president.

Harriet observed him closely, and she was struck by the remarkable resemblance of Thurston Howard to Clark Gable. But why hadn't she noticed it before? Gable had been her favorite screen star when she was growing up. She had cried when he died. It was truly amazing, the resemblance. Thurston even had the actor's broad mustache. She had to talk to him.

Later, at the buffet luncheon, she got her chance. He was sitting alone at a table with a plate of food in front of him, but he wasn't eating.

"Mind if I join you?" Harriet said, dropping into a chair.

"Not at all," he said, rising and sitting down again.

She was gratified to see that he was pleased.

"Shall we talk about the president of Ecuador?" she said.

"Please let's not talk about him, Mrs. Clayton."

"Harriet."

"Harriet," he said, smiling.

My God, she thought, he even has Gable's strong, masculine voice. And that wonderful smile the actor had. This was a man.

He was looking directly into her eyes with feeling. What did she know about him? Not much. She knew that he was a widower, with no children. He had taught at Harvard, made a reputation for himself with a number of books that had impressed her husband enormously. Two weeks after Wendell Clayton was elected president, he chose Thurston to be his national security adviser.

"Mr. Howard—"

"Please call me Thurston, Harriet," he said, again with that bright Gable smile.

"Thurston, do you miss teaching?"

"Very much. But I love being here in the White House. After being here, at the center of power, it's going to be tough to go back to Harvard."

They chatted for ten minutes and when Harriet got up to leave she said, "Thurston, would you take me to lunch tomorrow?"

"It would be an honor and a pleasure, Harriet."

Thurston took Harriet to a small Italian restaurant, about ten miles from the White House. That is, Thurston directed the chauffeur of the armored limousine to the restaurant. Another car followed behind them.

Of course the lunch was not very pleasant for both of them. Secret Service agents sat at a table fifteen feet from them. Thurston felt uncomfortable, and Harriet was disappointed.

Except for a few banal remarks about the restaurant, the food, they said little during the meal. Although the agents seemed to be ignoring them, they knew that they were being carefully watched by three agents, while the other agents scanned the room of the restaurant.

Harriet was thinking as she looked at Thurston, I want this man. I want to be in bed with this Clark Gable of a man. God, what a man. Built like Gable, with his broad shoulders.

Harriet was sure Thurston was thinking the same thing. Yes, she could see his desire for her in his eyes. He wanted her, he passionately wanted her.

And they were just right for each other, almost the same age. He couldn't be more than forty-eight or forty-nine, she thought. But how could they arrange to be alone? Never again in the White House, she swore.

"Why are you looking at me that way?" she murmured softly.

"Because I love your red hair, your bright blue eyes, your dimpled chin, your high cheekbones . . . . and the shape of your body."

He had spoken so low that she just barely caught the words.

When they were driving back to the White House Thurston said, "Harriet, could you manage to get away for the night, the whole night?"

The words thrilled her, but she casually said, "Why do you ask that question?"

"Because I want you to spend the night with me in my house."

"Don't you have an apartment here in Washington?"

"Yes, but when I can get away on weekends I go to this small mansion I own a couple of miles from Charlottesville. It's a beautiful old pre-Civil War house with a swimming pool and a dozen acres. The place is called The Elms.

"How far is it from Washington?"

"About a hundred miles. Say a two-hour drive."

"Are my bodyguards also invited?" she asked, smiling.

"We drive out there in my car, just the two of us."

"You want to show off your nice old house to me?"

"Yes . . . and I want you to stay overnight. Two elderly black servants look after it, a husband and wife. They've lived in that house for over forty years. I promise you that when you walk into the place you'll think you've been transported back more than a hundred and fifty years."

Harriet was thinking. She would have to sneak out of the White House, and to do that she would certainly need the help of her press secretary, Gussie Frazer. She could trust Gussie. She knew all her secrets, even about Wendell's impotence.

Gussie had been a newspaper woman. She had worked for Harriet when Wendell Clayton was governor of their home state. And when he was elected president, Harriet had hired Gussie to handle her public relations. Yes, she could surely trust Gussie with her life, or her reputation.

"What do you say?" Thurston said, breaking into her thoughts. "I promise you a unique experience."

How could she say no when he was smiling at her with that Gable smile? Yes, it would be a unique experience to have his handsome man make love to her.

"When?" she said.

"This Friday, about six o'clock, come to my office. I'll get rid of my staff early. I'll have a veil for you to wear when we drive off the White House grounds."

"Thurston, I love romantic intrigue."

"Of course if some stupid international crisis breaks out, we'll have to make it for another time."

"I'll be there."

At five o'clock that Friday, Gussie went into the Oval Office and informed President Clayton that the First Lady had come down with a fever. He dropped everything and went to see how his wife was feeling. Gussie had told him that Harriet was in a bedroom down the hall from the president's bedroom.

"Darling, how are you?" Wendell said as he walked into the room. It is very bad?"

"I feel terrible. I thought it would be better for me to sleep alone tonight. I'm afraid with this nasty fever I might keep you awake with my tossing and turning."

"All right. Do you want to see a doctor?"

"No, no doctor. I think it's one of my twenty-four hour fevers. I should be all right by tomorrow."

"Try to sleep, darling. Take something."

"I will, and darling, would you tell them I don't want any dinner. I have no appetite at all."

"All right, Harriet," Wendell said. He kissed her on the cheek and left.

Thurston drove down the highway. It was a soft summer night. Harriet was enjoying the ride through the Virginia countryside. They went thru quiet, sleepy little towns with small wooden frame houses, some of them partly covered with ivy. Harriet felt that she was going back in time. The deeper they got into Virginia, the further back in time they seemed to go.

It was twilight when Thurston turned into a long dirt road lined with elm trees on both sides. In the distance, Harriet could see the lights of the house through the branches of the trees that made a cathedral-like vault over the road.

"Now you know why it's called The Elms," Thurston said. "Oh, by the way, you are Miss Evans."

"Won't the servants recognize me?"

"Of course, but they won't say a word."

They turned a curve at the end of the avenue of trees, and there was the house. It was a three-story, slightly gray building, with four slender fluted columns. Virginia creeper covered one side of it. Standing in front of the open doors on the broad porch were the two servants, Esther and Ben, her husband

They got out of the car. Harriet smelled the scents of honeysuckle and magnolia in the warm night air. The stars appeared very close, and the bright crescent moon seemed to hang only a few feet above the old mansion.

Thurston introduced the servants to Harriet. Ben was dressed in the style of a butler's uniform of over a hundred years ago. Esther wore a red bandana on her head, and a plaid apron over her brown cotton dress.

When Harriet stepped into the house she really felt that she was back in the Old South. The old furniture, the shiny wooden floors, the dark portraits on the walls—it was all so enchanting, beautiful. What gracious lives those long-dead people must have lived, she thought.

"Thurston, I don't know what to say. It's—it's marvelous."

"There's more," he said.

"More?"

"Didn't I promise you a unique experience? Now you go on upstairs with Esther. I have something to talk over with Ben."

Esther led Harriet up the broad staircase with curving mahogany banisters on each side. They entered a small bedroom. On the bed was a blue satin gown.

Picking it up and holding it out to Harriet Esther said, "Miss Evans, Mr. Howard wants you to wear it."

"He wants me to wear this gown?"

"Yes, ma'am, that's what he told me over the phone."

Harriet took the gown and held it in front of her. "Why, this dress must go back to the days before the Civil War."

"The style does, but not the dress, Miss Evans."

"It's lovely."

"Do you want me to help you with it?"

"No, Esther, thank you."

"Mr. Howard will be waiting for you on the porch," Esther said, and left the room.

A small bathroom adjoined the bedroom. After freshening up, Harriet pt on the gown. She looked at herself in a full-length, oval-shaped mirror and was pleased with what she saw.

When Harriet stepped out on the porch Howard was looking up at the stars. She couldn't believe what she was seeing. Clark Gable had come back to life. Thurston was dressed as Rhett Butler was when he appeared for the first time in "Gone With The Wind."

"Good evening, Mr. Rhett Butler," Harriet said, walking over to him.

When Thurston turned around, he caught his breath. He stared, speechless. Harriet saw everything she wanted to see in this man's eyes. Love. Admiration. Desire. But there was also a little sadness.

Thurston found his voice. "Harriet, you gorgeous creature."

"Thank you, Thurston. You know, you make a magnificent Rhett Butler."

"I'm so glad the gown is a perfect fit."

"When you first saw me, I detected sadness in your eyes."

"That was my wife's gown. She wore it at our wedding reception. The whole thing was my aunt's idea. She wanted the wedding party here in this house, and all the guests had to wear the style of clothes of the Old South. My aunt was quite a character. I remember she said to me that night as she watched our guests dancing, 'Thurston, they aren't dead, they've all come back to live for this one night.' I was so happy that night. I was looking forward to a long and wonderful life with my wife, my Julia."

Harriet knew that the happiness didn't last long. Thurston's wife died of a heart attack only three years after they were married.

"You must have been very happy with her for those few years," Harriet said.

"Yes, I was. When Julia died I vowed that I would remain single for the rest of my life. But I know now that a man should never make a vow like that."

"No, he shouldn't."

Thurston brightened suddenly. "Hey, let's have our mint juleps. Ben brought them out a few minutes ago."

They sat down at a small table and clinked glasses. This wasn't real, Harriet thought. The smell of honeysuckle and magnolia, that moon shining through the trees—and Thurston Howard-Clark Gable-Rhett Butler sitting beside her and talking to her about this old house and some of the people that had lived in it.

Ben came out on the porch. "Mr. Howard, Miss Evans, dinner is served," he announced.

The dining room was illuminated only by the candles on the table. As soon as they sat down, Ben came in from the kitchen with a steaming tureen on a tray.

"Smells like turtle soup to me, Ben," Thurston said.

"That's what it is, Mr. Howard," Ben said, and returned to the kitchen.

Thurston poured chilled Chablis into thin-stemmed wineglasses. "Harriet, you are in for a special treat. Esther is a great cook. Now, let's have this turtle soup."

The soup was followed by broiled lobster that had been taken out of Chesapeake Bay that morning, roast duck, and baked ham.

When Ben brought out the plates of homemade ice cream, Thurston said, "Ben, we'll have the coffee on the porch, please."

"Yes, sir."

When they were seated out on the porch and sipping their coffee, Harried smiled at Thurston and said, "If I'm dreaming, please don't wake me up."

"I promise I won't wake you up until tomorrow morning."

"Unfortunately it has to be very early."

"Unfortunately."

"Thurston, I have never been happier than I am at this very moment. I want to thank you."

"Harriet, I thank you for the privilege of making the woman I love happy."

"No, no, you mustn't say that."

"Harriet, I don't care that you are married. That doesn't matter two cents to me. I love you. I've loved you since the first time I saw you. Why I waited so long to say this to you, I don't know. Maybe it was my southern upbringing. Another man's wife, behaving like a gentleman and all that muck. The hell with it. I love you, Harriet, I love you."

"Oh, Thurston, Thurston."

"Let's go inside. I want to play for you."

He took her across the large foyer into a small room. An old-fashioned piano stood in a corner with one candle burning on it. Thurston sat down on the piano stool and Harriet dropped into a chair at his side.

Thurston played a medley of Stephen Forster songs, beginning with "My Old Kentucky Home" and followed by "Oh, Susanna," "Come Where My Love Lies Dreaming," "Ring Ring De Banjo," "Old Black Joe," "Beautiful Dreamer," and ending with the hauntingly beautiful "Jeannie With The Light Brown Hair."

"How did you like that?" Thurston said, getting off the stool.

"Thurston, that was lovely," Harriet said, rising from the chair.

"Come," he said, taking her hand.

They walked out of the room, across the foyer and stopped at the foot of the broad staircase. They gazed into each other's eyes.

Harriet said, "Thurston, there's something I want you to do."

"You don't have to tell me what it is," he said, taking Harriet in his arms, sweeping her off her feet and carrying her up the stairs.

"Thurston, I love you," she said, her voice hushed and tender.

For the next two years Harriet spent many nights at The Elms. When Thurston had too much work and had to work late hours for weeks, they had to be satisfied with snatching a few hours together in his apartment, which was five miles from the White House.

As she lay beside her sleeping lover on that Saturday morning, Harriet thought, How wonderful those two years were. But in six months everything would come to an end. Could she divorce Wendell and Marry Thurston? In January she and Wendell would return to their home state. Wendell would go back to his law practice, and she—what would she do? Divorce her husband and marry Thurston?

But she hated the thought of divorce. It was an admission of failure, and she hated to fail at anything, though she had reason enough to leave Wendell, even if she didn't want to marry Thurston. But she did, oh, yes, she did.

But there was something else. The thought of leaving the White house depressed her. The center of attraction. Waited on hand and foot. Every wish promptly satisfied. It was the closest thing to living like royalty in America. And, oh, those glittering state dinners for visiting heads of state!

No, she could not give it up. She had to have many more years of it. This kind of life was like an addiction. She just couldn't do without it. No, no!

She had to go on enjoying the excitement, the glamour, the attention. But now she also wanted the power, the power to dictate her will.

Was this life in the White House to be blown away just because Wendell was going down to defeat, had bungled away the presidency? Was this life she loved so much to be blown away like a puff of smoke—gone with the wind?

But it wasn't going to be blown away. It didn't have to be, it didn't. She hadn't really been thinking seriously before. But now she was thinking seriously.

She sat up in bed, her eyes wide open. Yes, yes, that was the way it had to be. Wendell had to die. He had to be killed. And then she would . . . yes, yes. Why not? She was so excited, her face tingled.

Harriet nudged Thurston. "Darling, wake up."

Thurston opened his eyes and looked sleepily up at her. She bent down and kissed him on the mouth. She loved the feel of his mustache on her lips.

"Now are you awake?"

"Hey, I like that kind of wake-up call. What time is it?"

Harriet turned to look at the clock. "It's seven-thirty."

"We'd better get hopping."

"Thurston, there's no need to rush back to Washington today, remember?"

"Oh, yes, I forgot. Your husband flew down to Texas yesterday to have a strategy meeting with the governor, and he'll be back tomorrow

"The trip is a waste of time. Texas is lost, and so is the election."

"You don't think Wendell can turn things around?"

"That loser? Maybe Harry Truman could've done it in his prime, but don't expect a 1948 upset victory. My husband's political career is finished, or will be in January."

"So you think it's that hopeless?"

"Thurston, what will you do?"

He sat up. "Go back to teaching, I suppose," he said sadly. After pausing for a moment he added, "You know, for the last two years I've had two dreams."

"Two dreams?"

"Yes. The first one is to have you for my wife. And the second dream . . . to be secretary of state. Your husband should never have picked Courtnay Bennington for the job. He is ignorant of foreign affairs, and he gave the president lousy advice."

"Well, he raised a lot of money for Wendell's presidential campaign."

"I know. But he's still nothing but a dumb Wall Street lawyer who's unfit to hold down a junior position at the State Department. He's the reason why your husband is in trouble all over the world. And that's why, come November, Marshall Edwards is going to clobber President Wendell Clayton."

"Darling, you are so right. He should've chosen you as his secretary of state."

"Damn right," Thurston said bitterly, "but I was no name, and I didn't raise millions of bucks for him."

"Thurston, how badly do you want those two dreams to come true?"

He looked her straight in the eye. "Darling, I'd do anything to have you for my wife. And I've hankered so long to be the boss at State, it's become like a pain that won't go away."

"There's a way for your dreams to come true."

"How?"

Harriet didn't answer him.

"Tell me—how?"

"Wendell has to die."

"Harriet, what're you saying?"

"My husband is going to lose to Marshall Edwards. I'm sure you agree with me that his victory in November would be a disaster for the country."

"I do."

"So my husband can perform a noble sacrifice for this great country of ours. He can . . . die for it."

"And what's he going to do, slip on a banana peel and break his neck? Are you hoping for a convenient accident?"

"No."

"So what are you getting at?"

"The president has to die tragically."

"Harriet, I'm in a fog. Could you speak a little plainer?"

Her face was grim, her lips a thin line. "Wendell Clayton has to be killed."

"Assassinated, the president?"

"Yes, yes, assassinated. The country needs a strong-willed leader who can act decisively—do the things that have to be done to get things back on track."

"And who will that leader be?"

Harriet took a deep breath before answering. "I will be that kind of leader. And when I am elected president, I will appoint you my secretary of state. And one year after Wendell is dead, you and I will be married."

"Harriet, my head is spinning. Let's say Wendell is killed by some crazy assassin, how can you step in and run for president in his place?"

"Don't you see? I'll be the gallant, grieving widow taking up the banner my husband dropped when a bullet ended his life. That will appeal to a great many Americans."

"And if the Party bosses don't go along with you?"

"Then, damnit, I'll run as an independent and screw up any chance their man has of winning. I'm sure to get plenty of support from the women's groups. Thurston, it's certainly worth the try. Let's do it!"

"Are you saying we have to arrange Wendell's assassination?"

"Yes, for the good of the country."

Thurston was silent. Yes, he wanted Harriet for his wife. And, yes, he wanted to be secretary of state. But kill the president?

"Well, Thurston, do you want those lovely dreams to come true?"

"They are . . . powerfully attractive dreams . . . ."

"Aren't they? Well, what do you say, 'Rhett?' Are you the man I think you are?"

"Yes, by God, I am!

"Darling!" she said, kissing him on the mouth.

"So how do we do it?" he asked.

"You have to arrange it."

"Me? How?"

"Otto Henterman."

"How does the Director of the CIA come into it?"

"Doesn't he have killers in that organization?"

"Yes, but I don't know . . . ."

"Darling, you told me you and Henterman were good friends. I'm sure we can convince him to come in with us. He knows that when my husband leaves the White House, he loses his job as top man of the CIA."

"And I know that would break his heart. He's been with the CIA for twenty-five years. I know Otto. It's his whole life. he'd be lost without it."

"You two go back a long way, don't you?"

"We sure do," Thurston said. "I was in the CIA for three years. Two of those years I was with Otto in Afghanistan in the early eighties. We gave the Moslems weapons, supplies and money to fight the Russians. Let me tell you, we were in some tight spots together. Yes. We sure do go back a long way."

"Have you kept up your contact with him?"

"We meet quietly for lunch every few weeks to discuss problems of mutual interest, and to reminisce about those hairy years in Afghanistan."

"Do you think we can trust him?"

"Self-interest is his strongest motivation. Yes, I think we can trust him. But you have to promise him that if you are elected, he keeps his job as long as you are in the White House."

"He'll have that promise."

"Okay, so now what do we do?"

"We have to move fast," Harriet said. "We're at the end of July. In a few days Wendell will start his campaign with a nine-day trip through a number of southern states. Maybe something can arranged."

"Maybe, maybe. Harriet, you have to realize this isn't like hunting deer. The president always has a lot of Secret Service agents with him when he mingles with the crowds. It's going to be tough, damn tough."

"Let's see what the professional has to say. Call Otto and tell him to come here?"

"Today? Now?"

"Yes, now, now! Thurston, I'll need at least two months to get my campaign for the presidency going in high gear. We have to get going. There's no time to lose. Call Otto!"

"Okay, I'll try his office first. If he's not there, he's sure to be at his home in Fredericksburg."

"Tell him you have something very, very important to discuss with him. No details, just something very urgent."

"It's a good thing we're alone in the house," Thurston said.

Ben and Esther had gone to visit a sick relative in Halifax, a town about ninety miles away. They would be back the following day.

The night before, Harriet had cooked a delicious supper of breaded veal chops, baked potato and dandelion. The First Lady was a very good cook. Thurston complimented her on the meal.

They both got out of bed. Thurston picked up the receiver of the phone by the bed and began dialing.

As Harriet walked out of the room she said, "Darling, what would you like for breakfast?"

"Make it poached eggs and bacon."

It was a beautiful sunny morning. Birds chirped in the trees. Thurston led Otto down the dirt path to the outdoor pool. They were wearing bathing trunks. Harriet was swimming slowly from one end to the other. The men got in the water at the shallow side of the pool and Harriet swam to them.

She stood up and looked from Thurston to Otto. Neither of them spoke. "Have you told them everything?" she asked.

"Otto said that if it was something private, he didn't want to discuss it in the house. He's afraid of bugs."

"I have to protect myself," Otto smiled genially.

He was big, fat and bald, with a lot of gold teeth. His face was long and heavy, with small eyes and a crooked smile. Harriet didn't like him. She had met him twice, and each time he made her feel uncomfortable. But she had to deal with this man, she decided, if she was going to achieve her ambition.

"All right," she said, "tell him."

But before Thurston started to speak, the Director of the CIA held up his hand. "Hold it. First of all, let's swim out to the middle of the pool. All these bushes could hold bugs."

They went out to the center of the pool, which was five feet deep. They stood in the water facing each other.

"Satisfied?" Harried said.

"No quite. We have bugs small enough to fit under a bathing suit without making the tiniest wrinkle. I suggest we all remove our swim togs. Oh, and one more thing, we all speak in a low whisper."

The men took off their bathing suits and tossed them across the pool, about them feet away. Harriet kept hers on.

"Aren't you going to do the same?" Otto asked, smiling and showing a lot of glinting teeth.

"Look here, I'm the First Lady, and I'm not going to—"

"Hey, First Lady, I take it you're in on this thing, whatever it is. Am I correct?"

"Yes."

"So?"

Harriet sullenly removed her one-piece suit and flung it angrily over her shoulder. "Does that satisfy you?" she said, glaring at Otto.

"Not exactly," Otto said, ducking under the water and moving slowly around Harriet and Thurston.

"Did you get an eyeful," Harriet said when he came up. She was fuming. How she hated this man.

"I didn't see any bugs, if that's what you're referring to. So, okay, Thurston, old buddy, let's hear what you got to say."

Thurston told Otto everything. He talked for ten minutes. Harriet watched Otto carefully. When Thurston said that the president had to be killed, he didn't bat an eye.

After Thurston was done speaking Harriet said, "Well, Otto, what do you think? Can it be done?"

Otto didn't answer her. He looked from Harriet to Thurston. She began to worry. Would he inform the president?

"Otto, talk, say something," Thurston said impatiently.

"You say if you are elected, I get to keep my job for as long as you are in the White House?"

"You have my word on it."

"Your word," Otto said, wrinkling his face.

"What the hell you want me to do, put it in writing?"

"Come on, Otto, throw in with us. You got everything to gain," Thurston said. "You want to go on being the Director of the CIA, or do you want to be canned by Marshall Edwards?"

"Okay, okay, I'm in."

"You made a wise decision," Thurston said.

"You won't regret it," Harriet said.

"Yeah, okay, but there's just one hitch."

"What's the hitch?" Thurston asked.

"I can't order my killers to do the job. These men and women aren't machines. They aren't contact killers, or ordinary street killers. I couldn't order one of them to take out the president. They'd rat on me, and in no time I'd be in hot water and sure to spend the rest of my life behind bars. And of course I'd take you two down with me. No, the CIA can't bump off Wendell Clayton for you."

"So where does that leave us?" Harriet asked anxiously, a cold feeling gripping her heart. Wendell had to die. She had to be president.

"Otto, are you telling us it can't be done?" Thurston said.

"No, I didn't say that."

"Will you stop beating around the bush and tell us how the president can be eliminated!" Harriet demanded furiously.

"We have to bring the Director of the FBI in on this."

"No!" Harriet said frightened. "I don't want too many people involved in this . . . project. The fewer, the better."

"She's absolutely right," Thurston said.

"Hear me out," Otto said. "Mrs. Clayton, where does your husband go after he makes the trip through the South?"

"Back to Washington for a few days, and then eleven days campaigning in half dozen northern states, with two days in New York City and ending with a rally at Madison Square Garden.

"Okay, that's all I need to know."

"Otto, do you think it's safe to bring Paul Dirker into this?" Can we trust him?"

"No, Dirker has the morals of an alley cat. He has no principles. But he does want to go on being the Director of the FBI. He has botched a few cases, and the Press has been after his scalp. A few senators have demanded that he resign, and if he doesn't, Marshall Edwards has publicly stated that if he is elected president, he will fire Dirker. And let me tell you, that would kill him. The lug has had the job for years. I think I can persuade him to help us."

"But how can Dirker help us?" Harriet said, puzzled. The FBI didn't have killers, and the CIA did.

"Mrs. Clayton, we have to go out of the government to do this job. Dirker has valuable contacts with the New York Mob. This has to be a Mob hit."

"A Mob hit?" Thurston said. "I don't understand why—"

"Thurston, old buddy, don't ask questions. Leave everything to Dirker and me. You see, I got some dirt on the Director of the FBI."

"Like what?" Harriet said.

"Like film of him in action with two underage girls. But I don't want only to threaten to expose his passion for young girls. Mrs. Clayton, if he can get the job done, can I tell him he will go on being the boss of the FBI?"

"Yes, if I'm elected."

"I think you will be elected. The country is in a radical mood."

"Thanks for the vote of confidence," Harriet said, smiling.

"Folks, this conference is ended," Otto said.

"I'm hungry," Harriet said. "Let's have lunch. Thurston, do you have any mushrooms in the house?"

"You'll find all you want in the cabinet above the sink."

Harriet walked to the side of the pool and climbed out on the ladder. "Gentlemen, how about a mushroom omelets for lunch?"

"Love it," Otto said.

"Sounds good to me," Thurston said.

"And with it a nice chilled Chablis."

Both men stood silently in the pool and watched the naked Harriet walk up the dirt path to the house.

Just before she disappeared behind a row of bushes Otto said, "Thurston, you know something."

"What?"

"The First Lady sure has a first-rate ass."

But there was a snag. Paul Dirker told Otto that the killing couldn't be accomplished.

"Why not?" Otto wanted to know. "You got the top crime organization in New York City to do the job. What's the problem?"

"Yeah, Louey Tesoro's outfit in Brooklyn is the best, the most efficiently, run crime family in the country. But it still can't be done, and I'm not going to ask him to try."

"Have you contacted him yet?"

"Of course not. I'm not going to him with an impossible job. The president has just too damn much security around him. What with the horde of government agents, he has the local police. That means cops on roofs, motorcycle escort, helicopters—a real army. I can't find a chink in the security."

"Do you have something on Tesoro to make him do the job?"

"Oh, I got the goods on him, but I won't force him to do it when I know there's no way to get through that goddamn tough security screen around Clayton. Otto, we need a break."

The break came eight days before the president arrived in New York City for the rally at Madison Square Garden.

Harriet and Wendell were flying aboard Air Force One and alone in their private compartment. They had just left Philadelphia and were going to Boston for two days, and then for a few days in Vermont and New Hampshire.

"Harriet, I'm going to reveal a little secret," Wendell said.

For days she had been nervous and edgy. Thurston had told her about the conversation between Otto Henterman and Paul Dirker. The prospects for the success of their plan looked very bleak. And the days were slipping by.

"What's the secret?" she asked.

"I want to tell you something that only three people know."

"It must be a very important state secret."

"No, it's nothing like that," the president laughed. "You know I haven't seen my good friend Cardinal Devaney in months. So, when we're in New York I'm going to pay him a courtesy call, spend an hour with him at his residence on Madison Avenue."

"Is that the big secret?" Harriet asked.

"The secret is that I don't want the visit to be public. I don't want people to think I'm angling for the Catholic vote."

"So before we return to Washington, you want to see him. Fine."

"Harriet, as I said, I don't want the public to know about the visit. So, on the morning after the rally at the Garden, I'm going to visit Cardinal Devaney without the usual security. The Press will be told that I'm heading straight for Kennedy Airport from our hotel. So now you are in on the secret, and that makes only four people, who know, me, you, the chief the Secret Service detail, and the cardinal."

"So security will be down to a minimum, is that it?" Harriet asked, excitement growing in her.

"Yes, no police escort. There will be only three cars. Our car will be sandwiched in between two cars with government agents. I hope you can keep a secret."

This was it, Harriet though, this was the break they were hoping for. She would get this information to Thurston as soon as they landed in Boston.

"Darling, of course your wife can keep a secret," she said, smiling brightly.

FBI Director Paul Dirker sat in room in a small midtown Manhattan hotel located on a side street. Dirker had been waiting for almost an hour. He was sitting at a table that had on it a bottle of whiskey, two shot glasses, and a thick package in a manila envelope. Across from him was a chair for his guest.

Dirker had a medium build, with broad shoulders and a barrel chest. He had a snub nose, narrow eyes, heavy eyebrows, and a round, pugy face.

There was a low knock on the door.

"Come in," Paul said.

Louey Tesoro walked in. He stood by the door looking at Paul. He was wondering why the boss of the FBI had asked for this private meeting. Was he out for a bribe?

Louey was short and thin. He had a narrow face, shiny black hair, and deepest eyes. His long, beaked nose almost reached down to his pale lips.

"Lock the door," Paul said.

"Yeah, sure."

"You're not carrying, are you?"

"Nothing, like you said." He didn't move away from the door.

"So come on in."

Louey walked slowly around the room, glancing down into lamp shades, up at the ceiling, behind two paintings on the wall, and finally under the bed. He came over to the table. Paul was grinning at him.

"What's so funny?" Louey said.

"You."

"Yeah? Why?"

"I got your home bugged, every room. And your clubhouse in Brooklyn, and the one you visit in Little Italy. We got you complaining to your wife last week that the linguine was too soft. About a month ago in your clubhouse you said that if Monk Mecelli didn't button up his lip, he was going to receive a lot of flowers that he'd be too dead to appreciate. Oh, yeah, we also got bugged the apartment of that young Swedish babe you visit every Wednesday afternoon. You know, to look at you I'd never think you went in for kinky sex."

Louey leaned across the table and pointed a bony forefinger at Paul. He was boiling mad. "Dirker, get your stinking nose out of my ass! We live in a democracy! I got a right to my privacy!"

"Calm down, Louey. And sit down."

He sat down. He picked up the bottle and looked at the label.

"How do you know I like Jack Daniels?"

The Director of the FBI laughed.

"Son of a bitch," Louey said, pouring himself a shot and quickly downing it. He stared at Paul with murder in his eyes.

"Louey, I was only trying to establish my credentials. You can't be sent to prison for those things I mentioned. But we can put you away for a long stretch for dealing in illegal drugs."

"What're you talking about?"

"Five weeks ago, on a Sunday morning, you drove all over Central Park in your car for eighty-five minutes talking a dope deal with a Mexican gentleman by the name of Jaime Ortiz. We know all about him. He's been in the drug business for years. It sure sounded like a whopping big deal. You two were talking in the millions."

"Dirker, you got nothing on me! An actor imitating my voice!"

"Louey, we got a few other things on you. Like illegal gambling, loan sharking—"

"Dirker, you can't fame me!" Louey shouted angrily.

But Paul saw he was worried. Beads of sweat broke out on his forehead. He poured himself another drink and gulped it down.

The Director of the FBI pushed the package toward Louey.

"It's all there, Louey, and it's all yours to keep, or to burn."

Louey leaned back in his chair. "What's going on here?"

"Listen to what I have to say."

"How much?"

"I don't want any money."

"You want me to turn stoolie—forget it, Dirker."

"That's not what I want."

Louey leaned forward with his arms resting on the table. He looked relieved, and he was smiling. "Oh, I know what you want."

"Tell me."

"You want somebody killed."

"Yes."

"Who? Some guy you can't get evidence against, and you'd like to see him dead. The government wants this guy dead. That it?"

"No, that is not exactly it."

"So who is this bird?"

Paul remained silent. Now he was sweating. Yes, he was going to do it, he was actually going to put a contract out on the president of the United States.

"Well, Dirker, are you going to give me the name of this guy?"

"Louey, I want you to kill President Clayton."

"Dirker, you are outta your skull, crazy-mad!"

"Louey, you have to do it."

"It can't be done."

"It's been done in the past, and it can be done again."

"Why do you want him dead?"

"That's no concern of yours. Just do it."

"But Clayton has too many people around him. Agents, police—no, it's too risky."

"Louey, do this job for me and these tapes are yours. And I'll give you the location of every bug we have on you. How about it?"

Louey stared down at the package. "I wish I could say yes, but—"

"You'll say yes after you've heard what I have to say. There won't be any risks involved. You'll have an edge."

Dirker told Louey about President Clayton's planned discreet visit to Cardinal Devaney. He gave him the day and the time.

"Louey, what do you say now?"

"Well, yeah, maybe it can be done. I'll have to put my best marksman on it."

"Your very best."

"And you're sure only three cars?"

"Yes. The president will be with his wife. She will be wearing a white coat. Clayton has been wearing a bulletproof vest on the campaign trail, but I don't think he'll have it on that morning for his visit to the cardinal that morning. Still, just to be on the safe side, tell your man to hit him in the head."

"Yeah, sure."

"You do know where Cardinal Devaney's residence is?"

"Of course I do. It's on Madison Avenue, behind St. Patrick's Cathedral."

"Anything else you need to know?"

"No, I got it all."

"So we're all set."

"You know . . . I had a lot of guys rubbed out in my time . . . ."

"This is the big one."

"Me, Louey Tesoro, ordering a hit on the President of the United States of America," he said musingly and with a certain pride and wonder in his voice.

The Director of the FBI filled both glasses.

"Louey, let's drink on it."

When the presidential party was in Monpelier, Vermont, the state capital, Harriet had told Gussie to buy her a white spring coat.

"Why do you want another coat, Harriet? You have the black ones and the brown one."

"Please get me the coat without asking any questions. Don't get me a gray coat. It has to be snow white."

Harriet was going to wear that coat the day her husband was killed. She had to make sure that she got some of Wendell's blood on the coat. The bloodstains would show up more vividly on a white coat on color TV.

As the presidential car moved slowly up Madison Avenue, Harriet turned away from the window and cast a quick glance at her husband. The president was relaxed and happy. Wherever he went in New York City he had received a tremendous response from the people that was gratifying and encouraging to him.

And the rally at Madison Square Garden last night had been a big success. The crowd had been enthusiastic and cheered wildly when he appeared on the platform. And after his speech, the people rose to their feet and gave him a rousing ovation that lasted ten minutes.

Wendell was talking to her, but she didn't hear what he was saying. It was as if his voice was a long way off. She heard words but they sounded indistinct, muffled. She was thinking, I've been married to this man for twenty-three years. Yes, it was better that they had never had any children. It made everything so much easier.

Now they were only a few blocks from Cardinal Devaney's residence, and suddenly she could hear what Wendell was saying. He was speaking confidently for the first time in the campaign, telling her that after that great rally he really believed that he could turn things around, beat Marshall Edwards, and they would remain in the White House for four more years.

Harriet knew that wasn't true. Her husband was going to lose the election. He didn't stand a chance. He had been a poor, weak president, and now the people were going to turn him out.

But Harriet had the grace and the decency through her ruthless ambition to be president to feel compassion and pity for this pathetic man, soon to be dead.

The car slowed down and stopped in front of the old Gothic building where Cardinal Devaney lived. A dozen Secret Service agents were standing on the sidewalk when President Clayton and his wife came out of the car.

The cardinal was standing on the top of the front steps with one priest, waiting to greet the president, who was talking to the chief of the government agents.

A few people across the street recognized the president and cheered and clapped their hands. He turned to face them and waved his hand. At that moment a bullet from a high-powered rifle split his head wide open like a ripe watermelon. Wendell Clayton was dead before he hit the ground. Harriet screamed and knelt down. Cardinal Devaney rushed down the steps. The Secret Service agents ran across Madison Avenue with guns drawn. The wail of a police siren filled the air.

Cardinal Devaney tried to pull Harriet away from the president's body, but she shrugged him off, raising his head and shouting, "They killed the president, they killed my husband!

It took two agents to drag her away from the body. She resisted them fiercely, but they were able to get her into the car. They got in with her and the car immediately drove off for Kennedy Airport.

Two hours later, millions of Americans watched on TV as the casket containing the body of the president was slowly raised up to the rear door of Air Force One on a lift.

When the casket disappeared into the plane, the TV cameras shifted to Harriet Clayton. She was standing at the foot of the steps to the plane with two government officials. They were talking to her, but she wasn't saying anything. She seemed to be in a daze. The front of her white coat and one sleeve had dark blood stains. The heart of every American watching went out to her.

In Washington, when it was officially confirmed that President Clayton had been killed by an assassin's bullet, Pete Fennelly was sworn in as president by Supreme Court Justice Anson Brookridge.

One hour later, the TV stations reported that the new president would address the nation before a joint session of Congress that night at nine o'clock.

In her apartment in the White House, Harried was furious when she heard the announcement. She was alone with Gussie. She had told Gussie only an hour ago that she intended to run for president.

She paced angrily up and down the room. "Gussie, you know what that Fennelly is going to announce tonight, don't you?"

"That he is going to run for president?"

"Did you ever hear anything more ridiculous in all your life? That fathead run for president—I'd rather see that simpleton Giddings win the election."

"Harriet, how can you stop him?"

"By beating him to the punch, that's how."

"What do you have in mind?"

Harriet told her, and before Gussie walked out of the room she said, "Tell Thurston I want to see him right away."

At two-thirty that afternoon Gussie hastily called a press conference. There were eight TV cameras in the room and more than a hundred reporters.

Before Gussie could read from a prepared statement one of the reporters asked, "Gussie, can you give us any information on Mrs. Clayton?"

"Yes, yes, Dr. Martin Seward is with her. Mrs. Clayton is not under sedation. I want the American people to know that this brave lady is bearing up remarkably well considering the horrible, traumatic shock she has experienced. Also with Mrs. Clayton is her late husband's good friend, national security adviser Thurston Howard."

Another reporter got up and said, "Gussie, has Mrs. Clayton—"

"Please, please, I'll answer all your questions in a minute. Please allow me to read this statement from Mrs. Clayton."

There was immediate silence in the room. Gussie began reading the prepared statement. Every few seconds she looked directly into the TV camera that was in front of her.

"Mrs. Clayton wishes to express her heartfelt thanks for the many expressions of sympathy she has received in this country and from around the world. She would like very much to express her gratitude personally on TV, and is therefore asking the TV networks for twenty minutes of air time. Mrs. Clayton would like to speak tonight at seven o'clock. That is the end of the statement. Now I will take questions."

Harriet had put the executives of the TV networks on the spot. They could not refuse the request of the grieving widow of the slain president. If they did, the American people would condemn them for being callous, cruel and mercenary. Of course they granted Harriet the time.

For three hours Harriet and Thurston worked on the speech she would make that night. She told him that she wanted to come across to the American people as sincerely as possible. And because she wanted to seem to be speaking spontaneously, she would not read the speech, she would memorize it. With coaching from Thurston, she rehearsed it eight times.

When she appeared on TV that night she was wearing a simple black dress. She wore no makeup. She wanted to look as haggard, as grief-stricken, and as pitiful as possible.

Harriet spoke for thirty-eight minutes. Twice she broke down, too shaken and overcome with emotion as she told of those terrifying moments of the assassination. And there were long, awkward pauses, when it seemed she did not have the strength to go on. But somehow she found the courage to continue.

Tearfully, she recounted her husband's political career. First, mayor of their hometown, then senator in Washington, followed by one term as governor. And then the supreme achievement—President of the United States.

Harriet saved her dramatic announcement for the last few minutes.

"My fellow Americans, my beloved husband had been planning to develop new ideas in domestic and foreign policy. This is what he told me the night before he was killed. He had a noble vision for a better and greater America. But the dark forces of reaction killed my husband to crush that dream. Help me to fulfill that dream of our martyred president. The evil forces in this country killed him, but we must not allow them to kill Wendell Clayton's spirit. For I know it still lives and breathes in the hearts of millions of Americans.

"My friends, there is only one way to perpetuate the memory of President Wendell Clayton, a man who gave his life for his country, and that is to see that the vision he had for this nation becomes a reality. Yes, I am reaching out with my grieving heart for your support. Ladies and gentlemen, I want to continue the work of my husband, and I am pledging to you tonight that I intend to carry on his fight by running for president of the United States. God bless all of you, and God bless America."

Sitting in the Oval Office with his domestic adviser, President Pete Fennelly almost fell out of his chair when Harriet announced that she was running for president in her husband's place.

"That bitch!" he shouted. "Who the hell does she think she is? Running for president—she's crazy, and I'm going to tell her so, the egotistical bitch!"

He went up the stairs to her apartment two at a time. He was going to tell Harriet the political facts of life. He was going to run for president, not her, and he intended to inform the American people of that fact when he addressed the joint session of Congress that night.

But when he stood facing Harriet and looking into her hard-staring eyes, his courage failed him. He tried bluster, but she cut him short with a wave of her hand.

"You run for president? Don't make me laugh. That's what the American people have been doing for over three years—laughing at you. You have been the most inept, comical vice president this country has ever had. You caused my husband's administration a lot of embarrassment with your foot-in-the-mouth remarks."

"You can't talk to me that way! I'm president and I demand—

"A bullet made you president, not the American people. Don't even think of running for president. You'll lose, and you'll lose big."

"I can win, I know I can win!"

"Pete, for once in your life use your brains. I will run with or without the Party's support. Yes, I'll run as an independent like that blockhead Horace Giddings. And I'm sure to take millions of votes away from you. So how could you possibly beat Marshall Edwards? Pete, you are a dead duck before you start running for the White House."

"So what am I supposed to do, let you step in and run for president, just like that?"

"Pete, how about a deal?"

"What's the deal?" he asked suspiciously.

"You get the Party bosses to support me, and I promise that if I am elected I will serve only one term. And when my four years are up, I will do everything in my power to get you elected president. What do say?"

President Fennelly thought over Harriet's proposition.

"You really don't think I have a chance?"

"With three candidates running against you? Impossible. Pete, as my vice president, I'll do what I can to improve your public image. I'll give you important assignment, more responsibilities, send you on important trips abroad. And believe me, if you can learn to keep your big mouth shut and avoid talking like an ass, the American people will see you as a future president."

"Okay, you got a deal. How can I help?"

"Arrange with the big boys to have a convention to nominate me as our Party's presidential candidate."

"On such short notice?"

"And make sure the convention is in New York. That was where my husband was killed, and that's where my nomination will make the greatest impact."

"Harriet, you're a better politician than your husband was."

"I'll have to be if I'm going to beat Edwards."

In ten days the convention was organized and the delegates poured into the Big Apple. President Fennelly made the nominating speech. The next day Harriet won a stunning victory. Every delegate voted for her, and there was a tumultuous demonstration on the convention floor that lasted thirty-five minutes.

Three days later, Harriet started a twelve-day campaign tour of the Midwest. Then back to Washington, where she had established her campaign headquarters in the new Ben Franklin Hotel, with a suite of rooms for herself on the twenty-third floor.

After resting for two days, she was back on the campaign trail, crisscrossing country twice in fifteen days. Thurston always traveled with her as her adviser on foreign matters. They were careful to avoid any intimacies. A few times when they were alone for a minute, they embraced and kissed, but that was all. The important thing now was to win the election.

Three weeks before the election the polls showed Edwards still ahead by one percentage point, but the experts all said it was too close to call.

Ten days before Election Day Harriet made her last campaign trip, this time visiting cities in Kentucky, Tennessee, Arkansas, and Missouri.

She arrived back in Washington with two days to go. When she and Thurston walked into the suite Gussie greeted them with a whoop and a holler. The press secretary was now Harriet's campaign manager.

"Harriet, congratulations!" she said excitedly. You are the next president of the United States!"

"Gussie, what's happened?" Thurston asked.

"Calm down, Gussie, and give us the news," Harriet said.

"NBC just came on with a bulletin with the last poll figures. You are ahead of Edwards by four percentage points! Harriet, you are the next president of the United States!"

"You did it, Harriet, you pulled off the political miracle of the century," Thurston said, "God, I'm so happy for you."

"We all did it, and I'm very grateful to both of you," Harriet said.

"Edwards must be wondering what hit him," Gussie said.

"And how are you feeling, Mr. secretary of state," Harriet said.

"Secretary of State Thurston Howard—yes, I like it very much."

"Gussie, what about you? I want to give you a nice plum. What will it be? Commerce? Labor? Transportation?"

"Secretary of Commerce Gussie Frazer sounds nice to me."

"You got the job. I think this calls for a little celebration. Gussie, call down for a couple of bottles of champagne."

On Election Day Harriet voted early and returned to her suite at the Ben Franklin Hotel with Gussie. Thurston had to attend a national security meeting.

At three o'clock the head of the Secret Service agents outside Harriet's suite told her that Teddy Wilton was asking to see her. She had tried to get President Fennelly to fire him as his press secretary, but he had refused. For some reason he liked the young man.

For weeks Teddy had made a pest of himself, asking to have a private meeting with Harriet, but she had refused to see him. She now thought it best to see Teddy and get rid of him once and for all. She asked Gussie to leave the suite. She didn't want her to hear what Teddy might say.

Harriet was standing in the middle of the living room when Teddy came in. His face was pale and drawn. She was shocked to see how much weight he had lost.

"Harriet, thank you for seeing me."

"I'm Mrs. Clayton to you, Mr. Wilton," Harriet said frigidly.

"Darling, that's no way to talk to me."

"I am not your 'darling.' Now, what is it you have to say to me? I have a very busy schedule today."

"Why are you so cold to me? Once we meant so much to each other. Once we were so close and I—"

"Teddy, stop your jabbering and get to the point."

"All right, I will. I want you to know that I always think of those unforgettable nights in the Lincoln Room."

"And I want to forget them. I think of those nights with shame and disgust. Do you hear that, shame and disgust!"

"No, no, Harriet, my darling," Teddy cried piteously. "Don't say things like that. Those nights are sacred to me. Why are you so cruel to me?"

"Because you are a despicable creature."

"Harriet, I love you. I shall always love you, no matter what you say to me. Nothing can destroy my love for you, and I know if we could spend a few nights together you would learn to return my love for you."

"Stop talking rubbish! If that's what you came to say to me, I'm going to demand that you leave."

"Harriet, my darling, life without you is unthinkable! I'd die without you."

"So die! Teddy, you are a deluded fool. We have been through for over two years. You were nothing more than a shallow, passing infatuation. I had need of a male animal, and you served my purpose."

"But that isn't the way it is with me, Harriet," Teddy said, falling down on his knees and throwing his arms around her legs. "I adore you! I worship you, my heavenly being!"

Harriet shoved him away from her and he fell to the floor.

"Teddy, you make me sick! You make me want to puke!"

"Harriet, you are the whole universe to me. I want you to be my wife."

"You are crazy! Get up of the floor and stop groveling at my feet. Christ, don't you have any pride?"

"Harriet, my adorable one!"

"Get up," she shouted, kicking Teddy away from her.

"Yes, yes," he cried joyfully, "kick me, beat me! It's your right! You are my goddess and I am your slave, your worshiper! I deserve to be kicked and beaten for daring to love you, my adorable goddess! There will never be another woman like you in all of God's creation!"

"Get up off the floor and stop babbling like a crazy fool."

"Harriet, I love you!"
"Piss on your love."
"I'd give my heart's blood for you!"
"Shit on your heart's blood."
"I'd burn in hell for you!"
"Burn, burn!"
"Harriet, I will never stop loving you, never!"

She turned away from Teddy in disgust and walked to the other end of the room by the windows. She heard him sobbing. She was tempted to call in the government agents and have him thrown out. But she was afraid Teddy might resist violently and cause a terrible scene, and she knew that there were always a number of reporters outside her door. It had been a mistake to see this unbalanced young man, she thought.

After five minutes Teddy stopped crying, but he didn't move off the floor. Harriet was gazing out the window at the Washington Monument. Now she turned around and looked at Teddy, who was lying with his arms spread-eagled on the floor.

"Teddy, I want you to leave. You are grown man, behave like one. Please leave me."

Teddy got up off the floor. He took out a handkerchief and wiped his eyes. He stood looking at Harriet across the room.

"Goodby, Teddy."

He walked slowly and with stiff dignity toward the door. Before he opened it he said, "Harriet, you belong to me. If I can't have you, no one else will, I swear it."

That night, Harriet, Thurston and Gussie had finished their dinner and were having their coffee when ABC announced at nine-forty that Harriet Clayton was the projected winner of the election.

They all rose to their feet. For a few moments no one spoke, and then Thurston said quietly, "Harriet, congratulations."

Gussie kissed her on the cheek and said solemnly, "President Harriet Clayton."

"Thank you, both of you, thank you so much," Harriet said with tears in her eyes. "Gussie, I think it's too early to go down to the ballroom and thank all those people who worked so hard for me. You go down and tell them as soon as I receive Marshall Edwards' telegram conceding defeat, I'll be down to speak to them."

"That shouldn't be too long," Gussie said, going out.

Thurston threw his arms around Harriet and kissed her on the lips. When he dropped his arms and drew a little away from her, she embraced him passionately and covered his face with kisses.

"Thurston, my body is tingling all over. God, it's been so long since we . . . . Thurston, I want you to sleep with me tonight."

"Harriet I'm dying for you, but don't you think we should wait a little longer?"

"Thurston, if I had to sleep alone tonight, I'd go crazy. And what better way to celebrate my victory."

"You're right, Harriet. That's the best way to celebrate your unprecedented victory."

And so on a cold, windy day in January, with dark clouds filling the sky, the first woman in the history of the United States was sworn in as president.

Thurston rode with Harriet in the limousine up Pennsylvania Avenue. For the new president, it was the happiest day of her life. She waved and threw kisses at the cheering crowds of people lining the sidewalks.

"Thurston," Harriet said, "there's only one thing to make my happiness complete."

"Harriet, you have it all."

"No, I don't. I don't have you. Darling, I want to be your wife."

"You will be, at the end of the year."

"No, I don't want to wait that long."

"But we promised we'd wait—"

"Thurston, I want to be a June bride. Please say yes."

"But, darling, what will people think?"

"Who cares what they think. I'm president, and I can do as I please."

"Okay, Mrs. President, if that's what you want."

"And there's something else I might as well tell you right now."

"What's that?"

"I intend to run for a second term."

But you gave your word to Pete Fennelly that you would not run for a second term."

"And what if I did?" Harriet said defiantly. And, smiling, she added, "Isn't it a woman's prerogative to change her mind?"

"You devious darling!"

"That empty-headed dummy will never be president."

"Never?"

"Never. Darling, after I have served two terms, you will run for president. And I predict that you will be a two-term president like your wife."

"Sweetheart, you scheming woman, I love you."

"Think of it, I'll be in the White House for twenty years. Let anyone try to break that record."

"Harriet, you are one hell of a woman! You got more balls than any man on planet Earth!"

"Thurston, I want to have our honeymoon at The Elms."

"The perfect place."

"And our first night as man and wife, we'll dress as we did the first night I was there, won't we?"

"Of course."

"Darling, we're going to have a happy life together."

"A wonderfully happy life."

"Now, to show our fellow Americans what a very democratic person they chose to be their president, let's get out of the car and walk a little in the street."

"You sure you want me to walk with you?"

"Yes. I want the public to get used to seeing us together."

When Harriet and Thurston got out of the car, a dozen Secret Service agents made a semicircle behind them, with more walking on each side of them.

Harriet walked in the middle of the street with Thurston at her side, occasionally moving over to the sidewalk to shake hands with people on the sidewalk. The agents kept their eyes on the hands reaching out to President Harriet Clayton.

After they had walked for about a mile Thurston said, "Harriet, I think that's enough. Let's get back inside the car."

"Okay, I just want to shake a few more hands," she said, going toward a crowd of people on the corner of the block. Thurston and the agents followed closely behind her.

Harriet shook hands with a few men and women, and suddenly she found herself standing in front of Teddy Wilton. He seemed to her very bulky in his heavy winter overcoat.

"Well, well, Teddy, are you here to congratulate me?" she asked cheerfully, holding out her hand.

"Yes," he said, taking her hand in a firm grip, his face expressionless. "I congratulate you."

"Thank you."

"I have something else to say to you."

"Please let go of my hand."

"Harriet, I love and adore you. And now we'll be together forever. Nothing will ever part us."

"Let go of me, you lunatic!"

Thurston and four agents lunged forward to grab Teddy, but before they could reach him he pressed the button in his overcoat pocket. There was a deafening explosion. Harriet, Thurston and nine other people were killed instantly by Teddy' bombs.

And so ended the short presidency of Harriet Clayton.

Time Was His Enemy

1

Jeff Stanish woke up hating to get out of bed. The long day loomed in front of him like some dreaded monster about to pounce on him. Or some bleak dark tunnel. A tunnel that would end only when he went to sleep. The waking hours were like a heavy burden he had to drag along with him all the live long day. Sometimes he wished fervently that the day was only four hours and the night twenty hours. Maybe he could sleep all that time.

Time! That was the problem, Time! Some nights in his dreams, when his overmind knew that he was dreaming, and he was observing his dream like a speculator at a sports event, he still experienced that anguished depression of time hanging over him like some huge boulder about to fall down on him.

But why didn't it fall down and crush him! Put him out of his misery! Why did it go on tormenting him with the heavy weight of time?

Jeff was thirty-four years old. Up until the time he had inherited his maiden aunt's estate of more than a million dollars in stocks and bonds and her nine-room country house, Jeff had not at all been aware of time. Time went on smoothly in his carefree life. The days went by one after the other, and he was not conscious of time. It was an amorphous, intangible thing, having no substance, no solidity. Jeff was too busy to notice the passing of time. He always seemed to be doing something—his job, his social life.

All that changed when Jeff came into his aunt's money and property. Two days after Aunt Lily's burial Jeff got a phone call from her lawyer, a Mr. Coleman Headly. He asked Jeff to come to his office.

When he was seated in front of Headly's desk he was informed that he was his aunt's sole beneficiary. All he had to do was sign some papers.

Outside the office building, Jeff was like a man in a daze. He was overcome with emotion at his good fortune. Over a million dollars! And a large house all to himself in the country! He could quit his job and never have to work again! Never have to ride the buses in the morning! Never to be chained to a desk for hours!

"I'm going to be in paradise," Jeff shouted to the passing strangers in the street. They grinned at him and thought he was crazy.

A week later Jeff moved out of his two-room apartment and drove in his ten-year-old Toyota the forty miles to his new home in the country. On his way there he promised himself that he would buy a new car.

After parking the car in the garage, Jeff walked completely around the house and then walked up the porch steps and into his home. He went through all the rooms with a great feeling of pride of possession. Everything was all his, all the statuettes all over the place, the paintings on the walls, the furniture—everything!

Then, with a jaunty step he went outside. He had three acres around the house, lots of grass, a few old oak trees and a half-acre pond that was two feet deep. Jeff smiled at the leaves floating on the surface.

Looking around he yelled with pleasure and pride, "Mine, all mine! I am the lord and master of everything I can see." And I'm free as a bird!"

Yes, Jeff was free as a bird. Freedom was precious to him. He had not married because he did not care for the responsibility of raising a family.

To him, married life, a wife, having to support a family, filled him with horror and dread. That life would be like a prison. The bedroom, with the same woman to sleep with every night, would be like a prison cell. That was not for him.

Jeff had acquired his revulsion for marriage from the many times he had visited his married friends, who had, in his opinion, made the fatal mistake of tying themselves to a woman. It was a deep and befalling to Jeff how a man could be happy with one woman. For himself, it would be a life sentence of misery.

A number of times he sat in the living room with one of his married men friends and was disgusted at what he saw. Howling, restless, snot-nosed brats running around all the time, wanting to climb all over you like affectionate dogs, and always asking for this and asking for that. At one time the guy's wife breastfed her baby in front of Jeff. How gross!

The last time he went to visit one of his friends he left strongly confirmed in his opinion of marriage. It spelled three words: Unhappiness, monotony and madness.

Jeff could not understand why men got married. The explanation eluded him. He tried very hard to figure it out, but could not come up with a satisfactory answer. Once the word "love" occurred to him, but he pushed it aside as a mushy emotion, not worthy of serious consideration.

Once another thought popped into his head.

"Did my buddies, those fools, get married because they believed they would achieve some kind of immortality through their children?" Jeff asked himself.

Jeff had always followed the bachelor's ideal life—love 'em and leave 'em. It was impossible nowadays to get strongly attached to a woman. Seduction was unnecessary. All the girls were so willing. When you asked a girl for a date, and she said yes, she was virtually saying, yes, I'll go to bed with you.

There was no chase, no hunt. And no fun. A man did not have to use his masculine charm, wit or wiles. The cultural winds had eradicated in women their most endearing trait that made them all the more desirable—their sexual modesty. And also their virtue. A man wanted to feel big when he took a woman, like a conqueror taking a city after it had fiercely resisted him. Today, women were like cities that willingly surrendered and allowed themselves to be plundered.

That was not exactly how Jeff thought about women, but it sums up how he felt about them. There had been so many of them in his life that he could not remember them. He could recall names but the faces that went with the names were all blurred.

Jeff always made sure the girls did not know where he lived. He never gave them his phone number. He had heard about too many guys who had trouble with girls after they dumped them. They would phone all hours of the day. They would stand outside their apartment buildings, and they would make life hell for those men.

That would not be for Jeff Stanich.

He was careful how much he spent on a date. He took the girls to cheap restaurants a neighborhood movie theater and then straight to his apartment without any pretence of wanting to show her something. After a few hours of sex, Jeff would walk the girl to a bus stop two blocks away. If she asked him to accompany her home, he would tell her that it was dangerous to be out late at night.

As for Jeff's eating habits, Jeff was a lousy cook. He had never used the kitchenette in his tiny apartment. For breakfast, he ate in the cafeteria down the block. At work, he would go out and have a soft drink and a bowl or soup or a sandwich.

Such had been Jeff's life before his aunt died.

2

So now Stan was living in this old house and with no need to earn a living. Aunt Lily had invested conservatively. She put her money in solid blue-chip stocks and a few public utility companies. They were safe, and they gave a satisfactory return on a regular basis. With her old-fashioned mentality, Aunt Lily shunned the new high-flying tech stocks. She did not understand the complicated contraptions they produced. The old maid had hated modern life. She had preferred to look backward, not forward.

But even with Aunt Lily's conservative investments, Jeff's yearly income came to between eighty and ninety thousand dollars a year. His biggest bill was his real estate taxes. They came to a little over eleven thousand a year.

Woodson, the nearest town to him, was eleven miles away.

His first morning in the house, Jeff made his own breakfast. That he could easily do. He had done some shopping in town the previous day. He made himself bacon and scrambled eggs and a pot of coffee. Before breakfast, Jeff had a large glass of prune juice. He had had a constipation problem since he was a teenager.

Now for Jeff his troubles started. But he would not be aware of his great problem for a little while.

Breakfast over, Jeff went into the living room. He switched on the TV. The screen came on black and white. Aunt Lily had not bothered to buy a color TV.

Jeff dropped into the stuffed armchair and watched and listened to the morning news. The usual things, robberies, murders, fires, wrangling between the political parties and the international goings-on. The same old stuff. Didn't it ever change? Jeff idly wondered. The only things that changed were the dates.

When the news broadcast was over, Jeff got up and tried all the other channels. Nothing that appealed to him. And Aunt Lily had not installed cable TV. Jeff asked himself if he should do it. He decided not to. It would be an unnecessary expense. Most of the TV programs were trashy—garbage.

Shutting off the TV, Jeff walked into the small library room. Hundreds of books were on shelves from the floor up to five feet high, all around the room. There was one deep leather armchair with a standing lamp over it.

Jeff browsed along the shelves. He was looking for murder mysteries, the only book-reading he did. He did not find any. There were books on all the religions of the world, on their theologies, and also books on theosophy, which Jeff had never heard of. There was not one novel. But there were at least a dozen Bibles, and five or six lives of Jesus of the conventional kind. Those books held no interest for Jeff because religion held no interest for him. Both his parents had been atheists, and so he had had no religious upbringing.

There were many books on gardening, knitting, crocheting, astrology, animal life and bird watching.

Jeff walked out of the room, disgusted at his aunt's reading habits, disappointed and suddenly feeling irksomely restless. He went outside and strolled around. Behind the house he saw the straight rows where Aunt Lily did her gardening, all overgrown now with weeds and grass. There were a few drooping stalks of some kind of vegetables which Jeff did not recognize. The hell with gardening, he told himself firmly.

He went over to look at the pond. The water was clear and he could see right down to the pebbly bottom. For the first time he noticed some small fishes darting about in the water. They would not make good eating, he thought. There was nothing to them. Did Aunt Lily feed them? he asked himself.

After walking slowly around the grounds for fifteen minutes, Jeff returned to the house, standing outside and looking at the garage attached to it.

He opened the door and went inside. Standing next to his Toyota was a dusty jalopy, a Plymouth, at least thirty years old, Jeff thought. It was dark when he arrived yesterday, and he had not had a good look at it.

He looked in the window. The key was in the ignition. Did the old thing still run? Jeff sat behind the wheel and switched on the ignition. The car roared into life. He saw that the tank was more than half full.

Turning on the windshield wipers Jeff thought he would go for a drive, maybe drive into Woodson. He did not know the place too well. The few times when he visited his aunt, he had not spent much time in the town. Mostly he had gone there to help with Aunt Lily's shopping.

In a short time he was driving through Woodson, and in three or four minutes, he was out of it and back on the country road. He turned around, thinking he would park the car and explore the town on foot.

He found a space on aside street, and walked down main street. It was a nice little town, with plenty of trees on the sidewalk, attractive storefronts, and a few bars and restaurants. Jeff was glad to see a Chinese restaurant. He was partial to Chinese food.

He wandered around some more, and when he saw an open bar, he went inside. He sat on a stool at the bar and ordered a beer, dropping down a five-dollar bill.

The bartender eyed him curiously.

"New in town?" he asked.

"I've been here before, but not for a couple of years. Lily Frayn was my aunt. She left me the house."

Jeff could see that this piece of information made a big impression on the bartender.

"Oh, so you're living in the house now, sir?"

"Yes, I was my aunt's sole heir."

"Lucky for you."

"Say, what's the population of this burg?"

"Forty, forty-five thousand. Why you asking?"

"Uh . . . is there a good whorehouse in town?" Jeff asked. He had decided not to get involved with women on a social-and-sexual basis. He did not want the bother, taking them out and spending good money on them and having to listen to their empty, inane chatter, when all he wanted was the temporary use of their bodies to satisfy his carnal needs when they came upon him.

"Well," the bartender said, "we got two cheapie, cut-rate joints like that in the poorer section of town. They have mostly jaded, overage sluts. But if you're willing to spend money, and want high-class, fresh young ass, there's Viola's establishment. All the big shots go there, the business leaders, the political bosses, and even our honorable mayor."

"And this Viola is the madam of the whorehouse?"

"That she is, and a very refined lady. For around twenty years Viola worked in one of the dumpty cathouses in town. She was a hardworking, clean-cut whore, never took drugs or boozed it up, and she was a regular churchgoer, never forgetting her roots. She had ambition and a goal. Viola saved her money, and one day she had enough to open her own place. You got to hand it to her, she made something to herself."

"Where's the house?" Jeff said.

"You thinking of going there? Like I said, it's expensive."

"Just give me the directions to the house."

"It's two miles out of town, on Route 19. You can't miss it. You can see the big white house through the trees. It's on a rise about a quarter of a mile from the highway, up a dirt road. The house was once owned by a wealthy old family. They died out, except for a drunkard. He took Viola's money and disappeared."

"Thanks for the information," Jeff said. He finished his beer and left the change from the five dollars.

He got back in the Plymouth and drove home. Once inside the house he wondered what he should do. Was it too early to try Viola's place? He would go there that night.

He dropped into the stuffed armchair in the living room. In a few minutes he was asleep. When he woke up Jeff saw by his wristwatch that the time was ten minutes after four.

He felt hungry. Going into the kitchen he opened the refrigerator and saw a package of chopped meat, and a package of chicken parts. He made himself a thick hamburger and ate it at the kitchen table. He had two cans of beers with it.

He returned to the living room and sat down in the armchair. He sat there, tapping his feet on the floor and every fifteen minutes glancing at his wristwatch.

At six-thirty, bursting with impatience, he got up, walked quickly out of the house and got in the car, heading for Route 19. Seven or eight cars were in the parking space outside the brothel.

Jeff went up the stone steps of the broad porch, rang the bell and waited. Immediately the door opened. Standing in front of him was a tall, smooth-faced elderly man in butler's garb and wearing white gloves.

With his gray eyes staring at Jeff the man asked in a soft, cordial voice, "Yes, what do you want?"

"I want to come in, that's what I want," Jeff said. He saw a stout, middle-aged woman behind the butler-dressed man.

"Who sent you?"

"Nobody sent me. I heard about this place from a bartender in town, and—"

The woman stepped in front of the elderly man and said, "What is your name?"

"What's my name got to do with it?"

"I want to know your name, sir," the woman said sternly.

"It's . . . Jeff Stanick. Lily Frayn was my aunt. I'm now living in her house, and I intend to make it my permanent home."

"Oh, so you're the nephew she left everything—come in, come in!" the woman said, smiling brightly. "You are most welcome! Philbert, you can leave us. Please come in, Mr. Stanick."

The butler disappeared.

"Thank you," Jeff said, stepping into the ornate foyer. It had marble statues and tapestry-covered walls.

"My name is Viola. I hope we shall be good friends. Come, make yourself at home." She was dressed in a long sequin gown.

She led Jeff down a short carpeted hall and into a spacious room. It had a vaulted ceiling with a sparkling chandelier hang-down from it. More than a dozen men and young girls were seated at tables. The men were playing cards, the women watched. A bar with a black bartender was in a corner against the wall. On the walls were paintings of naked women in various lascivious poses.

Clapping her hands Viola said, "Ladies, and gentlemen, this is Mr. Jeff Stanick. He is Lily Frayn's nephew. Please make him welcome."

Most of the men merely nodded and went on playing cards. Two f the men came up and shook hands with Jeff, and so did a few of the girls. Jeff saw that the girls were all dressed in cotton housecoats. The way they clung to their bodies, he did not think they had anything else under them.

Viola introduced Jeff to one of the girls, a very pretty redhead, and left them. Her name was Denise.

"Would you like to have a drink?" Denise said.

"I can get a drink in a saloon. I didn't come here for that."

"Come with me."

They went up a staircase to where the bedrooms were. An hour and a half later, thoroughly sated, Jeff left Denise in the bedroom and went down the stairs. The butler was standing in front of the door.

"The fee is three hundred dollars," he said.

Well, Jeff thought, the bartender said that it would be expensive, but it was worth it. Denise had given him everything he wanted. But next time he would try another girl. Jeff liked variety in his sex.

As he drove back home, feeling gratified and elated, he said out loud with great joy, "I think I'll try all the girls! Aunt Lily, I thank you!"

And try them he did. Jeff made it a practice of visiting Viola's place three and sometimes four times a week. He always waited for the night to come. He knew that Viola was open for business after two o'clock in the afternoon. But for some reason daytime sex did not appeal to Jeff. He firmly believed that the night was made for sex. It seemed unnatural to him to engage in sexual activity when the sun was shining brightly in the sky. This prejudice was a peculiarity of Jeff's character.

He was enjoying a vigorous sex life at night, but the mornings and afternoons were a different matter. The mornings were tediously long, and the afternoons were brutally boring.

It became a habit with Jeff to sit in the living-room armchair and wait with nervous impatience for the time to go by so that he could get up and make himself some lunch. He was grateful when he could fall asleep and have a midmorning hap.

But then there was the long afternoon confronting him.

3

"Well, which girl would you like this evening?" Viola asked Jeff. She had developed a great fondness for him. He had given her thousands of dollars of business since he had started coming to her establishment five months ago.

"Would you like Sally, or Debra? They are both available."

"I've already had them four or five times," Jeff said sullenly

The madam could not understand his grumpiness. He had always been very cheerful, polite and smiling. Lately, he seemed to be annoyed about something. What was it?

"Well, then, who do you want tonight?" Viola asked.

"Someone here I haven't had."

"You don't man . . . me?"

Why not, Jeff thought. Maybe seasoned meat might be a pleasant change from all the young girls he had in this place.

"You want me to entertain you?" Viola said, flattered and pleased. Of all the men who visited her place, only the mayor had expressed desire for her.

"That's what I want," Jeff said.

But the older woman was a disappointment. Jeff realized it was not her fault. Everything he asked her to do, Viola did, and with the skill she had acquired in that line of work over the years.

Jeff drove back to his house a worried and anxious man. What was happening to him? Was sex beginning to pall on him? But why should it? He was still a young man.

In a sudden panic and starting to sweat, Jeff asked himself, But if I don't have sex to look forward to at night—. He could not complete the thought. It was too horrible to contemplate.

The routine continued for Jeff. Breakfast over, he sat in the stuffed armchair and waited for the morning to go by so that he could start making lunch. And then back to the armchair and waiting to go to town, eat in a restaurant, and then on to the brothel.

One morning he turned on the TV. The incessant gabbing with no point to it all, made Jeff so angry he got up, turned off the TV and put his foot through the screen.

That afternoon he wandered into the library. For the first time he noticed on a shelf close to the floor books on philosophy. There were dozens of them, going all the way to the ancient Greeks and up to modern times.

He was hoping those books would help to enlighten him, explain something to him, but exactly what Jeff was not sure. But after going through all the books he was as lost as ever, and left without answers.

As he walked out of the library, never to return again, he was thinking, What did all those dead men know? Nothing. It was all guess-work and speculation on their part. Why was there a universe, and why did we exist? For what purpose?

As the weeks went by, and Jeff became more obsessed by all the time he had on his hands, with nothing to do, he began to be aware of a strange development in him, in his body. Days had gone by and he had not felt the pricking of strong sexual desire, the craving for a woman.

Like a sick man and trying to find an antidote, he went that night to Viola's place. But it was not good. The girl he had, Freda, an attractive twenty-year-old with flaming red hair, did not really rouse him. He had her once, mechanically, and without much pleasure and quickly left.

That night he had very little sleep. Three times he woke up, and he would stay awake for hours. The thought that terrified him was the whole day he would have to face.

That morning, sitting in the armchair, Jeff finally began to see what his problem was. It was Time. He thought of time as a Being, something alive, an enemy, a relentless enemy.

Somehow, some way, he would have to defeat this hostile and hateful foe. It was out to destroy him, he was sure of that. But why? Why did Time choose him to persecute?

Jeff could not answer that question.

As the days went by, he became bitter and resentful. Why had God, fate, signaled out to him to suffer like this? He had not been a bad, wicked person. He liked girls, sex—was that a great crime?

So why me? Jeff asked himself.

Things did not get better as the days went by. He forgot about the brothel. It seemed to Jeff that his libido was extinct. But he was not too sure. Sometimes a feeble flicker of sexual feelings came over him. He tried to spur it on, imagining naked girls all around him.

But gradually, slowly, that sexual feeling died out in him and he was left brooding in anguish.

However, Jeff was not left in peace for long. For while his libido grew weaker and weaker, his consciousness of Time intensified ever more sharply, causing him more acute suffering.

The mornings were unbearable as he sat in the armchair, hoping they would end. The same with the afternoons. But it was the nights that were hellish beyond endurance.

Jeff would howl in agony like some wounded beast. Sometimes he would beg Time for mercy, pity. But when he saw that Time had no mercy, no pity, he would curse every passing second.

Jeff could not understand how Time could be so unrelenting, so inexhaustible. The seconds, hours, days went by, but there was always more Time. Time was like a tidal wave that kept coming and coming and coming and . . . .

In his desperation, Jeff turned to religion. On a side table in the living room was an old, heavy family Bible. He read the Old Testament from beginning to end. But he got no help from it. All the killing plagues, drowning, massacres, bloody wars, stoning to death found religious infractions disgusted and sickened him. He wondered why this was called the Holy Book. It should be called the Book of Horrors.

He took the Bible outside, set it on fire and watched it burn to ashes with great satisfaction. He scooped up the ashes and threw them into the pond.

But that did not solve his massive problem, dealing with Time. There was no escaping it. It was all around him, under him, over him. It was like an invading army, coming closer and closer but never actually reaching him.

But it was always there, a menacing threat.

For a whole week Jeff took to going to town and getting drunk. In a hazy stupor he would drive back to the house. Once he was tempted to crash his car into a tree to end the tormenting fiend's Time's grip on him. But he resisted the temptation—and went on suffering.

How Jeff hated to return to that empty, quiet, Time-ridden house. It was time like this when he wished that Time was a person he could take hold of, bet to death, strangle with his bare hands. Or that Time was an animal that he could shoot to death.

Oh, how wonderful it would be to be able to kill Time! But he could not. It did not have a body that he could destroy, or burn, as he did with the Bible.

Time, that silent, creeping, remorseful tyrant. It would not set him free. It enjoyed torturing him. It was a brutal sadist!

One night, unable to sleep, he sat up in bed and shrieked, "I'll get you yet, Time! You'll see! I'll find a way to kill you! You are not going to get the better of Jeff Stanick!"

But the next moment he was thinking, What's the matter with me? Am I going crazy? Is it all my deranged imagination? Why have I become obsessed with time? I have to get out in the world, do things, be with people.

As Jeff drove back to the big city where he was born and where he grew up, he was joyfully confident, supremely certain that he was doing the right thing. He would book himself into a hotel for a month, do things, be with crowds of people.

And when he registered in a fine hotel and saw two pretty girls sitting in the lobby with their shapely legs crossed, he felt a sudden hot sensation in his groin. Was his sex desire coming back to him? He was sure it was! he told himself. And how grateful Jeff was.

But the trip turned out to be a losing disaster. He tried everything to wipe from his mind his Time-obsession. But nothing worked. He went to plays. The performers on the stage did not move him. With the movies it was the same. What did he care for the plight and the problems of the characters in the film? He had his own much bigger problem—Time!

Jeff decided to give sports a shot. In the stadium he thought he was in a madhouse, among lunatics. Every few minutes they screamed like maniacs.

When he returned to the hotel, shaken and unnerved, an attractive young blonde got up from her chair and smiled at him, running her tongue across her lips. Jeff nodded and she followed him to the elevator.

But it was no go sexually. Some desire was in his mind, but his lower body did not respond. He gave the woman fifty dollars and told her to leave. The next day he checked out of the hotel.

Dispirited and dejected, Jeff knew why he had been beaten. It was Time that had defeated him. Time had been with him all the way, in the car, in the hotel, in the theaters, in the ballpark, and when he was in the hotel room with the prostitute.

But as he got closer to home, he began to shake off his despair, his sense of defeat. A furious anger began mounting in him. Why did he have to go on being a passive victim of Time? He did not have to, by God, no, he did not have to submit meekly to Time's torture and persecution of him!

When Jeff stepped out of the car and strode briskly into the house, he was a renewed man, full of fight, boiling over with wrathful hatred of Time.

Standing arrogantly in the living room, with his hands on his hips, Jeff declared out loud, "I'm not taking this lying down anymore, Time! I'm going to give you the fight of your life! You have tormented me long enough! Now it's my turn! I'm going to get my revenge! I'm going to make you suffer the way you made me suffer all these months!"

However, Jeff found out all too soon that it was easy to make that boast, it was another matter to carry it out. His enemy was an elusive prey. It was invisible, it had no substance, but what a massively heavy presence it was!

In the weeks that followed Jeff knew that he had the battle of his life on his hands. His enemy was cunning, his enemy was powerful, not in a forceful way, but in a subtle, cagey way. It had patience, and it had—all the time in the world!

Slowly, the fight went out of Jeff. Now every day was painful for him, his daily Via Dolorosa. All day long he had to drag his cross, Time, on his back, or so it seemed to Jeff. But for him there was no Golgotha, no death to end his suffering. It would go on and on, until he died. And he was only going on thirty-five! He could live to be seventy-five, eighty years old! And all those years he would be suffering worse than the poor damn souls in hell!

Some Time-obsessed days of the week were worse than others. But for some puzzling reason Jeff could not explain to himself, he had a particular horror of Sunday afternoons.

Why was that? he kept asking himself, all week as the fearful day rolled around. How he dreaded the long, boring Sunday afternoon. Sometimes he thought it would never end.

But when it mercifully did, he had to face the bleak prospect of getting through the night. How grateful he was when it was time to go to bed. Sleep did not come easily to him because he could sense the presence of Time in the bedroom. Sometimes he was able to read himself to sleep.

4

A startling thought occurred to Jeff one day. How come he was the only one who was agonizingly aware of the burdensome presence of Time? Or was he? Could there be others who were similarly afflicted with Time-obsession? And they kept it to themselves, and suffered silently?

No, Jeff, did not think so. He was the only one who was so keenly, so intensely, so painfully conscious of Time. But maybe he was all wrong about time. Maybe all this problem was a mental disorder.

But a frightening experience he had a day later convinced Jeff that Time was no phantom in his mind. It was objectively real. It did exist as a being.

This was the bad experience he had. One night, he was walking slowly over his grounds before going to bed. A bright moon was in the dark clear sky. Suddenly Jeff heard behind him the snapping of twigs and the sharp crackling sounds of leaves being stepped on. Turning around, he saw a huge hound stalking him. It had fiery red eyes. A long tongue hung out of the large, foam-specked mouth. Jeff could see and hear clearly the sharp clicking sound the beast's gleaming teeth made.

Jeff began to walk faster, and then broke into a run. Behind him he heard the hound chasing after him. And now he heard it growl, its big teeth in those massive jaws snapping.

Fifty feet head of him was an old oak tree, with low-hanging branches. If he could only reach that tree and climb up it before the beast caught up with him!

When it was only ten feet behind him, Jeff took a flying leap on the lowest branch and was able to scramble higher to safety.

Jeff was trembling and drenched in sweat when he turned around and looked down at the ground. He saw nothing. The beast had vanished, disappeared.

That fact convinced Jeff of one thing—Time had the power to materialize itself! Yes, Time could do that! But if the Beast-Time had caught up with him, what would it have done to him?

Jeff was sure it did not want to kill him. No, it wanted him alive, so that it could go on making his life a hell.

He got down from the tree and walked at a fast pace back to the house, all the time warily looking around him. There was absolutely no doubt in Jeff's mind that Time had assumed the appearance of that fearsome animal. He wondered what other shapes it could take. A human being? No, he did not think so.

As he stepped into the house, a painful thought came to Jeff. Tonight was Saturday. And tomorrow would be . . . Sunday. Once again he would be confronted with that dreaded desolate dreariness—Sunday afternoon. It deadened his spirit, crushed his soul, stifled him, made him wish he could stop living.

During that long, seemingly endless Sunday afternoon, a hand of ice seemed to grip his heart, and did not let go until the sun went down. But the aftereffect following the horrible Sunday afternoon was almost as bad. He continued to sit in his armchair like a man paralyzed, dumb, all the life drained out of him.

Jeff asked himself how long he would have to go on suffing like this. Was there no way to purge himself of his Time-obsession? Was there any hope for him?

He thought of God. Would prayer help? But to Jeff God seemed remote, far away. And Time was so close, so oppressively close. It was a ruthless and relentless enemy. It would take more than prayer to defeat time.

5

After a long night of hard thinking, Jeff woke up the next morning with a fresh, an intellectual outlook on his problem. He remembered in the books he had read in the library how so many great thinkers had grappled to understand Time—from St. Augustine to today's astrophysicists. And they were all stumped, confounded. Not one of them came up with a satisfactory answer.

The questions that seemed impossible to answer were did Time have a beginning? Would Time ever end?

The second question attracted Jeff powerfully. Would Time ever end? The end of Time . . . . That might be the solution to his problem—his Time-bondage. Somehow, for him, Jeff, Time must end. But how to accomplish that mighty feat?

If only he could kill Time! he thought desperately. If only he could get his hands on it! It had appeared to him as a dog. The dog he could not fight. It was too big, too ferocious. If only it would show himself as something he could fight!

And one day Jeff had his chance. It happened toward sunset. He was walking deep in the woods, about a half mile from his own grounds.

A thick mist hung in the air. Jeff glanced around him suspiciously. Yes, yes, he was sure of it! Time was near him, over him, all around him!

Jeff stopped in his tracks. There was fierce hatred in his eyes as he stared all around him. His hands reached out as if to grab something.

"Show yourself, you old bastard!" he shouted frantically, angrily. "Stop hiding from me, coward! Come on, come on, face me like a man! I'm ready for you! Let's fight it out."

And it seemed to Jeff that a mist near a tree took a shape that almost resembled a human form. It had a head, shoulders, arms, a torso, and legs.

With a furious cry of joy and exultation, Jeff charged toward the tree. In a matter of seconds he had it! He had Time by the throat! And now he would kill it, strangle it, destroy this enemy that had caused him so much suffering!

But his enemy fought back. Jeff fought with all the strength that was in him. He knew that this was his one change to be free of his oppressor. And so he fought as one possessed, and so did his foe. They rolled on the ground. Once Jeff thought that he had won, that the life was being strangled out of Time. But Time fought back with renewed force. And for a few moments Jeff feared that Time would kill him.

On and on the life-and-death struggle went. Suddenly, Jeff lost consciousness. When he woke up, lying on a pile of leaves under a tree, it was morning. Bright sunlight filled the forest.

Slowly, Jeff got to his feet. He felt pains and aches in every part of his body. He saw bruises on his bare arms. He looked around, hoping to see—what did he expect to see? Time sprawled dead somewhere near where he was standing?

There was nothing. Only leaves, broken twigs, patches of grass and trees, trees, trees.

Jeff had to face the terrible truth. Time had escaped him. He had it in his hands! He had the chance to kill Time! And he had let it get away!

Jeff returned to the house in deep despair. He realized now with bleak certainty that he would never, that he could never, beat Time. Time was unconquerable, unbeatable. Who was he, a mere mortal, to think that he could get the better of Time?

In the days and weeks that followed his titanic fight with Time, Jeff went downhill. He stopped bathing, shaving. He had little appetite for food. He would spend whole days in the armchair brooding over his miserable fate. There was not a minute of his waking hours when Jeff did not feel the goading presence of Time.

One day, sitting in the armchair, unwashed, in smelly, filthy clothes, passing his hand through his scraggly beard, an odd thought popped into his head. It did seem odd and strange to Jeff.

What if he got married? he thought. Sure, why not? Lately he had begun to experience faint stirrings of sex in him. Perhaps sensual desire was dormant in him? Not dead? A wife would be a distraction, get his mind away from thinking of his old enemy all the days of his life.

But would a wife truly help to free him from the totalitarian hold Time had on him? Actually liberate him from his Time-bondage? Jeff did not think so. Sex was short. The day was long.

No, a wife was not the answer. She would be of no use to him in his struggle with Time.

With that last hope gone, a grim idea came to Jeff.

"Death," Jeff said somberly out loud, looking around the living room, and smiling. "Yes, you old bastard, Time! That's how I will defeat you and end Time in my life, by killing myself! When I'm dead, you will no longer be able to torment me, persecute me, torture me! I'll be free, free of you at last!"

With that encouraging thought, Jeff got up and walked resolutely into the kitchen. In less than a minute, he had the long carving knife in his hand.

But with the knife gripped tightly in his hand, Jeff paused, as a disturbing notion came to him, something he had not taken into consideration.

What if there was life after death? What if the religious teaching and belief that human beings were endowed with an immortal soul was true? And if that belief was true . . . he, Jeff Stanich . . . his spirit . . . would live forever. And Time would continue its unrelenting, brutal reign of torture over him.

But was it really true that people had a soul that survived the dissolution of the body? No, it wasn't true! Jeff told himself. The belief in immortality was based only on human egotism. Men and women could not face the cruel, cold fact that death was the end, the total extinction of the self that made up a person. There was no afterlife. After death, there was only a corpse in a lonely grave, and the maggots having a feast.

As Jeff brought the sharp, shining knife up to his throat, he shouted in a joyfully defiant voice, "The victory is mine, Time! I will defeat you with one swipe of my hand! You will no longer be able to persecute me, torment me, torture me. I win, Time, I win! This is the end of Jeff Stanich!"

And he did it, he cut his throat free ear to ear. The blood flowed thickly and freely from the deep, broad fatal wound. Jeff dropped the knife and fell to the floor. As he lay dying he was smiling and murmuring happily, "At last, at last . . . an end to my suffering . . ."

And he died.

But to his horror Jeff found himself very much alive in the Great Beyond. To his dismay and consternation, he found out that it was true. Humans did have an immortal soul. And that meant he would go on suffering from Time-bondage for all of eternity.

SEXUALIS ANONYMOUS

As he slowly got off Nadine's hot, sweaty body Justin sadly admitted to himself that the deep satisfaction he had always felt after a vigorous bout of sex was no longer there.

Why? he wondered.

Every time when he rolled off a woman he had experienced that wonderful euphoric exaltation, that complete and total peace of mind, that supremely happy sensation of well-being. And for more than an hour after, he felt he was walking on clouds.

What he felt now was none of those things. At that very moment he was gripped by a deep sadness, and what was worse, a sense of disillusionment, futility, and also an overwhelming weariness.

But, Justin asked himself, was this the first time that this aching disillusionment, futility and weariness had come over him after sex? No, he realized. Those unpleasant feelings had been coming on for weeks, but he had ignored them by plunging once more into the whirl of sexual adventures.

But, really, was it worth it, that sexual activity of a few minutes and ending with that most powerful of all pleasurable physical sensations? Why should all that be the centerpiece of a man's life? Was a man truly and fully a man whose life was dominated by sex?

Should sex be a man's all-consuming passion? Wasn't he diminished as a man by being a slave to sex? Wasn't a man's mind capable of rising higher than mere bodily sensations?

As Justin pondered those questions he heard Nadine mumble sleepily, "Oh, you marvelous man, do me again . . . do me again . . . ." And she dropped off once again into a deep sleep.

Justin got off the bed and walked in his bare feet to the bathroom to wash up. He looked down at his body with a scowl. He felt sticky. And he had a musky odor about him. The smell of a woman.

In the bathroom Justin stared with dull, tired eyes at his reflection in the mirror of the door of the medicine cabinet. He saw a man that was very unhappy with himself. The mouth tried to smile, but Justin saw deceit in that weak smile. Who was he kidding? That seemed face looked too old for a man that was only thirty-four years old.

He turned on the water, but he did not wash himself, just stood there, gazing at himself in the mirror. The hell with it, he thought, turning off the water.

Should he go back to Nadine? How skilled she was in stimulating a man's jaded desires, and bringing him back to life for another round of sex.

But would that dissipate his gloomy thoughts? They were sure to come back, just as bad as ever. And then he would have to go back for more sex and—

No, that was not the answer.

So, what was the answer? Justin asked himself.

Why had he given himself so totally to a life of sexual pleasure?

The answer came to Justin with a kind of raw, stark truth that he could not deny. The allure of sex is a female trap. The huge promise of sex turns out to be a cheat and a swindle. The deeper he goes into that trap, the deeper a man is burying himself in a living death.

A powerful truth rang in his head. A woman's body is a man's grave. All women are graves on two legs.

Damnit, he said to himself, he had to be honest. The hard, cruel truth was that a woman's vagina is a man's tomb. All the time a man thinks he is having a great time feasting on a woman's body, a man is really imprisoning himself in that tight, hot, fleshy tomb.

A woman destroys a man's substance, sucking the soul out of him, until he is no longer a free man. He is an automaton, or a puppet, jerked around here and there. And the woman's vagina-trap was the puppeteer.

A real man had to free himself of that tyranny. It was his moral duty to break out of his slavish bondage. And he had to go all the way! Man had to declare his sexual independence of woman—the age-old tyrant!

Yes, that was it! Woman was the temptress who corrupted man by the forbidden fruit she had between her legs. Man had to renounce that fruit forever! All women were in their true, innate natures whores who lured men away from their real destiny.

And what was man's real destiny? Man's destiny was union with the Divine Mind. But how could a man unite himself with that Mind when he was draining himself dry physically and spiritually in that opening in the female's body?

The Divine Mind had implanted some of that divinity in man. But every time he experienced those bestial orgasms he was losing part of that divinity in woman's stinking, filthy sump hole.

Men had to start living celibate lives. That would be difficult, but not impossible. All they had to do was use their willower.

And how were they to do that? By getting their minds off women. Stop thinking carnally and start thinking mystically—about the Divine Mind!

Wait a minute! he told himself, getting up from the bathtub. Where did he get all this dippy, crackpot stuff about the Divine Mind?

And then he remembered the book he had read a month ago. The title of it was "You and the Cosmic Mind."

A more silly, goofy book it would be hard to find. Justin could not understand how he could have read it all the way through. He tried to remember the name of the featherbrain who had produced that mystical hogwash.

Justin had been brought up a Catholic, but somewhere along the way he stopped believing all that religious stuff. However, just for old time's sake, and out of respect for his parents, he attended Mass about a dozen times a year. During the service he experienced pleasant nostalgic feelings about the time when he was a body. But that was all he felt. The religious part, the miracle that was supposed to be going on at the altar, did not touch him at all.

So Justin had the good old-fashioned belief in God, and let it go at that. Trying to make contact with the mind of God here on earth was in his opinion a waste of mental effort. Maybe there was something after death, and maybe there was nothing, just the body turning into bones and then into dust.

Okay, so there was no soul in man yearning to be united to that daffy Divine Mind idea. But, Justin told himself, he was still a pitiful sex addict. And he had to free himself of that demeaning addiction! And he could do it only by going all the way—total sexual abstinence!

As Justin walked out of the bathroom he was supremely confident that he could beat this addiction. He felt as if a heavy burden had been lifted from his shoulders, a burden he had been lugging around for too many years.

How long had he been in the bathroom? Ten minutes? A half hour? Was Nadine awake? Sleeping? Justin realized that he was going to face his first test, the test that would show whether his willpower was made of glass or iron.

Nadine was sleeping. Her naked body was sprawled diagonally across the bed, her legs parted wide. He averted his eyes from Nadine and glanced down at his body. Justin smiled. He was pleased and gratified at what he saw. His main sexual organ remained soft, flaccid, limp.

He had passed his first test with flying colors!

Nadine's eyes began to flutter, and in a few moments her eyes opened. She smiled up at Justin, sticking out her large pink tongue and moving it slowly over her upper and lower lips. She threw out her arms to him invitingly, her hips gliding sinuously on the sheets.

"Better get dressed," Justin said curtly.

Nadine quickly sat up, a shocked expression on her face. She turned to look at the clock on the night table.

"But it's only a quarter after seven! We have plenty of time found one more—"

"I have some work to do in the gallery," Justin broke in. He was the owner and manager of a small art gallery.

"Justin, fifteen or twenty minutes can't make much difference!" Nadine said peevishly.

"Will you please hurry up and get dressed. I have an artist coming early to should me some of his paintings."

"You never let business interfere with pleasure before!" Nadine said, deeply offended.

"So I've changed!" Justin said in a hard voice. "Get dressed!"

Nadine saw Justin meant what he said. She knew from past experience how determined he could be. But . . . still, this was so unlike him. Slowly she got up from the bed and began to put on her things. Justin returned to the bathroom.

A half hour later, after Nadine had left in a huff, and Justin had showered and shaved, he paced up and down his living room, wondering seriously what he was going to do with this . . . illumination he had received. Yes, that is what it is, he told himself. Not a heaven-sent message. Justin congratulated himself on wisely seeing through that delusion.

He stopped his pacing and said, "All thoughts are manmade. They are the product of the brain cells in the human skull. The Jewish writers who had written the Old Testament and the Christians who had produced the four Gospels all were firmly convinced that the words they put down were divinely inspired. They were only acting as God's secretaries, taking down his dictation. The same with the prophet Mahomet. He sincerely believed that the words that came from his mouth were straight from heaven. "All baloney! I don't believe it!"

Justin continued his pacing. The jist of his illumination was simply that men had to free themselves from the bondage of sex. That was wise, sensible and rational—nothing divine about it.

Even at that moment Justin felt exhilarated. He had made the conscious decision to cut women out of his life. He was sure he could do it. How trouble-free life would be from now on.

Again Justin stopped pacing and a bright thought came to him. Were there other men in the same plight he had been in? Were there men who were hounded by that mad, frenzied craving for sex as he had been? Justin was certain there were many men who would like to escape from the sex hounds of hell.

"And I'm the man who will help them do it!" he exclaimed confidently, invigorated by a strong desire to help those men who suffered so grievously from their sex addiction.

But how was he to reach those men? Go public? Preach his message of total sexual abstinence to men on street corners? Would he be locked up in a booby hatch for having such a radical idea? And trying to get men to accept it? He knew what the authorities would say. If all men did as you, Justin, did, what would become of the human race? It would become extinct in a very short time.

But all that was irrelevant and beside the point. The important thing was that men had to be free, free of the torment of sexual craving, once and for all!

But Justin realized that he had to be careful. No matter how right he knew he was, those reactionary politicians might find a way to lock him up.

So the sensible thing to do was to start modestly and discreetly. Yes, he had to be careful. He would begin with all his male friends, that is those who were single and were in the throes of a rip-roaring sex life. That would be the sensible course.

He began to think of his plan of action. Going over to a small desk in the corner he sat down and began to write down the names of his bachelor friends.

When he was done, he moved his finger down the list. He had the names of fifteen men. How would they receive his message? Would they laugh at him? Mock him? Tell him that he was crazy? Or would they thankfully embrace his grand idea?

The first thing he had to do was get all those swinging males together and spring his message of sexual liberation on them. He thought of his art gallery, but he quickly rejected that place for a meeting.

The place had to have a solemn dignity to it, a religious atmosphere.... He had it! He would go to his old neighborhood and speak to the pastor of the church he attended when he was young. Justin had not been in that church in almost twenty years. He hoped that Father Malloy was still there.

This was the beginning of a great and noble crusade!

Two days later Justin was sitting in the rectory of St. Joseph's R. C. Church with Father Malloy, who was gray-haired man of sixty. They reminisced about the time when Justin had served as altar boy.

"And, Justin, I say a prayer for your mother and father every day. I want to thank you again for the stained-glass window you put up in their memory."

"They were wonderful parents."

"Now, why have you come to see me, Justin?"

"Ah . . . I want to ask a favor of you."

"Name it."

"I would like to have the use of your church basement for two nights a week."

"For what purpose?"

When Justin told him, the old priest was startled, and he showed it, smiling and shaking his head.

"What's wrong with my idea?" Justin asked.

"Don't you think that's an ambitious project?"

"But hasn't the church been teaching the same thing to single people?"

"Yes, for centuries, with mixed results."

"Well, anyway, that's why I want the use of the basement. How about it?"

"Justin, have you gotten religion?"

"Father, this has nothing to do with religion. My mind has told me that men should banish sex from their lives. Sex is a fraud. It's just not worth all the fuss and bother for a few moments of pleasure. Men should cut it out of their lives."

"Their whole lives?" Father Malloy asked, frowning.

"Yes, yes!"

"Justin, do you know how hard it is to go without sex? I know, believe me, I know. Yes, many priests fail and drop out, but most of us remain faithful to our vow of celibacy."

"Father, can I have the basement, yes or no?"

"Yes, you can have it. On which night?"

"I'd like to have it for two nights."

"Two nights?"

"Yes, the dangerous nights, Friday and Saturday, the date nights."

"I'm sorry, you can't have Friday. Saturday is okay."

"Why can't I have Friday?"

"That's when the drinkers have their meeting."

"Alcoholics Anonymous?"

"Yes."

"How about Thursday night?"

"No, that's when the drug addicts meet."

"How about Wednesday night?"

"Wednesday night is fine."

"Thank you, Father," Justin said, taking out a roll of bills. "This is for the church."

Father Malloy riffled the money, his eyes opening wide.

"Justin, you've been very generous. I'm very grateful. Say, what are you going to call your group?"

"Sexualis Anonymous."

"Very appropriate. Good luck, Justin!"

One week later the first meeting of Sexualis Anonymous was held. Justin was pleased at the number of his friends who showed up, fifteen of them. True, he had not told them over the phone the reason for the meeting, nevertheless he was happy to see the men seated on the metal folding chairs in front of him. He stood on the short platform and smiled down at them.

And then two women walked in and were about to take a seat.

"This meeting is only for men!" Justin shouted angrily. "Will you ladies please leave at once!"

The women left.

And then Justin launched into his speech, explaining the reason for the meeting and why men would be happier without women in their lives. But halfway through his talk he was discouraged to see the men begin to get up and leave. And when he was done, there were only six men left.

Justin shook off discouragement and smiled at the remaining six. Well, he said he was going to start modestly.

"Men," he said, "I am very glad you have stayed. Now here is what I want everyone of you to do. I want you to come up to this platform and make this statement: 'I confess that I am a sexual addict. I freely admit it. I cannot do without women. And I do not want to get married. I want to have sex with as many women as possible before I die. I live for sex, I hunger for it, it's on my mind day and night. All my dreams have to do with sex. Yes, I am a slave to sex. But I swear before all of you tonight that I want to break the shackles of sex. I want to get back my freedom as a man. I want to be liberated from the degrading bondage of sex. This I swear with all my heart and soul!'"

And so it happened. All six men came up to the platform individually and spoke those words, with some prompting from Justin. After they had all spoken, Justin got up on the platform again, smiling broadly. This was better, much better than when those men walked out on him, his friends, with insulting remarks like "Justin, you have gone off the deep end!" And "You belong in a padded cell!" And "Give up sex? It's my whole life! You might just as well tell me to stop breathing! Man, Justin, you have lost touch with the real world!" And the worst of all: "Justin, tell us the truth! With all that screwing, you've become impotent! You can't get it up anymore, and now you want us to stop having our fun!"

As Justin gazed down at the six men he took a good look at each of them. They were Alex, Romeo, Chris, Victor, Herb and Jasper. He was very proud of them. It took a lot of courage for them openly to admit their weakness, their shameful addiction. But Justin could see they looked very glum. He had to boost their morale.

"Men," he said, "you showed good sense by staying. Let the others go on with their empty, sex-driven lives. We have chosen to take a different path—freedom from sexual bondage! I want everyone of you to know how proud I am of you. You have taken the first step in breaking the shackles that bind you. You have made your public confession that you are sex addicts. You were once weaklings. Now I want you to become men of iron! I know we are fighting a powerful, demonic forces in us—raw, demanding sensuality! We must use our willpower to the utmost! Think of the vagina not as a source of pleasure, but as your enemy! Think of it, think of it! It is only a piece of inert meat! It is not an unbeatable foe!

I say it can be beaten, and once beaten, you will be free, free forever of that demon sex!"

"It isn't going to be easy, giving up the girls . . . sex," Chris said.

"I didn't say it was going to be easy, but the sacrifice will be worth it. You will all be getting back your self-respect, like drug addicts who break the habit, their dependence on drugs, Something just occurred to me. I think we should all tell our stories, I mean how we got so deeply hooked on sex. I think that would be a great help in breaking our sex addiction."

"What's your story, Justin?" Alex asked.

"It's very simple. I was searching for mother-love in vaginas. My mother never showed me any love. I could see how much she cared for my older brother, her first-born. My mom practically ignored me when I was growing up. Whatever my brother wanted, he got. Me, I got the back of my mother's hand whenever I asked for anything. And so I tried to find that love I never had in women."

"How could you be sure that that was what motivated your sex drive?" Victor said.

"Everytime I had an orgasm I would shout hysterically, 'Mommy, I love you! Please love me! Love your little Justin!' Of course over the years I stopped crying out like that, but that didn't decrease my voracious sexual appetite. Well, that's my story. What about the rest of you? Alex, you start."

"I went through a bad period, an abnormal time in my sex life. It happened in my second year in college. Up to that time I was okay, plenty of girls in high school and the first two years in college. Well, it happened this way. This maintenance guy asked me to come down to his workshop to help him with something. I must have been pretty naive, or dumb. Anyway, before I knew what was happening, he was doing me from behind. It hurt like hell the first few times, but then I began to like it. And then of course he wanted me to do him the same way."

"Did you try to break off with him?" Victor asked.

"Yes, lots of times, but I always went back to his workshop. I really felt guilty about what had happened to me. I come from a conservative Protestant family in the Bible Belt, and I used to think how they would be hurt if they ever found out about what I had become. All the time I was involved with this guy I seemed to have lost my desire for girls. One night I made up my mind I was not going to go on with that kind of unnatural sex life. I picked up one of the college girls in a bar and spent the night with her. And from then on it was one girl after another. The maintenance guy came to me one day and tried to get me down to his workshop. I told him to get lost, and when he grabbed my arm to force me to go with him, I punched him in the nose and told him to stay the hell away from me. But the fear of sliding back to that kind of sex preyed on my mind. And that's now I developed my mad craving for girl sex."

"Chris, what's your story?" Justin said.

"My father wanted me to be a big league baseball player. That was his great ambition for me. All he talked about was baseball, baseball, morning and night. He would brag to the neighbors how his son was going to make it to the Bigs and how proud he would be. But I never got beyond the minor leagues, not even reaching Tripple-A. I just plain wasn't good enough, so I quit baseball when I was twenty-seven and still a minor leaguer. I went to work in my father's furniture store as a clerk. Every day in front of the customers he would insult me, calling me a failure. 'Look at him, look at him!' he would shout at me with the store filled with customers. 'My son, the bush leaguer!' Well, in desperation I turned to sex to get some relief from my father's contempt. I got three girls pregnant, and my father had to pay for the abortions. That made him mad as hell. Just for spite, I got a fourth girl pregnant and left home and came to live in this city. But sex had its powerful hooks in me and sleeping with girls just about became a career with me. That's my story."

"Romeo, what about you?" Justin said.

Getting to his feet, Romeo said angrily, "Look at me! I'm a shrimp! Thirty-one years old and I'm not even five feet tall!"

"You shouldn't feel bad about that," Alex said. "There are a lot of short men in this world. It's what's inside you that counts."

"You can talk like that, Alex. You're over six feet tall. And what about my name, Romeo? I'm supposed to be the great lover boy."

"So to compensate for being short, you became very sexually active?" Chris asked.

"Yes. Mother Nature shortchanged me on my height, but she more than made up for it in a different way."

"How do you mean?" Justin said.

"Mother Nature equipped me with one hell of a lollapalooza of a pecker! With my clothes on I'm just a runt. But naked, I'm the fulfillment of every women's dream. And I can go all night!"

"Romeo, I think you are making this all up." Alex said.

"You don't believe me?"

"No," Alex said.

"I'll bet my penis is bigger than any two penises in this room put together!"

"Prove it!" Chris said.

"Okay, I will!" Romeo said, starting to pull down his zipper.

"No, no, Romeo, I for one believe you. I slept with one of your girlfriends a few months back, and she told me all about you."

"Which one?"

"Rosalie. She said that night with you was the most unforgettable sex experience of her life. She said in the morning she was sore and exhausted. You didn't give her a minute's sleep."

"Well, that's my story," Romeo said, sitting down with a heavy sigh.

"But I don't get it," Alex said. "You haven't told us why you are renouncing sex for good."

"I'm doing it because I don't want to go on leaning on my humongous penis to prove to myself I'm a man! I am a man, all four feet and eleven inches of me!"

"Herb, you're turn," Justin said.

"I'm thirty-three years old and still living with my parents. Taking a girl to a hotel room has become too expensive for me."

"Why couldn't you bring the girls home and use your own room?" Chris said.

"Look, my mother and father are very strict orthodox Jews. When I asked them if it was all right for me to have a girl in my room for the night, they almost jumped out of their skins. So, what was I supposed to do, have a girl up against a wall in a dark alley? I got my pride."

"Jasper, what about you?" Romeo asked.

"About six months ago I made a trip to Burma and spent two weeks in a Buddhist monastery. I talked to old monks who had been in that monastery since they were kids. They had never had sexual relations, all their lives—never! I couldn't believe it, but I knew it was true. They were sincere believers in their religion, always at their prayers. The great Buddha had taught his disciples that the way to nirvana—freedom from worry, anxiety and suffering—as to extinguish all passion, all desire in oneself. That is my goal. Yes, I'm going to give it a shot! I know I'm just as good a man as those monks!"

"Good luck!" Herb said.

"Victor, that leaves you," Justin said. "What's your story?"

"My story is briefly told. I'm a Catholic priest. I can't say that I am an ex-priest or a former priest. You know what Catholics say, once a priest, always a priest. It was the confession box that seduced me from my vow of celibacy. Every Saturday afternoon I had to listen to all those men and women tell me that they had sinned sexually and told me how truly repentant they were—until the next time they came to confession. And some of them were so graphically vivid about their sex lives that listening to them got my blood boiling. I began to look forward to Saturday afternoons. A couple of times I even had an orgasm listening to those erotic confessions. One day a woman confessed to me that she had been unfaithful to her husband for the last six months. When I gently reproved her and asked her why, she said that her husband was cold, unresponsive to her caresses and whatever she tried to arouse him. She burst out crying that he as a pathetic, inadequate lover. Out of pity I asked her if she would like to try me. That was the beginning of the end for me as a faithful priest. Through that confession box I had all the women I wanted. I must have had half the women in the parish. But my conscience began to bother me. One day I looked at myself in the mirror and said, 'Victor, you are a despicable hypocrite!' And I left the Church. But I didn't give up sex. However, for many months I've felt a strong desire to return to the priesthood. I must give up sex! I want so much to celebrate Mass once again with a clear conscience.!"

"Okay, we've all told our stories," Justin said. "We've all been frank with each other. That's a very encouraging sign. I have every confidence that we shall succeed in our difficult but not impossible endeavor. Does anyone have anything to say before we break up this meeting?"

"I have a question," Chris said.

"What is it?" Justin said.

"Let's say I'm alone in my apartment."

"Okay, so you're alone in your apartment. What's the problem?"

"The problem is I'm thinking of Melanie. I have seven or eight girlfriends, but Melanie is sort of my steady, or you might say my favorite. You see what I'm getting at?"

"Yes, yes," Justin said.

"So what do I do? There I am, thinking of me and Melanie in bed and—"

"Stop thinking of her!" Justin urged in a loud voice.

"But supposing I can't. What then? Supposing I'm so fired up that I'm tempted to call up Melanie and invite her over. What about that?"

"My advice to you is to you is what I've already said—stop thinking of Melanie! Get her out of your mind!"

"But I can't! That woman is in my blood! Tell me, what should I do?"

"What do members of AA do when they are tempted to hit the bottle?"

"They phone for help from the members of AA." Alex said

"And there's your answer, Chris," Justin said. "You call for help from three or four of us, no matter what hour of the night, and the night is the most dangerous time, and we'll come running. Before we leave here we'll have each other's phone numbers."

"Justin, I have a question," Romeo said. "Supposing I'm having a hell of a tough time resisting my number one girlfriend, Erica. She has hair like spun gold, and a body that would knock your eyes out. Erica, loves to please. She can satisfy a man eight different—"

"Okay, okay!" Justin said. "We get the picture. You are alone with this female, is that what you're saying?"

"Yes, that is exactly what I'm saying."

"Romeo, my advice to you is don't allow yourself to be alone with a female at any time. That is the cardinal rule of Sexualis Anonymous."

"Justin, I'd like your opinion on a situation," Jasper said.

"What's the situation?"

"The doorbell of my apartment rings."

"Okay, so it rings."

"I have to answer it, open the door, right?"

"Well, of course you do."

"And when I open the door I see Bea."

"One of your female friends?"

"For whom I have a particular fondness. She's built just the way I like them, plump, big-breasted and always ready for action. Bea says she wants to talk to me. Should I be rude and not let her in?"

"Talk to you, baloney! Women's wiles, women's wiles!"

"But, Justin, maybe she means it. Bea is very intellectual. She might want to discuss something non-sexual with me, like philosophy, politics, or Italian Renaissance art."

"Don't you believe it! When a women is alone with a man, she has only one thing on her mind—sex! A woman is a sex savage. She has only one nature, and it is permeated and dominated by sex We men are completely different. We have two natures, a sexual, or physical nature, and a nonphysical nature, or to be more specific, we men have souls."

"Justin, I think you are going to far about women not having souls," Victor said.

"Well, maybe you're right," Justin conceded. "What I should have said was that man has a more spiritual side to him than women. Women get pregnant, have babies. They are absorbed more in their bodies than men are."

"Say, Justin," Herb said, "I'm a little dry and could use a few beers."

"Okay, we'll break up the meeting. Now, remember what I said. Stay clear of all your girlfriends. Don't let them get you alone. Think of your pride and self-respect. You can be a man without being a fornicator. The next meeting will be Saturday night."

"Saturday night without Erica," Romeo said sadly.

"It's going to be tough, tough!" Victor said, and the rest of the men echoed his sentiments.

"Men," Justin said, "to fortify ourselves and to give us a little extra strength, I think we should end the night with all of us going up on the platform and admitting that we are sexual addicts once again. We'll make it a practice of ending all our meetings that way. Good night, and good luck to all of us!"

"We sure as hell will need it," Chris said.

A week later, when Justin was about to sit down to his dinner, the doorbell rang. He went to the door and opened it. It was Nadine. She had a stern expression on her face.

"Oh, Nadine," he said, "I was just about to have my supper and—"

Nadine walked brusquely past him and went into the living room, followed slowly by Justin. He caught a whiff of her perfume. It had a strange, exotic scent to it. He had never smelled it on Nadine before.

When she turned around to face Justin, she put both hands on her hips, thrust out her breasts and shook her head, all the time with that hard look.

"Uh . . . Nadine, why are you shaking your head?"

"Justin, don't play dumb with me. You haven't called in days. Did you find someone else to play with?"

"No, I haven't."

"So what's the explanation? For the past six months we've been seeing each other two, three times a week. I've slept here so often I thought you were about to ask me to move in with you. What's happened? Why have you cooled off?"

"Nadine, I . . . ." Justin thought about telling her everything. But of course she would think he had gone crazy, like all those men who had walked out on the first meeting of Sexualis Anonymous.

"Justin, damnit, tell me the truth! Have you found someone else?"

"No, I swear to you there is no other woman."

"Justin, I know you have brought other women here. How do I know? Because I've spent many a night outside this apartment building. But you always dropped those women after a few weeks. Now, will you be honest with me? Have you fallen in love with some floozy that pleases you more than I do?"

"Nadine, believe me, I am not seeing another woman."

"You are lying. She is coming here to have dinner with you, and then the bitch is going to sleep over with you, in that same bed where you and I—"

"Come with me," Justin said, interrupting her. He led Nadine into the dining room. "See, the table is set for one person. I am having veal stew and a lettuce salad."

"She's coming later!"

"No one is coming later, Nadine. After I have my supper I'm going to write an article for an art magazine, and then I'm going to hit the hay."

"But, Justin . . . this is not you, the sex-hungry man I've known all these months. Do you actually want me to believe that you have gone without sex for a whole week?"

"Nadine, I have been celibate since we last slept together."

"'Celibate', that word means no sex, right?"

"Yes, no sex."

"But that's unnatural, abnormal, unhuman, for a healthy man in the prime of life to go without sex for seven whole days."

"I swear to you on my mother's grave, I have not had any sex since you and me . . . ."

Nadine knew how much Justin had loved his mother. And how much anguish he had suffered because she had not responded to his love. Many times when they were lying in bed, Justin would ramble on, with a sob in his throat, about how his mother lavished so much affection on his older brother, but turned her back on him. So when Justin swore on his mother's grave, Nadine had to believe him. But what had brought on this celibacy craze? she wondered.

"Okay, Justin, okay, I'm convinced. I believe you. I know that you are not lying. But why? Justin, are you sick? Did you pick up something from one of those tarts?"

"I do not have any disease."

"So how long do you intend to do this celibacy thing?"

"For the rest of my life."

"No, my darling, no!"

"Yes, yes!"

"But why, Justin, why?"

"Because I have come to realize a momentous truth."

"And what is this momentous truth?"

"Sex is a fraud, a cheat, a great big swindle—and a debasing and degrading addiction to all men. For a few moments of delirious pleasure he loses, gives up his real manhood. And furthermore—"

Nadine listened to Justin in shock and disbelief. She asked herself, Was this the man she had known so intimately all these months? Was this the same man who had made such passionate love to her so many, many nights?

"Nadine," Justin said, "you have been staring at me for almost a minute without saying a word. I can see it in your face. I know what you are thinking. You are thinking that I have lost my marbles, that I have a screw loose. Well, I can't help that. This tremendous idea came to me, and I intend to live by it, till the day I die!"

"But people get all kinds of weird ideas, Justin. They have delusions. Maybe this idea is just something your morbid fancy thought up, though why it should come to a normal, healthy person like you I will never understand."

"Nadine, I am not delusional, and there is nothing weird about my desire to live a sexless life. I will be a better man for it, a stronger man, and, yes, a truer man. And I'll tell you something else. I have started an organization to help men get rid of their sexual addiction."

"What do you call this organization?"

"Sexualis Anonymous."

"How many men have joined this crazy outfit?"

"There's nothing crazy about it, and six men have already joined Sexualis Anonymous."

"Why are they?"

Justin gave Nadine the names of all the men.

"You hold meetings, like AA?"

Justin told her where and on what nights.
"Good night, Justin. I'll be seeing you."
"No you won't! Nadine, you stay away from me!"

Nadine sat at a table in one of the private rooms of Gallagher's Bar. Seated around the table with her were the girlfriends of the men who had joined Sexualis Anonymous. The waiter had just left after serving the drinks, but they remained untouched. No one spoke. A heavy silence seemed to hang in the room.

"Nadine gazed at each of the women. They sat there, grimfaced, silent, worried. Present were Lola, Melanie, Erica, Alison, Cora, and Bea.

"Come on, girls, the situation is not hopeless," Nadine said.

"But what can we do?" Bea said. "I call up Victor and soon as he hears my voice, he hangs up on me."

"Same with me," Lola said. "I've phoned Alex a dozen times, and he always says, 'Lola, stop calling me!'"

"How I miss my Romeo!" Erica said in a pitiful voice.

"Five times," Alison said tearfully, "I've waited outside the building where he lives. I know when he gets home from work. And when I tried to talk to him, he tells me to stay away from him!"

"Same with me," Cora said, with tears running down her cheeks. "Jasper has just lost interest in me."

"Chris won't even let me talk to him when I run into him in the street," Melanie said in an anguished voice. "Soon as he sees me, he turns around and goes the other way."

"Girls, we're all in the same fix."

"Justin has left you too?" Erica said.

"So all our men have left us for another woman," Bea said.

"No, we did not lose our men to women."

"But what other reason could there be?" Cora said.

"Ladies," Nadine said, "what I'm going to tell you is the truth. You will find it hard to believe, but it is the God's honest truth. We have lost our men to a wacky idea."

"What wacky idea?" the girls all asked at once.

And Nadine told them. When she was done, the six girls stared at Nadine in stunned silence for several moments. And then they all gulped down their drinks.

"Nadine, that's the craziest thing I have ever heard!" Bea said. "I can't believe my Victor can go without sex! And for the rest of his life?"

"My Romeo might just as well try to go without food!" Erica cried.

"I want my darling Alex holding me in his strong arms!" Lola wailed.

"If Chris doesn't come back to me I don't know what I might do to myself!" Melanie said, wringing her hands.

"No, no, Melanie, you mustn't talk like that," Nadine said.

"Girls, I just found out something," Cora declared with deep emotion.

"What's that?" they all asked her.

"I love Jasper!" Cora sobbed. "God, I love the man! Yes, it isn't only the sex! I love Jasper and want him back with me!"

"I feel the same way about Herb!" Alison moaned. "My life will turn into a wasteland without him!"

"Nadine, how can we get our men back?" Bea said.

"Think of something, Nadine!" Lola cried desperately.

"Come on, Nadine, you're the brainy one," Erica said.

"Tell us what we have to do." Cora said.

"And we'll do it!" Melanie said.

"Show us the way!" Alison pleaded.

After thinking for a minute with the girls' eyes glued on her, Nadine said, "Okay, here's what we'll do. They refuse to talk to us on the phone, and they turn their backs on us in the street. So here's what we will do. We will go to their meeting and have it out with them. Talk to them."

"Make them see how wrong they are!" Lola said.

"Talk some sense into our men!" Bea said.

"Make them see the light!" Melanie said jubilantly.

"Nadine, when is their next meeting?" Alison asked.

"This Saturday night."

"What a surprise they are going to have!" Erica said.

"We'll break up that meeting and each of us will be enjoying a normal Saturday night with our man!" Cora said.

"This calls for a toast!" Nadine said. "Waiter, waiter, bring us more drinks!"

Things were not going so smoothly as Justin had hoped when he started his anti-sex crusade. Standing on the platform he could see how unhappy the men were seated in their chairs. Herb and Romeo sat hunched over, staring wide-eyed at the floor with their mouths open. He knew what was on their minds. Alex and Chris kept crossing and uncrossing their legs and shaking their heads. As for Jasper and Victor, twice already they had risen from their chairs and walked restlessly around the basement.

Rome and Victor had told Justin, each privately, what agonies they were suffering. Already three times in the last week Alex and Chris phoned him after midnight and told him what torment they were enduring. Herb had told him he had been tempted twice to call up Alison and invite her over to his place. And outside St. Joseph's, as Justin was going down the basement steps with Jasper, he had said with pain showing in his face, "Justin, if I can't spend a night with Cora, I'm going to explode!"

Justin felt sorry for all these troubled men. But his pity for them did not sway him. He was determined to carry on, even as he thought of the restless nights he was experiencing. If only he could get Nadine out of his mind! Nadine . . . her soft, warm body . . . those perfectly shaped breasts . . . those long legs that rose up to—No, no!

Tonight he had to give the men a good strong pep talk. Yes, stiffen their resolve, give them the inspiration to fight that damned burning sex urge. And the talk would do him a lot of good too.

Justin began as he always began his talks with the words "I am a sex addict."

And that's when the girls walked in, aggressively led by Nadine. In fact there was a determined and aggressive look about the girls behind her.

"No, Justin, you are not a sex addict, you are a fool!" Nadine said.

All the girls were now standing in the space between the platform and the chairs. All the men got to their feet.

"Nadine, you and all these ladies have no right to be here," Justin said. "This is a private meeting, for men only! Get out!"

"No," Nadine said.

"I want you to leave this instant!" Justin said.

"Sure we'll leave, but with our men!" Bea said.

"And you can't stop us!" Lola said.

"Justin, this insanity has gone on long enough!" Alison said.

Justin stepped down from the platform and looked at the men. They were staring with hungry eyes at the women. He knew that he would have to take drastic action or all would be lost. But what could he do?

"Men," he said, "don't give in to your desires! Remember your self-respect! You'll be giving up your pride in your true manhood for a few moments of pleasure. They are not worth it!"

"Men, don't listen to Justin babbling his idiotic rubbish," Nadine said. "He's taken leave of his senses. Girls, grab your man and I'll grab mine and we'll put an end to this crazy Sexualis Anonymous tonight!"

There now ensued much tugging and shoving. The girls screamed, the men shouted and chairs were knocked over. Victor and Jasper ran all around the hall to avoid being grabbed by Bea and Cora. Alex and Herb picked up chairs and held them up as shields against the hard-charging Lola and Alison. Rome and Chris flailed away violently with their arms to beat off Erica and Melanie. And all the time, while trying to avoid being embraced by Nadine, Justin was exhorting the men not to surrender, to fight, fight, fight! At the same time Nadine was urging the ladies not to give up, that they would surely win this battle!

Father Malloy heard the racket and thought a riot had broken out in the church basement. He immediately dialed 911. And in a matter of minutes, four patrol cars and a paddy wagon were outside the church. Somehow or other the cops were able to get the combatants to pile into the wagon and drive them to the police station.

And even in the police station the struggle between the men and women went on. There was shrieking, yelling, accusations and counter-accusations. The desk sergeant could not make head or tail of what was going on. First he put his hands to his ears. Then he raised his arms up in despair and asked one of the police officers, "What the hell is going on here? Why did you bring these lunatics to me and not to a bughouse?"

"Well . . . Sergeant, they were disturbing the peace."

Dropping his arms the Sergeant said, "Release these maniacs, throw them out! They are disturbing my peace!"

Once again the ladies were gathered around a table in a back room in Gallaher's Bar. Glum faces stared at Nadine, who was looking glumly back at them.

"Your plan turned into a fiasco, Nadine," Erica said.

"A complete disaster," Lola added.

"We were lucky we didn't get time in jail," Bea said.

"But we'll succeed next time, won't we?" Lola asked hopefully.

"What next time?" Melanie said skeptically.

"But we can't give up!" Alison said, picking up her drink and taking a short sip.

"Nadine, it's your responsibility to do something!" Bea said

"Why is it my responsibility?"

"Because it's your man, Justin, who got our men all screwed up about sex," Erica said.

"Yes, with all his screwy ideas," Lola said.

"Well, what about it, Nadine?" Melanie said

"You have to take some positive action!" Cora said.

"All right, girls, all right. You have a point."

"So, what are you going to do?" Erica said.

"Attack the head, and the body dies," Nadine said thoughtfully.

"What do you mean?" Bea asked.

"Attack the head and the body dies, the body being Sexualis Anonymous. Yes, I'll get Justin when he's alone and seduce him out of all this anti-sex drive. And I'm going to do it tonight!"

"Hooray!" the girls shouted happily.

"Pour on the oomph!" Lola said.

"As only you know how!" Cora cried.

"Show Justin no mercy!" Alison said brutally.

It was almost midnight when Justin walked out of the bathroom after taking quick cold shower. He went into the living room drying himself with a large bath towel. He looked at his naked body in the big mirror on the wall and shook his head. He was getting a little thick around the middle.

Justin had arrived home late. He had had an exhibit for a very talented young artist. There had been a large crowd and he had sold a number of the artist's paintings. When people were starting to leave, an art critic said that he wanted to say a few words about the exciting developments in art that were going on in South America. But the few words turned into a long speech, and it wasn't until past eleven when Justin could close the gallery and head for his apartment.

When Justin was about to return to the bathroom, the doorbell rang. He angrily flung away the towel. He was sure who it was. Nadine, of course. It had to be Nadine. Would she ever stop pestering him? Why couldn't she get it through her skull that he was through with <u>that</u>?

Justin stood looking at the door and hearing the persistent ringing. Well, Nadine could ring all night! He was not going to open that door, no matter how long she kept it up.

The doorbell continued to ring.

Maybe he should open the door? What as he afraid of? Didn't he have confidence in himself? Nadine was only a female. And he was a man! A man who was going to live a brave, new, different kind of life! He, Justin, was a sex pioneer, yes, a sex trailblazer, opening up a new path for other men to follow him.

He rushed into the bedroom, quickly put on his bathrobe and returned to the living room. Then he walked slowly toward the door to the apartment. The doorbell was still ringing.

Justin opened the door.

God help me, he said, inwardly gasping and gulping in wonder and fear. Nadine had never looked more gorgeously beautiful and more irresistibly desirable. Justin was afraid he was going to break down and cry, so overwhelmed was he by her radiant beauty.

And it all was her own natural loveliness. She wore hardly any makeup except for a little rouge. God, those luscious, pink lips! And those long eyelashes! And the way Nadine was dressed accented her tantalizing figure. She had on a tight-fitting, low-cut blouse that almost made Justin's mouth water as he gazed at the deep cleavage. And her skimpy skirt went only a third of the way down those heavenly thighs, those thighs that had so often wrapped themselves—Stop, stop! he told himself. It was obvious what Nadine was trying to do. She was trying to break his will! Yes, seduce him from living a pure, sex-free life. Well, she was not going to succeed!

"Nadine, what are you doing here?"

"As if you didn't know," she said, smiling coyly and walking past him into the living room. Justin followed Nadine like a man mesmerized, his eyes riveted on her undulating buttocks. He blinked his eyes, shook his head and cursed himself.

When Nadine turned around to face Justin, she was still smiling that coy smile. A great fear came over him.

"Why are you doing this to me?" he asked weakly.

"Because I want to save you from this passing morbid fancy."

"It is not a passing morbid fancy! It's a stupendous idea! It means freedom, liberation from the thralldom of sex, and of the despotic hold women have had on men with that deathtrap—their bodies!"

"That is twaddle and rubbish. Justin, come to your senses. Be the man you once were. We could be so happy. Enough of this idle chatter. Come on, let's go into the bedroom. Or would you prefer here, on that couch?"

"Nadine, get out!"

For answer, Nadine unbuttoned her blouse and dropped it on the floor.

"That won't work!" Justin said, reaching for the cell phone on the coffee table. "I know what I have to do. I have prepared for just such an emergency. I'm going to call for help!"

But before Justin could hit the buttons, Nadine pulled the cell phone out of his hand and threw it behind the couch.

"Goddamn you!" Justin said, pushing her to the floor and running into the bedroom. He got through to Alex. "Alex, I'm in big trouble! Nadine is here, half naked and I need help desperately! Call three or four of the other guys! And for God's sake hurry, hurry! I don't know how much longer I can hold out! Condition Red, condition Red!"

Justin put down receiver with the intention of locking the bedroom door. But when he turned around, there was Nadine, standing in the doorway, a little groggy, rubbing her head, but smiling.

"Justin, give it up. Before they get here you'll be like putty in my hands."

Justin picked up the book on the night table and held it over his head. "Nadine, you stay away from me! I mean to defend myself!"

"Is my great big Justin afraid of his little, harmless Nadine?" she said, coming toward him.

"Stay away from me!" Justin said, dropping the book and leap-over on the other side of the bed.

"Darling, let's do what men and women love to do together more than anything else. Let's make love."

"You mean let's do sex!" Justin said, picking up a pillow, and when Nadine reached out for him, he hit her on the head and got past her.

He ran into the living room. When were those guys going to get here! He was relieved to see he had left the apartment door open when he let Nadine in.

And then he felt Nadine's hands on his neck. He twisted out of her grasp, pushed her away and ran into the kitchen. Round and round they went around the kitchen table. And then Justin saw his chance and made a break for the bathroom, Nadine managing to pull off his bathrobe.

When he got to the bathroom he tried to lock the door, but Nadine was too fast for him. She burst in, knocking Justin back and they both fell into the bathtub, Justin struggling frantically to break out of Nadine's embrace.

But even as he struggled to fight off Nadine, Justin felt his resistance to her waning. Her bare breasts were pressed up against his chest, she was trying to kiss him on the lips, and she was trying to wrap her legs around his hips.

"Nadine, please, stop!"

"No, no! You are mine, all mine!"

"Don't you have any feelings of shame?"

"When it comes to you, I am completely shameless!"

Justin knew that he was almost at the end of his power to resist Nadine. A warm sensation was beginning to stir in the lower part of his body. Where were his friends!

And then Justin heard voices in the living room.

"Chris, there's nobody here," he heard Romeo say.

"Let's check the other rooms," Chris said.

"I'm here, in the bathroom!" Justin shouted.

And immediately Chris, Romeo, Herb and Jasper rushed into the bathroom. For a few moments they were like men petrified when they saw the violent struggle going on in the tub. They stared and stared in speechless awe.

"Stop gaping like a bunch of clucks and do something, you guys," Justin yelled. "Get this creature off me!"

Justin's words snapped the men into action. It took all four of them to pull Nadine off Justin. They carried her into the living room. But it was not easy. Nadine fought them all the way, scratching and biting, damning them all to hell.

Romeo found Nadine's blouse and somehow got it on her. Then the men formed a circle around her. Justin came into the living room with a towel around his waist.

"Justin," Nadine pleaded, "if you'll get rid of these thugs and give me five minutes alone with you, I'm sure I can straighten you out."

"Nadine, I don't need your kind of straightening out. I am already straight as an arrow. But I must admit, Nadine, you almost had me. Guys, thanks for coming to my rescue. I'll do the same for you. Sexualis Anonymous lives on!"

Once again the girls had a meeting. This time it was held in Nadine's apartment. They sat around the kitchen table drinking coffee and looking very unhappy as Nadine gave a full report of her unsuccessful attempt to seduce Justin.

"I was sure you would make it with him," Bea said.

"We were all counting on you, Nadine," Lola said.

"That Justin must be made of stone to be able to resist you, Nadine," Alison said.

"That's not true, Alison," Nadine said. "I almost had him. Just one more minute and—"

"And what happened?" Melanie said.

"Four of his friends came in and spoiled everything."

"But how did they know to come to Justin's apartment?" Cora said. "How did they know you were with him?"

"They are using the same method used by AA," Nadine said.

"What method is that?" Erica said.

"Don't you know," Melanie said.

"No, I'm not an alcoholic.

Melanie explained how AA members help each other when they are tempted to drink. Individually they were weak, but collectively they were strong.

"It all looks so hopeless," Cora sighed.

"Nadine, what do you say?" Bea asked.

"Individually weak . . . collectively strong . . . ." Nadine murmured.

"What are you saying?" Alison said.

"Girls, we have been using the wrong tactics to get our men back," Nadine said."

"What wrong tactics?" Cora asked.

"When we went to their SA meeting the men were all together, right?" Nadine said, looking around the table.

"Uh . . . what's SA?" Erica said.

"Sexualis Anonymous, that goofy club Justin created to keep the men faithful to his scatterbrained no-sex-for-men idea."

"Oh, yes, I understand now," Erica said.

"Go on, Nadine," Lola said, "you were talking about tactics."

"Wrong tactics," Melanie said.

"Yes, we have to use the right tactics," Nadine said.

"How do we do that?" Melanie said.

"We have to attack our men individually and simultaneously! That way they will not be able to call for help. They each will be too busy defending themselves. And, girls, we'll go all out using all our weapons."

"What weapons?" Cora asked innocently.

Nadine got up from her chair. "Come on, Cora," Nadine said, moving her hands down her sides to her thighs. "With all this! With our bodies! Yes, girls, we'll use our bodies like battering rams to knock down that wall of anti-sexual rubbish Justin has built around himself and those deluded dopes that follow his daffy teaching?"

"Nadine, we can't miss!" Bea said.

"Flesh and blood will always beat stupid ideas!" Alison said.

"And how!" Melanie said. "Flesh and blood came first, long before men started thinking and dreaming up their wild crackpot ideas!"

"When do we do it?" Lola demanded impatiently.

"Slow down, slow down. We have to plan this thing carefully, like a military operation. Today is Wednesday. We'll do it this Friday night. At precisely eleven-thirty we commence our attack. At that very moment each of us will be ringing the doorbell to our guy's apartment. Timing is critical. We'll synchronize our watches before we go on our separate missions. Do you follow me so far?"

"Yes, yes!" all the girls said.

"Okay, now here's the most important part. When our man opens the door, what do you think he will see?"

"Alex will see me!" Lola said.

"And Victor will see me!" Bea said.

"And Romeo will—" Erica started to say but was interrupted by Nadine.

"Hold it, girls, hold it! When our men open that door they are not going to see a female dressed in ordinary street clothes. They are going to see each of us in a—bikini!"

"Nadine, you are a genius!" Melanie said.

"Their willpower will melt like butter in a hot oven!" Cora said.

"I'll have my Romeo back in my arms again!" Erica said.

"I can see Herb falling into my arms at the sight of me in my bikini!" Alison said.

"And, girls, we have to tell our men we'll settle for nothing less than marriage! They have had their fun long enough. It's time they became husbands and fathers."

"You are one hundred percent right, Nadine!" Bea said.

"Hey, we're forgetting something," Lola said. "It's November. we can't go walking in the streets in bikinis."

"No problem," Nadine said. "Wear a coat. But after you ring that doorbell, take it off and when that door opens, be ready to pounce!"

"Like a mountain lion!" Erica said.

"Oh, one more thing," Nadine said. "With those bikinis, wear high-heeled shoes!"

Friday night and Justin could not sleep. He rolled over and looked at the radium-dialed clock on the night table. It was almost thirty minutes after eleven. His body was on fire with desire. He got out of bed and was about to go to the window when the doorbell rang.

"Damn!" he said out loud, but deep in the recesses of his mind Justin was glad to hear that sound.

Before he opened the door he said, "Nadine, it's you, isn't you?"

No answer.

"Nadine, I'm not opening this door until I hear your voice!"

"Yes, Justin, it's me."

Justin gritted his teeth, braced himself and opened the door.

Nadine walked in without saying a word. Justin thought he was seeing a dream in motion. He averted his eyes from her as he followed Nadine into the living room.

When she turned around to face him, still silent, Justin was puzzled, and in spite of himself, he could not take his eyes off her.

Finally Justin coughed and said, "Well, aren't you going to say something?"

"I am making my statement this very moment."

"Nadine, it won't work. Yes, I can see you with my two yes. Yes, you are a ravishing beauty. And, yes, I am tempted, but at the very same time I am fighting against that temptation with all my moral might! I defeated you the last time you were here, and I will do it again in the same way!"

"Calling for your friends to come and help you will not do you any good this time."

"What do you mean?"

"You'll see."

Justin looked around for the cell phone but did not see it. He thought it might be in the bedroom. Just then the phone in the kitchen rang. He ran to answer it, followed slowly by Nadine.

When he picked up the receiver he heard Romeo's hysterical voice. "Justin, Justin, come over s fast as you can get here!"

"Is Erica there with you?"

"Why the hell do you think I'm calling you! She walked in a couple of minutes ago in a bikini and, oh, Christ, she's taking it off!"

"Romeo, throw her out! Be a man! Fight it!"

"No use, no use!" Romeo said helplessly. "Erica is tempting me beyond my strength! I'm a goner, a goner!"

"No, Romeo, no!" Justin said, but the line had gone dead.

He put down the receiver, and then when he saw Nadine coming up to him, he quickly dialed a number.

"Victor, Justin! Come quick, quick! Nadine is here again! I need help, right away!"

"No use," Victor's choking voice came over the phone. "I need help myself! Bea is here with me . . . God, what she's doing to me! I'm sunk, sunk!" And he hung up.

Justin put down the receiver, and immediately the phone rang.

This time it was Jasper. "Justin," he said in a panic-stricken voice, "get to my place right away with some of the guys! Cora is here and I don't think I can hold out much longer! Save me!"

"Hold out, Jasper! We'll be there in twenty minutes!"

". . . Justin, don't bother! I don't want to be saved!"

Before Jasper hung up the last words Justin heard were, "Cora, my darling! Come to me, baby, come to me!"

Justin dropped the receiver and turned to Nadine. He expected to see her gloating at him, to have an expression of arrogant triumph on her face. Instead he saw pity for him, and something else. What was it he was seeing? . . .

"Nadine, you engineered this whole thing, going after us all at once, didn't you?"

"Yes, I planned it all."

"Why, why?"

"Because I love you, Justin," she said, coming closer to him. "I did it out of love for you."

"Love for me . . . ? Out of love for me?"

"Yes, my darling. I love you, you and only you."

"Love . . ." Justin said like a man in a trance, staring at Nadine. He seemed to be seeing her for the first time. Her eyes . . . there was a deep mystery in them that would take a man a lifetime to explore, to try to understand.

As he continued to gaze silently into those sparkling, mysterious eyes his mind seemed to expand, opening up to receive an illumination from—where? What was this magical feeling that was filling his mind? Slowly the answer came to him. So this is love, he told himself in wonder and amazement, when you want one woman above all the other women in the world . . . until the day you die . . . .

Justin experienced a lightness in his mind and body, as if a heavy burden had been removed from him. He felt cleansed, purged of his promiscuous sexual addiction. He was a different man, with a new, changed nature. Love for Nadine had transformed him.

"Nadine, I love you," he said. "Will you be my wife?"

"Yes, yes!" she said, falling into Justin's arms.

The seven couples flew to the beautiful island of St. Lucia in the Caribbean. They were married in a chapel by the sea, and they enjoyed themselves so much on their honeymoon that they stayed an extra week.

And that was the end of Sexualis Anonymous.

The Imp Of Life

BY

DOMINICK RICCA

Ex-Father Norbert Kerry sat on the windowsill of the cheap apartment, boiling with raging fury and bitter resentment at the degrading and humiliating injustice done to him. That very day he had been unfrocked as a Catholic priest with solemn ceremony by his Eminence, Bishop Giles Wellmore, the bishop of the diocese.

As he left St. Paul's Church, which had been packed to the choir for hundreds of Catholics to witness his disgrace, an elderly priest handed Kerry an envelope with a kindly, sympathetic smile.

Outside he opened it and counted ten fifty-dollar bills. He stuffed the money indifferently in his pants pocket, ignoring the people staring at him as if he were some freak and walked hurriedly down the street. Did they know, those men and women, condemning him with their looks, what anguish he was suffering, yes, and actual physical pain?

And now, sitting in that apartment and gazing blankly down the street, he wondered about the old priest who gave him the money with that smile, an understanding smile, now that Kerry thought about it. Had he also with . . . women? But he had not been found out, caught and ceremoniously given the heave-ho by the Church, like him.

Thinking about the way he had been treated, and the reason for it, his seething anger returned. Kerry knew in his heart that he was not personally responsible, or even to blame, for his sexual behavior. All right, misbehavior in the eyes of the Church.

Kerry recalled Bishop Wellmore's words when he had that private meeting with his Eminence: "For your shocking and promiscuous lustful life, you are not fit to be a priest in the church founded by Our Lord and Savior Jesus Christ! You have dishonored yourself and the priesthood! Such licentious behavior cannot be tolerated! Kerry, you have been given many chances to amend your life."

"Eminence, may I say something?"

"Something in your defense? There is nothing you can say in your defense! A number of times we have sent you on spiritual retreats in monasteries, and with priests skilled in giving moral counseling to priests who have fallen into evil ways. The Church over the centuries has learned much about the weakness of the flesh, and how to deal with it. But all those times in the monasteries didn't help you. Nights you sneaked out of the monastery to find a female. So the retreats didn't do any good. Then, at great expense, I sent you to a psychiatrist to cure you of your wild, ungovernable passion for women. But what was the result? You seduced the psychiatrist! I don't know what—"

"Eminence, I didn't seduce her, I tell you. She—"

"Silence when your bishop is speaking! Kerry, I was about to say I don't know what to do with you. But I do! You have made abundantly clear to me that the celibate life of a Catholic priest is not for you. Time and time again you have despicably and shamefully used the confessional to seduce dozes of the wives and single women of your parish. In all my years as bishop of this diocese I have come across some pretty bad priests, but I must say you take the cake. I just don't understand how—"

Kerry wished he could put his hands to his ears, but he had to stand there, listening to this blistering tirade from Bishop Wellmore with rising anger, and gritting his teeth. He remained outwardly calm, but what he wanted to do was shout loudly and forcefully that he had not seduced all those women. And he most certainly had not used the confession box to inveigle them into having liaisons with him by artful persuasion.

For a long time Kerry had listened with sorrow and pity in his heart to these unhappy women as they sobbed out in the confessional their grievances against their sexually selfish, crude and cold husbands and boyfriends. Those men did not make love to a women. All they wanted was to achieve an orgasm as quickly as possible. They satisfied themselves, but they left the women in a maddened condition of sexual frustration and despair.

And so out of compassion, when Kerry invited these women to a small room at the rear of the rectory to talk out their problems, they agreed with alacrity, so desperately unhappy were they.

At first Kerry thought of talking to the men, but on second thought he did not think that was such a good idea. They might resent his interference. And they were sure to be very angry to know that a priest possessed intimate knowledge of the kind of sex lives they had.

At first Kerry offered those women sympathy and advice. But the holding of hands and the friendly, encouraging pats on the back and the women tearfully told their sad story led to passionate embraces, kisses and . . . before Kerry and the women knew what was happening, they went all the way. Sometimes he had them on a chair, or pressed up against the wall with their legs wrapped around his hips.

Kerry was such an affectionate, patient, considerate lover that the women started coming late at night to the rectory, sneaking into his room from the backyard. They were so careful and quiet that for months the other priests and even the housekeeper were not aware of what was going on. Some nights Kerry entertained the women individually, but occasionally, when three or four females came to him together, he had them in pairs.

But one night the housekeeper, unable to sleep because of her painful piles, happened to look out the window. She was aghast to see two women leaving Father's Kerry's bedroom, and two more climbing through the window.

Of course she informed the pastor. For three nights he and another priest counted eleven women going into Kerry's bedroom. The pastor sent a full report to Bishop Wellmore, who summoned Kerry to his office.

"Yes, I had sexual relations with all those women," Kerry frankly admitted.

"All those women? Father Kerry, how many in all?"

"I don't know for sure, your Eminence."

"A rough estimate!"

"Well . . . let me see . . . . You want only the married ones?"

"What does it matter? Married or single—how many?"

"I think there were more married than single ones."

"All together, how many?"

"Hard to say. Maybe between thirty or forty. Make it around thirty-five."

"And how long have you been carrying on this way?"

"Three or four months."

"How could you do it!"

"Eminence, I am in good health, and I'm a young thirty-eight years old."

"I am not talking about your health and age! How could you, a Catholic priest, descend into living the dissolute life of a libertine, behaving like a—like a Hollywood actor!"

"Eminence, it wasn't like that all. You see I was only—"

"I don't want to hear it! Kerry, you are through as a priest!"

"Bishop, what are you saying?"

"I am going to unfrock you, Kerry, that is what I am saying."

"For having sex with women?"

"Isn't that enough reason? Your scandalous behavior proves to me that you are an unworthy priest, a man who is not fit to wear the vestments, preach in a pulpit, and above all, say Mass!"

"Because I had sexual relations with those females?"

"Because you had immoral sexual relations with those women. When you became a priest you took the vow of celibacy. It sickens me to think of the numbers of times you violated that sacred vow."

"Bishop, you are not being fair."

"How so?"

"Since I have been in this diocese you have transferred five priests to other dioceses out of the state because you learned that they were fooling around with the altar boys."

"That's an entirely different matter, Kerry. I had to get rid of them to avoid an embarrassing scandal in my diocese. If the story got out about those wayward priests confidence in the Church would have been shaken. Public image is of incalculable importance."

"Did you inform those other bishops that you were dumping boy-loving priests on the, Eminence?"

"That is an impertinent question, and you have not right to ask that of me, a bishop!"

"So priests who like to sodomize young boys are tolerable in Mother Church, but not priests who enjoy having normal sexual relations with women, eh, your Eminence?"

"Now you are being insolent! This interview is over! Get out of my sight!"

"So here I am," Kerry said, talking to the walls of the room, "my priestly life is over and done with, after fourteen years of dedicated service to the Church, given the bum's rush."

It was all so unfair! He wanted to go on being a priest!

Kerry was as certain that he was not to blame for his passion for women as he was that God existed. Yes, he was innocent, just as surely as God existed.

The proof of God's existence was his creation, as Kerry saw it. Those over-intellectualized philosophers who asserted that the existence of God could not be proved were nincompoops and dumbheads, or just plain fools. They might as well say that the sun does not exist. Or the moon. Or the mountains, the seas, the land and all humans and animals—that the whole universe created itself. When ever did a building build itself?

Okay, Kerry told himself as he watched with straining eyes from the window a woman with a sinuous gait strut down the street. Christ, how those fat buttocks moved up and down!

Okay, God exists.

And so does the Imp, the Imp of Lust!

Yes, by heaven, the Imp exists! This tremendous belief came to Kerry when he was praying in the parish church two days before he was to be unfrocked. It came to him in a flash, like a blazing revelation, like a tiny explosion, illuminating his mind and making everything so clear. Whether this was a message from God, Kerry was not sure. But he was sure of the truth of this astounding idea that came to him.

When he rose from his knees he knew with a fierce certainty that he had had some kind of mystical experience. The existence of the Imp had been revealed to him, to Norbert Kerry!

All those months he had been tumbling those women in bed he realized he was sinning. But to ease his conscience he told himself, I am giving some comfort to those unhappy women. Still he suffered pangs of remorse.

But when he found out about the Imp of Lust, what an amazing relief he felt, as if a great burden had been lifted from his guilt-racked conscience.

Kerry thought of telling Bishop Wellmore about the Imp. But, no, he could not. The bishop would have laughed in his face, told him he was out of his mind.

From that day in the church Kerry was positively and firmly convinced that he could not restrain his sexual cravings. They had to be satisfied. Why? Because of this despotic Imp—demon, thing that was inside him, whipping up his carnal desires, and demanding imperiously to be obeyed. Kerry was sure that if he did not obey this relentless tyrant inside him, he would go crazy.

Yes, there was no doubt about it. He was powerless to resist this living force inside his body, stirring up his raging sex hunger. His uncontrollable lust was not his fault. He was entirely blameless. It was the Imp of Lust!

How good it was for Kerry to know that he was a victim, not a sinner. How refreshing that knowledge was to his Catholic conscience. Could you blame a man for having a hereditary disease, say like leukemia? Of course not!

He, Kerry, was compelled to obey the Imp, or go mad. That was indisputably true. People who dammed, tried to repress their sexual needs, did go crazy. He had heard of nuns and priests ending up in mental institutions, raving blasphemously in their lunacy, the nuns screaming obscenely that they wanted "My Lord and Savior Jesus Christ to screw me to death!" And the priests, panting heavily as they vigorously masturbated, shouting, "I want to shove this big cock up the Virgin Mary's cunt!"

But this Imp of Lust . . . just what was it? What did it look like? What shape did it have? Where in the human body was it? It had to be small, since it had never been seen by human eyes.

Could he get rid of it? Cut it out like some cancer? Remove it with some kind of treatment? Chemotherapy? Chemosurgery?

But, hold on, he told himself. Did he want to get rid of the Imp? He was not sure. That was something to think about.

Was it possible that the Imp was more than only a slave-drive-demon inside him? Or was it more like the libido, which not only gave humans their sex drive, but also stimulated ambition, creativity, the desire to perform well in any endeavor, the burning need to achieve a goal, make something of oneself, to succeed in life, to be somebody?

Kerry turned away from the window. His mind shifted to a different thought, took on an historical dimension. Since men had conceived of moral codes, which they believed were heaven-sent, they had been trying, with spotty success, to live up to them.

Husbands and wives, and unmarried men and women had vainly down through the centuries tried to live up to the sexual teachings of their religions. And falsely blaming themselves for falling short, thinking that they were struggling against some evil inside them.

That was wrong, so very, very wrong! It was not their evil nature. They had no evil nature. It was the Imp of Lust, inflaming their whole bodies with lascivious yearnings.

But, Kerry pondered deeply, What exactly was the Imp? Was it a wicked creature inside all of us? A demon as he had thought? Or was it simply and unmorally like a part of God's creation, like the sun, the stars, the rivers, the oceans?

But even if it was morally neutral, like Niagara Falls, it also had power, like that body of water, over humans. But not all humans. Some it mastered, totally controlling them. And some were able to master the Imp.

But the question was, Why was that so? Could the answer be that certain people who came under the total and complete domination of the Imp of Lust had, or were born with, an exceptionally powerful creature inside them? And that was why they failed to defeat it, becoming sexual addicts, like himself, Kerry?

"Yes, that might be the answer!" Kerry said out loud, getting up from the windowsill and walking excitedly around the room. "I have great sexual potency because I have inside me a very potent Imp! That would explain why some men and women have stronger sex desires than others. Mind doctors tell us that women with a ferocious sexual appetite are afflicted with nymphomania, and with men, something called satyriasis."

But that was all bunk! Those psychologists and psychiatrists were all wet! This seemingly abnormally powerful sex drive was not caused by a sick mental condition! No! It was the extra-powerful Imp of Lust working its will on its host—the man or woman!

"And that is what it is in my case!" Kerry declared to the walls of the room with a broad, happy smile. "No normal man could have had all those women I had in one night, and many times! My record was five in one night. And when those women left me, dazed, weak as kittens and blissfully satisfied, they thanked me with tears in their eyes, and gratefully kissing my hand. And, incredibly, I was fresh as a daisy and strong as I was when the night of love began. What was the answer to my outstanding sexual prowess? Flesh and blood could not do it alone. No, it had to be the Imp of Lust, driving me on, like a ruthless taskmaster!"

So, the mission ahead of him was plain enough, if he wanted once again to be a priest. He would have to find the Imp inside him, or locate it in the human body. Somehow he must get his hands on an Imp. Take it to Bishop Wellmore and show it to him, prove to him that he, Kerry, was not responsible for his sexual behavior.

By God, that would be the day, when he took the Imp to the bishop, held it under the nose of that stuffy, moralistic man and proudly declared, "See, see, here it is! The Imp of Lust! That is what prodded me to live that runaway, lecherous life! I was not to blame! I demand you take me back as a priest! I cannot live if I cannot be a priest and say Mass."

And if Bishop Wellmore refused to see him, he would go to Rome, demand to have an audience with the Pope, and with a number of cardinals from the Curia present as witnesses, show His Holiness the Imp of Lust! And the Pope, known for his goodness of heart and his sense of justice, would restore him into the good graces of the Church!

"And I will once again be a Catholic priest! I will once again be able to say my daily Mass in a church with hundreds of worshipers present. And I will once again preach the message of Christ from a pulpit!"

But, getting a tight grip on his enthusiasm and optimism, Kerry sat down in a chair and began to think calmly. All that he had been thinking of was easier said than done. He would first have to find the Imp. That could take a long time. it would be like, not quite, but like trying to find a vaccine to cure a disease, as Salk and Sabin did with polio.

He had to find the Imp! He would be going on a sort of voyage of discovery, like Christopher Columbus. Only he would not be venturing out into the mysterious sea. He would be seeking that Imp in the human body.

And there was only one way to do that. He had to study medicine, yes, become a doctor. It might take years, this search, but maybe he might be lucky and it would not take that long. But however long it took, he would succeed, he had to succeed!

So, the first thing next morning Kerry went to an employment agency. First, he had to get a job. He told the man at the agency that he had done counseling work in his previous line of employment. That was not a lie. He had done a lot of counseling as a priest.

That very day he was interviewed for a job as a social worker by a city welfare department, and was hired right away. Four months later, with the money he earned, he was able to enter a small medical college in town.

All the months Kerry was working for the welfare department and going to the medical college, he was not living a celibate life. But he had promised himself that when the Church welcomed him back as a priest, he would live up to the vow of celibacy

In the meantime he saw no reason or objection to continue having sexual relations with those women of the parish, married and single.

He had them come to his apartment, a parade of females . . . Agnes, Irene, Hilda, Olga, and so many others whose names he had difficulty remembering.

Even when Kerry was engaged in sexual activity he was thinking of the Imp. In the height of his sexual transports he tried with all his mental might to <u>feel</u> exactly where the Imp might be in his body, but with no success.

One Wednesday night, while resting on the short couch after a long bout of lovemaking, Kerry told Irene (his favorite) about his belief in the Imp, based on the experience he had had in the church. They were both naked.

Sitting up on the couch Irene said, "Father, that is the craziest thing I have ever heard!"

"Irene, I've told you many times not to call me 'Father.' You do it even when we're making love. Remember, I've been unfrocked. Let's go by the rules of the Church."

"Sorry, I keep forgetting. But that is a cockeyed notion. Where did you get it?"

"Don't you listen to me? It came only my head from somewhere outside me head."

"Well, get it out of your head. It—this experience you said you had—was only a dopey religious delusion. I repeat, get it out of your skill."

"I can't."

"Why not?"

"Because I believe with all my heart and soul that I know I am right."

"How do you know for sure?"

"Because I feel it in my bones that what I am telling you is the absolute truth! The Imp of Lust exists, just as surely as your beautifully shaped breasts exist! It's in all humans, male and female. If we can get hold of it we can train it to do our bidding, and not hold us humans in sexual bondage to do Its bidding. Yes, that's what we must do. The Imp is like some jungle beast that must be trained, like a tiger or a lion."

"Jesus, Father, I mean Norbert, I never thought of it that way. You're so earnest about it, so serious, you got me half believing in what you say."

"Irene, now you're showing some sense. I want to find the Imp, show it to the Church authorities and prove that my sexual behavior was not my fault. It was the Imp, lashing me into acting that way."

"But, Norbert, where in the body is this Imp?"

"I don't know. That is what I have to find out. In a few weeks I'll start to work on cadavers at the medical school."

"And you say I have the Imp, in my body?"

"Every human being."

"And this Imp is what gives me this mad craving for you?"

"Irene, not for me—for sex! Any man with a big, stiff penis would do."

"Norbert, don't talk like that about my feelings for you! You make it sound all so crude and dirty! You make me feel like a sex-crazy tramp—that I would go to bed with just any man. That's not true! I come here to you because our relationship is precious to me!"

"I hope you aren't talking about love."

"And why not?"

"And then what? Marriage? You want to tie me down with the matrimonial ball and chain?"

"I wasn't talking about marriage, Norbert."

"Good. Get the notion of any kind of permanent relationship out of your head. I'm on the trail of the Imp, and I'm not going to be diverted by a nagging wife and a bunch of squalling kids."

"I wouldn't nag you . . . if we got married."

"No ifs about it. I'm staying single. The Church doesn't allow priests to get married. That would be un-Christ-like. Now, let's get back to—the Imp!"

"Okay. Uh . . . you said I have this Imp in me?"

"Yes, somewhere in your body."

"Where in my body?"

"That's what I'll be trying to find out when I start dissecting dead bodies in a little while."

"At the medical college?"

"Where else? Here? Irene, you can ask the silliest questions."

"Do you have any idea how big this thing is?"

"No idea at all," Kerry said, thinking. "Maybe it's very small, like a tiny minnow."

"It could be even smaller," Irene said.

"How small are you talking?" Kerry asked, wrinkling his brow.

"I don't want to discourage you in your hunt for the Imp, but it could be small as a bacteria."

"Bacterium, singular, Irene."

"Right. So, supposing it's that small, how could you see it with the naked eye when you cut up those corpses?"

Kerry was so startled by the question that he got up from the couch and stared down at Irene with a puzzled expression.

"I never thought of that. Irene, you got a point there."

"If what I'm saying is true, all your cutting up of those bodies will be a big fat waste of time."

"You're right."

"Well, what's the sense of looking for something you can't see with your two eyes?"

"I know what I'll do! I'll use a microscope!"

"In front of all those students, and the medical instructor?" Irene said. "They'll all think you're a bit eccentric."

"They sure will."

"And you can't tell them you're looking for the Imp. Then they'll be sure to think you've gone loco."

"Yes, my belief in the existence of the Imp of Lust is on the radical side. There's almost something supernatural to it, I think."

"So how do you get around that problem?"

"Let me think," Kerry said, scratching his head, thinking hard and walking around the room. Irene watched him. Kerry went to the window and looked out. Suddenly he turned around and said, "I have it! We'll sneak a body out of the medical building!"

"We?"

"Yes, I'll need your help. I'll slip into the building, go up to the refrigeration room on the third floor where the cadavers are kept and get one of them."

"Where do I come in?"

"You wait outside by my car. I'll lower the body down to you with a rope."

"I don't want to touch it!"

"You won't have to. Just stand guard over it until I come out. I'll put it in the car."

"Are you getting both sexes?"

"What do you mean?"

"Are you going to get a male and a female body?"

"Hey, that's something I didn't think of. I'll get a man and a woman."

"Norbert, when are we going on this ghoulish, harebrained caper?"

"There's nothing harebrained about it. And it most definitely is not a caper! It's all in the cause of science, and to get me back to being a priest of the Roman Catholic Church!"

"Okay, I'm sorry if I offended you. So when do we do it?"

"I already know the layout, but I want to make sure of that third floor and how I'm going to sneak into the building late at night. Maybe I'll be able to leave a window open on the ground floor."

"When do we pull it off?"

"Tomorrow night."

"That means we have plenty of time to put the Imp of Lust to work," Irene said, smiling.

"Yes, we have lots of time to do a little imping."

It was twenty-five minutes after midnight. Irene sat in the car looking nervously around her. What was taking him so long! He had gone around to the back of the building almost a half hour ago. And then Irene remembered that Kerry had told her to keep an eye on the third-floor window. She could not get a clear view of it because Kerry had parked the car near an oak tree. Irene stepped out of the car, leaned against the fender an gazed up at the building. The window was closed.

Walking a few paces away from the car, Irene glanced down the long dark street. She was glad to see that the lamppost was more than a hundred feet away. Did the medical school have a night watchman? she wondered.

Irene's eyes went back to the window. After a minute she saw it opening. Kerry stuck his head out.

"Irene, I can't see you," he said in a low voice. "Are you there?"

"I'm here!" she shrieked up at him.

"For God's sake, don't shout!" he hissed down at her.

"Do you have them?" Irene called up softly.

"Yes, two of them, right here at my feet."

"Norbert, I was getting worried. What took you so long?"

"I had to open a dozen drawers before I found what I wanted with my flashlight."

'But all you wanted was a male and female. Didn't they have plenty of them?"

"Sure, but I wanted a young male and female."

"Oh, yes, I forgot you mentioned that."

"Most bodies were of old men and women, many of them derelicts," Kerry said.

"Let's hurry up and get out of here!"

"I'm tying up the first body with the rope I brought."

"Which one is this?" Irene asked.

"The female, and here it comes."

Irene stepped back and watched as Kerry slowly lowered the body. When it was lying at her feet she hunched down and saw that it was a very pretty young woman, about twenty-five years old. Irene straightened up and turned her face away. She did not move. She was frozen with fear and dread.

"Irene, are you untying the rope?" Kerry said, after waiting for a minute. "I want to send down the male cadaver."

There was no response from Irene. Kerry flicked on his flashlight for two seconds down on her. In those few moments he saw Irene standing perfectly still over the body.

"Irene, why are you standing there like a zombie! Untie the rope! I need it to send down the male!"

But Irene remained motionless, like someone in a state of hypnosis.

"Irene, do you hear me? Untie the rope!"

"I don't want to touch it."

"This is no time to be squeamish. It can't hurt you."

"I'm not touching it."

"You don't have to, with your hands. Just roll it over and pull the rope at the end of the knot. Then all you have to do is yank the rope from under the body. The quicker you do it, the quicker we'll be out of here."

Very cautiously Irene turned over the body with her foot. Then, kneeling down, she gingerly freed the rope from the dead woman. Jerking the rope twice she, "Okay, Norbert."

The operation was repeated again, and three minutes later Kerry cam down and placed both cadavers in the back seat of the car. He parked the car in the back alley of his apartment building, and without Irene's help carried the bodies over his shoulder one at a time up the back stairs and into his apartment.

He put the female cadaver in the refrigerator. It was a snug fit, but after removing a few things and bending her double, he was able to squeeze her in. The male body he placed in the bathtub. Then he went to the bedroom to get his surgical knives and the microscope.

"Norbert, I don't want to watch you when you're . . . you know," Irene said."

"Suit yourself," Kerry said, "Watch television. I'll be a long time working on the male."

He carried on the male."

He carried a side table into the bathroom and placed the knives and microscope on it. There was one more thing he needed—a garbage can for the body parts when he was done examining them. Going down the back stairs again, he picked up a large empty can and carried it into the bathroom.

After saying a short prayer, Kerry got to work.

He started dissecting the body slowly, piece by piece. Every time he cut off a piece of meat he carried it over to the table and placed it under the microscope. After a close, minute examination, and finding nothing, Kerry felt with the fingers of both hands, hoping and praying that he would find that Imp of Lust. When he was sure there was nothing, he tossed the piece of meat into the garbage can.

It was tedious, painstaking, bloody work. After four hours Kerry was down to the head. He had to use a heavy carving knife to crack open the skull. He spent a half hour on the brain before giving up. But he was not discouraged. He knew with absolute certainty that the Imp was somewhere in the body! Looking down at all the lumps of flesh in the garbage car, he decided he would examine them again tomorrow.

That night in bed with Irene he told her that he would go over the male body one more time, and then get to work on the female.

"Kerry. I hate to throw cold water on this . . . what do you call it?"

"Research. I'm only doing what scientists have done for centuries, I'm trying to find out something about the human body."

"Well, just suppose that this . . . Imp of yours doesn't exist?"

"Again you're casting doubts on the Imp's existence! And the Imp isn't my Imp! God created the Imp! I believe that just as I believe that Jesus Christ rose from the dead! And that not fifteen minutes ago you and I had sexual intercourse. Now, please, Irene, no more of your skepticism regarding the Imp."

"Well, okay, I sure as hell can't deny that we had sex a little while ago, but . . . ."

'Irene, it's been an exhausting night for me. Let's get some sleep."

After spending hours on the female cadaver the next day, Kerry hated to admit to Irene that he had found nothing.

"But I know that the Imp is in there—somewhere!"

"Whatever you say."

When they were having coffee and apple pie that night after supper, Irene looked at Kerry as he poked at his piece of pie. And he had eaten very little of the veal stew she had cooked. She wondered what she could do to cheer him up.

"Kerry, what will you do now?"

"I don't know."

"Will you give up?"

"Never!"

"Are you going to get rid of those body parts in the garbage can?"

"No."

"They're beginning to smell."

"I'm not throwing them away—yet."

"You aren't going to try to get more bodies, are you? You saw in the newspaper that the police were investigating the disappearance of those corpses from the medical school."

"Forget about the school. I phoned them and said I couldn't continue going there because of health reasons and was thinking of moving out West."

"So now what?"

"I don't know. But I do know this—the Imp exists! It exists somewhere in the human body, and I must find it!"

"Norbert, did you examine thoroughly every inch of those bodies?"

"I think I did, but sometimes I got a little impatient, and, well, moved on to another piece of meat, or another organ."

"Did you break open the bones?"

"I did, and ran my fingers through the marrow."

"Kerry, I was thinking . . . ."

"Come on, let's hear it."

"How carefully did you examine the sexual parts of the man and woman?"

"You mean the penis, testicles, and the individual parts of the vagina—the clitoris, labia majora and the labia minora?"

"I know what the clit is, but what are those last two things you mentioned?"

"They are the outer and inner folds of skin bordering the vulva—the female genitalia."

"Did you cut open those parts?"

"Most of the penis."

"But not all of it?"

"No."

"And the female's private parts?"

"I did the labia majora and the labia minora."

"But not the clit?"

"No."

"Well?"

Hitting his head with the palm of his hand Kerry said, "Say, Irene, maybe you got something there! How could I have been so negligent? Let's go into the bathroom! I'll dig the penis and clitoris out of the garbage can and cut them open!"

They went into the bathroom. After rummaging around with both hands in the can, Kerry found the penis, the scrotum and the clitoris. He placed them on the table and picked up the scalpel.

With Irene at his side Kerry proceeded to cut open the scrotum, and then the testicles. Nothing. He had sliced the penis open the full length, but had stopped at the head. Now, with a deep sigh he very slowly cut the head in half, and there it was, the Imp of Lust—at last! It was embedded in one of the halves of the head of the penis.

What a unique thrill it was for Kerry and Irene! The first humans ever to see the Imp! For several moments both of them were speechless with amazement at this fish-like thing.

Finally, overcome with emotion and dropping to his knees Kerry cried out, "I thank Thee heavenly Father, for revealing the Imp of Lust to me!"

"Kerry, make sure. Put it under the microscope."

"Yes, you're right," Kerry said, getting up and cutting out the Imp and placing it reverently on a glass and under the microscope.

What he saw seemed to send an electric shock through him. The Imp was small as a marrow, and strangely, with a face that resembled the wrinkled face of an infant just out of its mother's womb. Kerry stared at the dead thing in wonder.

"Let me look," Irene said.

"Go ahead," Kerry said.

"Peering down at the Imp," Irene said, "What a queer-looking thing it is."

"The Imp!" Kerry said. "I have discovered the Imp of Lust! Once again I will be a priest. I now have the proof to show the Church that I was not responsible for my sexually promiscuous behavior. It was the Imp of Lust that drove me into the arms of all those women!"

"But, Norbert, how can you be sure this is the Imp of Lust?"

"It has to be!"

"Couldn't it be an abnormal growth in the penis?"

"Well, yes, but I don't think so."

"Are you going to cut open the clitoris?" Irene asked.

"Oh, yes. Here goes."

Kerry slit open the clitoris, which was exceptionally long and thick. And there is was, the female Imp of Lust.

"This Imp is even bigger than the male Imp," Irene said with a puzzled frown. "I wonder why."

"I have a theory, but a theory based on experience, my experience with all the women I have had. The longer and thicker the clitoris, the bigger the Imp, and the greater the woman's sexual desire."

'Norbert, do I have, you know, my clit?"

"Yes, you sure do. Yours is the grandest of all the dozens I have ever seen. That would certainly account for your voracious sexual appetite, and mine too. I must certainly have a great big Imp in my penis."

"Norbert, why don't you try to get a live Imp?"

Irene's suggestion startled Kerry. He stared down at the two dead Imps, thinking, thinking . . . a live Imp. An actual living Imp! That would be something. Indeed it would. But what would he do with It?

Irene was ready with an answer.

"Norbert, if you could get your hands on a living Imp, maybe you could train it."

"Train it to do what?"

"I should have said domesticate it, teach it to control itself, restrain the mad lust that sometimes takes over the lives of men and women. Wouldn't that be a great boon to the world, to humanity?"

"It certainly would, if we could tame that living sexual powerhouse, that has the potential to cause so much trouble between men and women. Yes, taming the Imp would be a wonderful improvement in human relations. With the Imp under control, human beings could concentrate on higher matters than always fantasizing about sex all the time, like spiritual things, or in developing strong cultural interests in literature, art, the opera, the ballet and so on. With a leash on that beast-like Imp there is no telling how high the human can reach. To the very heavens!"

"Norbert, you could make millions, millions with this discovery of the Imp!"

"Irene, I am not in this for the money! How many times do I have to tell you? My goal is to prove to the Church that it is the Imp in me that drives me to act in a sexually sinful way, that I am not personally to blame. Irene, I just thought of something."

"What's that?'

"Perhaps the Church, the Pope, will not want to hear or acknowledge my discovery of the Imp."

"And why not?"

"Don't you see it? If the Imp is responsible for our sexual behavior, or misbehavior, and it is, the Church cannot blame anyone for acting the way they do. Personal responsibility goes out the window. That could put the Catholic Church out of business, and I don't want the Church, which was founded by Jesus Christ, the Son of God, to disappear."

"So now what? Do we keep this marvelous discovery to ourselves?"

"Irene, we're getting ahead of ourselves. Let's first get our hands on a live male and female Imp."

"And how do we do that? Any ideas?"

"I have to give this some thought. Let me think . . . ."

"I have already thought of a way we could get our hands on live imps."

"Irene, I hope you're not thinking of killing a man and a woman and taking out those little creatures before they die?"

"No, nothing that drastic."

"So, what do you have in mind?"

"This town is full of derelicts. We could invite a man and woman up to this apartment for a meal, put knock-out drops in their drinks, and we have them, prisoners, but alive."

"And remove their imps while they're out cold?"

"Sure. Go to work with your scalpel and do the job neat and clean. And the two wouldn't know a thing."

"No. I'd want to keep them, observe them, see how they act without the Imp, the sex motor, in them."

"For how long would you keep them?"

"A few days."

"But you couldn't keep them knocked out all that time—not in this small apartment."

"I know what I'll do. I'll rent a house, somewhere out of town, in the country. It'll put a strain on my finances, but I think I can swing it. First thing tomorrow morning I'll go to a real estate office."

The real estate agent told Kerry that he did have something for him, but the house in the country would not be ready for occupancy for a few days.

In the meantime Kerry wanted to satisfy himself about something. He was curious to know whether or not the dead Imps he had still retained any aphrodisiac power. Kerry remembered an elderly druggist who had a small drugstore in his old neighborhood. His name was Jenks. Jenks was an old-fashioned druggist who still compounded some of his own medications.

Before Kerry went to the drugstore he pounded the dead dried-up imps and put the powdery stuff in a glass jar.

Jenks did not recognize Kerry when he walked into the store. it had been over twenty years since he moved out of the neighborhood. Jenks was no in his seventies, white-haired, with a face deeply lined, and slightly bent over.

"Yes, what can I do for you, young man?" Jenks asked.

"First of all I want to know if you still do your own compounding."

"Yes, a few times. How did you know about that?"

"I used to live in this neighborhood, about a block from here."

"What's your name?"

"Norbert Kerry."

"Oh, yes, I remember your father. How is he?"

"Dead."

"And your mother?"

"Also dead."

"So your name is . . . ."

"Norbert."

"Well, Norbert, I see you have a jar there with some kind of powder in it."

"Yes, I want you to analyze it. A friend of mine just returned from Bolivia. He said the natives down there use this powder as an aphrodisiac. I would like to know how effective it is."

"What luck! I've had a half-dozen men come in and tell me what the Viagra pill does nothing for them, absolutely nothing. I have a small oven in the back. I'll take this into pills and see how they work on those men."

"When will you know?"

"Come back in about a week."

"Any charge?"

"No charge. I'll do this for old times' sake."

Three days later Kerry and Irene moved into an old furnished, tumbledown farmhouse. It was fifteen miles from town, and just what Kerry wanted. Because of its rundown condition, Kerry got a cheap monthly rate from the real estate agent.

He was particularly glad to see that there was a small cabin behind the house. He would have an important use for it. Here is where he would house the derelicts. Of course he was eager to get his hands on live imps and see what he could do with them. But there was also something else he had in mind, something he wanted to find out. How would humans act when the Imp was taken out of them? Would the loss of the Imp have a severe impact on their emotions as human beings?

Kerry fitted out the cabin with beds, tables and a few chairs. Now he was ready to begin his experiment on the derelicts. But first he wanted to find out from Jenks how those pills worked on the impotent men.

Soon as he opened the door to the drugstore, Jenks came quickly over to him from behind the counter. He was very excited, his eyes sparkling.

"Mr. Kerry, all those men reported spectacular results from the pills I gave them!"

"They were good?"

"Good! Those men rave on and on about them! They all told me they had erections that lasted for hours, hours! That stuff is pure magic! It's what every man has dreamed of, an hours-long erection! And those happy men told me how crazy-wild their women went! It's what every woman has always wanted—a nonstop penis, or one that could stay ramrod-stiff for hours! Those pills will bring down heaven on earth, heaven on earth, I tell you!"

'Well . . . that's fine. That's all I wanted to know. Thanks. Goodby."

"Goodby! You can't just leave me!"

"Why not?"

"You have to get me more of that stuff! Find out the name of the plant it comes from! I want to patent the stuff! We'll go in business together. I'm sure I can financing! We'll both make a fortune! Fifty years I've worked behind that counter for peanuts, peanuts! Now, at last, I'm going to be a rich man!"

Kerry saw that Jenks was half out of his mind. It would be no use to tell him that he couldn't bring any more of that powder. He was afraid he would have a mouth-foaming lunatic on his hands.

"Well . . . Mr. Jenks, I do have the name of the plant."

"Thank God, thank God!"

"But . . . I can't remember it off hand. I have it written down at home. I'll go get it and bring it to you right away."

"Hurry up! We mustn't waste any time! I've always wanted to know how it felt to live like a millionaire!"

That night Kerry and Irene drove to town and went down to skid row. They went up and down the dark streets for ten minutes. Every once in a while Kerry stopped the car, got out and looked at a sleeping vagrant in a doorway, and returning to the car, shaking his head.

"Just what are you looking for?" Irene asked, the third time he returned to the car.

"I want a young man and a young woman. So far, all I've seen are old men."

And just as he spoke, a man and woman came staggering up the block. They were not too shabby, and both appeared to be in their thirties.

Stopping the car Kerry leaned out the window and said, "Hey, you two, how about joining our party?"

"Party?" the man said. "Sure, I always like a party!"

"Me too!" the woman said. "I never pass up an invitation to a party!"

An hour later, the man and woman were unconscious from the drugged rye whiskey Kerry gave them. After anesthetizing their private parts, he removed the Imps from the penis and the clitoris. Then he quickly sewed up those organs and carried the man and woman into the cabin, making sure the door was double locked.

When he got back inside the farmhouse he saw Irene staring down at the Imps, who were moving slowly around in a metal basin filled with alcohol. To Kerry they seemed healthy enough.

"Well, what do you think?" he asked.

"I don't know what to think," Irene said, frowning. "I tried talking to them, but they just went right on swimming, indifferent to the sound of my voice. How are supposed to train them?"

"Irene, we have to be patient, like when you train a dog."

But after four days of trying Kerry could not get the slightest response from the Imps. There seemed to be no way to communicate with them. Even tapping on the basin had no effect on them. It was all very frustrating and discouraging.

And after the fifth day Kerry had to admit failure.

'It's no use, Irene. It's impossible to train the Imps. They are untrainable. They are like a force of nature. You might just as well try to control a tornado, or a hurricane. And that's the way it is with these Imps."

"I have more bad news for you," Irene said.

"What about them?"

They don't look right."

"What's wrong with them? "You've been feeding them, haven't you?"

"Yes, I've been passing in trays of food through that slot you made in the door. But they aren't eating, not much, anyway. They both look pale and weak, sort of feeble."

You've been watching them through the peephole?"

"Sometimes for a whole hour."

"Well, what do they do?"

"Nothing, nothing at all. They just sit moping all day on a chair, just moping with a stupid, blank expression on their dead faces."

"What about, you know . . . sex?"

"No. No sexual activity at all. Most of the time they sit with their backs to each other. The man shows no interest in the woman, and likewise with her. It's eerie watching them, spooky. All they do is stare into space and occasionally letting out heavy sighs. Weird."

"No kissing, fondling?"

"Nothing, nothing. They might just as well be two logs on chairs. I'm not even sure they are aware of each other, though I might be wrong. A couple of times I saw them gazing at each other with an intent look in their eyes, as if they were trying to recall something."

"What do you think the problem, Irene?"

"Isn't it obvious? They are like a machine without a motor, a car without a battery."

"What do you want me to do?"

"Kerry, you know what you must do! What you have to do! Give those two back their humanity! Give them back their Imp! If you don't, they will wither away and die!"

"I suppose you're right."

"Kerry, I know I'm right. It would be criminal of you if you don't give them back the life-force, the Imp! If you don't, they will go on living, but it will be death in life! Without the Imp, they have no feelings, no desire—nothing!"

For a couple of days Kerry thought over Irene's words. If what she said was true, he owed it to the couple in the cabin to restore to each of them the Imp.

But first he had to see for himself. The next time he fed them he put a heavy dose of sleeping pills in their water. An hour later, Kerry looked through the peephole. Both of them were sprawled out asleep on the bed, with their clothes on. He entered the cabin and undressed them.

After a few hours the man and woman woke up. Observing them outside the door through the peephole, Kerry saw them get slowly off the bed. They glanced at each other for several moments and then went to sit on a chair and stared down at the floor.

Kerry could not believe what he was seeing. But it was true, true! They were both coldly indifferent to each other's nakedness. No, it was not that, Kerry realized. They were oblivious of the fact that they had no clothes on.

Kerry thought he would try something.

"Hey, you two in there!" he called into the room. "You are both in nude! Can't you see? Both of you, naked, naked!"

The man and woman looked at each other for a moment and then turned their eyes away, once again staring down at the floor.

"Hey, mister, what's your name?" Kerry asked.

After thinking for a little while the man said meekly? "Uh . . . Elmer."

"And you, miss, what's your name?"

"My name is . . . Ivy," she answered listlessly. "Elmer, take a good look at Ivy." Elmer eyed Ivy impassively. "Well, what do you see, Elmer?"

"I . . . see a . . . person."

"A woman, Elmer, a woman! And she's naked, nude—got not a stitch of clothing on her! Take a good, look at that woman!"

After gazing at Ivy for a few seconds Elmer said casually, "Yes, I see that she is a naked woman. So what?"

Kerry banged on the door twice in anger and said, "Elmer, you're a man and Ivy is a female! Don't you see her pretty breasts and the hair between her legs?"

"Yes . . . yes. So?"

"So why don't you act like a man?"

"Oh, yes," Elmer said, scratching his head. "Yes . . . I seem to remember something . . . vaguely . . . ."

"Elmer, think, think! Try to remember! What did you do when you were in a situation like this with a female person?"

"Hell, I always got on top of her and . . . enjoyed myself. But for some reason I just don't have any . . . yen for that sort of thing, no desire at all."

"What do you have any desire for? What would you like to do?"

"Oh . . . sit here and . . . just sit here. What else is there to do?"

"Elmer, would you like to get out of this cabin?"

"What for?"

"To get back your freedom, man, your freedom! To get back to living the life of a free man—do what you want to do, go where you want to go."

'But I don't want to go anywhere, do anything. I'm satisfied to stay right here where I am. I have enough to eat, a comfortable bed and time to sit around and . . . ."

"Ivy, what about you?"

"I feel the same as him. I like it here. It's so nice to do nothing all day and, and think."

"Ivy, what do you think about?"

"What do I think about?"

"Yes, what thoughts do you have?"

"Oh, you know, thoughts about . . . things . . . ."

"Elmer, would you like to have a TV?"

"A TV?"

"Yes, a TV set."

"Where?"

"In the cabin—so you can watch TV!"

"Why should I want to do that?"

"To watch interesting shows, to be entertained."

"I don't have any desire to be entertained. I like things just the way they are in here. It's so nice and quiet and peaceful and . . . ."

"Ivy, I could get you big TV with a wide screen. You could watch all those wonderful shows. What do you say?"

"Don't bother. I like things just the way they are. And besides, I'm too busy . . . thinking."

"Listen to me, you two. I have you locked up in this cabin. You are my prisoners. Would you like me to set you free?"

"Free to do what?" Elmer asked.

"I'm very happy here," Ivy said.

Kerry walked away from the cabin shaking his head. He felt guilty, remorseful. He had destroyed Elmer and Ivy as human beings. They had no desire for anything beyond eating, sleeping and sitting around "thinking."

"I can't leave them in that nonhuman condition," he said to himself. I have to give them back the Imp. If I don't, what would become of them? I can't keep them here indefinitely, and it would be cruel to turn them loose the way they are now."

Again Kerry put Elmer and Ivy into a deep sleep with sleeping pills. With Irene helping him, he performed the operation of putting back the Imp in Elmer's penis and Ivy's clitoris.

Before leaving the cabin Kerry left them lying naked side by side on the bed, with the light on. A few hours later, Kerry and Irene returned to the cabin and took turns watching the couple on the bed through the peephole.

At four o'clock in the morning Irene said, "Kerry, take a look, take a look! Boy, are they going at it!"

Kerry put his eyes to the hole. He was pleased and very happy to see Elmer and Ivy engaged in a very vigorous act of sexual intercourse, with a lot of body movement and vocal expressions of pleasure.

"Wow, what action! Her legs are up on his shoulders!"

"Let me see, let me see!" Irene said.

Kerry stepped aside and she put her eye to the hole.

After a few moments she said, "God, now she's on top of him and bouncing up and down like crazy!"

"Come on, let's leave them to it," Kerry said.

"But I want to watch them!" Irene said.

"And I say let's go back to the farmhouse. We aren't perverts—voyeurs."

"Okay and straight into the bedroom. I'm in the mood for love!"

"Irene, you are going to be looking up at the ceiling all night!"

"No, only half the night! We never tried it with me on top!"

About sunrise Kerry and Irene were awakened out of a sound sleep by loud banging and shouting from the cabin. They both dressed and went out to see what the racket was all about. As they approached it they heard the angry voices of Elmer and Ivy. They were demanding to be released.

"Let us out!" Elmer yelled in a furiously angry voice, kicking on the door.

"What's the big idea, keeping us locked up in here like prisoner!" Ivy shrieked.

Kerry said through the locked door, "Please calm down, both of you. This has been all a terrible mistake. I'm . . . well, a sort of scientist, and I wanted to perform a little, simple experiment on both of you."

"What kind of experiment?" Elmer asked.

Kerry did not know how to answer the question, and Irene said, "It was supposed to be a—a mind experiment."

"What the hell is that?" Ivy said.

"That doesn't matter," Kerry said. "I changed my mind. I'm sorry I locked you up."

"How long have we been in this shanty?"

"Only overnight," Kerry lied.

"Well, how about opening the door?" Elmer said.

"Uh . . . you aren't sore, are you?" Kerry said.

"Sore as hell!" Elmer said.

"Damn sore!" Ivy said.

"Would two hundred dollars apiece take away that soreness?"

"Make it two hundred and fifty and we'll forget the whole thing." Elmer said. "Now hurry up and open this goddamn door!"

Kerry drove them back to town. Irene went into the farmhouse and got started on breakfast. When Kerry returned Irene saw that he was troubled about something. He ate his ham and eggs in sullen silence and went into the living room, followed by Irene.

He dropped into an armchair and stared straight in front of him. Irene took a chair against the wall and watched him. She could see he did not want to talk, did not want to be disturbed as he thought and thought.

After fifteen minutes of silence Irene asked, "Norbert, did you enjoy the breakfast I made?"

"Breakfast? What breakfast?" Kerry said, leaning back in the chair, a happy, strangely exalted expression on his face.

Wondering what was the matter with Kerry, Irene sat in a chair across from him and watched him. Kerry was absorbed deep in thought, smiling and shifting restlessly in the chair.

Suddenly he jumped up and said, "Irene, do you realize what I have done?"

"What have you done?"

"I have made the greatest discovery since 1492!"

"You mean the Columbus thing?"

"Yes! And in my opinion, my discovery tops his! He only discovered land! I have found out what makes humans tick! What makes human beings human beings. What gives them the will to live, to love, to fight, to work! What makes them interested and curious about the world around them! What makes them angry, hate! What blows up their egos—the whole spectrum of human emotions!"

"You found all that out?"

"Yes, by observing how Elmer and Ivy acted without the Imp, and how they behaved once they got back the Imp. Irene, I have made the most stupendous discovery in the history of the human race! But I was wrong about one very important fact. The Imp isn't one-dimensional! It isn't the Imp of Lust! It's the Imp of Life! Irene, has enormous implications and possibilities for human beings! I'm going for a walk to think this out."

"Do you want company?"

"No, stay in the house."

"I won't say a word, just walk quietly beside you."

"Irene, I have to be alone!'

Kerry walked in the woods for hours. As he walked, he began to get a proper perspective on the findings of his experiment with Elmer and Ivy. Yes, he told himself, he had made the greatest discovery in the history of scientific research. It could go a long way toward improving the character of men and women.

But he had lost sight of something that was personally important: His return to the priesthood. He must once again celebrate Mass in church! He must once again give to the people the Body and Blood of Jesus Christ!

The Church must be informed of his amazing discovery! He now had positive proof that his sexual misbehavior was not his fault. He was only acting under the powerful control of the Imp of Life!

When he returned to the farmhouse and entered the living room, he saw Irene with a book in her hand. She looked expectantly up at him.

"Go on reading," he said.

"Well, what did all that cogitating do for you?"

"It told me what I have to do. I'll be in the kitchen, and please don't disturb me. I have some writing to do."

Kerry got a tack of sheets of paper and sat at the kitchen table with a battered old typewriter he had found in a closet days ago. After a minute of prayerful meditation, he began to type.

And after three hours of writing and rewriting, he was done—a full and comprehensive report of his great discovery. In it he showed in broad outline, first of all the existence of the Imp of Life and how it controlled all of human behavior.

He mailed the report to Bishop Welmore's diocesan office and waited. He did not have long to wait. Three days later a long black limousine drove up the dirt road and parked in front of the farmhouse.

Kerry came down the porch steps as the chauffeur opened the door on the passenger side of the car and the bishop stepped out. He looked at Kerry with a kind of wondering curiosity but said nothing. Kerry showed him into the house.

When they were seated in the living room, Kerry asked Bishop Wellmore if he would like something to drink? A cup of coffee? Tea? The bishop shook his head. Irene came into the room.

"Nothing," Kerry said, dismissing her. She left.

"Who is she?" the bishop asked.

"She . . . lives here."

"With you?"

"Yes, Eminence."

Sighing deeply the bishop took out of the breast pocket of his coat Kerry's report.

"Kerry, is this true?"

"Absolutely, Eminence. You can believe me when I say that it is based on the soundest scientific research. I can demonstrate the truth of my discovery before your very eyes."

"But this is horrible, most horrible!"

"Why do you say that?"

Ignoring the question Bishop Wellmore, greatly agitated, said, "I have E-mailed this report of yours to the Holy Father!"

"You did?'

"Of course he had to know about this fantastic discovery of yours."

"What was his response?"

"I don't know what he thinks, but I can well imagine. All I know is that he wants to speak with you right away. He ordered me to charter a private plane. You are going to Rome!"

"Me?"

"Yes, you!"

"When?"

"As soon as you can pack a bag. The plane is already waiting for you at the airport."

"Are you coming with me?"

"No, you are going along to see His Holiness."

Ten hours later Kerry was walking down several long corridors in the Vatican. In front of him, behind him and on each side of him, escorting him, but Kerry felt, really hemming him in, were six tall, burly Dominican monks. Their faces hidden in their cowls, they did not say a word to him. Leading the way were two Swiss Guards armed with halberds.

Presently they entered a long, narrow room. At the far end of it Kerry saw a man sitting slumped over on a chair with a high back. As he got closer he saw that the man was dressed in a costume that was completely white.

Twenty feet from the man in the chair, the Swiss Guards stepped aside and moved away. The monks also stopped. One of them gestured for Kerry to move forward.

Ten feet from the sitting man Kerry stopped, awe-struck. He was standing before the Pope, God's Vicegerent. A sudden chill ran through his body. The lighting was much better than it had been in all the halls he had passed through with his escort. For some reason he turned around to look at the monks. He still could not see much of their faces, but he did see that their robes bulged at the hips.

So, they areal armed, Kerry thought, recovering his natural self. Now he felt that instead of seeing before him the head of the Church founded by the Son of God, he was looking at a Mafia boss. But that unnatural feeling passed when he turned his attention back to the Pope.

"You may approach," the Pope said in a feeble voice in English, but with a slight accent.

Kerry stepped forward five paces, the Dominicans moving with him but remaining behind him.

"Closer," the Pope said, extending his hand.

Kerry obeyed and dropping to his knees he kissed the Pope's hand, thrilled and overcome with reverent emotions, in spite of the Dominican gun-toters.

Rising, Kerry said, "your Holiness is most kind and gracious to receive me . . . to grant me a private audience."

"Bishop Wellmore informed me that you are an unfrocked priest," the Pope remarked.

"Yes, Holy Father."

"You like the ladies too much, is that it?"

"I admit that, yes."

Leaning back the Pope said sorrowfully, "An old problem with our priests down through the centuries." And then brightening, he added, "Well, it could be worse. At least you never had anything to do with boys?"

"Never Holiness, never!"

"That is another persistent problem the Church has been plagued with. That penchant for boys . . . I wonder where our priests acquire it . . . . It is a particularly nasty sin."

"Holy Father, if I may say so, I think it is more than a sin! It's a rotten perversion! I swear to you my preference has always been for the ladies!"

"Always? Did you have sexual relations before you became a priest? Answer me honestly. It would be . . . understandable . . . before you felt the holy vocation to become a priest."

"Holy Father, I was a virgin when I took my priestly vows."

"A pure virgin male when you took your vows! Splendid, splendid! But not even with, you know . . . your hand?"

"Not even that, Holiness. My life changed when my religious zeal waned and my interest in the ladies began to soar."

"How did that change come about?"

"The life was so lonely and I reached out for . . . human warmth . . . ."

"You mean sexual pleasure."

"Holy Father, those females practically thrust themselves on me. The married ones were dissatisfied with the performance of their husbands in bed, and I got the same complaint from the girls with boyfriends. And it would have broken your heart to hear the single women tell how frustrated and unhappy there were having to repress their sexual desires.

"Where did they tell you these things?"

"During confession, Holiness."

"That was very naughty of you to use the confession box for that purpose, my son."

"At first I tried to do my duty like a good shepherd of souls. But when I was alone with them, outside the confession box, well, from sympathy and spiritual consolation . . . I began to give them what they really hungered for. At first I told myself that I was offering them Christian charity. But later I began to realize what a hypocrite I really was. However, I could not stop. Holiness, those young, attractive women . . . the things they loved to do! I never heard of such sexual practices, even in the seminary. You could call it a powerful and revealing education."

"And so your downfall as a priest was complete. And when you were found out, you were given many chances to reform yourself, all to no avail. And so you were unfrocked, and properly so."

"All that is true, Holy Father. Yes, I admit that with shame and regret. But, as you saw in my report, based on the purest science. I was not to blame! No, it was and is the Imp of Life in me!"

"And in all humans?"

"Yes, of course, Holy Father."

"And what becomes of personal responsibility for our moral behavior, my son?"

"Well, I haven't thought that far ahead. I don't know how to answer you."

"Then I shall answer for you. If human beings can point the finger of blame at this Imp of yours—"

"It is not my Imp! God created it, and placed it in all of us, just as he did the soul! The Imp exists just as surely as your nose, ears, lungs and stomach exist. Holy father, I do not relish contradicting you, but I insist that the reality of the Imp of Life is an indisputable scientific fact. Even if you proclaim ex cathedra the non-existence of the Imp. All the awesome spiritual authority and moral insight Almighty God has bestowed on you as Keeper of the Keys cannot deny the truths of science."

"The Dominicans behind Kerry made a move toward him for speaking so audaciously and defiantly to the Pope, but he stopped them with a wave of his hand.

"Oh for the days when the Pope had the Inquisition to back him up!" the Pope cried in frustration. "But today we have to act like gentle Christians. An Innocent III would know how to deal with you. I wish could shut you up as Urban VIII shut up Galileo. What does it matter to the men and women on this earth whether they live in a geocentric or a heliocentric universe? Does the difference change their lives in any significant way? Not a bit! But I can't do to you what another Pope did to Galileo. My hands are tied. However, it really does not matter, since what you say in your report has no scientific basis. The Imp of Life! What lunacy, what fantasy!"

"Holy Father, I swear to you the Imp exists!

"I have spoken!"

"Please, I implore you, allow me to perform before your very eyes the same experiment I did in America."

"You mean lock up a man and woman, two robustly sexually active people and—"

"Yes, yes, Holy Father! I will take out of them the Imp, and you will see how the very life goes out of them."

"And then when you give them back this so-called Imp of Life, you want me, the Holy Father, the head of Christ's Church, to witness a man and a woman fornicating?"

"It's the only way to convince you that—"

"Never, never! Pornography in print and on film is bad enough, but you dare to suggest I view pornography in the flesh!"

"But if you want to find out the truth you have to be, well, open-minded. All I'm asking is that—"

"Enough! I am ordering you to destroy this report of yours. You must not publish it. Even though I'm sure everything in it is preposterous rubbish, there is danger in it to the Church. Infinite harm can come from it if Catholics read it and come to believe in your crackpot theory of this Imp of Life. Why it could mean the end of the Catholic Church. You would be putting me and all that army of cardinals, bishops, priests out of business. What would become of us? What would we do for a living?"

"Holy Father, I don't' think the truth can ever hurt the Church."

"It is not the truth I fear! It is this monstrous fallacy of yours. You are dismissed! You have wasted too much of my valuable time already. I don't know why I had your bishop send me a mentally deranged person. The audience is over!"

Kerry took one stop forward to make one last desperate plea, when he was grabbed by the monks and hustled out of the room.

Ten minutes later he was leaning against one of the pillars of the columns that stretched out from St. Peter's and wondering vaguely what he was going to do next. It was about eleven o'clock at night. He looked out from the shadows of the columns and saw a bright moon in a clear sky.

The Pope had ordered him not to go public with his report which proved the existence of the Imp of Life. Should he obey him? But he was an unfrocked priest, no longer under Church discipline. Still, all those years as a priest meant something to him. he had been kicked out of the priesthood, but he was and would always be a Catholic

So, what should he do? He would decide that question when he got back to the States. But how? He had only a few hundred dollars on him, not enough to buy a plane ticket.

"Hey, Norbert Kerry," a voice whispered behind him.

"Who's that?" Kerry said, turning around.

The outline of a man appeared in the semidarkness. He was of medium height, had a stocky build, a wore a fedora, and had his hands in his coat pockets.

"How do you know my name."

"I know all about you, Kerry."

"What do you know?"

"I know that you are a defrocked priest of the Catholic Church. But I am not interested your status vis-à-vis your church."

"And what is it about me that interests you?"

"Your discovery."

"You mean . . . ."

"Yes, the Imp of Life."

"How did you come by all this information about me, and about the Imp? Who told you all this?"

"Our man in the Vatican."

"You have a spy in the Vatican?"

"Yes, one of the Dominicans who escorted you to that slumbering, half-comatose deluded old fool who believes that he is God's viceroy here on earth>"

"I resent that slur on the Holy Father!"

"Sorry if I offended you. Anyway, the Dominican is a secretary to one of the cardinals in the curia. He tipped me off about you and your report, but not the exact nature of your discovery."

"A spy in the Vatican . . . that sure beats me. But a spy for what country?"

"I am a sort of middle man. I work for countries and corporations."

"Are you working for a country or a corporation now?"

"Both."

"Name them."

The man mentioned a country in the Middle East and a corporation in the United States.

"You must be doing all right for yourself. I'm impressed.

But what's your business with me? What do you want from?"

"First of all I have informed the leader of that country I mentioned. He wants a full and complete report of your discovery, and the experiment you carried out. That is all I am at liberty to say."

"Uh . . . could you show your face? I don't like talking to a man without a face."

"Surely," the man said, stepping away from the columns and into the silvery moonlight.

Kerry saw that the man was of Middle Eastern origin. He had a mustache, dark complexion and a beaked nose.

"Are you a Muslim?"

"I believe that there is no God but Allah and Mahomet is his prophet. One day there will be only Muslims in the world."

"And what about all the other religions?"

"They will be blown away like a mist before the hurricane of Islam. All this is written in the stars. The extinction of all those false creeds in their kismet—their destiny. Only the true religion will prevail—Islam!"

"You think so?"

"I know so!"

"Well, that's one man's opinion. Right now I have an immediate problem on my hands. I want to get home, but I don't have enough money."

If you agree to the deal I am prepared to offer you, your money problem will be solved."

"What's the deal?"

"I have chartered a plane to take you to the country I mentioned. The president wants more information on this great discovery of yours. He thinks it might be useful to him."

"That man is an unelected president," Kerry said, "He is a dictator, a tyrant!"

"He is not a tyrant! He rules by the love of the people!"

"So you say."

"Okay, okay, I'm in no position to argue with you. If I go to this country, how much do I get?"

"One hundred thousand dollars. I have the money on me in a money belt. What do you say?"

"Tell me something, what's in it for you?"

"I will receive twenty-five thousand dollars."

"So you aren't doing this out of religious conviction, for the sake of your precious Islam."

"Since ancient times man have been able to combine devotion, to religion with self-interest. There is no moral conflict."

"Sad to say, I think history bears you out."

"Well, do we have a deal?"

"You got yourself a deal."

"Fine. My car is five minutes from here."
"First the money."

Four days later the Pope was cursing himself for not believing Kerry's report, for being a hidebound skeptic. He had with him in his office his Secretary of State, Cardinal Rasaclli, and the head of the Dominican Order and of the Holy Office, Cardinal Hentzeler. Both men could plainly see how furious His Holiness was as they stood in front of his desk. He was wide awake, alert and sitting up in his chair.

Cardinal Rascalli, a pragmatic and hardheaded man, had persuaded the Pope to conduct the experiment proposed by Kerry to prove the existence of the Imp of Life.

The Pope wanted to be sure, positively certain, that the Imp was the motivating force in all of human behavior. He wanted to observe with His own two eyes what effect the loss of the Imp would have on a man and a woman famously known for their strong sensual appetite.

Turning to Cardinal Hentzler he said, "I want for this experiment a man and woman have a reputation for being big on sex. Any suggestions?"

"Let me think . . . . Yes, I know the two who would be perfect!"

"Who are they?" Cardinal Rascalli eagerly asked.

"Name them!" the Pope demanded.

"The pop diva Lila Spearling. Thrice married and changes her boyfriends faster then she changes her hairstyle."

"And the man?" His Holiness asked.

"That's easy—Guilio Defanzano, the big movie star. He doesn't marry them. he loves them and leaves them. Two or three times a year he's involved in a sex scandal."

"What kind of sex scandals?" The Cardinal said.

"Oh, usually involving other men's wives, underage girls, and . . . I hate to mention this."

"What, what?" the Pope asked excitedly. "That bad?"

"He sneaked into a convent at night and abducted two nuns. But when the police arrested him, the nuns refused to testify against him."

"Did the nuns return to the convent?" the Pope wanted to know.

"After living that dolce vita for two months with Defanzano? Holiness, you have to be kidding!"

"That dissolute couple will be perfect for the experiment," Cardinal Rascalli said.

"Can we get our hands on them, Hentzeler?" the Pope asked.

"Fortunately, they are both in a movie that is being filmed here in Rome, and the gossip columns report that they are having a sizzling affair."

'You read the gossip columns, Hentzeler?"

"Well . . . as head of the Holy Office I have to keep up with what's going on in the world. I know that Spearling and Defanzano are shaking up—I mean they are spending their nights together in the Hotel Roma."

"Hentzeler, get them!" His Holiness ordered. "Tell your Domini-boys to hop to it!"

Within thirty-six hours the sex-driven singer and the actor were locked up in a room with a two-way mirror, after having their Imps removed.

And then His Holiness with Cardinal Rascalli and Cardinal Hentzeler watched to see what happened. And they saw very little activity on the part of the man and woman. They sat around all day bored, listless and totally indifferent to each other."

"Amazing, amazing!" the Pope exclaimed. "They are like dead people."

"I've seen severe cases of depression, but this beats them all!" Cardinal Rascalli said.

"Almost a total loss o fall human feelings, and not much appetite, even when we sent in gourmet meals," Cardinal Hetzeler commented in amazement.

"All right, we've seen how humans act without the Imp," the Pope said impatiently; "now, Hentzeler, give those two in there a strong sedative, put them to sleep, and have the doctor give them back the Imp."

"I'll put something in their wine," Holiness."

Four hours later the Pope and the two cardinals had their noses pressed against the two-way mirror. Popeyed, fascinated and agape, they stared at Spearlig and Defanzano making love. They went flopping all over the room. First they were on the bed, and then their violent gyrations carried them to the floor, the couch and then on the stuffed armchair. On an on they went, the diva almost hysterical with pleasure, and the actor grunting and snorting like a maddened bul.

After an hour they were still at it, and the Pope said, "Mother of God, that ma is not human!"

"He's a ferocious beast!" Cardinal Rascalli said.

"And that woman keeps begging him for more!" Cardinal Hentzeler said. "How much can she take!"

"And he's been inside every aperture in her body!" the Pope said in wonder.

Stepping away from the mirror Cardinal Hentzeler said, "Holiness, are you now convinced that the Imp does exist?"

"Yes, yes," the Pope said, his eye glued to the glass.

"I think we have seen enough," Cardinal Rascalli said.

"Yes . . . I suppose so," the Pope said, moving slowly and regretfully away from the mirror.

"In an hour or so those two will have exhausted themselves and they'll drop off into a deep sleep," Cardinal Hentzeler said. "I'll have my monks return them to the hotel."

"Yes, Hentzeler, you do that," the Pope said, thinking.

"Well, Holiness, what do you say now?" Cardinal Rascalli asked.

"I say I should never have let that unfrocked priest out of here!" the Pope said angrily.

"Yes, that was a mistake," Cardinal Hentzeler ventured to say. "We should have first performed the experiment to see if there was any truth in his Imp theory, which we now know is a scientific fact."

"Are you blaming me?"

"No, no, Holiness. I'm . . . ah . . . agreeing with you. We should have kept that priest here."

The Pope looked at Cardinal Hentzeler and said, "Well, what's to be done now?"

"Well, Holy Father . . . I . . . ."

"I want no hemming and hawing! I want action! That man must be found and brought back to me!"

"If we can locate him and he refuses to come back, what then?"

"Stop raising petty objections!"

"You mean? . . ."

"Yes, I want him—dead or alive!" the Holy Father said grimly. "Gentlemen, don't you see what a danger his discovery represents? It's a menace, a very dangerous menace. If this ever got out, it would cause a moral revolution in human behavior. People will believe they are not responsible for what they do. They will do as they please and not heed the teaching and admonition of the Church. Without responsibility, there can be no sin, no forgiveness, no judgment after death. And what's even worse, no need for the Atonement, Jesus' sacrifice on the cross! And no need for the Church! The whole fabric of all religious teaching on morality, sexual morality, will be doomed if we don't get our hands on that priest and silence him before he promulgates his pernicious discovery to the world!"

"Holy Father, do you think it's that serious?" Cardinal Rascalli asked.

"Certainly it's that serious, Rascalli! Don' t you have an ounce of brains in your head? Hentzeler, I mean business! Get cracking! I'm ordering you to get the full machinery of your organization on this job! Top priority, top priority!"

"What are your specific orders, Holy Father? Do you really want him dead or alive?"

"I don't think that would be a good idea, now that I think of it. What would I do with that trouble-making priest? Keep him in a dungeon in Castel San 'Angelo, as the Popes used to do with their enemies in the good old days? And for how long? He might escape and blab to the whole world about papa tyranny. No, Hentzeler, I want him silenced for good. Turn your Dominicans killers loose! Yes, the death of that man is surely justified! For the good of the Church founded by the Son of God, the American must die!"

Cardinal Hentzeler leaped into action in compliance with the Holy Father's stern command. He put two hundred Dominicans monks on the job. They were divided into groups of the, all of them armed to kill.

For days they scoured Rome relentlessly day and night, covering every street, going from north to south and from east to west. They question all their stoolies. But even with all their zeal and tenacity, they failed in their mission.

After weeks of this massive manhunt Cardinal Hentzeler reported his failure to the Pope, whose only comment was a muttered, angry curse.

"Holy Father, the man seems to have vanished without a trace. It's as if the earth swallowed him up. My Dominicans tried, I want you to know they tried to find that creature. He can't be in Rome!"

"Maybe the Devil snatched him down to hell!" the Pope said wrathfully. "That would be too much to hope for. But, no, that would not make sense. That Fallen Angel would like to see our church destroyed, and that limb of Satan, that unfrocked priest, could succeed in doing just that if we don't find him! Where is he? What are his diabolical plans? He is out there, Hentzeler, out there plotting the ruin of the Church!"

"Your Holiness, should I call off the search for that renegade priest?"

"Yes, no use going on with it. But where is he! Christ in heaven, where is that traitor!"

7

At that moment Kerry was languishing in a prison cell.
Here is what happened to him.

He was taken swiftly to the capita of that Middle Eastern country and brought before the dictator. The dictator demanded to know the exact nature of Kerry's discovery, and to prove to him how true it really was.

Kerry complied with a demonstration showing how a man and a female acted without the Imp in them and then with the Imp back in their bodies.

The dictator was deeply impressed and completely convinced.

"May I go home now?" Kerry asked.

For answer the dictator said to his bodyguards, "Lock up this American!"

On the second week of his incarceration Kerry asked the guard outside his cell what the dictator was going to do with his discovery.

The guard smiled and said, "He is going to destroy American with it."

"How can the petty tyrant of a small country destroy the one superpower in the world?"

"I should have said he is going to sexually and emotionally destroy Americans."

"What's that supposed to mean?"

"At this moment our factories are manufacturing thousands of powerful laser guns that will render the Imp of Life sterile and incapable of performing its normal functions. Our glorious Leader is going to swamp America with his men, who will be armed with this laser gun, which will operate silently."

"And what will they do with that weapon?"

"With that weapon, these fanatically loyal and dedicated men will zap high government officials, including your president, everyone in Congress, all top military people in the Pentagon and around the country—"

"This is insane!" Kerry shouted angrily.

"And all the business leaders in commerce and industry, and in television and Hollywood. And we will not forget the newspapers. All your important people, the brain power of American that keeps that decadent, rotten country of yours running, will lose all interest in life, and wont' give a damn about anything but sitting around and doing nothing. And when that happens, America will be ripe for a takeover by our people!"

"You will not succeed in this fiendish plot against my country!"

"And who is going to stop our great Leader? We will do the same thing to all the countries of the world! Yes, all the high and the mighty of the other nations will be zapped without even knowing it with our noiseless laser guns, and we will be the masters of the world!"

"Not if I can help it"

"You? Ha, what can poor you do in that cell?"

Kerry realized what dire danger America and the rest of the world were in. Somehow he had to get out, escape and get back to the States and warn the President of the impending catastrophe.

A week later Kerry noticed that the guard was looking very glum. By this time he had found out his name.

"What's wrong, Abdullah? Why are you looking so unhappy?"

"I heard from one of the workers in the government laboratory that the scientists are having trouble getting that laser gun to work properly. Already three of them have been executed."

"Maybe they'll never get it to work."

"Shut up, American!" Abdullah said, shaking his clenched fist at Kerry.

Three days later the guard was smiling.

"They made a breakthrough, American!" he crowed. "They got those laser guns going. They tried them on the most violent convicts and they turned into lambs! And now they're going into production! American, the mighty United States, is doomed!"

Kerry knew there was no time to lose. He had to act fast. That night an idea came to him. It was the one chance he had to escape.

In the following days Kerry won the confidence of Abdullah by making criticisms of American, and even going so far as to express hatred of his country.

"The United States is a materialistic, godless country made up mostly of moneygrubbers!" he said to the guard. "Abdullah, I wish your inspired Leader succeeds in is crusade! Islam is the religion of humanity. The religion of American is the dollar."

"Do you mean every word you have said?"

"Yes, and you can do me a favor. Could you bring me a copy of the Koran, in English?"

"You think you want to convert to Islam, become a Muslim?"

"I think I'm beginning to lean that way. Worshiping Allah is a lot better than worshiping the dollar. And I like the idea of having more than one wife."

"Yes, the Prophet allowed believers to have four wives."

"Four wives! What a time a man could have!"

"But they can be a burden."

"How many do you have, Abdulla?"

"I can afford only two."

"Do you get much sleep nights?"

"Very little. How my wives fight over me," Abdulla said sadly.

"Don't forget to bring me the <u>Koran</u> next time you come on duty."

"I'll see if I can find on in English."

And it was the <u>Koran</u> that got Kerry his freedom.

Here is how it happened.

Late one night Kerry pretended that he was puzzled by a passage in the holy book. He got up from his chair and went over to the bars, holding the book in his hands.

"Abdullah, could you please explain a couple of sentences to me. I'm a little confuse," he said.

"Of course," the guard said, coming close to the cell.

Just then Kerry said, "Hey, Abdullah, look, you relief is coming." And when Abdullah turned around, Kerry whacked him over the head with the book and knocked him out cold. Kneeling down he grabbed the keys on the guard's belt and opened the cell door.

After quickly donning Abdullah's clothes and slipping his revolver in his pants pocket, he walked out of the cellblock. Kerry saw with relief that the prisoners in all the other cells were sleeping.

Walking down a dimly lighted hall, he opened a heavy metal door and found himself outside the building. It was nighttime. By the light of a bright moon he spotted a panel truck. He said a prayer to St. Anthony that the key would be in the ignition, and it was.

The sentry at the gate waved him on and within minutes he was speeding down a highway. Days before he had casually asked Abdullah where the nearest airport was. He told Kerry that there was a small one six miles south of the prison.

For the next few minutes he kept asking himself, Was he going north or south? And then on the right side of the road he saw the airport. He turned into it and drove until he saw a small two-seater on the runway, just about to take off.

He braked the truck, jumped out of it, and with the gun in his hand ran over to the plane.

Above the roar of the motor he ordered the pilot to fly him to Israel, pointing the gun at his head.

"You can put down that gun," the pilot said. "That's where I'm going."

"You're flying to Israel?"

"I'm getting out of this slaughterhouse of a country. Our great leader is on one of his periodic killing purges of the armed forces-the whole military establishment. It's a habit with him to ensure the loyalty and devotion of everyone who wears a uniform. He pretends that he has uncovered a military conspiracy against the government and then proceeds to shoot a couple of thousand officers-generals, colonels, captains and lieutenants. I'm a lieutenant in the air force. This will be our beloved leader's fourth purge in eleven years."

"How did you find out another one was coming up?" Kerry asked

"I head tonight from my cousin, who works as a clerk for the secret police, that there was going to be a big roundup of air force officers tonight. My cousin tipped me off that my name was on the death list. So if you're going to Israel, hop on!"

Of course as soon as the plane entered Israeli air space it was intercepted by Israeli jet fighters and forced to land. And in less than an hour Kerry was being interrogated by agents of the Mossad, Israel's intelligence agency.

Kerry told them of his escape from the Middle Eastern nation and of the nefarious plan the dictator of that country had for the ruthless Islamization of the whole world.

"You must get me to the President of the United States right away!" Kerry said. "I must warn him of the danger facing America! Something terrible is going to happen to him and thousands and thousands of Americans!"

"You are too late," one of the agents said. "A strange and mysterious condition has afflicted many people in your country."

"Oh, God, no! Tell me more."

"Already countless government and business leaders have become zombie-like in their behavior. The medical authorities are completely stumped and baffled as to the cause."

"I didn't think that dictator would work so fast!" Kerry groaned in despair.

"I'm sorry to have to tell you this, but . . . well, the President of the United States, it's all day long in the Oval Office quietly staring into space. And when aides come in with papers for him to sign, he tells them to leave him alone. Even the Secretary of Defense and the Secretary of State can't get him to do his job. And what's even worse, he refuses to sleep with his wife. They say she's turning into a nervous wreck."

"I'm certainly sorry for her," Kerry said. "What about the rest of the country?"

"A good part of it has come to a standstill. The stock exchanges around the country have shut down. Most of the brokers and investors have lost interest in money. America is fast approaching economic stagnation. Do you have any information bearing on this calamity? If you do, let's have it! Israel is very much dependent on American financial support!"

"Do I have information! I told you about the worldwide plot that lunatic dictator has to turn the whole human race into servile Muslims under his despotic rule, but I haven't told you how he intends to do it. Here is the whole story!"

And Kerry told the agents about his discovery of the Imp of Life and the experiment he performed. And he told them about the laser guns.

"But what can we do to counter these guns? He can use them on the people of Israel and walk into our country without any resistance from us. How can we stop him from zapping us into listless, apathetic creatures?"

"I think there is a way. But I don't think the people of your country have anything to worry about. It is my country, the United States of American, that he must first conquer. Then he will go after the rest of the world."

"So how are the Americans to protect themselves from these zap guns?" one of the agents asked.

"Fly me to Washington. I must speak to the President personally!"

But as he was flying over the Atlantic Kerry realized that talking to the President in his present condition would do no good. He had to talk to the Vice President, who had not yet been zapped.

Kerry arrived with a dozen of the Mossad agents, who with the help of the Israel ambassador to the United States, was able to speak with the vice President.

"Mr. Vice President, I know how to restored the President to the vigorous, strong-willed, energetic man he once was." Kerry said.

"For God's sake, tell me how! American needs his strong leadership! I don't think I'm up to the job!"

"It's simple. Get me a recently deceased young male. And I mean one who has been dead no more than twenty-four hours."

"Say, are you nuts?"

Once again Kerry had to tell the story of his discovery of the Imp of Life and how vital it was to every human being. Without it, they became like zombies, as the President was. And he told the Vice President about the dictator's evil plans.

"So you see now, Mr. Vice President, why I must have a fresh young male corpse."

"I'll get the CIA on it right away!"

And within two hours that agency delivered to the White House exactly what Kerry wanted. And he performed the operation on the President in the Oval Office, after injecting the President's penis with a strong shot of Novocain.

As Kerry cut open the head of the penis with eight Secret Service agents, the Vice Presidents, the Secretary of Defense and the Secretary of State looked anxiously on, the President gazed blankly and indifferently at the wall across from him.

When Kerry removed the zapped Imp from the presidential penis, happily startled to see that it was not dead, only knocked out and incapable of performing its normal functions.

"It's not dead!" Kerry cried, turning to the Vice President. "That means that all the Americans who've had their Imps zapped will, in time, return to their normal condition!"

"Fine, glad to hear it. That sure is good news. But get on with the operation!"

Kerry immediately complied, and in a half hour he had implanted the healthy Imp in the President's penis and sewed it up.

And now everyone in that room stood around the President of the United States to see what would happen. Would he penis reject the substitute Imp? And if it did, that would surely present the Vice President with a Constitutional crisis. He could not succeed the President while he was still alive. But was he truly alive? He was more like a contradiction—living a corpse!

For almost an hour there was a grim silence in the Oval Office as all the men stared down at the listless inert, dull-eyed President of the United States lying on the desk where Kerry had made the switch of Imps.

The Vice President wrung his hands nervously. The Secretary of Defense impatiently pounded the palm of his hand with is clenched fist. The Secretary of State maintained his usual polished poise, but there were beads of sweat all over his face. Some of the Secret Service agents eyed Kerry, who was calmly smiling, suspiciously.

And then it happened. The effect of the Imp the President had received began t kick in, to function. Everyone was astounded to witness what seemed to them a miracle, a complete transformation. It was like seeing a man who was half-dead come back to life, like seeing a light switched on.

The Vice President, who was religious man, thought to himself, This is how it was when Lazarus walked out of the tomb! He who was dead is now once again alive!

The President looked around at the men gazing down at him, momentarily bewildered. And then he jumped off the desk and stood straight and tall, shoulders squared and an angry expression on his face, and fire in his eyes.

"Why the hell are all of you looking at me as if I was someone from outer space?" he bellowed. "What's going on here?"

"It worked, it worked!" the Vice President cried. "Thank God, thank God!"

"What the hell worked, Sam? What are you raving about?"

"Mr. President, it's good to see you back to your old self, the Secretary of State said.

"Welcome back, Mr. President!" the Secretary of Defense said, pumping his hand.

"Welcome back from where?" the President said. "Have you all gone crazy? Why are all these agents here?" And pointing to Kerry he added, "And who is this man? Why is her wearing that hospital gown? Somebody sick here?"

The Vice President turned to Kerry. "You'd better explain," he said. "I'm too excited."

Kerry spoke for twenty minutes, and when he was done, the President said, "Well, Norbert Kerry, I guess I owe you my life, or at least I have to be grateful to you for giving me back my real self, my healthy body. Your discovery of the existence of the Imp is truly fantastic, fantastic. It offers all kinds of possibilities for benefitting the human race. American continues to lead the way in scientific research!"

"Thank you, Mr. President," Kerry said.

"But are you sure about this dictator's mad dream of world conquest?"

"Absolutely, sir. After he has eliminated America as a world power, made us sexually, emotionally and militarily impotent, he intends to go after all the other counties on earth. If he succeeds in laser-zapping the mighty United States into powerlessness, he will have nothing standing in his way. That madman will be master of the world."

"The hell he will! I'll blow him to bits with a nuclear missile!"

"But, Mr. President," the Secretary of Defense objected, "how can we get at him? He sleeps in a different palace every night."

"How many palaces does he have?"

"The CIA says fourteen."

"Okay, so we'll blast every one of them simultaneously with nuclear missiles. And just to make sure, hit every palace with two missiles!"

"But, Mr. President," the Secretary of Defense objected, "how can we get at him? He sleeps in a different palace every night."

"How many palaces does he have?"

"The CIA says fourteen."

"Okay, so we'll blast every one of them simultaneously with nuclear missiles. And just to make sure, hit every palace with two missiles!"

"It'll take four or five days to get this operation going," the Secretary of Defense said. "We'll have to get the precise location of al that dictator's palaces from our agents in his country."

"And n the meantime Americans will be getting zapped into that pitiful, apathetic condition, losing all interest in everything, including sex," the President said, seriously concerned. "That could hurt our birthrate, destroy marriages, increase our divorce rate and break up families. How can we protect the Imp in them from all those thousands of agents loose in our country and armed with those laser guns?"

"I think I know how," Mr. President," Kerry said. "You must go on TV right away. You have to inform the American people of the existence of the Imp in them, and the danger they face from the laser-zappers. And of course the public has to know about that crazy dictator's evil plans for world domination."

"Fine, but how can the American people be immediately protected against those fanatical zappers?" the President asked insistently.

"I have an idea, sir," Kerry said. "It's only a theory, but I think my plan will work. In your TV address to the nation, you must urge all adult Americans, for they will be the prime targets of the zappers, to carry with them a briefcase when they are in public."

"I don't get it," the President said. "How can a briefcase to any good?"

"Please allow me to continue, sir. They must carry this briefcase, which will contain a one-inch thick lead plate in front of them, at all times when they are in public. I am sure that lead plate will protect their Imp from the laser guns."

"I'm sure it will do the job!" the President said enthusiastically. "I'll tell all those adults to make sure they hold the briefcase in front of their groin area. "And there's one more thing. I'm going to order the FBI to move fast and round up all those foreign zappers! Mr. Kerry, you are America's greatest hero!"

For days, at the President's urging, all over America men and women could be seen walking around holding a briefcase in front of them.

But they did not have to do that for long, for a week after the President was restored to his normal self the awesome danger hanging over America and the rest of the world was over. The Middle Eastern dictator was sent violently into the next world when the nuclear missiles blew into smithereens his fourteen palaces. And in less than ten day s al the mad tyrant's agents in America were arrested and prosecuted to the full extent of the law.

And at a gala ceremony at the White House the President, on behalf of a grateful country, personally, pinned on Kerry the Congressional Medal of Honor. It was the first time a civilian had received that highest of honors. New York City gave Kerry a parade up Broadway, and he was feted in more than a score of countries around the world. At Buckingham Palace the Queen bestowed on Kerry an honorary knighthood.

But there was one person who did not join in the universal rejoicing—the Pope. Of course he was glad that the menace confront-the world had been removed. However, in his eyes he had a serious grievance.

Now he sat in his office fuming silently as Cardinal Hentzeler stood stiffly in front of the desk waiting nervously for the Pontiff to speak.

"It's not fair!" the Pope finally burst out angrily. "It's some kind of anti-Catholic plot!"

"What's unfair, Holy Father?" the Cardinal asked timidly. "What anti-Catholic plot?"

"The worldwide propaganda of silence!"

"Propaganda of silence? I don't understand you."

"Don't you, don't you?"

"N—no, Holy Father, I don't."

"In all the ceremonies and parades held in this man's honor for saving the world from the evil designs of that lunatic despot, who I hope is burning in hell, there has been not one mention that this great hero is a priest!" the Pope said with bitter resentment. "Not a word on TV, radio and the newspapers that he is a priest of the Catholic Church!"

"An unfrocked priest," Cardinal Hentzeler pointed out.

"Hentzeler, I want you to see to it that he is un-unfrocked. I want that man, say, what's his name?"

"Norbert Kerry."

"Father Norbert Kerry! I want Father Kerry on my side, in my—I mean in our Church! We should be immensely grateful to him. He saved Christian civilization, he saved the Catholic Church, and he saved my job!"

"But, Holy Father, if I may remind you, he was booted out of the priesthood for carrying on affairs with many woman, married and single. His behavior was disgraceful and unforgivable. We want only pure-minded, celibate men—"

"Hentzeler, will you stop taking like a backwoods Bible-belt preacher and remember that you are a high churchman of the Holy Roman Apostolic Church!" the Pontiff said irritably and very much annoyed. "Show a little worldly wisdom, a little sympathetic understanding for Father Kerry's behavior."

"But, Holy Father, all those women—the vows he took when he became a priest! Don't they mean anything?"

"Hentzeler, we are not all born with the same Imp of Life."

"Did I hear right, Holy Father?"

The Pope got slowly up from his chair and walked over to the high, wide window. It gave a fine, broad view of Rome. Hundreds of people were walking below in the great piazza in front of St. Peter's. the Pontiff beckoned Cardinal Hentzeler to join him.

When the Cardinal stood beside him he said, "Look out. Tell me what you see."

"Well . . . I see a good art of Rome . . . rooftops and . . . ."

"People. Many people."

"Yes, many men, women and children. What are you trying to tell me, Holy Father?"

"Hentzeler, are those hundreds of people down there all alike?"

"No, certainly not."

"Precisely. They all differ from one another in personality, tastes, interests, character and so on. Why? We now know that it is the Imp in them that makes them different from each other. No two Imps are alike. Father Kerry is a sexual athlete because he was born with an Imp whose sexual component is overly robust. Look at it this way: Some people have exceptional minds. They are called geniuses. That is they have an Imp with a powerful intellect. Some men are outstanding baseball players, football players, boxers and so on. That is the superior athletic Imp in them. The same is true of Father Kerry in the sexual sense. The sexual side of his Imp is . . . perhaps overdeveloped, and therefore this improper behavior with those women is really not his fault."

"Improper behavior fiddlesticks, Holy Father! Outrageous, scandalous behavior! Your Holiness, you are standing Catholic teaching on sexual morality on its head. This man has been unfrocked, and canon law—"

"Canon law be damned!" the Holy Father roared. "Hentzelr, get your mind out of the moldy Middle Ages and come up to the fresh air of the twenty-first century. Listen to me carefully. Why do we have canon lawyers? To twist into a pretzel Catholic morality, or make it jump through a hoop lie a trained seal whenever it is expedient or serves the higher purposes of the Church."

"But he was unfrocked in a valid manner.'

"Unfrocked, defrocked, what does it matter? An impediment can always be found that can make a seemingly valid marriage invalid. Isn't that true, Hentzeler?"

"Well . . . in some cases . . . ."

"Good, good! That's the way I like to her you talk! Get your smartest Dominican canon lawyers on the job right away. Those men could make St. Peter's do a jig."

"I'll see what I can do, Holy Father."

"You will see that Father Kerry is back as a priest in the Church or you'll find yourself running a mission in Botswana! By the way, who is the bishop responsible for kicking Father Kerry out of the priesthood?"

"It was . . . Bishop Wellmore . . ."

"Inform him that the unfrocking ceremony was invalid.'

"On what grounds, Holy Father?"

"Haven't you been listening to me, Hentzeler! That's for your learned canon lawyers to find out! Now get going! I want action—today!"

"I'll get on it right away, Holy Father."

"Oh, and one more thing. I want a big publicity buildup for Holy Father. I don't care how much you spend. Hire a top PR firm. I want the whole world to know that it was a priest of the Roman Catholic Church that saved it from that crazy dictator's crazy dream."

8

Everything came about as the Pope had ordered. Bishop Wellmore, standing in front of the TV cameras and with a score of reporters present, officially announced that the unfrocking of Father Norbert Kerry was invalid because of an impediment. He did not specify just what the impediment was. And when a reporter asked him about it, the Bishop went into a long, rambling speech about the intricacies and complexities of Catholic canon law. When he was done talking, all the reporters were so dazed and befuddled that the question regarding the impediment remained unanswered.

As for the publicity campaign on behalf of Father Kerry, it was a sweeping success. His Holiness was pleased and gratified that now the whole word realized what it owed to a priest of the Roman Catholicism.

And finally, the great day arrived, the major event of the year in the United States: On a bright Sunday morning Father Kerry celebrated his first Mass in St. Paul's Church since being reinstated to the priesthood.

Sitting in the front pews were the President of the United States, three cardinals, eight bishops, the Pope's special nuncio, an abbots and monsignors galore. And of course the church was filled to capacity, for the parishioners were happy to see the very popular priest back with them.

And at that solemn moment when Father Kerry looked out at all those people with the raised Host in his hand, he was filled with a joyful, spiritually exhilarating rapture. Once again he was a Catholic priest in good standing, honored, loved and respected by all these good people who came to witness his moment of triumph.

Among the hundreds of smiling faces Father Kerry saw more than a dozen pretty young ladies smiling at him and . . . winking. A thrill of happiness shot through him. God was good! The world was a wonderful place!

But those women winking at him . . . should he wink back? Well, should he? And then he saw Irene, and she too was giving him a deliciously wicked wink. And without thinking, he winked back at her.

The Gold Digger Must Die

1

Gwen Welton, editor of a popular women's fashion magazine, was hard at work at her desk. It was a little after nine-thirty in the morning and Gwen was already halfway through a long article she was pounding out on her typewriter for the next issue of "Woman's Fashions."

Gwen had been using that machine for ten years, and it wasn't only because she was fondly attached to it and had an old-fashioned streak in her. She was a firm believer in spontaneous writing. She didn't like using the word processor that was on a table in a corner of her office under a plastic cover. Gwen thought that there was something dishonest, coldly calculating, about using a word processor. Writing should come from the heart, not the brain.

At five to ten her phone rang. Gwen wrinkled her brow in annoyance. She had given her secretary strict orders to hold all calls until ten-thirty. "Even if it's the President of the United States," she had told her.

When the phone went on ringing for twenty seconds Gwen picked up the receiver with an angry jerk. "May, didn't I tell you—"

"It's Mrs. Edmund Worthing. I told he that you were too busy and couldn't be disturbed, but I couldn't put her off. She's demanding to talk to you. She sounds very . . . emotional."

"Emotional?"

"Yes."

"Put her on."

Edith's voice came over the line in a rush, desperately frantic. Sobbingly she cried, "Gwen, Edmund asked me for a divorce this morning!"

"No!"

"Yes, yes, Gwent, it's true!"

"When exactly did he? . . ."

"Just after we'd finished breakfast and the servant had cleared the table and left the room. Edmund got up from the table, looked at me for a moment, and then spoke those awful words."

"Did he give a reason why he wants to break up your marriage?"

"Edmund was very frank about it. He says he's fallen in love with a woman, fifteen years younger than you and I."

"Did he mention her name?"

"Yes . . . Arlene Swinton."

"Oh, her! This I find hard to believe. How could Edmund be so ignorant? Doesn't he know that woman has a notorious reputation all over cafe society as a gold digger? Her specialty is middle-aged men. I just don't understand how Edmund could fall for a brazen creature like that."

"Gwen, we have to stop Edmund from divorcing me and marrying that woman!"

"Yes, yes."

"But how, Gwen, how?"

"We have to find a way. Give me time to think . . . ."

"Edmund sounded so madly in love with this woman. And he says she loves him."

"Don't you believe it. I know this 'Arlene Swinton.' She's been trying to land a wealthy husband ever since she came up to Manhattan from Brooklyn four years ago when she was twenty years old. Her real name is Mable Bottly. And, yes, she has stunning good looks, a knockout. I've seen pictures of her in the papers, always with rich, mature men. In love with Edmund! Bottly wants to get her hands on a chunk of his six-hundred-million-dollar fortune."

"Gwen, we have to stop her! Edmund can't love a woman like that! He has too much character. It's only a temporary lapse, an infatuation.

"Edit, it's an old story with men. As they get older, they have to prove to themselves that they are still attractive to young women. Their egos make them blind to the dollar signs in the eyes of those grasping females. Men . . . they grow old, but some of them never grow up."

"Before Edmund left for the office this morning he said that in two days he's leaving for Europe on some big business deal. I know he was lying to me. He didn't dare look in my eyes when he said it. I'm sure he's taking this Mabel-Arlene woman with him. Edmund said he would be gone at least a week. No business deal ever took him away that long. Oh, Gwen, Gwen, my heart is breaking!"

"And you think I'm not suffering along with you? This is dreadful, dreadful. All these years we've had this marvelous arrangement, and now this scheming cutie comes along and threatens to spoil everything. Well, Edith, she's not going to do it! I'll stop her, even if I have to—"

Gwen didn't finish the thought. But it was in her mind very seriously. She was just as angry and upset as Edit. Dear Edit, the anguish she must be enduring.

"Gwen, what were you going to say?" Edith asked.

"Not over the phone. We have to get together and talk this problem over."

After hanging up Gwen leaned back in her chair, the article forgotten. She thought back over the long years of friendship with Edith.

They had been best friends since they attended the same Catholic college. All those four years they were inseparable. They roomed together, went always and only on double dates and studied together.

Gwen majored in journalism. Edith didn't know what she wanted to do. She had been brought up by a wealthy aunt when her parents died in an automobile accident. She knew she would not have to go to work, find a job when she left college, and so Edith studied psychology

After they graduated, Gwen got a job as a newspaper reporter. Edith went to live with her aunt in her mansion on the Hudson, an estate forty miles from New York.

When Edith was twenty-three the aunt arranged for her to marry Edmund Worthing. He was the young CEO of a mid-sized computer company. Of course Gwen was one of the bridesmaids.

As a lover Edmund was sexually overbearing, domineering, and overwhelming. Every morning Edit woke up with aches and pains. She wished that she could get pregnant so that she could get some rest from Edmund's insatiable appetite for sex, and his violent lovemaking. But after three years no babies came. Edith began to fear going to bed.

One day she called Gwen, who was now working for a fashion magazine, and invited her over for tea for the following Saturday. Edith and Edmund were living in a townhouse on the Upper Eastside.

They had the tea in the library. Gwen immediately saw how distressed her friend was. And she saw that Edith wanted to tell her something but didn't know how to begin.

"Edith, I can see you have a problem. What is it?"

"I'm . . . so embarrassed to talk about it."

"Edith, I'm your best friend, so tell me. What is this all about? Have you and Edmund been fighting? Is there another woman?"

"I wish to heaven it was something like that. No . . . we never fight, never have cross words. I don't even think Edmund is aware of my . . . problem. He is a dear, loving husband. But when . . . ."

"Go on, Edith, what are you trying to tell me?"

"When we're in bed he becomes a . . . different man. He's like a madman . . . so violent, so different from what he is when we aren't in bed. I don't feel he's making love to me. It's more like he's raping me. I love him for his kindness, the expensive gifts he's always giving me, and his good looks. But . . . in bed, every night, so many times. He's just too much for me."

"But, Edith, you do get some pleasure out of it, don't you? I mean, you are sexually satisfied, aren't you?"

"Oh, yes, yes. No complaints on that score. But . . . sometimes when I tell him I've had enough, he ignores me and goes on and on and on . . . . In college, after three or four times, the boy would roll over and go to sleep. But Edmund—he's too much for me. I was thinking . . . if he had someone else . . . that might take the pressure off me. You know what I mean?"

"Edith, I'm not sure I know what you mean. Exactly what are you trying to tell me?"

"Gwen, you're a mature beauty. At our dinner parties I've seen Edmund looking at you with that certain gleam in his eyes. I'm sure he's attracted to you. Yes, I know he has a yen for you. And . . . ."

"You want me to make a play for Edmund?"

"Would you, darling, would you? I'd be so grateful. If my husband had you fir his mistress, my dearest friend, I'm sure I wouldn't mind one bit. In college we shared boyfriends, so why can't we do the same thing with my husband?"

"But this is different. Have you forgotten your marriage vows, in church?"

"Gwen, stop being an old-fashioned Catholic. This is the twenty-first century, forty years after Vatican Two. Pope John had all the windows of the church opened to let in fresh air."

"But instead garbage came flying in."

"Let's get back to my problem."

"Edith, are you sure this is what you want?"

"Yes, but we mustn't let Edmund know that I'll know about it. Let it be our little secret. If Edmund knew I was aware of what was going on between you and him, I don't think he would get as much pleasure out of having sex with you. You know, forbidden fruit is the sweetest fruit."

"Edit, are you positive this is what you want?"

"Yes, don't let me down. Please do this for me. I remember how many times you told me when we were in college that you would never marry. You said that the hassle of married life wasn't for you. You loved your independence too much. But I also recall that you said you weren't going to deny yourself the pleasures of sex. Well, believe me, with Edmund you will have a ball in bed. What a versatile lover my husband is. He knows how to please a woman in so many exciting ways. Gwen, darling, say you will do this for me. Do it for your dearest and best friend. Since we've known each other intimately for over twenty years, I won't feel Edmund is being unfaithful to me, that he's committing adultery."

"But he will be doing just that."

"Gwen, I'm not talking about morality, I'm talking about how I will feel. So, say it. I want to hear you say you will do this for your old pal."

"Well, if this is what you want . . . okay, I'll do it. Invite me over for one of your formal dinners. I'll wear my slinkiest décolleté gown. And I'll start right in by making goo-goo eyes at Edmund when we're having the cocktails. I'm going to give him the sexiest come-on a man ever had.

"Darling Gwen, I love you!" Edith cried happily, throwing her arms around her dear friend.

A month later, Gwen was able, thanks to Edmund's generosity, to move out of her modest apartment on the lower Westside to a luxurious six-room furnished love-nest overlooking Central Park.

Naturally Gwen and Edmund could not be seen alone together in public. Once in a while they went to have dinner in a small restaurant across the river in Brooklyn Heights. But mostly they ate in Gwen's apartment. She prided herself on her cooking.

As for Gwen's social life, Edmund, ever thoughtful, saw to that. He had one of his vice presidents, Adrian Grantwell, devilishly handsome and gay, act as Gwen's escort around town. With Adrian's taste for boys (of legal age) Edmund was sure he had no cause to worry.

It was a perfect arrangement. Adrian liked to be seen with a lovely woman at play openings, art exhibitions and dining in the toniest restaurants in Manhattan. And Gwen was a glamorous companion indeed. She dressed elegantly, now that she could afford to wear the fashionable clothes she wrote about.

Gwen had a radiant sex appeal. It tickled Adrian to see men casting envious looks at him. Whenever a man at one of the many parties they went to asked Gwen for a date, she would always say, "Thank you so much, but you see, my heart belongs to Adrian."

This arrangement went on smoothly and enjoyably for ten years to everyone's satisfaction. Edmund was getting all the sex he wanted from two very desirable women. Edith was grateful to Gwen for getting some relief from her husband's relentless sex drive. And Gwen enjoyed a richly satisfying love and social life.

Adrian was perhaps the happiest of the three. He had a lively social life, and a wonderfully happy private life with his boys. He really was a very conventional person, with a proper respect for what was right and decent—in public. He was a devout Episcopalian who lived with his parents, attended church every Sunday, and was active in church activities. His Christian conscience did prick him now and then when he thought what would happen if his parents ever found out he was gay. He knew that they would be crushed. He swore to himself that they would never find in downtown Manhattan. He made it a strict rule never to go to gay bars. Adrian always relied on pimps to supply him with the lads he so much adored. How he wished he could have openly married one of them!

Occasionally Edmund, Edith, Gwen and Adrian made it a foursome and went out on the town together. Edith prayed every night that things would go on like this for always.

And then Arlene Swinton came into Edmund's life and threatened to destroy her happiness. Something had to be done, and done quickly before Edmund got a divorce and married that woman!

Edith and Gwen met for lunch a block from the office building where Gwen worked. Gwen saw how worried and unhappy Edith was. They knew without even talking about it, that they had to come up with a plan to make Edmund change his mind about marrying Arlene.

When they were having their espressos Edith asked, "Gwen, have you thought of anything . . . you know, some way? . . ."

Gwen didn't answer right away. She was thinking how Arlene's appearance in Edmund's life had affected her. Now she understood why Edmund n longer came t have to dinner with her at her place.

Now he stayed less than an hour when he came to visit her. It was a quick drink, and then he would pull her into the bedroom for one hurried act of love, and he was gone.

Sometimes Gwen didn't see Edmund for weeks. After a steady diet of strong, frequent sex, having to go without it for many days was very trying for Gwen. She began to consider taking on a part-time lover.

"Gwen," Edith said, "I asked you a question."

"I heard you."

"Well, what're we going to do?"

"Hire a contract killer to bump off Arlene."

"Gwen, be serious."

"I am serious, sort of. It's the instinctive thing humans think of when someone creates a problem. Get rid of the person."

"But, Gwen, killing Arlene?"

"How else do we get rid of the bitch? I've got almost as big a stake in this are you have. With Edmund spending so much time with Arlene, I'm practically sex starved. Sometimes I don't see that husband of yours for weeks, and when I do, he does a rush job on me. He doesn't make love to me, he just quickly relieves himself in me, like a man having a bowel movement. Is it the same with you, Edith?"

"Yes, it is," she complained. "Exactly as you described it. One, two, three and it's all over. Gwen, we must get our lover back!"

"By killing Arlene."

"No, I've been thinking of another, less drastic way to get her out of our lives."

"Could you be a little clearer? What do you have in mind?"

"Maybe we could persuade her to go away."

"You mean buy her off?"

"Gwen, my aunt left me two million dollars in stocks and bonds, and that mansion on the Hudson I sold two years after she died."

"How much did you get for it?"

"For the house and the twelve acres I got four million. Today, personal worth comes to almost eight million dollars."

"Edith, are you willing? . . ."

"Yes, yes, I would pay any price to save my marriage, and to preserve this wonderful arrangement we've had all these years. We have been happy, haven't we, all three of us?"

"You're forgetting dear, sweet Adrian," Gwen said with a smile.

"Well, okay, he too has been very happy."

"How much, Edith?"

"How much what?"

"How much of your money are you going to offer Arlene to lose herself in Brooklyn?"

In a sudden spasm of despair Edith said, "I'd give her everything, every last penny I have! Yes, and even all the jewelry Edmund has give me over the years! Everything except my wedding ring! I don't want to lose Edmund! And it isn't only because I love him! There has never been a divorce in my family, never! We had had annulments, my brothers and uncles, but never one of those sinful, un-Catholic divorces! To me, the marriage vows are sacred, inviolate!"

"Edith, I agree with you completely," Gwen said firmly. "All these divorces will be the ruination of the American family. I think we Catholics will be the saviors of American family life. But . . . about handing over all your wealth to that gold digger . . . I think that's a bit too much."

"What do you suggest?"

"Let's start with three million, and see if Arlene is satisfied with that. I'll get in touch with her and get her to meet with you to talk things over."

"No, no, Gwen, I don't want to see that creature! I don't want to talk to her!"

"You want me to do the negotiating, is that it?"

"Would you, darling? You are so much more the woman of the world than I am. I wouldn't know how to talk to that person. I'm sure you can get her to accept the offer."

"Edit, if she doesn't bite, how high can I go?"

"You already know the answer to that question. My entire fortune and the jewelry!"

"Okay, I'll try, Edith. But I'm not sure that I will succeed."

"I don't understand. Why would Arlene turn down all that money?"

"Edith, be realistic. Arlene know that Edmund is the owner of a computer company. And she probably keeps a sharp eye on the financial pages and knows down to the dollar how much Edmund is worth. All your money and diamonds might seem like chicken feed to her. But maybe I'm wrong. Maybe Arlene is only modestly greed and your top offer will be enough to satisfy her mercenary heart. We'll see."

2

Through a gossip columnist Gwen was able to get Arlene's phone number. When she called, the voice on the line came over thick and sensual. Gwen got right to the point and said that she was calling on behalf of Mrs. Worthing on a matter that would be of great financial interest to Arlene. Would she care to meet in a bar?

"Why don't you come up to my place?" Arlene suggested.

"Okay," Gwen said, startled by the invitation.

The address she gave impressed Gwen. It was a Park Avenue apartment building in the upper sixties. The doorman, looking like an admiral in full dress, opened the door for her and she rode the elevator up to the fourteenth floor.

Arlene opened the door to her ring and led her into a spacious duplex condo. They walked through several rooms. The place was exquisitely furnished. There were Persian rugs on the floor, paintings on the walls—everything solid, beautiful and expensive.

As they entered the living room Gwen was filled with a raging envy. The apartment Edmund had give her was comfortable enough, but this! It must have cost him millions! Was Arlene worth it? Gwen wondered. Was she that good in bed? Was any woman?

Now Gwen understood clearly why Arlene had invited her here. It was to show off her swanky place. It was to show Gwen that she was playing for high stakes. This was a shrewd, calculating woman, Gwen thought. She had already scored points. She was not going to be bought off so easily.

They sat down on a sofa in front of a coffee table on which were tow tall glasses, a bottle of bourbon and a bowl of ice cubes. Arlene fixed the drinks, leaned back with a glass in her hand and smiled kittenishly at Gwen.

Now for the first time Gwen got a look at Arlene. She was just the kind of female she had expected. A platinum blonde, big-breasted, beautiful. And oozing sex from every pore of her voluptuous body. Looking at Arlene, Gwen thought, This was a woman God created for sexual romping and nothing else. She should always go around with a mattress on her back.

Arlene tossed off her drink in two gulps, poured herself another and said, "You mentioned on the phone that you had a message for me from . . . Mrs. Worthing. What is it?"

"You don't go in for any chitchat, do you?" Gwen said, taking a short sip from her glass and putting it down on the coffee table. She never did like bourbon.

"What for? Life is too short. So, what did you want to see me about?"

"Come on, Miss Swinton, or do you prefer Bottly? Full real name Mable Bottly of Brooklyn, isn't it?"

Arlene's eyes blazed with fury. She slammed her glass on the coffee table, shattering it. "I am Arlene Swinton, and don't you forget it!"

"Okay, okay, Arlene Swinton. You must have some idea why I wanted to see you when I mentioned Mrs. Worthing."

"I do, I do."

"And what do you think it is?"

"It's obvious, of course. The wife wants me to break off with her husband."

"And what is your answer?"

"No, no, no. I love Edmund."

"You love his money!" Gwen said, flaring up angrily. "You cheap gold digger!"

"Not so cheap, sister," Arlene said, smiling sweetly. "A high priced."

"At least you're honest."

"Sure, I'm an honest gal. Okay, I'll be frank with you. I've hooked a lot of small fish for peanuts. This time I've got my hook in a big one, and now I'm going to haul him in. I've been wined and dined and paid off by a lot of rich guys. But all they wanted was my body for a few nights of sex. This time I've hit the jackpot, and I'm going to make the most of it. Edmund told me he craves my body like a heroin addict craves his drug. He says he wants to sleep with me every night, and he's proposed to me, and I said yes."

"He's not even divorced yet," Gwen said, beginning really to hate this woman.

"A minor technicality."

"Arlene, Mrs. Worthing is willing to pay you three million if you disappear, blow this town, get lost."

Arlene placed her hands over her breasts and moved them slowly down to her hips. "Is that all you think this is worth?"

"Four million."

"No."

Gwen decided to go the limit, including her own jewelry that Edmund had given her. Surely that would be enough for this tart?

"Arlene, you can have eight million dollars, and over a million more in diamonds. What do say?"

"You aren't even close to my price. I keep myself informed on money matters. Last week there was an article in one of the financial magazines on Edmund. The article stated that my lover is worth close to a billion dollars."

"That's an exaggerated figure," Gwen said.

"So maybe Edmund is worth only eight hundred million! That's still a lot of dough! Sister, I'm playing for big stakes. I have to get mine while my body is still ripe and tasty. I've given Edmund the best time in bed he's ever had. He's told me so many times. Now he wants me for his wife. After a few years of marriage with that middle-aged man and a child, I'll dump him for a whopping settlement and by myself a handsome young stud for a husband. How I hate the smell of these men so many years older than myself!"

"You bitch, how much do you expect to get out of Edmund?"

"A hundred million, and not a penny less."

"You aren't a bitch! You are a rotten bitch!"

Arlene got up from the sofa. "This discussion is over. Tell Edmund's wife that she can have her precious husband back in a couple of years."

3

It was the day after Gwen's meeting with Arlene. Gwen sat at her desk feeling lifeless, mentally numb and physically paralyzed. She stared at the blank page in the typewriter with only one thought in her head. She had failed. Arlene was going to take Edmund away from her and Edith. That creature was going to take away their happiness and bring down on them misery.

The door to the office opened and Edith walked in.

"We'll Gwen? How did it go? I've been on pins and needles waiting for your call. Tell me, for God's sake, what did she say?"

"Edith, close the door."

After she had closed the door, Edith, still very much distraught, asked, "Gwen, what did she say?"

"Edith," Gwen said calmly, "get a grip on yourself. Sit down."

Sitting down in the chair in front of the desk Edith said, "Gwen, tell me! How did the meeting go with Arlene?"

"It didn't g. she turned down my offer."

"You went the limit?"

"Yes, and I even threw in my diamonds. We were never in the ballgame."

"What do you mean?"

"Arlene's plan is to marry Edmund, have a kid by him, and then divorce that chump for a big payoff. She doesn't love Edmund. That money-grubber is incapable of love. To Arlene Edmund is only a money tree, and she's going to shake it for all she can get. And then she's going to find herself a handsome young stud and live happily ever after, the bitch."

"Gwen, where do we go from here?" Edith asked, in a voice pathetic and desperate. "We have to do something to stop Arlene!"

"Steady, Edith, steady. Don't go to pieces."

"So what can we do?"

"You haven't forgotten that first solution I mentioned, have you? At the time I think I was a half-joking, but since having that face-to-face with that vile gold digger . . . ."

"Gwen, I want my husband back, but . . . murder?"

"How else can we get rid of that creature? She's playing for keeps! Well, we have to play for keeps too!"

"Gwen, we are practicing Catholic. I receive communion every month, and I know you do too. We can't go against our religion by killing a human being."

"Arlene, a human being? That's a moot point. But, darling Edith, what's this got to do with religion? We have a serious problem to deal with. We are trying to figure out a way to save our marriage. And I say killing Arlene is the way to go. Come to think of it, I think there is nothing religiously wrong with that solution to our problem. We kill Arlene and save your marriage. What could be more moral?"

"Well, yes . . . there is something to what you say, when you put it that way. It would be morally justified, wouldn't it, Gwen?"

Gwen nodded yes, but she didn't have morals on her mind. Lately she had been nervous and jumpy. And she knew why! It was because Edmund was spending so much time with Arlene! He had no time for her. When was the last time she'd had sex? Days and days. She was not a woman made for eh eelibate life. Twice Edmund had called her at her apartment to say he would be coming around to see her at her apartment to say he would be coming around to see her, but right now he was busy.

"Busy with what?" she had asked him once.

"With business. What else?" he had laughed.

And Gwen wanted to come right out and say, "You mean with that whore, Arlene!"

Gwen's mind focused back on the office. She saw Edith looking down at the floor with a sorrowful, pensive expression. Her face was pale. It had lost that healthy glow. There were lines under her eyes. Edith too, like herself, was being cheated out of her sex life with her husband. That Arlene must be a devouring beast in bed! She drained Edmund dry, leaving nothing for Edith and herself. Yes, that's what that creature was, a beast that had to be destroyed. It menaced a happy marriage, and a wonderful relationship of many years she had had with Edmund. Killing Arlene could not be called a crime. It was a moral necessity!

Edith straightened up in her chair and said, "Gwen, if we o this—this—"

"Kill the gold digger."

"Yes . . . uh . . . how do we do it?"

"We get somebody to do the job?"

"We couldn't do it . . . ourselves?"

"Out of the question. You'd be the first logical suspect, and I'd probably come under suspicion too. I'm sure the police would find out about me and Edmund. And under grilling from those tough police detectives we'd be sure to crack and confess. So we can't do the killing ourselves."

"So we have to get someone to . . . do it."

"Right, a professional."

"A professional who kills for money? Are there such people?"

"Edith, you sweet, innocent darling! Of course there are. They are called contract killers. You pay them so much money, and they do the job. I think the going rate these days is ten thousand dollars for a rubout."

"I'll put up all the money."

"Slow down. It's not that simple."

"I don't understand. I have the money."

"Fine, swell. But we have one problem. We have to find the person to blow away that gold digger."

"How do we do that? You don't know? . . ."

"Edith, how can you think that of me? I don't hobnob with underworld characters. I've always been a law-abiding person . . . until now. The problem is making contact with a killer for hire."

"Gwen, maybe we could ask a bartender. They meet all kinds of people. What do you think?"

"Too risky. I've read about husbands, wives and business partners who went to bartenders for a killer. He informs the police, and they have an undercover cop pose as a contract killer. They get the person who wants somebody dead offering money for the job, and the husband, wife or business partner gets ten to fifteen years in prison. No, we can't do it that way."

"So how are we going to get rid of Arlene?"

"I'll have to think of about it. Give me a little time."

4

Three days later Gwen was still thinking about it as she sat in her apartment slumped in a stuffed armchair in front of the blank TV screen.

She felt angry, depressed and frustrated. That gold digger had to be killed! For so many years Edith and she were so happy, until Arlene came into Edmund's life. In this city of eight million people there had to be any number of contract killers. But how did you get in touch with them? With a real killer, and not an undercover cop.

The phone on the small table beside her rang.

"Hello."

"Gwen, Gwen darling, wonderful news!" Edith said, happy and excited.

"Don't tell me you've found someone to do the job?"

"We don't have to do it! I just got a phone call from Arlene. It turns out she isn't as bad as we thought. She's had a change of heart."

"How could she? She doesn't have a heart!"

"Gwen, please listen to me. Believe me, she sounded sincerely unhappy over all the trouble and anguish she has caused me. She said she is deeply sorry for her immoral and dishonorable behavior. Arlene swore to me that she is giving up Edmund and going to live with a maiden aunt in South Dakota. She has come to hate the wicked New York scene. So you see we don't have to kill her. Isn't that grand?"

"Sure, if she means it."

"I know she does. And she's going to prove it. Edmund is going to her place tomorrow night. He already told me that he's going on a three-day trip to Chicago. He things he's going to spend a few hours with Arlene before he catches his plane. But Edmund won't be having any sex with Arlene.

"Our reformed gold digger wants me to go to her apartment, and right before my eyes she's going to tell Edmund that she's stepping out of his life and leaving town for good. And Arlene says that she is going to apologize to me for all the misery she has caused me, right in front of Edmund. Isn't she an angel?"

"Somehow I can't think of Mabel Bottly as an angel," Gwen said.

"Gwen, I'm going to hang up now. I'll call you tomorrow night and tell you all about it. I'm so happy, so happy! My prayers to the Little Flower, Saint Theresa, have been answered!"

Gwen got up from the armchair and walked slowly up and down. This was hard to believe about Arlene. What a remarkable transformation in a person. But what had caused it? Did that woman get religion all of a sudden? The woman she had met was hard as nails and out for all she could get in this world. This just didn't sound like the person who had callously turned down her offer of all that cash, and the diamonds. And yet . . . people did change for the better.

It was one-thirty in the morning. Gwen had had a few hours of restless sleep. The dream she had of herself and Edmund woke her up. Now she lay in bed, half-awake, trying very hard not to think of Edmund.

She was trying to get her mind on the fashion show she was going to attend tomorrow when the phone on the bedside table rang.

"Yes . . . who is it?"

Edit's sobbing, hysterical voice came over the line.

"Edith, what's wrong? What's happened?"

"Gwen, Gwen, everything is wrong! Arlene is a monster, a monster! I want to kill her! I want to strangle her with my own two hands! She's a witch! She should be burned at the stake!"

"Edit, get hold of yourself," Gwen said, sitting up in bed and switching on the lamp. "Tell me what happened."

"Gwen, it was horrible, sickening, revolting! That Arlene isn't human! She's a sadistic devil! She should burn in hell forever, forever! I never knew anyone could be so cruel, never!"

"Edith, for God's sake, stop this crazy raving and tell me what happened. Did you go to Arlene's apartment?"

"Yes, fool that I was to fall for her lies."

"Was Edmund there?"

"No, Arlene was alone. When I arrived she greeted me cheerfully, with a smiling face. She even embraced me and told me how sorry she was for having this affair with Edmund, and for all the pain she had caused me."

"And then what? Gwen asked.

"Well, then she said that Edmund would be arriving soon. Arlene said she thought it would be better for me if I waited in the bedroom. She wanted to talk to Edmund alone, tell him that she was going away, and that he should do the right thing and stick with me. 'I realized now that marriage is a holy sacrament, Mrs. Worthing, and I don't want to be the one responsible for breaking up your marriage,' the hypocrite said, as she led me into the bedroom and told me to wait in the deep clothes closet. I left the door open a crack."

"How long did you have to wait?"

"After about twenty minutes I heard voices through the open door of the bedroom, so I knew Edmund had arrived. And then—oh, the horror of it—after about five minutes, they entered the bedroom. They were stark naked. Edmund was carrying Arlene in his arms. He dropped her on the bed and began kissing her all over her body for three or four minutes. Then, when he had Arlene moaning with pleasure he plunged into her with a joyful shout, and Arlene screamed with delight. After his orgasm, he rolled off her and lay on his b ack. Arlene, like a tigress, was immediately bending over him, kissing and licking him until he was big and hard again. And then she got on top of Edmund, and they went at it like two sex savages, both of them shouting filthy, disgusting obscenities at each other."

"Edith, why didn't you stop them? Why didn't you run screaming out of the closet?"

"No, no, Gwen, that would have been the worst thing to do. I know my husband. Edmund has pride. If I had shown myself, humiliated him, he would never have forgiven me. I would surely have lost him for good. Yes, I was in torment seeing that I was seeing. Yes, I was revolted. Yes, I was furious with Arlene and filled with a murderous hatred of her for playing monstrous deception on me. But I'm glad I kept my head."

"And so you continued silently watching Arlene and your husband going at if ro—how long?"

"I think it was when they were going it the fifth or sixth time that I began to feel weak. Edmund had Arlene up against the wall, with her legs around his hips, not more than three feet from me. Then I stepped back into the closet, so I wouldn't see them. And then everything began to get dim, dark. I must have blacked out, fainted."

"Edith, how long were you unconscious?"

"I'm not sure. All I can say is when I regained conscious, I was in the middle of the bedroom, and Arlene was standing over me, naked, alone, smiling, gloating down at me."

"Where-where's my husband?" I said.

"Gone to catch a plane for a business trip in Chicago. He left a half hour ago. I've just had a lovely, refreshing shower. How did you enjoy the sex show I put on for you, my dear Mrs. Worthing? Wasn't that a spectacular performance I arrange for your entertainment? Aren't we a perfect sex match, me and my future husband? Before Edmund left he swore to me that he would have you out of his life in four months, and be free to marry me.

"You are an evil woman!"

"No, I am an ambitious woman. Now the show's over, so get the hell out of my home. Your future ex-husband promised to call me as soon as he arrives in Chicago to tell me how much he loves me and can't wait to get back to my loving arms."

"That's the whole sordid story, Gwen. How I hate that woman!"

Gwen was seething with rage at the unspeakable suffering Arlene had inflicted on her dear friend. That creature was no ordinary woman! She was a witch, a witch in league with the devil!

"Edith, I'm so sorry, so sorry for you. Arlene will pay with her life for what she did to you! The gold digger must die!"

"But how, Gwen, how do we kill her?"

"Leave that to me. Somehow, I'll find someone to do the job. That gold digger will die violently—and soon!"

5

But a week later Gwen, eating her lunch at her desk, had not thought of a way to terminate Arlene's life without implicating herself and Edith.

Sighing in frustration, she put down her ham and cheese sandwich, which she had hardly tasted, and picked up the can of ginger ale. And as she sipped the soda, Gwen remembered a date she'd had with Adrian two years ago.

As they walked out of that Spanish restaurant Gwen said, "Adrian, that spicy Spanish food gave me a big thirst. I feel like getting tanked up tonight. What do you say?"

"I'm with you! Let's get real high!"

An hour and a half later, and sitting in the booth of the second bar they went to, Adrian, who had a weak tolerance for liquor, was feeling boozy, maudlin, and in a mood to open his heart to Gwen. He told her of his absolute need for boys. His life would be a desolate wasteland without them. He told Gwen of the apartment he kept in Greenwich Village, where he took them.

Ordinarily, like a sophisticated, tolerant New Yorker, Gwen would not have said anything. But with a dozen Scotches in her, she spoke her mind.

"But, Adrian, I know that you are a devout Christian. Don't you see conflict between your love of boys and your religion?"

"No, Gwen, there isn't any conflict, because I know that Jesus Christ, my Lord and Savior, understands and loves me."

"How do you know that?"

"I know because Jesus told me so himself.

"When?"

"It . . . happened in my second year in college. I was troubled by my sexual orientation. Hard as I tried, I couldn't square it with my Christian conscience. It was a time of spiritual crisis for me. I couldn't renounce my faith. That to me was unthinkable. But I just couldn't, couldn't give up my gay sex life."

"So what did you do?" Gwen asked.

"I took my problem to my Savior. I went to the chapel on the campus. I was all alone, only me and the big wooden cross with my Savior nailed to it. Looking up into that suffering face, I prayed, prayed with all my heart and soul for guidance from my Redeemer. And then it happened, the miracle that ended my suffering. I saw Jesus open his mouth and say with deep compassionate feeling, 'Adrian, stop tormenting yourself. I understand. Follow whenever your desires take you. I love you. As long as you go on worshipping me as your Savior, I will not condemn you for the life you choose to lead. You have my promise that when you die, you will spend eternity with me in heaven.'"

Not believing for one moment the objective truth of what Adrian had told her Gwen said, "It's good to know that Jesus loves us, no matter what."

"Yes, but I do have one great fear."

"What's that?"

"My . . . parents."

"What about them"

"If they should ever find out that I . . . ."

"Love boy sex."

"Yes, if they ever learned about my secret sex life, they would be shattered. Gwen, they are such sweet, loving, wonderful parents . . . that if they found out about me . . . I couldn't bear it. I don't think I would want to go on living. I know how mortified and ashamed they would be. My mother, father, and I go to church together every Sunday, and we have Bible readings four or five times a week."

"Adrian, have they ever asked you why you didn't get married?"

"When I was younger, yes, but not anymore. When they did ask, I always told them I was too busy with my job, and too much involved in church activities. That answer seemed to please them, but I think they would have liked to see me married, having children, making them grandparents."

"Yes, I'm sure they would have loved that.":

"But, Gwen, if I could only make you understand! The very thought of being bed with a woman, and both of us naked, terrifies me! My blood runs cold, just thinking about it!"

Now, Gwen, sitting at her desk, staring down at her half-eaten sandwich, and thinking about what Adrian had told her about himself and his mother and father, suddenly jumped up from her chair, filled and excited with an inspired idea that flashed through her mind.

"That's it!" she said out loud. "Adrian is the answer, the solution! Adrian will kill Arlene!"

6

Eight days later Gwen and Adrian had dinner in the restaurant of the Plaza Hotel. All during the meal she wondered where she was going to tell Adrian she wanted him to kill Arlene. She knew how she was going to force him to do it—threaten to reveal his sex life to his mother and father.

When they came out of the hotel to the cool October air, Gwen saw across the street on the Central Park side a half-dozen buggies standing by the curb, the horses' heads drooping. She smiled to herself.

"How about a ride in the park?" she said.

"Sure," Adrian said, "I haven't done that in a long time."

When they were deep in the park and under the shadows of the trees, Gwen interrupted Adrian about the church charity he was organizing to say bluntly, but softly so the drier wouldn't hear, "Adrian, I want you to kill somebody for me."

Adrian almost fell out of the buggy. Gwen grabbed him by the arm and pulled him back beside her. After glancing at the driver, he stared at Gwen, cold fear in his eyes.

"Gwen, the way you spoke those words, I know you are serious."

"You got that right. Well, will you do it?"

"I don't have it in me to kill an innocent human being."

"She's anything but that!"

"Gwen, lower your voice, the driver."

Whispering harshly Gwen said, "She's a viper, a dragon, a devil!"

"A woman, you want me to kill a woman?"

"Yes,"

"No, never, never,

"You will do this for me, Adrian!"

"I will not! 'Thou shalt not kill.' Straight from the mouth of God. And I am a God-fearing Christian! I will never commit the crime of taking the life of a human being. You can't make me, no matter what you say or do."

"Even if I tell you parents that you are a queer, a homosexual, that you love to suck the penises of young boys, that you sodomize them and that they sodomize you?"

"Gwen, you wouldn't be so cruel as to tell my mother and father all those things about me, would you?" Adrian cried, panic-stricken.

"You goddamn right I would!" Gwen said ruthlessly. "And stop that sniveling. I'll go right to your mother and father and tell them you've been gay all of your sex life."

"They would never believe you. They know what a good Christian life I live."

"But they don't know about your apartment down in Greenwich Village, where you take your boyfriends and do very unchristian things with them in bed."

"They won't believe that of their son! I would deny everything you said! And they will believe their son!"

"Even when I show your loving mom and dad vide proof?"

"Gwen, what're you saying? You have . . . ."

"I do," Gwen said, lying. And she went on elaborating on her lie. "I hired a private detective to break into your apartment and install two cameras in your bedroom."

"How did he know where my apartment is?"

"Don't be asinine and naive. that's his job to find out things like that. The cameras got you and one of your handsome lads in two angles having a gay old time."

"In the last week . . . I did take two boys to my place," Adrian admitted sadly.

"And I have it all in vivid color."

"Gwen, please, please, I'm begging you . . . destroy that film, not for my sake . . . for my parents' sake."

"I will."

"Gwen, you're a real pal. I'll never forget—"

"When you kill this person. It's as simple as that. Kill this creature, and I promise to burn the film."

"Gwen, have a heart," Adrian said.

"Adrian, what's it going to be? You do the job, or I show the video to your mother and father?"

"Okay, all right . . . I'll do it," Adrian said in a beaten voice.

"Now you're acting like a man."

"Um . . . how am I going to . . . end this person's life?"

"With a gun!?"

"A gun!"

"Yes, you know, those things that shoot lethal lead."

"But I've never had a gun in my hand in all my life!"

Neither had Gwen, but, she thought, finding a gun club would be easy enough. She would take a few lessons, fire off a few dozen shots, and then instruct Adrian on how to use the deadly weapon.

"Adrian, that's nothing to worry about. I've handled guns all my life, or since I was in my twenties. My father used to take me hunting, and for a long time I was a member of a gun club."

"Gwen, why do you want this woman dead?"

"Do you really want to know?"

"yes, I want to know why she needs killing."

"Because she is a vamp who has seduced your good friend and mine with her highly charged sexual charms."

"Gwen, are you talking about Edmund?"

"Yes, Edmund."

"But I thought he was a happily married man."

"Adrian, this woman—"

"Her name, Gwen, her name."

"Arlene Swinton."

"I know her! I mean not personally. But I have seen her picture in the papers, and always with a different man."

"With a different wealthy man. She goes out only with men who are loaded. Her boy is for hire to the highest bidder."

"She does have a notorious reputation."

"Lurid would be a better word."

"Edmund sure has kept this relationship with that woman a secret."

"Yes, he's been very discreet. Months ago he set her up in a condo, and he's always careful about when he goes to visit her. Sometimes he stays with her for days."

"How does he explain his absences to Edith?"

"Business trips."

"Yes, the last three or four months he has been going on more of them than usual. But how did Edith find out about Edmund and Arlene?"

"Some weeks ago he said he was going to divorce her and marry that dirty slut. To Edith it came like a bombshell. How that woman is suffering. Edmund doesn't love that tart. He's acting like a lovesick kid. Arlene is just a drug to him, that's all. All she's interested in is squeezing millions out of Edmund, having a baby by him, and then dumping him for a young stud. She told me she's fed up with having to sleep with older men."

"Gwen, you talked to her?"

"Yes, I went to her place, acting for Edith. We made her an offer she could refuse, said she wanted bigger bucks, and she was going to get them from Edmund."

"Gwen, that woman is evil! She is breaking up a Christian marriage! She must be stopped!"

"You said it, Adrian, with a good killing."

"And I'll do it, with pleasure. It's the Christian thing to do. That marriage-breaking slut deserves to die! She is a terrible sinner! Her death will be divine retribution for hr wicked life!"

"Once Arlene is dead, her sex spell over Edmund broken, I'm sure he will go back to Edith and be a loving, faithful husband once again!" Gwen said with a blissful smile.

"Gwen, when do you want me to send that wicked woman to hell?"

"Easy, Adrian. We have to plan this thing very carefully. I have to show you where Arlene lives, and when is the right time to bump her off. Of course you know her by sight."

"After all the times I've seen her in the papers—you bet I do."

7

Three weeks later the body of Arlene Swinton was fished out of the lake in Central Park South. She had four bullet holes in her, two in the chest and two in the head. The police were in a state of complete bafflement. There were no clues and no suspects. It was a murder that would never be solved. Only Arlene's maid was at her funeral.

Gwen proved to be right about Edmund's attachment to Arlene. He did grieve over her death, but his grief lasted only a few weeks. He really didn't love Arlene, he had only a lecherous passion for her shapely body. And once that was gone, Edmund lost all feeling for her. Sexual bewitchment is not love.

And so this story has a happy ending, as all stories should for the good people in it. Edmund, Edith and Gwen went back to their old arrangement, and Edmund never again mention that nasty, un-Catholic word divorce again.

And Adrian Grantwell, deeply devoted to his religion and active vestryman, went on enjoying his gay life without any fears or anxieties.

Caiaphas

1

Joseph Caiaphas, high priest, sat in his small office with his secretary and special assistant Phinehas. They were taking a reckoning of the funds deposited in the Temple by wealthy merchants, the debt-bonds, and the income from the animal sacrifices.

The great Jewish Temple was more than the place in which dwelled the God of Israel. It was also a national bank. The money deposited in the Temple did not lie idle. It was lent out at interest. This made Caiaphas more than only the high priest. He was also a banker. And he took his responsibilities seriously.

He was the religious leader of his nation and also the leader of the Sadduccean aristocracy that ruled in Jerusalem. It was from this class the Roman emperor chose the high priest.

And for the Romans, the first duty of the high priest was to maintain peace in the land. But peace, Caiaphas realized, was hard to maintain with those fanatical Zealots carrying out guerrilla warfare against the Romans. They hid out in desert places. They attacked small Roman units on the road, they burned villages that cooperated with the Romans, sometimes murdering prominent citizens that were thought to be too pro-Roman.

Those Zealots caused Caiaphas much mental anguish. Didn't they realized how hopeless their cause was? Did they think they were like the Maccabees, fighting that ragtag Syrian army? Rome was the mightiest empire in the world, and with an invincible army. Rebellions against Rome would bring bloody disaster to Israel. That powerful Roman army would fall on the Jews like a mountain. Other people had tried revolting against Rome. All those revolts had been crushed, as the Jews had revolted when Herod the Great Died. Thousands had been killed in the futile bid for freedom by the Jews, and two thousand had been crucified.

But still those mad Zealots thought they could defeat the Romans, and once again Israel would be a holy, sovereign nation, with only God as its ruler and the high priest as his vicegerent.

These were the sad thoughts that troubled Caiaphas many a night. He was a man only in his forties, but already his hair was all gray, and his face had a careworn look. He did look old beyond his years.

Phinehas had got on a different subject from the finances of the Temple. Caiaphas' mind had drifted off, worried, concerned about the Zealots.

"That's why I think we should keep a watchful eye on this new troublemaker," Phinehas was saying.

"What did you say . . . troublemaker?" Caiaphas said, his mind focusing on the present. "What troublemaker, Phinehas?"

The two men were sitting at a desk. Both were Sadducees. But they were different in physical appearance. Caiaphas was tall, slender, with refined features and an open and frank manner about him. Phinehas was short, wiry, with a gaunt face and eyes that always seemed to be darting about. He was not intelligent, but he was cunning, a scrupulous Jew but a pitiless foe.

"Now, leaning close to the high priest, Phinehas said, "This new one is from Galilee. He goes by the name of Jesus, or Joshua."

"So, what about this Galilean? And what do you mean by this one?"

"You know, another one of those wonder-working preachers."

"Yes, yes, we have had enough of them. They gather a few hundred supporters around them an foolishly claim to be the Messiah. And that's when the Romans step in, kill the lunatic leader and some of his followers, and that's the end of the movement."

"But this Jesus is different. He doesn't go around claiming to be the Messiah. He's too smart, too cautious for that. He knows that if he did publicly proclaim that he was the Messiah, the Romans would pounce on him like a cat on a mouse. But I still think he is a danger to us."

"Why do you think that, Phinehas? He seems harmless enough to me. A fake healer and a chatterbox. Where do you see the danger?"

"Your eminence, I first heard of this Jesus or Joshua, or whatever he calls himself about a month ago. He comes from a small village in Galilee, called Nazareth. He first came into public notice when he was baptized by that derange fellow, John called John the Baptist. Jesus was baptized by him, and then he started on his own, always going around announcing and repeating the same words."

"And what are these words?"

"Jesus always starts his preaching talks with the word 'The time is fulfilled, and the kingdom of God is at hand. Repent and believe in the gospel.'"

Caiaphas smiled broadly and said, "That's it, just those words? And you think that makes this Jesus a menace to the peace for our land and the mighty Roman empire?"

"But don't you see!" Phinehas said grimly, his eyes glittering. "Think of those words—'the kingdom of God is at hand.' They can only mean one thing."

"And what is that?"

"The overthrow of the Roman rule over Israel! This Jesus believes that by some miracle we can rid ourselves of the Romans and be once again a free nation!"

"And is that how you interpret the words of this Jesus?"

"I tell you he is preaching sedition! He must be stopped! Already he had scores of followers, men and women. They go up and down Palestine with Jesus. Sometimes he draws hundreds of people to him in the villages and towns. They leave him exclaiming that never was heard in Palestine such a preacher, showing so much wisdom, such knowledge of the scripture. Every day his popularity grows and grows!"

"Calm down, Phinehas, calm down. But tell me, how do you know so much about this Jesus?"

"Well, I had two of my agents keeping an eye on this mad John the Baptist. When Jesus started going around with this talk about the kingdom of God, I had my agents switch to Jesus. We have to watch him!"

"Phinehas, I think you are getting agitated over nothing. This Jesus fellow is nothing for you and me to worry about. Let him spout his foolish talk about the kingdom of God. I see nothing seditious about that."

"Eminence, I tell you he is our natural enemy, the enemy of our class! So far, he has been to Jerusalem only a few times, preaching in the Temple precincts, and making a few score converts to his way of thinking. Most of his strength is in Galilee. There his followers are rabble, low-class people, people of the land. Galilee is a tinderbox of rebellion! It was in that region that Judas of Galilee started his rebellion when the Roman emperor ordered the census to be taken of our land. His message was that Jews should not pay taxes to a heathen ruler."

"Yes, I know all that. But his revolt was crushed and he was crucified. And that was the end of him."

"But not the end of his movement!" Phinehas said. "His spirit lives on among the Zealots who resist the Romans whenever they can."

"I disagree with you, Phinehas. Those Zealots are not zealous for the law. They are nothing but brigands, bandits, fighting futilely against the Romans. Well, I think we have done enough work for the day, Phinehas. Time for em to go home and enjoy my supper and relax with my family. Mahala has been a goof wife to me. She sees to it that cook prepares for me a feast every night. And she has given me two fine children, a nice balance, a boy and a girl."

"Yes, Lemuel is a good lad, very studious, and very serious-minded. A true Sadducean Jew! But as for your daughter, Davina . . . ."

"Caiaphas frowned, peering at his secretary.

"Yes, Phinehas . . . you have something to say about Davina?"

"Eminence, I hesitate to give you cause for anxiety . . . with all the cares you have, administering the Temple . . . having to get along with that Jew-hating Pontius Pilate . . . ."

"Phinehas, what are you hinting at? You have something to say about Davina?"

"Yes, eminence."

"Well, say it, I'm waiting!"

"Do you know where Davina has been these last few weeks?"

"Of course I do! She's been visiting with my sister in Jericho. I got a message from her yesterday. Davina should be in my palace when I get home. And it will be so good to see that lovely loving daughter of mine!"

Phinehas stared at Caiaphas but said nothing.

"Why are you looking at me like that?" the high priest demanded.

"I hate to tell you this, but Davina did not spend those weeks with your sister Uria. She stayed only two days and then left . . . ."

"Left?" Caiaphas said, puzzled. "But where did Davina go?"

"She went to join Jesus. Davina was with Jesus as he journeyed up and down Palestine . . . in the villages, in the towns . . . for all of seventeen days."

"Phinehas . . . your . . . agents reported this to you?"

"Yes."

"Are you telling me that my daughter is . . . ."

"Yes, eminence, Davina is a disciple of this Jesus. My agents witnessed how raptly she listens to Jesus when he is speaking to the crowds of people. And how close she stay with him when they are on the road."

"Phinehas, are you sure of all this?"

"I am."

"And just what does Davina believe about this Jesus?"

"One of my agents asked her directly just that question."

"And what was her answer?"

"The same answer my agent got from all of Jesus' followers and disciples—that he is the Messiah, the liberator who will drive the Romans out of Israel."

"No, no!" Caiaphas cried in anguish. "My daughter, my Davina, could never believe in such madness! That is not the daughter I raised! You must be wrong, Phinehas, wrong!"

"My agents don't lie, eminence. And you know . . . children develop minds of their own as they grow up."

"Tell me this, has Jesus publicly announced that he is the Messiah?"

"Certainly not. He's too cagey, to cautious to make such a dangerous announcement in public. The Messiah is the anointed one, a king. But only the Roman emperor says who is a king in his empire. Oh, no, you don't get this Jesus sticking his neck out like that! If he did, it would be crucifixion for him. Those Romans don't fool around. Rebel against them, and it's the cross!"

"And my daughter . . . earnestly believes that this Jesus is the one the Jews has been waiting for to free us from the pagan Roman yoke, to cleanse our holy land of these heathen occupiers . . . ."

"Pure madness, eminence, a religious delusion! Do you know how these believers in the Messiah think he is going to drive out the mighty Roman legions?"

"Go on, tell me."

"Legions of angels will descend from heaven and to battle with the Roman emperor's soldiers! There you have the insane hope and dream of these Messiah crackpots!"

"And you say Davina . . . my daughter . . . thinks like that?" Caiaphas said, a downcast expression on his face.

"Yes, according to my agents."

"Uh . . . how long is this Jesus fellow been spouting this kingdom of God nonsense?"

"Not too long, I would say three or four months."

"And he has many people with him as he travels up and down Palestine?"

"Usually twenty, twenty-five men and women."

"Men and women?"

"Yes, even many women have fallen under his influence, mature women, some of them fairly well off. They help to support Jesus and his wandering band of loafers."

"I see," Caiaphas remarked thoughtfully. "Now I understand why Davina asked me for sixty pieces of silver when she went to visit my sister, Uria, in Jericho. That money went to Jesus."

"Eminence, I know it's not my place to meddle in family matters . . . but . . ."

"Yes, go on, Phinehas, what were you going to say?"

"I can speak frankly?"

"Tell me what's on your mind!"

"Sir, can't you see how much damage this can do to you? The daughter of the high priest . . . a member of Jesus' group. You should see how he disputes Torah law with the Pharisees—turning our religion upside down! But that is not bad enough. It's this Messiah business, people believing that this Jesus is the Messiah that will certainly upset and alarm Pontius Pilate. I think . . . ."

"Yes, go on, what do you think, Phinehas?"

"You should have a talk with Davina. Order her to stop going around with Jesus and all those men and women. She is . . . how old in Davina?"

"Seventeen, two years younger than Lemuel."

"Seventeen years old! An impressionable age! Full of enthusiasm, foolish enthusiasm!"

"Yes, I will have a talk with Davina," Caiaphas said sadly.

2

Caiaphas walked slowly to the high priest's residence in the Upper City, some distance from the Temple. He was a man troubled and worried. Phinehas was right . . . the daughter of the high priest consorting with this rabble-rousing Jesus. Yes, he would put an end to it! But Caiaphas knew how willful his daughter could be, how obstinate.

The solution came to him in a flash. Davina must marry! Yes, that would put an end to her foolish attachment to this Jesus. What Davina needed aw a husband!

"Yes, that's the answer!" the high priest shouted out loud.

Caiaphas, when he left the Temple, had two of the Temple police walking slightly behind him as bodyguards. In the last few months the Zealots were becoming bolder. No longer confining their activities in the country, they had now to come to Jerusalem. Already they had stabbed to death a wealthy merchant and a member of the Sanhedrin, the highest court and council of the nation. Anyone that they deemed was too pro-Roman was marked for death. They hid their daggers in their robes, striking swiftly and disappearing in the crowd. The member of the Sanhedrin had been killed in broad daylight, and the killer got away.

Of course the high priest hated these Zealots, these religious murders, as he called them. Yes, he was unhappy that the holy land of Israel, Yahweh's Chosen People, was ruled by these heathen Romans. But what could be done about it? Sadly, nothing. Rome had the power, and all the Jews had was faith in Yahweh's providence that in good time they would be freed of these Romans. It had happened in the past, didn't it? Caiaphas told himself. Pharaoh was all-powerful, and yet Yahweh had delivered the Jews from his tyranny.

All that was needed was patience and prayer, and one day the rule of the Roman emperor would come to an end, and Israel would once again be a free and sovereign nation. That was the way t the kingdom of God! the high priest believed fervently.

But those fanatical Zealots did not see things that way. They had to storm heaven with violence! They had to kill not only Romans but also Jews, and all in the name of religion!

Outside his door, Caiaphas nodded to the Temple police and entered the house. He was greeted by his chief steward, Ephrom.

"Master, I hope you had a pleasant day, "Ephrom said, smiling pleasantly.

"Is my daughter back?" Caiaphas asked, without returning the smile.

"She arrived this afternoon, sir. She is in the lounge room with your wife and your son."

Caiaphas went straight to that room.

Soon as he entered, Mahala said, "My husband, you are late! We have been waiting dinner for you."

Lamuel and Davina both went up to their father and greeted him politely. He started hard at Davina, leaving her wondering why.

Caiapahs got through the dinner as quickly as possible and then stood up and said, "Mahala, I want to talk to Lemuel and Davina alone for a little while. Excuse us. Into my study," he added to his two children.

In the study, which had scrolls of scriptures from floor to ceiling, Caiaphas sat down, motioned his son to sit down in a chair, and to Davina to stand in front of him.

"Father, what's wrong? They way you've been looking at me since you returned from the Temple . . . . Have I done anything to displease you?"

"Davina, how did you enjoy your visit to Aunt Uria?"

"I always enjoy myself when I visit Aunt Uria."

"You were supposed to be with her for a few weeks, weren't you?"

"Yes . . . I was . . . ."

"But were you? Answer me that?"

"I was with her for some time . . . ."

"For weeks?"

"No, not for weeks."

"Tell me where you went when you left Aunt Uria!"

"Father, I can tell you where she went," Lamuel said.

"I want to hear it from her! Speak, Davina, tell me!"

"All right," Davina declared proudly, defiantly, "I was with Jesus."

"A daughter of mine, a daughter of the high priest, consorting with these drifters from Galilee! Why, Davina? Why? What is it you see in this man, this Jesus?"

"I see love, I see compassion! And I see a great hope for our people, our land!'

"Daughter, what're you saying?"

"Some of us think he might be . . . the One!"

"Are you talking about the . . . Messiah?" Caiaphas whispered fearfully.

"Yes, yes!'

"Has Jesus ever announced openly, in public, that he is the Messiah?"

"No, Father, but some of us do believe and hope he is."

"A vain hope!" Lemuel laughed. "Jesus is just another Messiah pretender. We have so many of them. They appear and disappear. Or the Romans kill them, and good riddance! Why can't people learn to accept Roman rule? Rome is the great power today, and that power will last for a long time."

"Yes," Caiaphas sadly agreed, "you are right, Lemuel, Rome is the great power in the world. But we Jews should not cease to hope that one day we will be a free and sovereign nation. Anything wrong with that, Lemuel?"

"It is unrealistic, Father. Those Zealots in the desert are fighting a hopeless battle against the Romans. They only cause a lot of trouble for us. I'm glad when they are captured and he Romans crucify them! That is how they should be treated, like mad dogs!"

"Lemuel, I think you have been spending too much time with Phinehas That is exactly how he thinks."

"I believe he is right, Father."

""Right or wrong, I have in my own family a problem that must be dealt with. Davina, I forbid you to have anything to do with Jesus, is that clear?"

"Father, I wish you could meet Jesus. You would change your mind about him. His very touch cures the sick, his words drive the devil out of people. And you should hear his wonderful parables! I am sure if you met Jesus, you would change your mind about him."

"Davina, I have the solution to your problem! Caiaphas said.

"What problem?"

"You need a husband! It's about time you got married! Lemuel is getting married in three months. Once you get married and start having babies, you will forget all these silly notions you have about Jesus."

"Father, my friend Baruch has said to me a number of times how he would like to have Davina for a wife," Lemuel said

"Yes, yes, he would make a good husband!" Caiaphas exclaimed. "He comes from a wealthy Sadducean family. They have much property in Jerusalem, and they had acres and acres of vineyards and fruit orchards. Lemuel, invite Baruch over for dinner tomorrow night."

"You think you two can settle my future for me, don't you! Davina cried furiously. "Well, I have something to say about it!"

"Davina, go to your room! Tomorrow you will meet the young man who will be your husband.

But the next morning it as discovered that Davina had left home. Some of her clothes were missing. The short not she left said only that she was a joining Jesus.

3

A week later, Caiaphas was standing on the balcony outside his office in the Temple. Looking down he saw hundreds of Jewish pilgrims making their way into the Temple, first to see the money-changers and then to buy an animal to sacrifice.

He was worried and distressed. In a few days Passover would begin. At such times religious feelings ran high, and as a precaution Pilate, the procurator, came up from his headquarters in Caesarea with a large contingent of soldiers.

That was what worried the high priest—that some hotheads would start trouble, and Pilate would have to intervene with his troops. And people would die needlessly. And there would be crucifixions—there were always crucifixions with these brutal Romans.

Looking over his shoulder, Caiaphas saw at a corner of the Temple court the Antonia Tower, built by Herod the Great to honor his patron, Mark Anthony. It was the garrison fortress of the Roman cohort, numbering some six hundred men. Even now he could see some of the soldiers looking down at the Temple courts.

Caiaphas worried that the peace would not be broken, that there would not be any unruly elements among the Jewish pilgrims who came to visit the sacred Temple from all over the Roman world this holy week of Passover.

And what caused the high priest's distress? He had not heard from Davina since she had left home. The last he heard, Jesus and his band of followers were in Bethany, a village two miles from Jerusalem. How was Davina? Caiaphas wondered anxiously. What was to become of her? And what were the aims and objectives of this Jesus? How much longer could he go on announcing that the time is fulfilled and that the kingdom of God is at hand? And just what was this kingdom of God Jesus kept babbling about? It was all so baffling and frustrating for the high priest.

Caiaphas dearly loved his daughter. He missed her. Yes, he loved his son too, Lemuel. But he was so self-confident, so sure of himself, so strong-willed. Davina was . . . softhearted, loving, vulnerable. She need him, yes, and he need her! If only she could get this Jesus out of her mind!

It was his fault that she ran away. He should not have talked about her getting married. That was very wrong of him. A father should not force his daughter into a marriage.

Phinehas came out on the balcony. He gazed across the vast Court of the Gentiles and smiled. Teeming crows were pouring through the double gates by the Royal Porch.

"Business will be brisk today!" he said, rubbing his hands together. "And in a few days, when Passover week starts, the Jewish pilgrims will be arriving by the thousands from all over the Roman Empire!"

"Yes," said Caiaphas, "and most of them will be sleeping in the fields. The few inns we have in Jerusalem have already been reserved by the wealthy visitors."

"Do you think we'll have any trouble with those Zealots?"

"I hope not, but you can never tell with those fanatics. But if there is, Pilate will know how to deal with them."

"When is the procurator arriving?"

"He sent me a message that he would be here in a few days."

"Ah . . . eminence, I heard about your daughter . . . Davina. Have you had any word from her since she left home?"

"No, all I know is that she went to join Jesus."

"The giddy fool! Davina will find out soon enough that Jesus is only another false Messiah!"

4

At that moment, Jesus and his followers were sitting on benches outside the home of Mary, Martha and their brother Lazarus, very dear friends of Jesus. Occasionally, Jesus enjoyed visiting with them, to relax after hectic days of preaching and miracle-working. And he did love the meals the sisters provided! And so did his disciples.

As Davina, Martha and Mary were in the kitchen preparing the evening meal (Lazarus was away) Jesus and his men were planning a really big event—Jesus' triumphal entry into Jerusalem the following day.

"Peter, do you think the authorities will try to stop it?" Jesus asked apprehensively. "Maybe arrest me?"

"They wouldn't dare!" Peter laughed.

"Jesus, you'll have mobs of people cheering you, wildly welcoming you!" James added."

"If they were foolish and stupid enough to try to arrest you, Jesus, there would be a riot!" John said.

"How are we going to do it" Jesus asked.

"You will ride into Jerusalem on a donkey," Peter said.

"All very symbolic," James said.

"And and in our holy scripture!" John said.

"The king comes riding into the holy city on an ass!" Jesus shouted happily.

And all the discipline shouted merrily back at him.

All except one—Judas Iscariot. He was not happy. In fact, he was very unhappy. In the last few weeks he had developed a fierce spite, a ferocious grudge against Jesus. He had been shut out of the inner circle around Jesus. Only Peter, and the brothers James and John were so favored. What had really galled Judas was the spectacular event he had not been allowed to witness. It had occurred two weeks back. Jesus led Peter, James and John up to a high mountain. Jesus' whole body shone with a blazing light, and he was seen talking with Moses and Elias.

And when they came down from the mountain, how the disciples raved at what they had seen! Jesus shining with a heavenly light, and Jesus conferring with those great prophets—Moses and Elias!

And he, Judas, had not been privileged to see it! Why not? Wasn't he just as good as those other three disciples? It was not fair! It was mean of Jesus not to take him into his inner circle!

As they were walking away from the mountain, Judas voiced his grievance to Jesus. He was hoping Jesus would show some sympathy.

"Judas, what're you complaining about? Don't I let you carry the bag with all the silver in t?"

"I know that, I know that. But sometimes you talk only with those three, shutting the rest of us out. And I don't like it!"

"Well, damnit, that's the way things are! You are much younger than those three. They have more maturity. See what I mean?"

No, I don't see what you mean! And I repeat, I don't like the way things are!"

"You don't?"

"That's what I said."

"So you know what you can do, Judas!"

"What?"

"You can leave—get of my life!"

But Judas was not ready for that. He could not quit Jesus. He believed too strongly that he as the Messiah and that with his wonderful powers he would drive the hated Romans out of Palestine.

The next day, Jesus' entry into Jerusalem was a great success. But Judas has one more complaint against Jesus. He was not allowed to hold the reigns of the donkey as Jesus rode into Jerusalem. Peter enjoyed that honor! Judas thought bitterly

But after Jesus got off the donkey and went into the Temple courts to preach, he got a surprise. A servant from Caiaphas came up to him, identified himself as the high priest's servant and said, "You are Jesus of Nazareth?"

Jesus was puzzled by the question. "Why do you ask me that? You know who I am?"

"Sorry, a mere formality. Is the answer to my question 'yes'?"

"I am Jesus of Nazareth."

"Joseph Caiaphas, the high priest, wishes to speak with you in private."

Peter had come up to Jesus and the servant. He heard the last words. "Jesus, don't go, don't go! It could be a trap!"

"You think so?" Jesus said.

"The high priest wants to get you alone! He's afraid to arrest you in public! The mob would go wild! He'd have a riot on his hands! I say don't go!"

"My master assures you save conduct," the servant said.

"Take me to your master," Jesus said.

Five minutes later, Jesus walked into the high priest's office. He had expected Caiaphas to be angry over the enthusiastic welcome Jesus had received from the multitude when he rode into Jerusalem on the donkey.

Instead, he saw the high priest pouring wine out of a flagon into two silver cups. Holding out one of the cups Caiaphas said, smiling and affable, "Would you join me?"

Jesus was surprised and puzzled. His first thought as to refuse the offer. But no, that would be rude, Jesus reflected.

"Thank you," he said, taking the cup.

"To what should we drink?" Caiaphas said.

"To the freedom of our people from heathen rule!"

"Isn't that too remote a toast, Jesus?"

"With Yahweh all things are possible!"

"You have great faith, Jesus. But as the high priest . . . I have to deal with the Romans. I have to balance my religious faith with a certain worldly temper. You understand what I mean?"

"I think I do. What do you say we drink to our people's happiness?"

"Yes!" the high priest said. "To the people's happiness!"

And they each emptied the wine cup in two gulps.

Putting down his cup on a bureau, Jesus said, "Why have you invited me here?"

"To warn you."

"To warn me?"

"And to make you an offer."

"What is this about a warning?"

"Jesus, today you involved yourself in a seditious demonstration. All those hosannas and mention of father David the people shouted at you—that was a Messianic demonstration! Are you claiming to be the Messiah?"

"No one has ever heard me speak those words."

"But why did you remain silent when the crowds practically called you the Messiah?"

"Can I help what they say?"

"You should have denounced, repudiated the things they said about you."

"What's the harm?"

"A great deal of harm to you, if Pilate had agents knowledgeable about Jewish beliefs. They will report you to him!"

"You spoke of an offer," Jesus said.

"Yes, I do have an offer to make to you."

"What is it?"

Caiapahs went over to the bureau, opened it and took out a large leather pouch. He brought it over to Jesus.

"This pouch contains one thousand pieces of silver. It is all yours if you will stop this aimless wondering up and down our land and proclaiming this nonsense about the coming of the kingdom of God! It is all unrealistic, claptrap rubbish! The emperor's legions will see to it that this mad, visionary dream of yours will never happen!"

"Is that what you think?" Jesus asked scornfully.

"Yes, because I have my two feet planted firmly on the ground!"

"And you think my head is high up in the clouds, eh?"

"Yes. But it isn't only because I think your message is all foolishness that I offer you this money. Don't turn it down. Go back to Nazareth, forget this crazy dram of yours! With the money I give you, you can buy a farm, get married, live a quiet, normal life. What do you say?"

Smiling, Jesus said, "First of all I am not a farmer, I am a carpenter."

"Very well, Jesus, move to Jerusalem. I'll see that you get plenty of work. In a year or two, you'll have a dozen men working for you."

"And I do not intend to marry. I must go on with my ministry. But I sense some personal reason for your wanting me to stop with my holy work. What is it?"

"I have a daughter."

"So you have a daughter."

"Her name is Davina."

"Oh." Jesus said, and stared at the high priest.

"She is one of your disciples, isn't she?"

"You could say that. Davina is very devoted to me. And she has been very . . . helpful."

"Financially helpful. Isn't that so?"

"Yes, I do accept financial support wherever can get it. After all, we have to eat and sleep somewhere . . . ."

"Dreams have to be paid for, don't they, Jesus?"

"Some o my women followers have been very generous."

"Jesus, won't you seriously consider my offer? I'm sure if you give up this insane dream of the kingdom of God, Davina will come to her senses, come back to me and . . . ."

"And what?" Jesus pointedly asked.

"What else? Get married, have children, as you should me doing!"

"The high priest has done me the honor of inviting me to speak with him privately. I do very much appreciate the honor. I think I do owe you something."

"Jesus, what're you saying."

"You love your daughter, don't you?"

"I have also a son. Yes, I . . . love Lemuel, but . . . . Davina . . . . she is my favorite chilled! I want nothing but happiness for her! She is throwing her life away on your—your—"

"Mad dream?" Jesus said, smiling.

"Mad and dangerous! Those Romans can be ruthless! They have already crucified thousands of us Jews! Watch out, Jesus, you don't end up the same way!"

"Don't worry, I'll be careful."

"Jesus, I know we seem to be on opposite sides. But in spirit we really aren't. sure, I'd like to see our people free of this heathen Roman rule. But I have to be realistic, fully appreciating the brute fact of Rome's power. As the leader of the nation here in Jerusalem, I have a responsibility and a duty to maintain the peace."

"At the cost of our religions humiliation," Jesus cries in an outraged voice. "Romans should not be lording it in Yahweh's holy land!"

"And how do you propose to rid our holy land of these pagans, Jesus?" Revolt? That would be a bloody disaster for us. Thousands of Jews would be killed, and in the end, the Roman emperor would still be our master. No, Jesus, all we can do is hope and pray that in God's good time Israel will once again be free."

"Yes," Jesus said sadly, "I'm afraid I have to agree with you, but I still think that if we make a fight of it, Yahweh will not abandon his people."

"By sending down legions of angels?" Caiaphas smiled.

"If you have the faith, it could happen!"

"If that's the way you think.:

"That is the way I think! Faith can move mountains!"

"And about my offer, Jesus?"

"I must refuse it. I have to do what I was born to do. But I do appreciate your concern for me. I . . . I'll talk to your daughter . . . Davina . . . see what I can do to persuade her to come back to you."

"Thank you, Jesus. I do miss her so much."

"Goodby, and thanks for the wine."

5

Soon as Jesus got back from Bethany, Peter, James and John crowded around him. They seemed very excited about something.

"Jesus, where have you been?" Peter asked

"I've been having a private chat with the high priest."

"Caiaphas!" all three men cried out together, with incredulous looks on their faces.

What were you doing meeting with him?" John demanded.

"Did he send for you?" James said.

"And . . . what happened?" Peter asked.

"Nothing happened. Caiaphas just wanted to give ma friendly word of warning. But what are you three so excited about?"

"Jesus, an hour ago a man by the name of Ezra came here, asking for you. He's a rough-looking character, a Zealot." James said.

"How do you know he's a Zealot?" Jesus asked.

"He says he's from Barabbas." John said.

"Barabbas, the powerful Zealot leader," Jesus said in amazement.

"Jesus, the Ezra told us that Barabbas wants to meet with you. Ezra is still waiting to take us to their desert hideout. What do you say?" Peter said.

"Now why would this Zealot leader want to meet with me? Jesus wondered. "We've all heard of his daring exploits, his hit-and-run tactics against small Roman units. What do you think, Peter?"

"I say let's see what he's got to say."

"Call this Ezra."

For almost four hours Ezra led Jesus and his three disciples across the desert. Once, when they climbed up and down a high hill, they caught a glimpse of the water of the Dead Sea shining in the moonlight.

Finally, they came to a group of large boulders. One of them had an opening. They walked down a crooked passageway until they saw the glowing light of a fire.

In a few minutes they entered a large spacious areas. A dozen men were seated around a smoking log fire. On the rock walls hanging from wooden pegs were swords, spears and metal shields. The men were passing around a jug of wine.

Ezra went over to one of the men and whispered in his ear. The man nodded, got up and walked over to the visitors. He was a tall, burly man, with broad shoulders, a scraggly beard and piercing dark eyes. He had an animal skin around his waist.

"Which one of you is Jesus?" he asked in a strong, commanding voice.

Stepping forward Jesus said, "I am Jesus."

"And I am Barabbas," the tall man smiled, showing gleaming white teeth. "Welcome, Jesus, you and your companions. You have walked for many miles. Come and sit down by the fire. You must be thirsty. Jabez, the wine jug! I hope you people are not too dainty to drink out of the jug!"

After Jesus and his disciples sat down and took a long swig of the wine, they sat looking across at these Zealots, these men of violent action who risked their lives in Israel's cause against the hated Roman oppressors and occupiers.

Jesus as seated next to Barabbas. He turned to him and said, "Barabbas, you have sent for me. Here I am. What do you have to say to me?"

"We must join forces, Jesus!"

"You want me and my disciples to go on raids with you against the Romans?" Jesus asked, aghast.

"Nothing so small as that!" Barabbas laughed, throwing back his head. "I have something much bigger in mind!"

"Bigger?" Peter asked curiously, frowning.

"What're you getting at?" James said.

"You have a plan, Barabbas?" Jesus said.

"Do I have a plan! I've been discussing it with my men for days! Jesus, do you know what you and I are going to do?"

"Tell me what you and I are going to do," Jesus said in an uneasy tone of voice.

"We are going to take over Jerusalem!"

Jesus, peter, John and James uttered one word together, and very loudly—"Madness!"

"No, no, it is not so mad as you think. "I have for hundred men under my command. Jesus, I was in Jerusalem when you rode into our holy city. It was a triumph for you! Hundreds of people greeting you as if you were the Messiah himself! With my men, and all the supporters you have, Jesus, we can easily take and hold Jerusalem, I tell you!"

"You really think it will be that easy for us to get control of Jerusalem?" Jesus asked skeptically.

"Yes, I do," Barabbas said confidently. "With my brave men and the Jerusalem mob with you, we can do it. You will take over the Temple. Your task will be to destroy the debtors bonds. Too long those rich Sadducean aristocratic moneylenders have exploited the poor! The day of reckoning for them is coming! Out with the pagan Romans. Out with the rich! The people of the land will be masters in the kingdom of God!"

With these rousing words, all the Zealots stood up and shouted as one man—"Amen, amen!"

"Jesus, you take over the Temple, and I and my men will take over the whole town! What a great victory for Yahweh! What a great victory for the Chosen People over those dogs, the Romans! Noah, hand me that wine jug!"

"Ah . . . Barabbas, I hate to put a damper on your premature victory celebration . . . but isn't there something you have forgotten?"

After taking a long drink from the wine jug and wiping his mouth, Barabbas asked, "What have I forgotten?"

"The cohort of Roman soldiers garrisoned in the Antonia tower—six hundred fighting men."

Barabbas laughed and said, "They will not be fighting men! Those soldiers will be sleeping men! This morning, my people will be delivering their ration of wine—all drugged!"

"I am impressed, Barabbas," Jesus said. "You have planned well. But do you really think we can take over Jerusalem?"

"I do, yes I do! We will strike three hours after sunrise!"

"When the moneychangers and the merchants selling the sacrificial animals are doing a thriving business, eh, Barabbas?" Jesus said.

"Exactly. Now let's get some sleep. We have a big day ahead of us!"

6

The attack on the Temple led by Jesus and the mob of supporters was spectacularly successful. The dozen Temple police were overwhelmed, simply brushed aside by the mob. The tables of the moneychangers were overturned, and there was a mad scramble for coins. The crates of the pigeons were broken open, the birds flying away. The oxen and sheep were turned loose and driven out to the courtyards. Animal feces covered the ground. The stench was overpowering. People were slipping and sliding all over this stinking filth. The moneychangers and the animal merchants were crying in despair. But not Jesus and his small army of followers. They were cheering and shouting their heads off. For them it was complete joyful pandemonium.

"Jesus," Peter reminded Jesus. "we have to destroy the bonds!"

"We have to find out where they are kept!" Jesus said.

And while Jesus was enjoying this great success, Barabbas and his hundreds of Zealots had taken over the holy city. There was only a feeble opposition to them. About fifty of the soldiers in the Antonia Tower (they probably had not drunk the drugged wine) came out to fight the Zealots. They were slaughtered to a man.

High up from a window in his palace, Caiaphas could see what was going on in the Temple, the frenzied activity, oxen and sheep wandering all over the Temple courtyards and making a mess with their droppings. Caiaphas could clearly see Jesus in command of the violent mob.

"Jesus has lost his head!" he cried in despair. "He is asking for trouble! And I can see all over Jerusalem armed men! They have to be Zealots! What's the matter with the soldiers in the Antonia Tower? Why haven't they come out to fight these rebels?"

Yes, the attack launched by Jesus and Barabbas enjoyed initial success. But it was short-lived. One Roman soldier made its defeat inevitable.

In the Antonia Tower was a small stable that held five horses. Seeing how hopeless things were with the Temple and the town in the hands of the rebels, this one soldier knew he had to get to Caesarea and inform Pilate, the procurator, of the dire situation in Jerusalem.

And so mounting a horse he was able to sneak out of the Temple gate that faced the Mount of Olives. Jesus' people were too busy looting and pillaging to notice him.

Once out of Jerusalem, the soldier headed south to Caesarea, riding hell for leather!

He did not have far to go.

For at that moment Pontius Pilate was three miles from the holy city. The procurator was riding at the head of four cohorts of infantry and three squadrons of cavalry, totaling in all almost three thousand men. Pilate always came to Jerusalem during Passover week. The powerful Roman force was a warning to any Jews who had any foolish thoughts of staring trouble this holy week.

As he rode, gazing straight ahead at the dusty road, Pilate was ruminating and reflecting bitterly since the time the Emperor Tiberius had sent him out here as the procurator over Judea.

Pilate hated the scorching heat, and in time, he came to detest the people. At first, he was intrigued by their strange religious beliefs. Later, he was repelled by them.

These Jews seemed to think they deserved special consideration! All over the Roman Empire in the cities and towns there were statues of the emperor. The Jews did not allow statues in their land! On the soldiers' standards there were images of the emperor. The Jews would not tolerate the standards to be brought into what they called their holy city, Jerusalem! Pilate was informed that the Jews would not tolerate any graven images. It was against their religion.

For months Pilate brooded over what he considered an affront and an insult to the emperor and to the majesty of Rome. He kept telling himself that he would not put up with the Jews' religious prejudices, convictions! No, he would not! Did they think they were better than all the other millions of subjects under Roman rules?

One day an idea came to Pilate. He would get the better of those Jews! He would show them who was master! They had to conform like everyone else! They had to show their loyalty to Rome and the emperor!

Pilate's plan was very simple. He would march his soldiers into Jerusalem at night, and have them set up their standards in a number of main points of the town. Once the Jews saw the standards, they would have to accept the fait accompli! Pilate assured himself.

In the morning, Pilate returned to his headquarters in Caesarea, smugly proud at the way he thought he had outsmarted the Jews.

But that afternoon the procurator was astounded to see thousands of Jews besieging his palace, men, women and even children! Pilate could not understand their highly emotional behavior, crying, mourning, bewailing.

"He sent an officer to find out why the Jews were causing all this ruckus. When the officer returned Pilate asked gruffly, "Well, why this uproar?"

"Sir . . . it's those military standards you had set up in Jerusalem . . . ."

"Yes, what about them?"

"Sir . . . the Jews are demanding that you remove those standards from their holy city. They say those standards offend their religious beliefs. And that is why they demand—"

"They demand, they demand! Images of our Emperor offend them! I'll show them! I'll show them who is master here!"

And going out to a balcony with the officer following him, he glared down at the hundreds of bewailing Jews twenty feet below.

"Stop this unruly behavior, I say!" he yelled down at them. "You are not going to have your way! Those standards will remain where they are! Now I order you to disperse and return to Jerusalem at once, do you hear, at once!"

The Jews cried up to Pilate that they were loyal to the emperor. But they would not tolerate those blasphemous standards to remain in their holy city.

Turning to the officer Pilate barked, "I want five hundred soldiers to surround those beggarly creatures down there, and with draw swords! If those Jews don't disperse, there will be a general massacre! I'll slaughter them all!"

Five minutes later, when Pilate's order was carried out, with the soldiers holding their swords over the Jews, the procurator was very well satisfied. He smiled grimly down at the mob, supremely confident that he would have his way with these Jews.

"Listen to me, all of you, I give you fair warning, if you are not out of here in one minute, I will order my men to slaughter all of you!"

Baring their necks, the Jews shouted up at Pilate, "Kill us, kill us all! But we will not back down! Remove those blasphemous standards!"

Pilate was stunned, shocked. These Jews were mad! Sick religious fanatics! Stubborn and incomprehensible! Pilate turned to the officer standing at his side. He was looking straight ahead, his face expressionless.

Beads of sweat broke out on the procurator's brow. His eyes opened wide as he stared down at the Jews. When he realized that he could not give the order to carry out his threat, a great wave of ferocious anger came over him. They had beaten him! These Jews were going to compel him, him, the procurator to give in to them!

"Order your men to put up their swords and return to their barracks," Pilate said to the officer in a low voice.

"And about the standards, sir?"

"Tell the Jews I will send orders to Jerusalem for them to be taken down today," Pilate said, walking back inside the palace, filled with a seething hatred of the Jews.

All day he brooded bitterly over his defeat. Those Jews had forced a Roman magistrate to do their will! How that galled the pride and arrogance of this Roman! But I will get my revenge! The procurator promised himself. He would kill Jews wherever and whenever he could!

In the next few weeks and months Pilate ordered sorties of infantry and cavalry to attack the Zealots in their desert strongholds. Most of the times these sorties ended in failure. But once Pilate's men were able to capture eight Zealots. He had them brought in chains to Caesarea and had them crucified in front of his palace. What sweet pleasure it gave Pilate to watch the bloody spectacle. From a window of the palace, while sipping wine, he enjoyed the sight of the Zealots dying their slow agonizing death on the cross.

And one more time Pilate was able to inflict death on Jews.

This time it happened in Jerusalem. Some Galileans were causing a disturbance in Jerusalem. Pilate did not care what it was about. Some more of their crazy religious nonsense, no doubt, he told himself. No matter. He had them killed in the Temple itself while they were at their devotions, mingling their blood of the Galileans with their sacrifices. That was the only way to treat the Jews! Kill them! They were not normal humans beings, with their strange, morbid beliefs!

7

Such was the man Pontius Pilate, who rode at the head of his troops up to Jerusalem for Passover week. He was a man with an obsessive hatred of the Jews. All the Jews he had killed so far had not assuaged his wounded Roman pride when he had to bow down to the will of the Jews over the standards.

As he rode, Pilate half-wished that the Jews would start some kind of trouble in Jerusalem this Passover weeks. Religious feelings among the Jews ran high at that time. Good, Pilate hoped! Let them start some trouble! It would give him an opportunity to kill more Jews!

Just them the soldier who was able to escape on horseback from Jerusalem came in sight of Pilate. He motioned to an officer riding behind him.

"Fabius, what do you make of this horseman riding toward us? Is he a Jew, or one of ours?"

Peering up the dusty road Fabius said, "He's a Roman soldier, sir, and riding as if all the hounds of hell were after him!"

In a minute the rider came up to Pilate, saluted and told what was going on in Jerusalem. "It's a bloody insurrection, sir! The Zealots have taken over the town and the Temple!"

"Fabius, bring up the cavalry, and order the infantry to double-march!" Pilate commanded.

Within not too many minutes Pilate's cavalry squadrons came galloping into Jerusalem, followed not far behind by the foot soldiers. The Zealots, surprised by this unexpected appearance of this powerful Roman force, were easily routed. Many of them were killed, but most of them made good their escape, including Barabbas. Pilate ordered the wounded Zealots killed. Only two were captured alive; their names were Hezekiah and Eleazar.

Jesus, seeing from a tall Temple building the complete defeat of the Zealots, gave warning to his supporters. They all fled through the Temple gate facing the Mount of Olives, Jesus and his disciples leading the panic-stricken mob up the hill and to safety.

Meanwhile, Pilate, gazing around him at all the dead Zealots lying around him asked Fabius angrily, "Where the hell were the men in the Antonia Tower? Why didn't they come out and suppress this insurrection?"

"Sir, I just came from there, and I can tell you why those soldiers didn't come out and fight the Zealots."

"And why didn't they, these brave soldiers?"

"Their wine had been drugged."

"Those Zealots, they are clever! But their scheme didn't work, thanks to me, me!"

"Sir, I found that that agitator, Jesus, lead a mob into the Temple, took it over and stopped all business. There was much looting and pillage. The moneychangers and the sellers of the sacrificial animals lost a fortune today!"

"A mob was able to take over the Temple, you say? And what was Caiaphas, the high priest, doing while his Temple was taken over by this mob?"

"I can't answer that, sir.

"Tell Caiaphas I want to see him in my residence in five minutes. No, make it a half hour. I want to bathe first, wash away all this goddamn grime and dirt!"

Bathed and with a fresh robe, Pilate sat at a desk sipping wine when Caiaphas walked into the room. The procurator did not stand up, nor did he offer the high priest wine. He was still in a foul temper.

"Well, high priest, what have you to say for yourself?"

"I . . . don't understand you."

"Don't understand me! Rioting, pillaging, looting your Temple, an insurrection in the town—and you say you don't understand!"

"But what could I do . . . there were hundreds of them. They easily brushed aside my Temple police. There are only a dozen of them on duty at one time. I couldn't help what happened."

"I was informed that the leader of that mob was a man by the name of Jesus. Do you know him?"

"Yes, I know . . . of him."

"Joseph Caiaphas, I want this Jesus arrested and brought before me to stand trial. He will be charged with sedition! He is a rebel against Rome!"

"Arresting him won't be so easy."

"Why?"

"Well, I don't know where he is. After today's action, I am sure he is in hiding."

"Find out where he is! Man, don't you use spies?"

"I never thought of spies."

"Fool! Get out! And find this Jesus, if you want to go on being the high priest and raking in all that silver the Temple business generates!"

Worried and anxious, all Caiaphas could think of doing was to call a council of the senior priests and a few members of the Sanhedrin. The high priest informed them that he had been ordered by Pilate to have Jesus arrested.

"That is not so easily done," one of the priests observed.

"Jesus certainly cannot be taken in the daytime, that's for sure," one of the members of the Sanhedrin said. "He is too popular here in Jerusalem, has too many followers. There would be a bloody riot."

"Pilate wants to try him on a capital offense—sedition. And knowing Pilate's hatred of us Jews, we can expect only one verdict," Caiaphas said sadly.

"Well, if we don't hand over Jesus to Pilate, we could lose our positions!" an elderly priest said. "If one man has to die to satisfy Pilate—so be it! Jesus must die."

Regretfully and reluctantly, Caiaphas agreed.

"But how do we find Jesus to arrest him?" he asked pointedly. He has to be arrested at night. But where does Jesus go at night?" Does anyone know?"

All the others shook their heads. The men sat looking across at each other, perplexed and stymied.

Just then a servant walked into the chamber and went over to the high priest. He stood at his side without speaking.

"Yes, Lamech, what is it? Can't you see we are having a very important meeting?"

"Excellency . . . there is a man outside wishes to speak with you."

"I can't see him now!"

"He says it is a matter of great urgency . . . concerning Jesus."

"Jesus!" the high priest exclaimed. "What is this man's name?"

"Judas Iscariot. He claims to be a disciple of Jesus and wishes to impart certain secret information concerning Jesus."

Glancing around the conference table Caiaphas declared, "I think we should see this Judas Iscariot. Lemech, show him in!"

A moment later, in walked Judas. He was Jesus' youngest disciple, a tall slender man with a soft, sensitive face and gleaming, piercing eyes that darted nervously around the chamber.

"Well, why have you come here?" Caiaphas demanded.

"I'm sure that after all the trouble Jesus caused in the Temple today, you want to get your hands on him, arrest him."

"Trouble!" a member of the Sanhedrin shouted angrily. "I have a business as a moneychanger! Those criminal ruffians, those looters, cost me three hundred pieces of silver! The way they were diving for coins when your Jesus overturned my tables! You damn right, he should be arrested!"

"And I lost over a hundred pigeons when that violent mob broke open the crates!" a second member of the Sanhedrin complained furiously.

"Speak, Judas, you have something to say?" Caiaphas said.

"I know you dare not attempt to arrest Jesus by day. But I can show you how you can arrest him by night."

"Explain yourself," Caiaphas said.

"I can show you where Jesus and his disciples bed down for the night."

"Where is that?"

"On the Mount of Olives. I will lead your men to the exact spot. It's near the tallest olive tree on that hill."

"And how much do you, Judas, want for this treachery, for betraying your master?" Caiaphas asked with a scornful smile. "Name your price."

"I don't want any of your filthy money!" Judas yelled angrily, outraged. "Keep your dirty money!"

"But . . . why are you, a disciple of Jesus . . . doing this?"

"I have my reasons. I'll be back here later tonight. Have your men ready. And make it a big, armed party!"

"Everything will be in readiness when you return," Caiaphas said. "And my advice to you, Judas, is that you flee Jerusalem after you have done your dirty work!"

"Flee?" Judas laughed bitterly. "After tonight . . . I will have nothing to . . . live for . . . ."

8

Meanwhile, Jesus and his disciples had made it back to Bethany. They were sitting on benches outside the house of their good friends the sisters Mary and Martha and their brother Lazarus.

The men were all feeling embarrassed and humiliated. They were all thinking the same thing. That enterprise in collaboration with Barabbas and his Zealots had resulted in total defeat! They had not counted on Pilate showing up with all those troops.

"What a fiasco!" the whole thing turned out to be!" Jesus could not help laughing. "The bold Barabbas and his brave Zealots driven out of Jerusalem!"

"And we in the Temple scattering like frightened children!" roared Peter. "We couldn't scramble up to the Mount of Olives fast enough!"

"It wasn't so funny, you two," Andrew, Peter's brother said. and added somberly, "Scores of those Zealots lost their lives today. Those Romans aren't soldiers, they're butchers! The Zealots who couldn't manage to escape, they slaughtered!"

"You're right, Andrew," Jesus agreed. "It was a bloody bad business. Too bad about those Zealots . . . martyrs for Israel. They died in a noble cause . . . ."

"What next, Jesus?" Peter asked.

"We are going back to Jerusalem."

All the disciples protested vigorously and loudly against such a move. It would be madness to return to Jerusalem after the events of the day.

"Jesus, after what we did in the Temple today, it would be dangerous for us to return to Jerusalem. The authorities will be looking out for us."

"I am determined to celebrate the Passover meal in the holy city!" Jesus said decisively."

"All of us?" Andrew said.

"Of course all of us! Peter, you already reserved that upper room for us two days ago, didn't you?"

"Yes, everything, the roast lamb, side dishes and I ordered four wineskins of the very best Galilean wine—good and strong!"

"So you see, we have to go back to Jerusalem—a little after sundown."

"But the danger!" Peter insisted.

"There will be no danger. We'll sneak into Jerusalem two or three at a time. Just make sure you keep your faces hidden."

"All right, Jesus, if that's the way you want it," Andrew said.

"That's the way I want it."

"But, Jesus, when we're done eating, we positively can't remain in the town. That really would be too risky."

"We couldn't stay in Jerusalem anyway, even if there wasn't any risk to us. With all these people here for the Passover from all over, the inns are packed. They'll be hundreds of families sleeping in the fields outside of Jerusalem."

"And what about us?" Peter asked.

"We'll bed down up on the Mount of Olives," Jesus said. And then he asked curiously, "Say, where is Judas? Where did he disappear to. Does anybody know?"

"Here he is now, coming up the road from Jerusalem," Peter said.

A few moments later, as Judas approached them, Jesus asked testily, "Judas, where have you been?"

"I . . . was in Jerusalem."

"In Jerusalem!" Jesus cried, flabbergasted. "What were you doing? Why didn't you run off like the rest of us? You could have been recognized as one of my disciples and been arrested, you fool!"

"Calm down, Jesus, calm down," Judas said. "There's nothing to get excited about. I was careful. I kept most of my face covered."

"But what were you doing?"

Judas had his lie ready.

"I . . . thought I'd do a little reconnoitering, see what was going on in town after all of you fled."

"And what did you see?"

"Pilate's soldiers patrolling everywhere. And sorry to say, a lot of dead Zealots. God, those Romans are pitiless! I saw them finishing off those Zealots that were wounded."

"You hear that?" Peter asked Jesus. "Maybe you want to call off our supper in town tonight?"

"I do not!" Jesus said. "We are having our Passover meal in Jerusalem! I don't care how many soldiers there are!"

9

"Let's have another wineskin!" Peter shouted. He was slightly tipsy, as were most of the other disciples. They were all having a very good time. The roast lamb was cooked to perfection, and the spicy side dishes made a man want to drink more and more of that strong, full-bodied Galilean wine.

Jesus was drinking moderately and eating lightly. Ever since they had entered this upper room, something had come over him. He could not put his finger on it . . . what was causing this vague feeling of dread . . . apprehension? What was it? Jesus kept nervously asking himself. What had brought on this sudden fear . . . this uneasiness?

There was one other person at the table who was not having a rollicking good time like the others, eating and drinking heartily.

Judas sat in brooding silence, taking short sips of wine and occasionally gazing across at Jesus. In a few minutes he would leave the party and . . . do it—lead those scores of men to where Jesus was.

Even at the dinner table he was not to have a place of honor! He was seated at the end of the long table, away from Jesus! Always treated as a nobody! Well, all right! Tonight he would have his revenge! Jesus would pay for not showing Judas Iscariot proper respect!

In a few minutes he would leave to join Caiaphas' men and lead them to where Jesus would be spending the night. Yes, he would do it! Tonight was his night!

And with the thought of his sweet revenge Judas got up and announced that he was going to visit a friend he had not seen in days.

"Will you be joining us on the Mount of Olives?" Jesus asked.

Looking straight into Jesus' eyes Judas said in a steady voice, "Yes, Jesus, I'll be there. You can count on it!"

And with those words, Judas abruptly left, none of the others even noticing that he had left. Jesus sat thinking. Suddenly he picked up the wineskin, filled his cup and drank the wine in one gulp.

An hour later, the dinner party ended when the last of the wineskins was flat, and they all trooped merrily out of the room and went down the flight of steps.

They walked in small groups to the Damascus Gate. Once out of the walls of Jerusalem, they turned right, and down the Kidron Valley, and then up to the Mount of Olives.

"I'm for sleep," Peter said on the edge of a grove of olive trees. And all the others sleepily murmured the same thing.

"Shouldn't some of us stay awake . . . on guard" Jesus suggested.

"What for?" Andrew said. "We're safe up here."

"Sure, no one knows we're here," James assured Jesus.

"Peter," Jesus said, shuddering, "I feel a damp chill!"

"I don't! You should've had more wine!" Peter laughed. "Then you wouldn't be feeling cold!"

Within a few minutes Jesus was left standing, looking down at his sleeping and snoring disciples. That strong Galilean wine! Jesus thought indulgently.

But as Jesus walked away from his sleeping disciples that worrisome feeling and cold dread he had experienced at the dinner came swept over him once again.

Jesus could not understand it. It was a strange, melancholy feeling. No, it was not fear, Jesus realized. It was something else. It was a sense of futility, that was it.

And what had brought on this sense of futility? Jesus knew the answer to that. It was the events of the day—that ridiculous fiasco in the Temple and the city. He and his supporters in the Temple fleeing for their lives, Barabbas and his Zealots routed by Pilate's troops—what a total and ignominious failure it was! What pathetic folly to attempt the takeover of the Temple and the city!

"And now what?" Jesus pointedly asked himself. What was he going to do now with himself? Go on preaching . . . indefinitely? For how long could he go on proclaiming that "The time is fulfilled, and the kingdom of heaven is at hand. Repent and believe the gospel."?

". . . is at hand," Jesus thought, shaking his head. For how long could he go on speaking those words of coming future happiness? Not too long . . . when . . . nothing happened.

So, what was he going to do for the rest of his life? He and Barabbas had tried to take the kingdom of heaven by storm. But Pilate had defeated them.

What next? What should he do? Jesus asked himself. Return to Galilee? Tell the disciples to do the same thing? For him it would be going back to being the village carpenter. And for them, back to their fishing jobs.

Just then Jesus saw many flaring torches snaking their way up the hill toward him. And a moment later he could discern scores of men carrying torches and lanterns only a few hundred feet below him. And they were armed! Well, if they wanted a fight, they would have it!

Jesus' disciples came to the upper room for the Passover meal armed with swords. They had stacked them up in a corner before they sat down to eat.

Before they left the upper room Jesus had asked Peter if they had enough swords to defend themselves in case they ran into any trouble. Peter assured Jesus that they had enough swords, and even an extra one for him.

And so, once the meal was over, Jesus and his disciples strapped on the sword belts and adjusted the swords on their hips. They had been careful to leave the building in small groups. In the dark, silent streets, as they made their way to the Damascus Gate, they passed two Roman patrols without incident.

Jesus realized that this armed band was coming to arrest him for trying to take over the Temple earlier that day. He and all his disciples were armed, Jesus thought gratefully.

Leading the arresting party was Phinehas, with Judas showing the way. Seeing Judas when they were only a few hundred feet away, Jesus yelled angrily, "Judas, what does this mean? What are you doing with these men?"

"Showing them were your hideout is, Jesus!" Judas cried joyfully. "And it means you are going to be arrested!"

"So you sold me out, you rotten double-crossing rat!"

"No, I didn't do this for money, Jesus! I did it because you didn't show a proper respect for me, Judas Iscariot! You shut me out of your inner band, never taking me into your confidence, treating me like dirt! Tonight, I'm having my revenge!"

"Seize him!" Phinehas ordered. "Bind him with your ropes!"

"You'll never take me alive!" Jesus cried, drawing his sword. And then shouting over his shoulder, "To arms, men, to arms! Wake up! We have a fight on our hands!"

As Jesus crossed swords with three men, the disciples dashed into the fray, with swords flashing.

But there were just too many of them, over sixty. What chance did twelve men have against such numbers? After only a minute, the disciples dropped their swords and took to their heels, fleeing for their lives.

Jesus was fighting bravely and manly with his sword holding off four men at one time. But when he saw the backs of his disciples, he was shocked. He could not believe they were deserting him.

"Come back, come back and fight! You craven cowards, weaklings! What kind of men are you!"

But, finally, Jesus saw he was fighting a hopeless fight. He was surrounded by six swords. It was futile to go on resisting.

Throwing down his sword he declared, "All right, I quit, I surrender. I'm your prisoner? Where are you going to take me?"

"To the palace of the high priest, to Caiaphas!" Phinehas grinned a mean grin at Jesus.

10

Jesus stood in the great hall of the high priest's palace. A dozen Temple policemen with drawn swords stood at one side. All the Temple priests were present.

Caiaphas came out of a side door with Phinehas behind him. The high priest approached Jesus, whose arms were bound behind his back. Phinehas went to stand with the priests.

Gazing at Jesus for a long time without speaking, Caiaphas finally burst out, "What madness possessed you to do it?"

Jesus did not answer. He remained silent, with his head bowed.

"Jesus," Caiaphas spoke softly, almost in a pleading voice, "have you nothing to say in your defense?"

"What defense could this rebel have?" Phinehas said. "He is guilty, like all those fanatical Zealots! He's probably a secret Zealot himself."

"I am not," Jesus said.

"Quiet, Phinehas!" Caiaphas shouted. "I am conducting this inquiry! Not another word out of you!"

There was silence in the great hall for several moments.

Again the high priest spoke.

"Jesus . . . don't you have anything to say?"

"Nothing."

"Was your attempt to take over the Temple connected in any way with the insurrection lead by Barabbas in the city?"

Jesus remained silent.

"A number of Roman soldiers were killed putting down that insurrection. If you were in some way involved in it, the procurator, Pilate, will deal harshly with you, as he surely will with the two captured Zealots. Is there anything you want to say to me that I could tell Pilate . . . to mitigate your guilt?"

"I have nothing to say."

Sighing deeply, Caiaphas said, "Phinehas, have the Temple police take Jesus down to a cell. He will face Pilate in the morning."

As Jesus was being lead away, Caiaphas called out, "Jesus . . . I . . . wish I could do something to save you . . . . But it's all in Pilate's hands."

Those few hours Jesus was in the cell he did a lot of thinking, hard thinking. Maybe he could save his life if he renounced his claim to be the Messiah when he came before Pilate for trial. He could beg for mercy, say he was sorry about the attack on Temple. It was just possible that Pilate might let him off with a scourging.

And then what?

What would he do with himself for the rest of his life? Those yellow-belly disciples of his had proved how useless they were in a crisis. They had abandoned him. Where were they while he was held a prisoner? Probably hiding in cellars like the cowardly rats they were!

So, if by some miracle Pilate did set him free, what would he do, where would he go? One thing Jesus told himself, he was determined not to return to Nazareth to live the humdrum life of a village carpenter! No, sir! Not that life for him! Not after those exciting times when he was traveling up and down Palestine with so many ardent men and women followers. Not after enjoying so much popularity with all those crowds of people that listened spellbound to his sermons and parables! Why, once, Jesus recalled, in the desert, the mob, bursting with enthusiasm, wanted to proclaim him king—the Messiah!

But, Jesus realized, he was not thinking clearly. If Pilate did set him free, he would have to return to Nazareth—a great big failure! And live that dull village life!

No, he would not beg Pilate for mercy! He would show no fear! Yes, when he was brought before Pilate, he would claim to be the Messiah! Yes, even if it cost him his life! He would die an agonizing death. But it would be a noble death! The death of a Jewish martyr!

Jesus of Nazareth, the carpenter, would join the glorious ranks of those Jews, hundreds of Jews, who had been crucified in the great cause of Israel's freedom!

11

"Are you the king of the Jews?" Pilate asked Jesus, expecting an emphatic and vigorous denial.

"Yes, I am!" Jesus defiantly proclaimed.

Surprised, Pilate muttered, "You are claiming to be a king?"

"Yes!" Jesus declared, deciding to lay it on thick. "And you will see this king, after you have killed him, coming down from heaven on clouds of glory and power to establish his kingdom, after he has destroyed your Roman Empire!"

"And how will you achieve that amazing feat—all by yourself, Jew?" Pilate sneered.

"No, with legions of angels!"

"You really have said a mouthful."

"A mouthful of Yahweh's truth!"

"Truth!" Pilate laughed. "What is truth?"

The scene was the broad patio of the Roman judgment hall. Pilate had decided to hold the trial of Jesus in public to show the Jewish people how Roman justice dealt with rebels and seditionists.

On one side of Jesus stood a squad of Roman soldiers. On the other side stood a score of the Temple priests, with Phinehas at their head. And down below the patio had gathered hundreds of Jews to witness the trial.

Jesus did not respond to Pilate's pointed question. He knew it would be useless to speak of divine truth to this heathen, this Roman. He lived in that gross world of the Roman Empire. Pilate worshipped a man, the emperor, as a god. No human being who would one day die and turn to dust should be worshiped! Jesus thought righteously.

"Let's get on with it," Pilate said. "You are accused of leading a seditious demonstration against the business of money changing and the selling of sacrificial animals in the Temple. You and your followers, with your violence and pillaging cost those business people a heap of money. Jesus, how do you plea?"

From the hundreds of Jews a chant went up—"Set Jesus free!"

But from the priests, and loudly and vigorously lead by Phinehas, the furious cry was "Crucify him! Crucify him!"

However, the demand for death from the priests was drowned out by the roar of the crowd of Jews to Pilate to pardon Jesus. Angry and frustrated, Phinehas went among the Jews, jingling a bag of silver and offering them money to demand Jesus' death. All the Jews, men and women, rejected the bribe with scorn.

"Well, Jesus, what have you to say?" Pilate asked Jesus. "Are you guilty as charged?"

"Yes, damnit, I plead guilty of being a Jewish patriot who hopes and prays that one day we will be free of Roman tyranny, oppression, having to pay taxes to a pagan government and seeing you Romans no longer polluting our holy land with your vile presence!"

Pilate smiled happily. He was going to do what he so much loved to do to Jews! Die that wretched, cruel death on the cross!

"Jesus, your own words have condemned you. I sentence you to be crucified! Take him out to that hill and nail him to the cross! And now bring out those two Zealots we captured in the insurrection! They also will be crucified with Jesus, one on each side of him!"

Pilate spoke those words with joyful glee. If only there were more Jews he could crucify!" he thought.

11

From the roof of the tallest of the Temple buildings Caiaphas stood and watched in the distance on hill the stark sight of three men nailed to a cross. He knew that Jesus was the one in the middle. Phinehas had come to report to the high priest.

"I stayed for fifteen minutes to see Jesus and those crazy Zealots getting nailed to the cross and watched them when they were hoisted up," Phinehas said with a pleased smile.

"Phinehas . . . don't you have any pity for those men, the suffering they are enduring?"

"They deserve to die! Jesus, the Zealots—they are all troublemakers! They are a threat to the social order, to our peaceful relations with the Romans! If they are not snuffed out, they will bring down on the Jewish nation catastrophe, bloody disaster!"

"Phinehas . . . what you say has some truth. But I have something else to say to you."

"And what is that, eminence?" Phinehas asked, smiling and bowing.

"Get the hell out of my sight!"

When he was alone, the high priest turned away from the grisly ghastly sight in the distance, praying for the men dying on those crossers.

Hours later, when Caiaphas was sitting in his office, brooding sadly ever the tragic and horrible death of Jesus and the two Zealots, Davina walked in. Immediately she saw how disheartened, and crest-fallen her father was.

Coming up to him and laying her hand on his bowed shoulders, Davina said, "He is dead. Jesus is dead." There was a cold finality to her voice. "I stayed to the very end. It was horrible, so horrible! They took so long to die! At the end, just before he died, I was shocked and disappointed at the last words he spoke."

"What were they?" Caiaphas asked.

"Jesus cried out, 'God, my God, why have you forsaken me?'"

"Well, Davina, that's the end of Jesus. He was just another pretender to Messiahship, like so many others who were killed or disappeared.

"Yes, Father, I think you are right. In time, Jesus will be forgotten. But, Father, I had such hope in him, such hope!"

"My daughter, don't despair. You still have your Jewish faith."

Three People

1

Jim and Linda were a young unmarried couple living together in a rundown apartment building on Tenth Avenue and Thirteenth Street. They had a seedy apartment, half of which was occupied by a bed, and the other half was their living room. The living room had a short, lumpy couch and three wooden armchairs picked up in a junkyard. In a corner by the window was a small stove, a refrigerator about two feet high, and a narrow round table with two stools. The sink was a tiny enamel basin, much chipped. A TV was near the couch.

Jim was today where he spent most of the day, and that was lying stretched out on the couch. A couple of empty wine bottles were under the couch. He glanced with bleary eyes at the half-empty bottle in his hand. Jim never bothered with a glass. He always liked to drink out of the bottle.

He had become addicted to the fruit of the wine out of frustration, because of his failure to become a successful writer. Ever since he was twenty years old he had been submitting manuscripts to publishers and agents, but all he got back were rejection slips. And so in his despair he took to the wine bottle for comfort and sleep.

An aunt had left him some money, but in no time it was all gone. Now Jim had to rely on his girlfriend to live. Linda supported both of them by selling her body for money while Jim slept off his daily daytime wine-drinking. This was what he was, a wine lush at twenty-four.

Linda worked the Westside, the Eastside, uptown and downtown. She did not want to become too familiar to the cops on the beats. Occasionally she even walked the streets of the Wall Street district at lunchtime when the stock brokers went out to eat. She knew how mad and angry those men would get over the activity of the Stock Market. And to get relief they would go with this attractive young girl when she gave them a big come-on smile. With those well-heeled customers Linda always upped her price from thirty dollars to sixty dollars.

But though Wall Street was a place where Linda could make real money, it was not good for her business. It did not have many hotels. Sometimes a broker or executive would take her to his office for a quickie on his desk, and if the stock market was going against him, curse it for being unpredictable and even curse Linda, taking out his anger on her, calling all kinds of foul names. One elderly white-haired man called her "a dirty, filthy whore who was worse than garbage." After having her, these men would ride the trains back to their homes in the suburbs, glad and happy to be with their loving wives and wonderful children.

There were days when Linda returned to the apartment with aching feet and no money. Sometimes, when business was very slow and the need for food and rent money was urgent, and the customer did not have enough on him to pay for a hotel room, Linda had to bring him to the apartment.

When this happened, Jim could get up slowly from the couch, taking his bottle with him and go into the bathroom in the hall and sit on the toilet seat for a half hour.

One time, half-drunk as he usually was, he returned too soon. He saw Linda and the man as a blurred writhing mass of arms, legs and bare buttocks, the man grunting and going up and down like a machine and Linda with her long shapely legs wrapped around his waist. Jim stayed and watched until the man was done.

Linda turned streetwalker after she was fired from her job as a sales clerk in a women's clothing store. She was caught trying to walk out of the store after work with four blouses under her dress.

"I'm not going to have you arrested, you thieving bitch!" the boss told her. "But don't try to use me as a reference when you go applying for a job!"

Linda became so downhearted by that threat that she took the easy way and went on the street. She turned prostitute because she loved Jim, and felt that he loved her. He really did not like what she did to earn money, but he was too much of a weak-willed sot to object.

This night Linda was getting ready to go out and walk the streets. She usually did not work nights, but that day she had not been able to make one customer, and the rent was due in few days.

Linda was giving herself a looking-over in the mirror that hung on the door of their apartment. She was always very careful about her appearance. Her hair had to be just right, and she made sure her makeup was on right. After all, those were the things that caught a man's eye. And being very pretty as she was helped too.

When she was satisfied with the way she looked, Linda turned around and went over to Jim, who was lying flat on his back on the couch. He did not bother to sit up as he looked her up and down.

"Well, do you think I look alluring?" Linda asked, smiling. "Do you think this honey will catch files? Is my skirt tight enough? How about the dress? Is the cleavage deep enough, or not deep enough? Well, damnit, say something, Jim! Show some interest, some appreciation, for crying out loud! I'm peddling my ass for you, goddamnit!"

Sitting up and smiling Jim said, "I love you, Linda! I hate the whole world, but I love you! Now give me a kiss before you go out and make us some money."

"That's all I wanted to hear, darling," Linda said, gratified and smiling. "In this room I'm your adoring sweetheart, but when I hit the streets I turn into a different person. No, not a person—a sex robot. How I despise those men! Most of them married and some of them Catholic priests and rabbis. How those so-called men of the cloth haggle over my set price!"

"Linda, how do you know some of those men are married? And about the clergymen?"

"They tell me, after they have emptied their filth into me! The priests say prayers after they are done and want to convert me. The rabbis want me to pray with them. And some men tell me about their wives."

"What rotten hypocrites," Jim said, smiling.

"And how bitterly remorseful they are when it's over, swearing they will never see me again, but they do, they certainly do!"

"What rats men are," Jim said.

"All except you, Jim, my sweet, darling Jim! How I love you! Hey, I better stop this gabbing and get to work. I'll try to be home before midnight."

"Where you working tonight? Off Times Square?"

"No, too many whores there. You have to fight for a corner. I'm going to patrol the Westside, from Fifty-ninth Street up to the Seventies. Not too many girls work that area."

"Good luck, sweetie."

"See you in three or four hours, honey," Linda said, bending down to kiss Jim on the lips. "I'll be thinking of you all the time, you adorable man!"

After Linda left, Jim dropped back down on the couch. He wondered idly how long his lazy, useless life would go on. Could he go on living this boozing life for years and years? And go on living off Linda?

"I'm even lower than a pimp!" Jim said out loud. "At least a pimp sometimes lines up the customers, pays his girls a decent salary, protects them. All I do is stay home, drink this cheap wine and sleep all day. I'm just a lowlife parasite! But how can I climb out of this rut! It gets deeper every day! What can I do to get my life back, for God's sake!"

That serious question roused him enough to rise with sudden energy from the couch and go over to a side table against the wall. His typewriter was on the table, a dust-covered plastic sheet over it. He removed the sheet and stared down at the machine with a frown.

"Damit, I'll get back to writing again!" he swore angrily.

And then he returned to the couch, picked up the wine bottles from the floor and emptied it in one gulp. And then he lay down on the couch. In two minutes he was sound asleep.

2

It was Sunday night, and Linda was dolling herself up to go out. Jim was puzzled. She never worked the streets Sunday nights.

"How come you going out tonight?" he asked, getting up from the couch.

"I thought maybe we could use the extra money. Lately you've developed fancy tastes in your wine-drinking. No more cheap wine for you! Now you buy wine that costs thirty, forty dollars a bottle!"

"Go ahead, blame me! That cheap wine is bad for my liver!"

"Now I have to work for your liver!"

"Stop your grumbling. When will you be back?"

"How do I know? If business is brisk, I might not be home until after midnight."

"That late? You know how I hate to sleep alone."

"Well, maybe I won't be that late. It's all according to the customers. Those guys don't like to be rushed. And sometimes they like me to put on a show, to get them worked up."

"What kind of show?" Jim asked sharply.

"Oh, nothing kinky. A belly dance in the nude, a very, very slow strip act. Things like that."

"Oh, okay," Jim said, relieved. "I was afraid those mutts might want you to do some of that depraved sadomasochism stuff."

"No, I'd never do that for any amount of money. Well, I'm off. Give me a kiss for luck. How I wish I could meet a rich guy who would pay me big money so we could move out of this dump and into a decent place!"

"How you going to meet a sugar daddy in the street?"

"You never can tell, Jim, you never can tell."

Tonight Linda thought she would work all along Central Park South, from Fifth Avenue to Eighth Avenue. It was a safe area, with plenty of pedestrians and street lights. And if the man didn't want to go to a hotel, they could do their business behind some bushes in the park.

Things were slow for Linda that night. In three hours she had only two customers. One man took her up to his apartment. His wife was visiting her mother in Queens. The second man wanted Linda to satisfy him with her hand, which she did behind a tree. And then he balked at the thirty-dollar fee Linda demanded, giving her twenty dollars and walking hurriedly away. What could she do? Call a cop?

About eleven-thirty, when Linda was about ready to call it a night, she noticed the same elderly-looking man passing her for the third time, and staring at her with a scared expression on his face.

The fourth time he was going by and eyeing Linda she asked him why he was staring at her. Did he want something from her? Linda knew from experience that some men were timid about approaching a streetwalker.

The man stopped and said shyly, "I . . . wanted to . . . I wanted to ask you . . . ."

"Ask me what?"

"Uh . . . are you just out for a stroll?"

"No, mister, I am not out for a stroll. I'm a whore, and if you can pay my price, I'm yours for a half hour."

Sweat broke out on the man's face. He looked terrified. Startled, Linda took a good look at him. He was short and slender, with thinning gray hair, a pale complexion and a beaked nose.

"Well, how about it, mister?"

The man coughed and answered, "Uh . . . would you mind coming to my house?"

"You live far from here?"

"Not too far. I live off Eighth Avenue, on Fifty-sixth Street."

The man's suit looked pretty expensive to Linda. She decided to ask for more than the usual fee. "The price is fifty dollars, and I do only straight sex, nothing else, got that?"

"Straight sex? I don't understand."

Linda did not know how to explain. She did not want to be coarsely graphic. This man looked like a gentleman.

Offhandedly she remarked, "I do only what men and women do to make babies. Now do you understand me?"

"Yes, yes, thank you. Uh . . . about the price. . . . I'll pay you two hundred dollars if you stay with me for an hour or so."

"Two hundred dollars!" Linda said. No one had ever paid her that much money. But this man probably wanted her to stay with him for a couple of hours. She would be getting home well past midnight. Jim would not like that. Bu two hundred dollars!

"Would you?" the man asked, a pleading tone to his voice. "I get so lonely since Rachel died four months ago."

"That was your wife?"

"Yes. She died so suddenly, heart attack. Now I'm all alone in my two-story house. All my children are gone, married, living in Florida, Arizona, and Ohio. And . . . the nights for me are so long, so . . . lonely . . . ."

Half out of pity and half for the money Linda said, "Sure, I'll go with you to your place. My name is Linda. What's yours?"

"My name is Abe . . . Linda. And I'm very pleased to know you."

"Same here, Abe," Linda said, sliding her arm under Abe's arm and stepping jauntily out toward Fifth Avenue.

As soon as they were inside the house, Linda asked Abe where the toilet was. She felt that her bladder was about to burst. She had not urinated since she went with that man to his apartment, two hours ago. Minutes before she met Abe, she was thinking about going into the park and squatting behind a tree.

After emptying out her bladder, Linda washed her hands and freshened up her makeup. When she returned to the living room, Abe was coming from the kitchen carrying a tray with a bottle of white wine and two long-stemmed glasses.

"Oh, are we going to have a party?" Linda asked cheerfully.

"I thought you might be thirsty," Abe said, handing Linda a glass. Before they drank he added cordially, solemnly, "To your very good health, Linda, and I hope very much that we will be good friends."

Linda was moved by the gentlemanly, old-world manner of the old man. As he looked at her over his glass, the thought that she had never seen such sad gentle eyes in all her life strangely came over her.

After they had had a second glass, Linda was sure Abe would take her into the bedroom to earn her money. But he did no such thing. He sat down on the silk-covered divan and patted the space beside him.

"Sit down, Linda. Let's talk."

Linda was puzzled. She wondered what in the world they would have to talk about. With all the other men, all they want to do was to get down to it, quickly shedding their clothes and roughly telling Linda to do likewise. No love-dovey sentiment for them, no pretence at showing affection, just the sex act, with the explosive finish. And then quickly getting dressed and rushing out of the room, leaving the money on the bureau. With that brusque kind of sex, Linda began to believe that men looked upon sex as just another biological function, like defecating and urinating.

Abe began talking about his life with Rachel, always referring to her as "my beloved wife." He told Linda how they met, fell in love, their happy life together, the children, a daughter and two sons, all professionals, a doctor, lawyer, and a registered nurse. It was all heavy, tedious going for Linda.

To lighten up the atmosphere Linda asked, "Abe, were you ever unfaithful to your wife?"

Abe leaned back, shocked by the question.

"Never, never!" he protested. "I never so much as looked at another woman that way, with desire for her! Rachel was the perfect wife, the perfect mother! I could never do such a cruel thing as cheat on my beloved Rachel!"

"Are you retired?" Linda asked.

"Yes, about four years ago."

"What did you do for a living?"

"I had a jewelry store on Seven Avenue and Twenty-third Street for over thirty years. I invested my money wisely, and when I was sixty-four I decided to sell the business. I had an idea of moving to California, but my wife liked New York too much and so we stayed here."

Half listening to Abe, Linda was thinking to herself that this was a nice old man who craved companionship more than anything else, someone to be with, to talk to. A vague, ambitious idea began to form in her mind.

But Linda wanted to get back to Jim, and so said, smiling and suggestively patting Abe's thigh, "Uh, Abe, I enjoy listening to you talk . . . but don't you want to . . . you know? . . ."

"Oh, yes," Abe said, as if remembering something. "You go into the bedroom first. It's down the hall, first door on the right. Get in bed. I'll join you in five minutes."

When Abe joined Linda in the dark bedroom she saw by the light in the hall that he was naked. Before he closed the door Linda got a glimpse of the old man's frail, skinny, slightly potbellied body and thin, hairy legs.

In the black darkness Linda pulled off the blanket, placed a pillow under her buttocks and spread her legs wide. But Abe did not mount her. Instead he lay down beside her with a happy sigh.

For a few minutes Abe did not move. Linda wonder what was the matter with him. All her customers always pounced on her like predatory, ravenous beasts. Was Abe impotent? Would she have to use her hands to stimulate him, rouse him?

Suddenly, Abe leaned over and kissed Linda ardently on the mouth. Linda was amazed, astonished. Not one of those men she went with had ever kissed her on the lips.

And then something even more amazing happened. Abe began to weep, softly, making low moaning sounds. Why was he crying? Linda asked herself. What was she supposed to do? Should she reach down for his organ and work on it?

"Abe, what is it? Why are you crying?"

"Ah, Linda, Linda, I'm crying out of pure happiness! I truly feel that I am once again in bed with my beloved Rachel! You won't believe how I was struck with awe when I first saw you on the street! I could not believe my own eyes! That's why I walked by you a number of times to make sure!"

"Make sure about what, Abe?"

"Oh, didn't I tell you when we were in the living room, Linda? How did I forget to mention something important like that!"

"Abe, would you please explain?"

"Linda, you have Rachel's face, the eyes, the mouth, the nose, even the hair! Uncanny, uncanny, that's what it is! It's—it's as if my wonderful wife, my beloved Rachel, has come back to life, back to me, me, her husband!"

Linda was deeply moved. But she had to get back to Jim! He was going to be sore as hell for returning so late. She had to hurry up Abe and get him back to the business at hand.

"Uh . . . Abe, I'm glad that my resemblance to your wife gives you so much happiness."

"So much happiness, so much happiness!"

"And I'm sure that you enjoyed making love to her, didn't you?"

"Yes, oh yes! She gave me so much pleasure! Rachel was very passionate in bed, so very passionate!"

"Abe, just imagine that I'm Rachel, here in bed with you, now."

"Imagine that you are . . . Rachel?"

"Yes, come back to life, back into your arms."

"Oh yes, yes, you are!"

"Abe, I'll show how passionate I can be, like Rachel. Abe, your darling beloved wife is waiting for you to make love to her! Come, Abe, show your wife how much you love her!"

"Yes, my beloved Rachel, I'll show you how strong my love for you is!" Abe exclaimed, and with a sudden burst of energy he got on top of Linda and joined himself to her in a passionate embrace.

Since he was an old man, Abe took a long time to have his orgasm. As he pumped vigorously up and down he repeatedly shouted how much he loved his wife, how much he enjoyed making love to her.

"Rachel, Rachel," he said, "you've come back, you've come back to y our adoring husband! Oh, but you were gone so long, too long! How bitter and lonely the nights were without you! Rachel, my darling, how happy I am that you have come back to me! Oh, how much pleasure you give me! Am I giving my darling wife pleasure?"

Linda, also sexually soaring, did not have to pretend that she was sharing Abe's pleasure. And so she sincerely shouted back, "Yes, Abe, you wonderful lover, I love you, I love you to pieces! Don't stop, go on, go on! For God's sake don't stop!"

"No, no, Rachel, I'll never stop!" Abe howled joyfully in his sexual rapture. "I love you, love you, Rachel! Say you'll never leave me again! Say it, Rachel, say that you will never leave me!"

"I'll never leave you!" Linda said. "Your Rachel will stay with you always, forever!" But even in the throes of her pleasure, Linda spoke those words calculatingly, with that idea she had in mind.

And when, finally, Abe had had his orgasm with cries of almost anguished ecstasy, Linda, who somehow had ended up on top of him, rolled off him and they lay side by side, panting and gasping.

But now that the sex pleasure was over, Linda felt disgust and shame. She had never had sex with a man as old as Abe. And he was such an ugly old man! How could she do it? For the money, damnit, for the filthy money!

For five minutes they lay in the dark room without speaking. A few times Abe took Linda's hand, squeezing it and bringing it to his lips and kissing it.

Abe said gratefully and after kissing Linda's hand for the third time, "Thank you . . . Rachel. That was the best ever, the best."

Linda got out of the bed and switched on the bedside lamp. She looked calmly down at Abe, at his scrawny body. He gazed lovingly up at her. Linda was thinking . . . what a bony, ugly body he had! Such a little old man . . . and yet he gave her sexual thrills she had never experienced with all those other Johns . . . only with Jim.

"What are you thinking, Rachel?" Abe said, smiling.

"Abe, it's over. The play-acting is over. I'm Linda, the whore you picked up in the street and brought home for sex."

Abe was aghast. "No, no, Rachel! My beloved Rachel is not . . . what you said. She is my good, virtuous, faithful wife!"

"Abe, come back to the real world. Rachel, your wife, is dead. I'm Linda, got it?"

Abe swung his legs around and sat up on the edge of the bed. For a moment or two he stared sadly down at the floor. Then, glancing hopefully up at Linda he said, "Yes, I know Rachel is dead . . . but can't I go on calling you Rachel? How happy it makes me feel, to believe that she is alive . . . ."

"Yes, I know what you mean, Abe. We all wish that we could bring back the dead we loved so much. I'm sorry, but . . . look, I have to get going."

"Oh, Rachel, can't you—"

"Linda, Abe, Linda."

"All right," he said regretfully, "Linda, can't you stay a little longer, please?"

"Abe, I'd like to but it's getting late and we agreed about the time and the money. We talked—you talked a lot before we got in bed, and your time is up."

"Rachel—"

"Not Rachel, Linda, Linda!"

"All right, Linda, I'll give you an extra hundred to stay with me one more hour. We don't have to do . . . sex. I just want to be with you. The loneliness . . . it's so unbearable that sometimes I . . . think of putting an end to it all . . . ."

"You talking suicide?"

"Yes, I am."

"Abe, get that crazy notion out of your head. Life, no matter how miserable, is always better than death. Death . . . I get the chills when I think of it. How I hate going to a funeral home. The flowers have a sort of sweet-sickening, ghoulish smell to them."

"I bought a lot of flowers for Rachel when she—oh, Linda, won't you stay a little longer?" Abe pleaded, his watery eyes sadder than ever.

Linda stood looking down at the pathetic old man. She realized she had power over him. Now that idea in her head became clearer, bigger. But she had to get back to Jim! She had never stayed out this late before. What would he think? she worried.

"I'm sorry, Abe," she said, starting to put on her clothes. Abe watched her quietly, very unhappy.

"I don't know why you can't stay with me a little longer," he murmured, sniffling.

At that moment, looking down at that pitiful old man, Linda realized again the power she had over him. His sorrowful question gave her the chance to put into operation the idea, the plan, that had been growing in her mind.

"Abe, I'll tell you why I can't stay longer with you, why I have to get home," she said, her voice quavering with deep emotion. "I have to get back to my brother. He . . . needs me . . . ."

"Needs you? Is he a child?"

"No . . . but he's sick and I have to take care of him, give him his medicine. A long time ago he had a nervous breakdown, and he needs me, really needs me."

"And your parents, Linda?"

"Dead, a long time ago. There's only the two of us."

"I'm so sorry, Linda, so sorry, for both of you."

"Thank you Abe," she said, a sob in her throat.

"How old is he, your brother?"

"A couple of years older than me. I have to take care of him. Because of his mental problems, Jim can't work. And he's weak too, physically, something wrong with his lungs. So how you know why I have to get back to him right away, Abe."

Abe got up and got into his pants. "I understand, Linda. You are a good sister to your brother. Yes, you have to go home. But it's late and I don't want you walking the streets or riding the subway at this time of night. I'll call car service for you. Sometimes I use this livery car service two blocks from here when I go down to the store."

"But didn't you tell me that you sold the business?"

"Yes, but the man I sold it to is young and inexperienced. I go down to help out three or four times a week. I do it to keep busy, not for the money. What would I do with myself, all day in the house?"

"You're right, it's good to stay active."

"I'll give you thirty dollars extra for the car service. You have far to go?"

"It's some distance," Linda said evasively, reckoning that the fare would cost no more than ten dollars with the tip. She would have twenty dollars more for her night's work.

"And you're sure the thirty will be enough?" Abe asked.

"Sure, it will be enough, and, Abe, you're swell."

By this time Linda was dressed and ready to leave. Abe reached for a woolen bathrobe on a chair and put it on. They went into the living room. Abe made the phone call to the livery service.

"He'll be here in five minutes," he said, dropping the receiver in the cradle. Uh . . . Linda . . . when will I see you again?"

"Tomorrow night?"

"No, tomorrow is the beginning of Sabbath, and it can't be Sunday, that's your Sabbath, right?"

"I guess," Linda replied carelessly.

Abe's eyebrows went up. "Linda, aren't you a Christian?"

"You could call me a Christian whore."

"Linda, stop using that nasty word when you talk about yourself! You are a good girl . . . sacrificing yourself for your brother."

"Well . . . to answer your question, I was brought up a Baptist, so I guess that makes me a Christian."

"Do you go to church on Sundays?"

"I haven't been inside a church in years, not since my parents died."

Shocked, Abe asked, "Linda don't you practice any religion?"

"What's to practice? We're born, we live for so many years, and then we die and our bodies rot in the ground."

"Oh, Linda, so young and so pretty and to talk in that cynical, materialist way! What a shame!"

"Well, that's the way I see life."

"Are you unhappy with your life?"

"What do I have to be happy about, the way I have to earn a living."

"But why do you have to do it . . . that way?"

Linda told Abe about the reason why she got fired from her job as a sales clerk and how it broke her spirit.

"I understand now. Linda, you are not a bad person. Deep down inside you have a . . . pure heart."

"A pure heart?" Linda smiled. "Abe, you're a funny guy. I'm beginning to like you."

"You are?" Abe said, his eyes glowing.

"Yes."

"Uh . . . so you wouldn't mind coming here Sunday night?"

"Sure, what time?"

"Say six o'clock? We could have supper together. I learned to be a pretty good cook since my beloved Rachel died."

"Yes, I think I'd like that Abe!"

"But, Linda, may I ask you a persona question?"

"What is it?"

"Will you be . . . working the streets until Sunday night?"

"I have to earn moving to pay the bills."

Abe showed the anguish in his face. In a voice full of pain Abe said, "Linda, how I hate to think of you in bed with all those strangers . . . rough men, with your face, the face of my Rachel . . . ."

"Abe, I understand your feelings. But, remember, those bills have to be paid."

"I don't want you to soil yourself with those men!" Abe said with sudden furious anger. "No, no, I won't tolerate it! Linda, I'll give you more money than I promised! I'll give you five hundred dollars right now! But you must give me your word of honor that no man will touch you!"

Linda was pleased and surprised by the proposal. It would be a relief not to have to walk her feet off until she saw Abe again. Five hundred dollars! What a lucky night this was, meeting up with this old man, she thought.

But she decided to be cagey. Abe would think better of her.

"Abe, that's very generous of you," she said, "but I can't accept your offer. That's so much money!"

Of course she was confident that he would insist. He did, and Linda put on a show of reluctantly accepting. Abe rushed happily back into the bedroom and returned with the money in twenty dollar bills.

Clutching the stack of bills Linda said, "Abe, I feel like an heiress! You are one hell of a sweet guy! See you Sunday night!"

"Linda, a kiss before you go . . . please," Abe asked shyly.

She threw her arms around Abe and kissed him hard on the lips. The old man embraced Linda in a fierce hug, his lips glued to Linda's lips. It was a long kiss, and it was she who finally broke away from Abe.

When Linda stepped out the door to the waiting car Abe said passionately, "Until Sunday, my darling!"

3

"Why you out so late!" Jim said querulously, getting up from the couch and switching off the TV. "Christ, it's almost three o'clock!" He was also very sore because he had finished all the wine in the apartment.

Linda said not a word, kissing him on the cheek, taking out of her handbag the fat roll of twenties and holding it in front of Jim's eyes.

"Wow, how much is it?" Jim said, his gleaming eyes on the money.

"Five hundred dollars, and all from one customer. He's a goofy widower, crazy about me. He took me to his place."

"Linda, he didn't have you do any dirty, perverted tricks, did he?" Jim asked anxiously.

"No, no, he's not like that. He's a nice sentimental old man."

"Where does he live?"

"Not far from Central Park. He owns this two-story brownstone. He sold his jewelry-store business a little way downtown, and still works there a few days a week."

"This old bird must be loaded!" Jim said.

"He is, believe me, he must have plenty of jake."

"What kind of man is he, this guy?"

"A short ugly little Jew, in his late sixties."

"A Jew and a geezer! How was it having sex with a man that old?"

"What does it matter? His money is good, and that's all that really matters, right?" Linda said, dropping the money back in her bag.

"I suppose," Jim agreed. "But how come he gave you so much money? This is the best night you ever had. Linda, did you tell me the truth, about this old guy not having you do any of that depraved stuff?"

"Jim, you know I wouldn't do it for any amount of money."

"Okay, I believe you, but you haven't explained why he gave you all that dough."

"Jim, he gave me all that money because he doesn't want me screwing for other men."

Jim frowned, puzzled. "I don't get it. Why not?"

"This will kill you. Abe, that's his name, thinks I resemble his dead wife. While we were doing sex he kept calling me 'Rachel, Rachel, my beloved Rachel!' Isn't that a scream?"

"Hey, Linda, you could be on to something," Jim said seriously. "I think you discovered a gold mine, my beloved Linda!"

"I think you really love me, Jim!" Linda laughed back at him.

"I take it this 'Rachel' is this sappy old fool's wife?"

"Yes, she is."

"And he thinks you look like his dead wife?"

"Maybe I do."

"Baby, this old guy is ripe for plucking! We're going to cash in on him! At last, we get a break!"

"I'm glad I don't have to walk my feet off the next couple of days. Sometimes I think those pavements are made of iron."

"I'll be able to treat my girl to a few dinners in a good restaurant for a change."

"Oh, so you're going to be big-hearted with the money I earn."

"Linda, come on, don't talk like that. You know how it breaks my heart to know that you go to bed with all those Johns. Show some consideration for my feelings, will you. Baby, you know how much I love you."

"And I love you, Jim, so let's not quarrel. I feel good tonight about the money, and about meeting this money-man Abe."

"Speaking of money, give me a hundred dollars. I want to buy a case of wine. I ran out tonight. And I'm not getting any of that cheap vino!"

4

It was eight-thirty that Sunday night. Abe had cooked a delicious pot roast dinner with stuffed cabbage, mushrooms in a tasty tomato sauce and potatoes. He had bought a chocolate layer cake for dessert.

Now they were lying in bed after sex. Abe sighed a few times contentedly, and every minute kissing Linda's hand. Again when they made love he called Linda Rachel. He even did it a few times at the dinner table. Linda no longer corrected him. She thought . . . if it made the old guy happy, what was the harm?

"Did I give my good little wife much pleasure tonight?" Abe asked, turning to look at Linda.

"Yes, yes, you really sent me up to the clouds!" she said, wondering how long she would have to stay with Abe and how much money he was going to give her tonight. She knew that she could not hope for the same amount that he gave her last time. Was it too much to expect that he would give her a hundred dollars?"

"Rachel, I was right up there in the clouds with you! Darling, you don't mind that I call you by my wife's name, do you? Please don't rebuke me when I say it, especially when we're making love."

"Abe, it's all right. Call me Rachel all the time, when we make love, when we're just talking like now—anytime."

"Oh, I'm so glad you said that! You've—you've brought Rachel back to life! You don't know how I suffered for months after my wife died. This bed was so cold without her. I felt like I was sleeping in a coffin. But everything is all right, now that you have come into my life. You even gave me back my appetite. How Rachel enjoyed watching me enjoy her good cooking!"

To Linda all this was the maudlin driveling of a silly old man living in the past. Why, she asked herself, was he so idiotically attached to his wife's memory? Was he so childish, so weak, that he could not face reality? But if that was the way he was, good for her and Jim. She would exploit this silly old man's weakness as much as she could, try to get as much money out of him as she could.

Abe's voice broke in on her thoughts.

"Linda, didn't you hear what I said?"

"Oh, forgive me, Abe, I was thinking of my brother. What did you say?"

"I want you to sleep over with me tonight."

"You mean all night—go home in the morning?"

"Yes, and I'll make you a good breakfast."

Linda's mind was racing, with dollar signs in it. Forget the hundred dollars! For sleeping with him all night, wouldn't the obsessed old coot give her at least—at least two hundred dollars? Jim was right, Abe was turning out to be a gold mine! Maybe she would not have to work the always hard, sometimes cold and sometimes hot streets anymore!

But Linda did not want to seem too eager, and she certainly did not want Abe to think she would easily fall in with his desires. She thought it best to play the loving, serious-minded, responsible sister.

"I don't know if . . . if I could, Abe," Linda said slowly. "I have to think of my brother. Jim might worry about me when I don't come home. He might even call the police."

"You could phone him, couldn't you, darling?"

"Yes, I could do that," she seemed to agree, thinking, But how much money are you going to give me for sleeping with you, damnit!

Abe answered her question.

"For being my wife all night, and having breakfast with me, the way I always did with Rachel, I'm going to give you . . . three hundred dollars.

"Abe, you are so good to me, so generous," Linda said, leaning over and kissing him on the cheek. "For the rest of the night and tomorrow morning, I'll be your affectionate Linda."

"Rachel, please . . . Rachel."

"Yes, Rachel. I'll be your affectionate Rachel, my sweet, darling, devoted husband!"

"How I love it when you talk like that!"

"Abe, are you ready to make love to your wife again?"

"Yes, my adorable Rachel! How I love to make love to you!"

Yes, sure, Linda thought. But she had a different word for it. But she had to admit, even to herself, that she enjoyed the long time it took Abe to have his orgasm. On top of giving her a long, heavenly ride, he paid very well!

The next morning Abe served a simple breakfast of orange juice, poached eggs on toast and coffee. Linda could see how happy he was, setting the table, breaking the eggs into the poacher, serving her.

As they were eating Linda asked, "Abe, did you make breakfast when your wife was alive?"

"Yes, that was my job," he smiled, fondly recalling the past. "And Rachel always had a nice supper for me when I got back from the store. I could smell the savory aroma the minute I walked into the house. How I miss her, how I miss her! But I have you now! Thank God I have you!"

Linda felt a sudden pity for the old man. She could not help feeling sorry for him, in spite of the hardness in her heart.

"Abe . . . you visit her grave?" she asked softly.

"Three, four times a year . . . . with flowers . . . ."

Linda visualized the old man standing by the grave, gazing somberly at the headstone with his wife's name and dates, remembering their lives together, and saying a prayer before he left.

As Linda was about to leave, Abe asked her if he could see her again in two days. When Linda said that was fine, he wanted to know something else.

"What is it, Abe?"

"You know what it is. Do I have to ask it?"

"Oh, that. Abe, after all, that's what I do for a living."

She saw the pained expression on the old man's face. He put his hand in his pocket and brought out a thick wad of money.

"Here, my darling wife, take this, all of it. Keep yourself pure for me. I get sick to my stomach when I think of those men . . . in bed with you."

Taking the wad of bills Linda said, "I will keep myself pure for you, Abe, my wonderful husband." She wondered how much money he had given her. He didn't even count it!

"Rachel, my beloved wife, I love you!" Abe cried joyfully, crushing Linda in his arms.

She thought she might as well play along with this foolish old man. Why not? He was paying her enough to play her part.

"Abe, you have my word . . . I'll stay home, take care of my brother, and go out only to do the shopping."

"My good and faithful wife!" His eyes lighted up with a sudden thought. "Darling, I would very much like to meet your brother some day."

"Sure, Abe, some day."

5

Abe sat behind the counter of the jewelry store, staring out through the plate-glass window. It was a busy street, with plenty of cars and pedestrians going by. This had been a very profitable location over the years. He had chosen wisely.

He was alone in the store. The owner had left early to take his wife out to dinner and a show. It was her birthday. Abe glanced up at the wall clock across from him. It was almost closing time, a quarter to seven. Most of the business was in the morning and afternoon, But you never knew when a customer might walk in to make a purchase before going home.

Abe thought of the one time he had been robbed. The robber must have known his routine. He had waited until it was close to seven o'clock to come in, knowing the cash register would have lots of money.

The incident appeared vividly in his mind. Even now, after all those year, recalling it, a chill went down his spine. He had been about to leave the store for the day when a man came in. He was short and dark and wore a wool-knitted cap and a leather jacket.

The man asked to see some engagement rings. Abe walked behind the display counter and bent down to get a tray of rings. When he straightened up to put the tray on the counter, he found himself staring at a big black shiny gun. It seemed enormous in the man's small hand.

"Back up!" he barked, taking a brown paper bag out of his pants pocket and emptying the tray of rings into it. "Now the cash register, and make it fast!"

Even a half hour after the man fled Abe's hands were shaking and he felt a terrible pressure in his chest. He reported the theft to the police, but the man was never caught.

A week later, Abe got a license to carry a handgun. He bought a .32-caliber revolver, and for a month went twice a week to a shooting gallery to fire off a dozen shots.

From then on he made it a practice to make money deposits twice a day in the bank down the block. And he always walked the short distance with the revolver stuck in his belt, the butt prominently displayed. And he always kept the gun handy, under the counter.

That was ten years ago. He was never robbed again. But now he did not bring the gun with him when he worked the few days in the store. It was home in a drawer.

Suddenly, Abe smiled. He was thinking of Linda. But he did not think of her as Linda. She was Rachel, his beloved Rachel.

And then, before he knew where it came from, a great big wonderful idea burst like a brainstorm inside him. What would his darling say? Would she go for it? If she said yes—how happy he would be! But would she say yes? She had to, she had to! His beloved Rachel had to stop degrading herself by walking the streets, going to cheap hotel rooms with those foul men! The images in his mind of Linda in bed with those men was a cruel torture to Abe. His beloved Rachel had to stop living that filthy, sordid life!

"Yes, yes!" Abe yelled defiantly in the empty store. "My Rachel has to stop living that immoral, sinful life! And I'm going to see to it that she does!"

And Abe bravely but with fear in his heart that Linda would reject his proposal told her of the idea that came to him in the store. She listened quietly and intently to the old man.

"Well, my darling, what do you say? Will you move in with me?" Abe asked, his voice trembling.

Linda did not answer right away. She bent her head, thinking. Abe watched her anxiously, biting his lip. His whole life, his happiness, depended on what she would say.

"Linda . . . I'll do everything I can to make you happy. We'll have a good life together. Linda, I don't want you living that other life!"

"Abe, what about . . . my brother? I can't leave him alone, my brother! Can Jim live here too?"

"Certainly, certainly. I wouldn't want to separate a brother and sister. Jim is welcome to live with us. I have four bedrooms upstairs. He can sleep in one of them."

"And you and me sleep together?"

"Why . . . yes."

"No, Abe, no. It would not look right. It would not be respectable. I have to consider my brother's feelings. He's an old-fashioned kind of guy, with old-fashioned notions of . . . morality. As a brother, I don't think he'd like it . . . me sleeping with you. I must have my own bedroom."

"But, my darling . . . ."

"Oh, it will only be for appearance's sake. Of course I'll come to your bedroom at night and spent a little time with you. Will that arrangement satisfy you, my sweetheart husband?"

Those last two words softened the old man's disappointment. Reluctantly, he agreed. But Linda had something else to say.

"Abe, a girl has to think of her future. I know that I won't have any expenses living with you . . . but I would like to be able to put something aside for a rainy day, you never know what the future holds."

"Yes, I see what you're getting at. I'll open a savings account for you in the bank where I have my savings."

"Uh . . . could you explain further?"

"Every week I'll deposit three hundred dollars in your account. Will that be enough?"

"How about making it fifteen hundred dollars a month?"

"Yes, I can manage that."

"And, Abe how about clothes? I wish I could throw away the shabby dresses and skirts and blouses I have. Abe, I haven't bought myself anything in almost a year! I want to look good for my darling husband when we go out together!"

"You're right, you're so right! I'll buy you a whole new wardrobe! Shoes, stockings—everything you need!"

"And incidentals . . . cosmetics too?"

"Yes, yes! I'll even buy anything Jim needs!"

"Swell, swell! Abe, I love you!"

"You mean it sincerely, my darling Rachel?" Abe asked, trembling with excitement and happiness.

"I said it, didn't I?"

"I want to hear you say it again!"

"Abe, my darling husband, your wife Rachel adores you!" Linda said in a loud, strong voice, deciding to pour it on. What the hell, they were only words to her, but if they made the old fool happy . . . .

"When can you move in, you and Jim?" Abe said eagerly, his eyes shining.

"Let me talk this over with my brother, and I'll let you know. I'm pretty sure that he'll go for it. But, Abe, remember what I said, we have to keep up appearances, for Jim's sake."

"Yes, I understand that, my darling. But don't make it too many days!"

6

"That daffy old guy wants you to live with him?" Jim said, amazed when Linda told him.

"He wants us both to live with him."

"And you'll be sleeping with him, I suppose, every night—that old man?"

"No, Jim, no. A couple of nights a week I'll go to his bedroom, that's all. I'll be spending plenty of time with you, but we have to be careful. After all, the crazy old man thinks of me as his adorable wife, his beloved Rachel, as he likes to call her, or I should say me. Jim, we've fallen into a good thing. Let's not spoil it by being careless."

"Yes, it sounds like a sweet arrangement, but I don't know," Jim said, shaking his head. He glanced around the room. It was small but comfortable, homey. And then what about his drinking? It was so nice on the couch all day, sipping wine, watching TV, dozing off. All that might change if he went along with this plan.

"Linda, I like things the way they are."

"Yes, you lounging on that couch all day, sopping up wine, and me walking my feet off and going to bed with any guy that has the price of my body!"

"Hey, don't talk like that to me! I'm not going to be like this always! You'll see, you'll see, one day I'll get back to writing and—you'll see!"

"Jim, forgive me for talking to you that way. You know how much I love you. Please say that you forgive me. And I know you'll get back to writing one day. Now, say you forgive your girl!"

"Okay, I forgive you."

"So, can we move in with Abe?"

"Linda, will I have my own room, with a sofa or couch?"

"Yes."

"And a TV?"

"And a TV. I'll talk to Abe about it. I'll tell him it soothes your nerves."

"And what about the money for the wine?"

"Abe will give it to me. I'll tell him you have to have the wine for medicinal purposes, that the doctor told you that you had to drink a certain amount every day."

"Will this old guy believe that story?"

"Jim, he believes everything I tell him! His beloved Rachel would never lie to him!"

Jim threw his arms around Linda, kissing her on the lips

"Linda, get those clothes off!" he shouted. "I got that urge for my bitch!"

"Jim, I worship you!"

7

Abe was shocked when he saw Jim's dissipated, blotchy face. But he said nothing. He sized up the situation immediately. Linda had a drunkard for a brother. And he would have to supply him with whatever it was he drank. From Jim's puffy, purplish-red face Abe judge him to be a wino. Good, he thought, wine is cheaper than hard liquor.

Abe did not by sign or word indicate to Linda that he knew the kind of contemptible weakling Jim was, living off his sister! He felt little pity for Jim. And he thought, his condition would make his life with Linda simpler, more convenient. Sure he would have a TV installed in this brother's bedroom. He would be out of the way most of the time, getting drunk on wine, watching TV and sleeping off his wine boozing.

It was just as Abe thought it would be. In the following days and weeks the old man saw little of the brother. Jim came down to breakfast ten or eleven o'clock, long after Abe left the house on those days when he worked in the jewelry shop, or when he went out shopping.

The only time Abe saw Jim was when he came down for supper, the supper the old man always cooked. Linda saw nothing about cooking. At the dinner table Jim maintained a moody silence for the most part, while Abe and Linda engaged in small talk. When Jim was done eating, he got up, said good night and returned to his room. To resume his wine-drinking, Abe was sure.

Abe insisted that Linda come to his bedroom every night, but not always to make love. Sometimes all the old man wanted to do was kiss and cuddle Linda and talk to her as if she were his dead wife. Linda did not object. Abe was prompt with his deposits in her savings account.

After staying with Abe for an hour or so, Linda returned to her bedroom. But she would not remain long. Twenty minutes later, she would leave her room and tiptoe down to Abe's room, listening at the door she had left open a crack. Soon as she heard his regular snoring, she quietly slipped into Jim's room.

Linda did get a certain physical enjoyment in her sexual relations with Abe. But with Jim it was not only sexual pleasure, it was love. How she loved making love with him!

When she looked hard at Jim's ravaged face, Linda felt great pity for him. But his body was still smooth and appealing, not like Abe's bony, flabby body. Jim was a bum, but he was her man, and she loved him passionately. Only death would part them.

Abe was glad when Jim returned to his room after he ate. There always seemed to be a kind of tension in the air when he was present. Or so it seemed to the old man.

When Jim was gone, Abe felt a sense of relief, that he could relax a little with Linda. When supper was over, Abe would take Linda's hand and lead her into the living room, take her in his lap and ask what kind of say she had had.

Of course Linda would not tell Abe that sometimes she spent hours in Jim's rom. She would tell him about her trip to the beauty salon, her stroll through Central Park and around the lake, or about the soap operas she watched that afternoon.

Abe would listen avidly to every word she said, relishing the sound of her voice, all the time kissing her on the cheek, or gently caressing Linda's breast and calling her by his dead wife's name.

But Linda was not being truthful to Abe about those walks she took. She had thought about something for days and decided, why should she lose a chance of making money with all the free time she had in the afternoons? Why not do a little streetwalking and earn some extra money?

Linda always made sure that she got back by five o'clock, take a shower, set the table for supper and help Abe out in the kitchen.

All went well for months until one night Abe woke up from his after-dinner nap. He usually slept for ever an hour, but for some reason that night he woke up after only ten minutes.

He glanced around for Linda. She always sat in an armchair across from him, either reading a book or watching TV. Linda was not in the room.

"Linda, Linda!" Abe called out, thinking she might have gone into the kitchen.

But Linda did not answer, did not come into the living room. Abe panicked, jumping up from his chair, going into the kitchen, and the dining room. Where was she? he wondered with a vague feeling of dread.

The reason for Linda's mysterious absence was that she met a man that afternoon near Columbus Circle. He took her to his apartment in an apartment building that was half a block from Abe's brownstone.

Linda was happily surprised when the man paid her. Her usual fee was thirty dollars, but because the man wore a well-tailored suit she demanded fifty for her services. But when she was about to leave the apartment, her customer handed her two fifty-dollar bills.

"Oh, thank you!" Linda smiled. "You're very generous!"

"And I want you to come back tonight, after eight o'clock."

"I can't come tonight. How about tomorrow afternoon?"

"I said I want you tonight! I haven't had a woman like you in bed since I went on a business trip to Milan five years ago. I have some work to do downtown, but I want to see you again in three hours! You're young, got a terrific body, and you gave me the best time since Milan!"

"I told you I can't come back tonight," Linda insisted.

"Damnit, that's when I want you! I get so tensed up with my business deals that I got to have some relief! You come back here after eight and I'll pay you two hundred dollars!"

Two hundred dollars! Linda thought. That was a lot of money. She could not turn down that much money. She was thinking fast. Abe always had that snooze after dinner. She could do it! I'll be gone only thirty or forty minutes at the most, she figured.

"All right," Linda said, "but only for a half hour. I have to visit my sick mother in the hospital."

"Sure, a half hour is all I need, and baby, you're going to earn your money!"

And so that night, Linda slipped out of the house right after Abe dropped off to sleep, almost running down the block to the apartment building.

Abe was still standing in the living room, puzzled not knowing what to think, when Linda walked briskly in, flushed, her hair mussed up, her eyes still shining brightly from the different exotic ways the man had made love to her.

"Oh, you're up!" she said, startled.

"Yes, I'm up! Where were you? Did you go out?"

"Uh . . . yes. It was so stuffy in here . . . I wanted to get some fresh air. I sat on the stoop."

"Is there a strong wind blowing?"

"Why do you ask that?"

"Your hair, look at your hair!"

Going to the mirror on the wall Linda said, "Oh . . . yes, there is a little breeze. It sure felt good on my face."

But from her nervous manner Abe was not entirely convinced that Linda was speaking the truth. And there was something about her explanation that bothered him, exactly what, he was not sure. Abe did not have a suspicious mind, but he began to suspect that maybe there were things about Linda he did not know.

For the next few days Abe did not go down to the store, phoning the owner that he was sick. He wanted to keep an eye on Linda. He had her come with him when he went shopping, and he accompanied her on her walks through the park. Abe could see how annoyed and irked Linda was by his constant presence.

Once, when they were walking out of Central Park to return home, Linda burst out peevishly, "Can't I have a little time to myself! Must you always be around me! You make me feel like a prisoner!"

"Rachel, my darling!" Abe said, stunned by her angry outburst.

Pulling her hand out of his hand Linda said irritably, "Rachel, oh God, I wish you would once in a while call me by own name!"

"What's the matter, what's wrong?"

"Nothing's wrong!" Linda said, boiling inside, thinking of the money she was losing these empty afternoons with Abe. "Let's go home, I'm hungry!"

Ten days after Linda's short disappearance, Abe was in bed, sleeping lightly, troubled by Linda's sulky moods, when he heard a noise in the hall of a squeaky door opening. Getting out of bed he went to the door, opening it a crack and looking out. Soon he began to hear soft moaning sounds. They were coming from Jim's room.

He stood there, transfixed, not knowing what to do. There was no doubt about the nature of the sounds. There were cries of joy, sighs of pleasure—the mingled sounds men and woman make when they are enjoying sex.

Abe remained at the door for a half hour. His patience was rewarded. He saw Linda come out of Jim's room. And she was naked! She went down the hall to her own room.

Abe could not believe his own eyes. He was shocked and appalled by what he had seen. Brother and sister were having wicked incestuous relations!

Abe went sadly back to his bed, filled with dismay, sitting on the edge, thinking. What should he do? Should he tell Linda that he had seen her come out of her brother's room, that he had heard those ardent sounds of love?

Abe recalled the books in the Bible he had read many times. Back then, thousands of years ago, the Hebrews stoned to death brother and sister caught having sex together, guilty of a serious offensive against the Law.

But mostly Abe was deeply grieved and disappointed with Linda. She was betraying him. For how long? How long were Jim and Linda lovers? Long before they even came to live under his roof, Abe was sure.

In the eccentric old man's mind it was not Linda, Jim's sister, who was committing the sin of infidelity, it was Rachel, Rachel, his beloved wife! Oh, it was cruel, unbearable, his Rachel, an unfaithful wife!

What should he do? Should he confront the woman he loved with her guilt, tell her that he had seen her leave Jim's room in the nude?

For days Abe brooded in agony over his problem. What should he do, what should he do! Some nights he knew that Linda went from his bedroom to Jim's! He suffered brutally when he stood at his open door, listening to them making love.

In the store he was glad when a customer came in to buy something. How happy it made him when a young couple came in to look with smiling, excited faces at the engagement rings. They always took so long to decide the kind of ring they wanted. Abe did not mind. He was as patient and helpful as he could be.

One day, when a couple bought an engagement ring and were walking out the door, holding hands, smiling into each other's eyes, lips touching, a solution to his problem came to him. He would ask Linda to marry him!

Yes, that was the answer! Surely when they were bound together in holy matrimony, Linda would stop having sexual relations with her brother, realize her duty to her husband.

Of course Jim would have to leave the house. Yes, he would have to move out. I'll find him a boarding house, Abe thought, and give him an allowance to live on. Maybe they would have Jim over for dinner once in a while. After all, they were brother and sister.

On his way uptown in the subway Abe rehearsed in his mind how he would propose to Linda. Should he do it right away, soon as he entered the house? Or should he wait until after super, when they were in the living room, alone, just the two of them?

Abe was so thrilled with his wonderful plan that he almost missed his station, laughing happily at himself.

As he went up the steps of the station a horrible thought sent a chill through him. Suppose Linda refused to marry him? She might, yes, she might, he thought understandingly. She was young, only in her twenties, and he was almost seventy.

But as he walked the several blocks to his house he convinced himself that Linda would marry him. She would not turn him down! He would tell her how much he loved her, how much he needed her. And he would promise to start an investment program for her! Yes, she would have a stock portfolio of a hundred thousand dollars! And he would invest more money for her month after month!

And when she said yes, he would tell her that Jim would have to go. He would say nothing about what he knew about them. No, that he would not mention. That knowledge would put a strain on their marriage.

But what reason would he give for wanting Jim out of the house? He would have to think of something. Would it hurt Linda if he told her that he knew about Jim's wine addiction and that he should go to a rehabilitation clinic for treatment? And once he got Jim out of the house he would make sure he never came back to live with them again.

What a wonderful happy life he would have with his Rachel! Maybe, maybe, God, could he really dream such a dream—maybe they would have a baby—a gift from God! Why not! Older men than he was had fathered babies.

Abe was sure everything would work out fine. He would propose to Linda, she would say yes. And then he would bring up Jim's wine-drinking. He had to stop. He needed treatment. He was a young man. He had to do something with his life. Was he going to spend the rest of his days in a wine bottle?

Perhaps he should have a long talk with Jim, in private, tell him that he needed professional help, maybe try to instill some ambition in him.

But when Abe walked into the house he could not find Linda anywhere. Not in the kitchen, the living room and the dining room. He even checked the toilet.

Was she upstairs in Jim's room, making love with that bum brother of hers? he thought with a sickening feeling. He hurried up to the second floor, walking in without knocking.

Jim was asleep, stretched out on the couch. Two empty wine bottles were on the coffee table. A third bottle was two-thirds empty. The TV was on. After turning it off he went over to the couch and looked down at Jim. His mouth was open and he was making snuffling sounds. The smell of wine came up from him.

Abe was disgusted by the sight of Jim. A sudden surge of hatred rose up in him. He was a lazy good-for-nothing bum, and Linda's lover—her own brother! Yes, he hated this man! Why couldn't he drink himself to death? What did his sister see in this wretch? He was rotten through and through.

Maybe he could tell him where Linda went. Roughly shaking Jim, Abe said, "Hey, Jim, wake up, wake up!"

"Who . . . ? What . . . ?" Jim said sleepily, sitting up and rubbing his eyes.

"Get up, stand up! Are you glued to that couch?"

Jim got off the couch and stood up. Scratching his head he said grumpily, "Why'd you wake me up? I was having a nice rest.

"I'd like to know what you were resting from! You spend most of the day lying on this couch. Don't you ever go out, for a little fresh air, exercise?"

"Don't worry about me. I can take care of myself. What do you want? Is supper ready?"

"No, it isn't. That's what I came to see you about. Linda isn't home. Did she tell you that she was going out?"

Jim knew that Linda had been going out on the streets to pick up some extra money. But of course he had no intention of telling Abe about that.

"She did say she was going out to do some shopping."

"Linda should've been home by now!" Abe said. "It's going on to seven o'clock!"

"Hey, what's going on up there?" Linda called from the first-floor hall. "I'm home! Jim, has Abe got back yet? I was delayed. I—"

"Shut up!" Jim yelled, running out of the bedroom and followed by Abe. Linda was at the foot of the stairs, looking up. "Abe's up here. We were . . . talking."

"I'm coming down," Abe said.

"I'm going to take a shower," Jim said to Abe. "Tell my sister I'll be down in twenty minutes."

As Abe came slowly down the stairs he asked, "Linda, where've you been?"

"Oh, I thought I'd take a walk in the park."

"Jim said that you went shopping?"

"He did? Well . . . I changed my mind. I'm sorry I got back a little late. I lost track of the time. Why don't you buy me a wristwatch?"

"I'll do that. I'm going into the kitchen and get started on our supper. Start setting the table."

Abe was not completely satisfied with Linda's explanation for being out. He noticed that she did not look him in the eye when she spoke to him. Also, he noticed that she moved slowly, as if she was tired, exhausted.

After the hot, delicious meal Abe felt a little better. He waited until he and Linda had been sitting quietly in the living room. Linda was reading the paper and Abe was watching her, thinking of what he was going to say to her.

Taking a deep breath and moving his armchair closer to Linda, Abe coughed and said, "Linda, would you please put down the paper? I have something . . . very important I want to say."

Linda put aside the newspaper and stared apprehensively at Abe. Was he going to question her more closely about her coming in late today? But she was relieved by what he said next.

"Darling, I've been thinking . . . about us, about our future together . . . ."

"And what have you been thinking about our future?" Linda asked, smiling.

"Call me old-fashioned, call me a fuddy-duddy . . . I—Linda, you know I love you, love you very much! I realize that you can't have the same feelings for me that I have for you. An old man like me . . . I know you can't . . . love me."

"Abe, you mustn't talk like that. You've been so wonderful to me, how could I help not loving you?"

"Linda, you mean that, you really love me?" Abe said, getting up from his chair, happy, excited, his eyes lighting up.

The real truth was that Linda did not love Abe. She felt pity for the old man, pity mixed with revulsion. Sometimes she wished she could spit it all out, have the satisfaction of telling this old goat, as she thought of Abe, what she really felt about him. When he took her in his arms in bed, her skin crawled. His arms were bony, and his hands always were sweaty. And his body had an old man's smell about it so strong that sometimes it brought on a wave of nausea to Linda's nostrils. And then when he mounted her! She felt shame, disgust. How different it was with Jim, her adorable Jim! Linda preferred those strange men she picked up on the streets. At least they were young, most of them. But Abe! Those hairs sticking out of his nose and ears! And when bouncing up and down on her belly, passionately and repeatedly calling her his dead wife's name! So sickening, so morbid!

But Linda could not tell Abe these things. She and Jim had a good thing going, living this free and easy life. And all she had to do was endure Abe's sexual embraces a few times a week. It was not too much to pay for the good life the old man provided for her and Jim.

And then Linda heard Abe's voice.

"And since I love you and you love me—oh, darling, it's so hard for me to get the words out. You are so lovely and young and I'm . . . an old man . . . ."

"Abe, what is it you want to say to me?"

"Linda, I love, I love my Rachel!" Abe said, tears running down his cheeks. "I must have her with me always, always! I love you!"

"Yes, you already said that," Linda replied lightly. "But just what is the important thing you want to say to me?"

"My precious darling," Abe declared, falling down on his knees and placing his hands in Linda's lap, "I want to marry you! I want you to be my wife!"

"Your wife!" Linda said, shocked and disgusted by the old man's words. She looked contemptuously down at Abe. He had dropped his head on her knees and was crying.

Raising his head and looking up at Linda, his face tear-streaked, he said, "Rachel, my love, my life, make me the happiest man in the world! Say that you will be my wife!"

His wife! Linda thought with angry contempt. How could this old man, this Jew, dare think that she would ever marry him! Never, never! She loved Jim, and someday they would get married! Her rage boiled over inside of her as she thought of Abe's proposal of marriage. The gall of the old Jew! Let him get in bed with her for a half hour a couple of times a week, yes. But not to sleep with this stinking old man every night of the week!

With her raging anger Linda lost all control of herself. She got up, roughly pushing Abe away from her. He fell over backward with a cry. Lying flat on his back he looked up at Linda, towering over him, her face blazing with furious anger, her eyes flashing fire, her crooked mouth showing her contempt.

Getting up slowly to his feet Abe said, "Rachel, my darling, what's wrong? What have I done to make you so angry, to knock me over like that?"

"Goddamn your Rachel! She's dead, buried and rotting in her grave!"

"No, no, don't say such things! But why are you so angry? What have I said that upset you so much?"

"What you have said, you silly old senile fool! Don't you know! I don't mind being your whore two or three times a week, but I will never be your wife, Jew!"

Abe staggered back, as if mud had been flung in his face.

"Darling, don't talk like that to me. I love you!"

"And I throw your love back at you like so much shit! That's what your love means to me—shit, garbage! How dare you love me, and expect me to love you, you runty ugly little Jew! I'll never marry a creature like you, never! I could never marry you!"

"Why, why?"

"I'll tell you why!" Linda said, laughing. She went out to the hall and called out, "Jim, Jim, come down!"

A few moments later Jim and Linda walked into the living room.

"What is it, Linda?" Jim asked, looking from Abe to Linda. "What's up, sis?"

"Can that sis stuff, Jim," Linda said. And pointing at Abe she added, "You want a laugh? This old man, this Jew, wants to marry me!"

"No!"

"Yes! Isn't that enough to bust your gut!"

"Darling," Abe cried piteously, "why are you being so cruel to me?"

"Abe, I got a piece of news for you. Jim is not my brother, he's the one man in my life, the man I love!"

Abe was stunned. He looked from one to the other, his mouth open. He seemed to have lost the power of speech, like a man paralyzed.

"Well, what've you got to say?" Linda said.

"Come on, old man, speak up!" Jim said, smiling.

Abe cleared his throat and said, "My love, it isn't true, say it isn't true. Jim isn't the man you love, is he?"

"Old man, I'm not your love! Do I have to tell you a hundred times! Jim is my whole life! I love him, adore him!"

"And there's something else you should know, old man," Jim said. "Linda has been visiting me in my room at night, right under your nose!"

"Yes, I know all about that, and I thought it was very wicked that brother and sister . . . ."

"Oh, so you knew about those visits, did you, Abe?" Linda said proudly. "Well, I'm glad, glad!"

"How could you do this to me, after all I did for you, giving you and Jim a home?"

"Mister, I don't owe you anything!"

"What will you do now, you and Jim?"

"What else can we do, now? that you know about us? Move out, before you throw us out."

Abe stared grimly at Linda and Jim for several moments as they grinned back at him. His face hardened, his lips were a thin line. There was a cold glitter in his eyes.

Turning away from Jim and Linda, Abe walked out of the room. A few moments later he came back. He had one hand behind his back. Linda and Jim were standing close together, looking lovingly at each other.

When Abe returned to the room, Linda and Jim turned to him happy, arrogant smiles on their faces. But when the old man brought his hand out from behind his back, and they saw the revolver that he was holding, the smiles faded from their faces.

"Abe, what are you going to do?" Linda said in a meek, frightened voice.

"I am going to punish you and Jim for your wicked deception," Abe said, firing two shots into Linda's chest, and two shots into Jim's chest. Both of them crumpled to the floor.

Abe sat down in a chair, the gun dropping to the floor. He gazed down at Linda's lifeless eyes staring up at him.

"Rachel, Rachel," he sobbed, "why were you unfaithful to me, your husband! I loved you so much, and you committed the worst sin a wife—how could you do that to me! You sinned against me and the Law! I had to punish you with death!"

For a few moments Abe wept quietly, turning his face away from the bodies at his feet. Then, glancing down at the floor, the revolver caught his eye. He bent down and picked it up. Gripping it tightly he cried out, "Rachel, my beloved Rachel, I can't go on living without your love, without you! I won't, no, I won't!"

The Resurrectionist

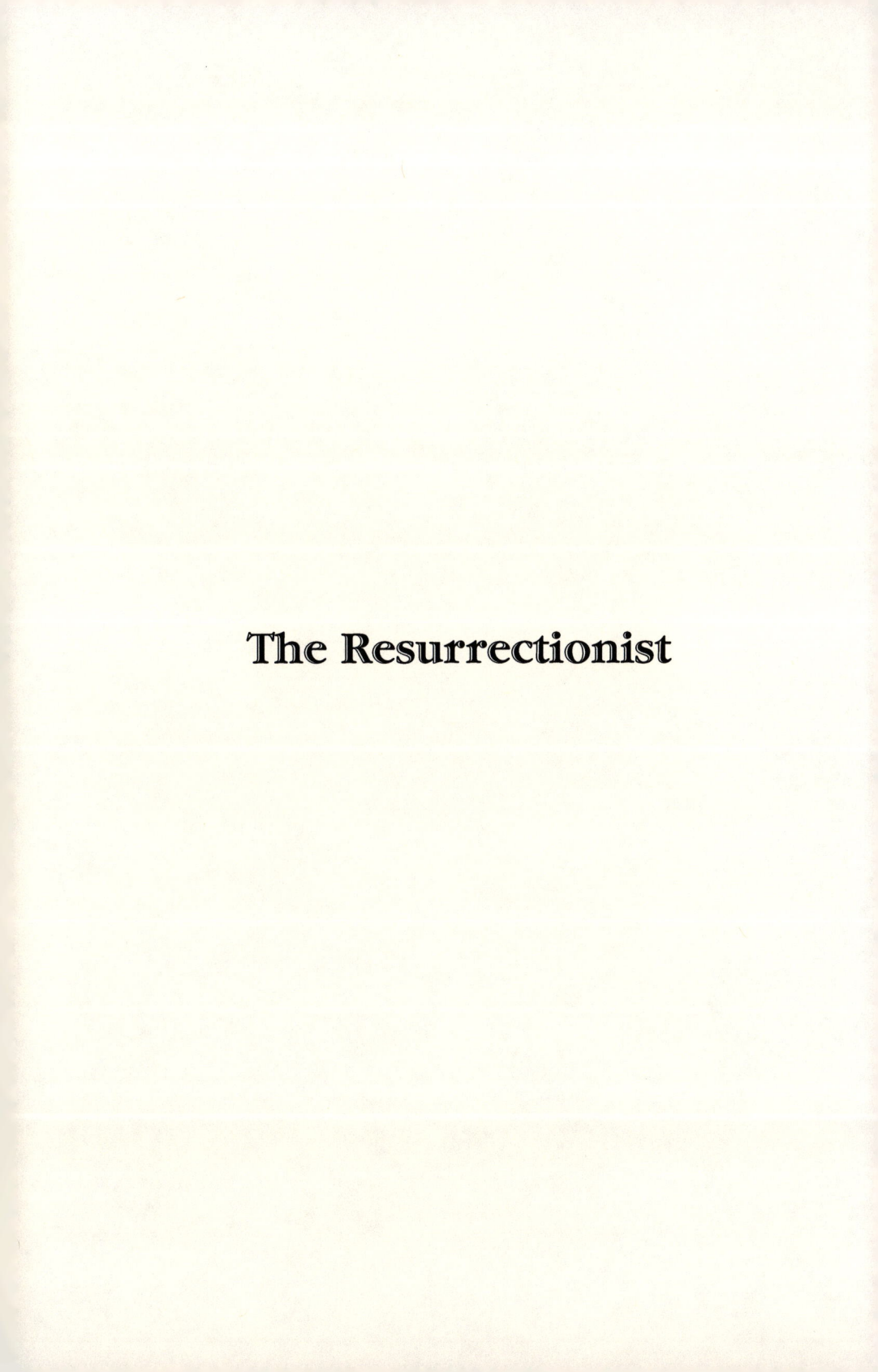

1

"Seventy thousand fans are on their feet, cheering, shouting, hoping Jolly Johnny Fortel can pull off a miracle play, as he has done so many times in the past. Only six seconds left, and forty-five yards to the goal line. Time for just one play, and everyone in this stadium knows it's going to be a pass. Can Jolly Johnny do it? We are going to find out right now. The players come out of the huddle. Johnny is calling the signals . . . a long count. There's the snap! Johnny backpedals . . . breaks out of the grip of a tackler, and there it goes, a long arching pass down the field. Turbel, that great pass receiver with those long arms, leaps up and—touchdown, touchdown! Jolly Johnny has done it again! No question about it, folks, he is the greatest quarter-back in pro football, a man who has led his team to three superbowl victories!"

In the stands, deliriously happy and thrilled was the brother of Johnny Fortel, Gilbert. He was madly hugging his girlfriend, Carol Sutton, and he was actually crying out of sheer joy.

Gilbert and Carol worked together in Memorial Hospital. Gilbert, Doctor Gilbert Fortel, was a cardiologist and heart surgeon and Carol always acted as the head nurse when he performed surgery.

They had been lovers for three years. Only six months ago Carol had moved into Gilbert's apartment. He had strong feelings for Carol, sometimes in the heat of passion declaring his love for her. But after the lovemaking, whenever Carol mentioned marriage, Gilbert was evasive, much to her disappointment.

Gilbert was very proud of his famous younger brother. Gilbert was thirty-two, Johnny, twenty-eight. Yes, he was proud of Johnny. He was more than a fabulously successful football player—he was a celebrity! But mingled with his pride in his brother was a little envy.

Every day Gilbert read in the papers about Johnny, and not only in the sports pages. His name was always in the gossip columns, linked with some supermodel or a Hollywood actress. And those wild parties he threw in his townhouse! They were more than wild—they were notorious! Johnny had it all, wealth (his contract ran into the tens of millions) fame and all the lovely girls he wanted.

Once Gilbert and Carol had been invited to one of those parties. Fifty guests drinking, stuffing themselves, and occasionally couples disappearing, going up to the bedrooms on the second and third floors.

And of course after the stunning victory that Sunday, Gilbert and Carol waited outside the clubhouse to congratulate Johnny. Waiting also for Johnny were seven or eight screaming young female fans.

When Johnny came out, the girls rushed up to him, howling with delight. He was certainly an All-American male. Tall, slender, and good looking? He was an Adonis.

Even with the girls all around him, he spotted Gilbert and Carol, waving to them to come over. Breaking away from the girls he said, "Gilbert, I'm throwing a party at my place. I want you and—what's her name?"

"My name is Carol, Mister Fortel," she said sulkily.

"Hey, what's this 'mister' business! Call me Jolly Johnny! Everybody does! Come to the party! We're going to have a real blowout! You'll meet the famous and the infamous! I don't discriminate—come one, come all! And all you girls are invited too!"

The females screamed with delight.

"We'll be there," Gilbert said, taking Carol's arm and starting to walk away. "Oh, I almost forgot—Johnny, that was one hell of a touchdown pass you threw! How do you do it, time after time?"

"What a question! I'm Jolly Johnny Fortel, one of a kind! I make them forget Montana, Marino, and even the great Johnny Unitas!"

2

When Gilbert and Carol arrived at Johnny's townhouse the victory celebration was in full swing. Most of his teammates were there, along with Johnny's many friends and girls, girls girls!

The broad long living room had a buffet table fifty feet long, with a bar at one end. Johnny had tired waiters to serve from one of the restaurants he frequented. Tables had been set up in the room and adjacent rooms. A DJ was loudly blasting out music.

Gilbert saw his brother surrounded by a dozen men and women, all laughing, joking and drinking. There was no way to get near him, so he and Carol joined the buffet line and got some food and drinks.

As the party really went into high gear, couples began to disappear up to the second and third floors where the bedrooms were.

When Gilbert saw Johnny about to go up the stairs, slightly tipsy, with three girls, and a bottle of whiskey in his hand he called out, "Johnny, for God's sake, take it easy!"

Turning around, staggering, with a girl on each arm, Johnny laughed and crowed, "Gilbert, stop treating me like your baby brother! I'm healthy as an ox and strong as a bull! And pretty soon these girls are going to find out why I'm called Jolly Johnny Fortel! Goodnight, Gilbert, and you too . . . Carol!"

And that was the last time Gilbert saw his brother alive.

The next morning, just as he was about to sit down to have his breakfast of ham and eggs in front of the TV, Gilbert heard the anchor man mournfully announce, "Today the sports world is in profound shock and grief. It has lost a Titan of football—Johnny Fortel is dead. The greatest quarterback the game has even seen died of a massive heart attack. The cause of—"

Gilbert had shut the TV. He was staggered by the death of his young brother. He could not believe it. He was so alive! So full of exuberant vitality! How could it happen?

But as Gilbert paced the dining room in his apartment, somewhat in a daze, he began to think as a doctor, a cardiologist.

The TV report on Johnny's death made no mention of what caused the fatal heart attack of an athlete in the prime of life and in good health.

But Gilbert was sure what caused his brother's death. Johnny had had a sordid death—in bed with those three girls. His surmise proved correct when, later that day, Gilbert talked to the doctor and the police who came to the townhouse. They found three hysterical, frightened girls and Johnny dead in bed.

3

Gilbert sat six feet from the coffin in which Johnny lay, Carol at his side. The sickly sweet aroma of many flowers pervaded the chapel from the many floral tributes. The place was packed with all the members of Johnny's team, sports writers and friends, sitting in chairs, standing against the walls and outside the chapel.

Gilbert, with Carol holding his hand, stared with steady, unblinking intensity at the body of his brother, that powerful, muscular body, once so so agile, now dead and cold in a coffin.

On the last day of the wake, when they were going to close the coffin, Gilbert broke down, crying like a child, kissing his brother's stone-cold face and hugging the stiff body. Carol tried to pull him away, but Gilbert shook her off. It took two of the hefty linemen to drag him away from the coffin.

And at the cemetery, clutching Carol's hand, Gilbert stood staring down at the open grave into which the coffin had been lowered, holding a single rose in the other hand.

All the mourners started moving away. Carol watched them leave. She turned to Gilbert. He was gazing down at the shiny gray coffin. She tossed her rose down into the grave.

"Gilbert, they are all leaving. Gilbert . . . Gilbert, drop the rose into it. Say goodbye to . . . Johnny . . . ."

"How can I say goodbye to my brother!" he sobbed.

Carol took the rose out of his hand and dropped it on the coffin. Holding his hand tightly, she got Gilbert to start walking toward where the cars were, but very slowly, all the time he kept looking back over his shoulder at the grave.

In the car, on their way to the restaurant, where all the others were going, Gilbert remained moodily silent, his face impassive.

The owner of the team was paying for the lunch in a swanky restaurant. That afternoon it was closed to the public.

Gilbert hardly touched his food, and neither did Carol, as she kept looking at him with serious concern. But Gilbert did have several vodkas on the rocks. Carol slowly sipped her one drink, a Manhattan.

At the beginning of the meal, Johnny's teammates spoke softly, But as the meal progressed, and the men ordered more and more drinks, they began fondly reminiscing about Johnny, his spectacular come-from-behind victories with only minutes to play. And his zany behavior, on and off the field. They all agreed there would never be another Jolly Johnny Fortel!

It was all agonizingly too much for Gilbert to hear. To listen to Johnny's teammates talking about him in the past—dead! Gone forever!

Gulping down his fourth vodka, Gilbert got up and said, "Come on, Carol, let's go to my place."

But Gilbert found no solace in sex. Rolling off Carol's body he lay down beside her, murmuring repeatedly, almost reverently Johnny's name.

Gently taking Gilbert's hand Carol said soothingly, "Darling, stop tormenting yourself. Accept Johnny's death."

"No, no!"

"Gilbert, you're going to drive yourself crazy if you go on obsessing over his death."

"This Sunday Johnny won't be playing. And why? Because he's dead! But he shouldn't be dead!"

"But he is dead, and there's nothing you can do about it."

Turning to Carol Gilbert pronounced ferociously, "Death is a bastard! I wish I could take Death between my two hands and strangle it! Kill it!"

"Gilbert, you're not talking sense, not thinking rationally."

"And you, Carol, are thinking conventionally! For how many hundreds of thousands of years human have servilely and supinely accepted death as the normal course of existence. We have abjectly resigned ourselves to the inevitability of death. Death is inexorable, relentless. We are all born to die. But why, Carol, why must we die someday?"

"Well . . . that's life . . . ."

"Wrong, wrong! That—dying—is an aberration! Death is unnatural!"

"Gilbert, what are you saying?"

"Carol, I say death can be conquered, and I'm going to conqueror it! Victory over death—what a blessing for humanity!"

"Gilbert, how many drinks did you have?"

"I am not drunk! I am talking with the brilliant mind God gave me! Death, your days are numbered!"

"Gilbert, you say that you are going to abolish death?"

"Yes!"

"How?"

"Carol, all the time I've been talking to you I've been thinking how to beat death."

"Tell me, this I want to hear."

"I will ignore that note of sarcasm. Carol, for the first three years I was in college I was majoring in electrical engineering. In my fourth year, I changed my mind. I wanted to be a cardiologist—a heart surgeon. But I still have a great deal of knowledge of the science of electricity."

"What does electricity have to do with you beating death?"

"I'll explain that another time. I do have one big problem—money! I'll need heaps and heaps of money to build the machine that will destroy death! But where am I going to get it?"

"Gilbert, why are you going to . . . to try to do this?"

"I'm doing it for two reasons."

"What's the first one?"

"I want to spite God! I want to show Him that he can't go on inflicting death on us humans while He goes on living!"

"And the second reason?"

"I've always wanted to be a billionaire! When I've invented my resurrection machine, I'm going to charge working people ten thousand dollars, and the rich a million dollars to come back to life! But I have to get the corpse before the undertaker drains the blood out of it. Remember what Dracula said, 'The blood is the life, Mr. Renfield.'"

"So that means, Gilbert, your resurrection machine will not be able to bring Johnny back to life."

"Yes," Gilbert said sadly, "it's too late for him. By now the maggots are feasting on that magnificent body of his."

Carol raised herself in the bed and leaning over Gilbert said with a slight chuckle, "Gilbert, you have been joking about this macabre project of yours . . . you know, beating death, haven't you?"

"No, I most certainly have not! Carol, all the grief and sorrow has left me! I feel, I feel rejuvenated! I'm going to whip death and thumb my nose at God! But where will I get the money I'll need?"

4

The answer to that questions came five days later.

The day after the funeral he had gone to the college library in town and borrowed four books on electrical engineering to brush up on the subject. As he read, he took copious notes.

It was two o'clock in the afternoon when his reading was interrupted by the ringing of his doorbell. Opening the door, Gilbert saw a tall slender, gray-haired man in a business suit with a briefcase in his hand.

"Mr. Gilbert Fortel?" the man said.

"Yes, I'm Gilbert Fortel."

"Mr. Fortel, I'm with the law firm of Ridgely, Porter and Feldman. My name is Otis Hanson. May I come in?"

"Yes, come in."

Once they were seated across from each other in the living room Gilbert asked, "Uh . . . why have you come to see me, Mr. Hanson?"

Opening his briefcase and taking out a folder, Hanson said, "Mr. Fortel, this is your late brother's will."

"My . . . brother's . . . will?"

"Yes. He named you as his sole beneficiary."

"I get . . . everything my brother . . . left?"

"Yes, Mr. Fortel."

"Go on, Mr. Hanson. What did Johnny leave me?"

"All his investments—bonds, stocks, annuities, mutual funds—totaling forty-two million dollars."

"My brother left all that to me?" Gilbert said in wonder and awe. "Forty-two million dollars—all mine?"

"Yes, and also his townhouse."

Gilbert was stunned, he could not speak. He was thinking of Johnny—and the fortune he had left him. Johnny had loved him, just as surely as he had loved Johnny!

As Gilbert thought back at the life he and Johnny had growing up, Hanson was taking some documents out of the briefcase. He looked at Gilbert, deep in thought.

"Uh . . . Mr. Fortel, I have some papers for you to sign. Mr. Fortel . . . ."

"Oh, excuse me. What did you say?"

"You have to sign these papers."

After he had done do, Gilbert asked, "Say, when can I move into the townhouse?"

"Today, tomorrow—any time you wish. It's your property."

Soon as Hanson left, Gilbert phoned Carol and told her to come right over, he had something very important to tell her.

5

An hour later, Gilbert and Carol were going over the townhouse, from the top floor down to the finished basement. Two servants and the cook watched them anxiously. They were worried about their jobs.

The basement was very spacious, over a hundred feet long, and nearly fifty feet wide. It had tables, chairs, couches and a bar in the corner. Sometime Johnny had his small parties down here.

As Gilbert looked around, very pleased and nodding his head, Carol asked, "Gilbert, what are you going to do about the maid, the butler and the cook? They sure looked worried."

Very firmly, he stated, "I'm going to fire them! With the plans I have in mind, I don't want them snooping around in this house! They have to go!"

"Gilbert, have a heart! They must have worked for your brother a long time. Now they'll be out of a job."

"Okay, I'll give them good references and a fat severance pay."

"How much?"

"What do you say to fifty thousand each?"

"Gilbert, that's very generous of you!"

"Now, Carol, about us and this house."

"Yes, go on, what about us and this house?"

"First of all, Carol, you are going to quit your job at the hospital, same as me."

"Why do I have to leave the hospital?"

"Carol, have you forgotten my colossal resurrection project?"

"Gilbert, you weren't serious about that, were you?"

"Yes, damnit, seriously serious! I'm going through with it! I have all the money I need to finance it, and I have this big basement for my laboratory. And to answer your question, I need a very capable assistant—Carol Sutton! You have helped me perform many heart operations, and very successfully! Now you are going to help me conquer death! I'll give the Bronx cheer to God, and start making that billion dollars!"

"Gilbert, I love you, but I do think you are mad!"

"Yes, madly confidence! In two weeks this basement will be transformed into my laboratory! And with all the equipment and tools I'll need! And one very, very expensive piece of equipment!"

"What's that?"

"A dynamoelectronic generator! A very powerful one—powerful enough to shock the dead back to life!"

"Gilbert, that is preposterous—insane!"

"Oh, I know it will take time—a lot of experiments with corpses."

"Experiments with corpses?"

"Yes, I will need corpses, freshly dead corpses, before the undertaker has drained the blood out of them."

"Gilbert, you are beginning to sound like Henry Frankenstein!"

"Carol, stop making fun of me. You are going to be living in this house, working with me."

"Uh . . . about the corpses, where will you get these . . . freshly dead people?"

Frowning, Gilbert said, "I have been giving that considerable thought. And I think I have the solution to that problem. I remembered that my roommate's father in college was a Mafia boss."

"So how does that help you with the corpse problem?"

"Over the years I've kept in touch with Angelo. Before we graduated, Angelo told me his father wanted him to join the mob. He told his father bluntly and positively that he was not going in for a life of crime. Angelo went on to law school. He's done all right for himself. He works for a Wall Street law firm, has a nice house in the country, a wife and four kids. I'm sure Angelo can help me get in touch with his Mafia father. For a price, the father will find me the kind men I need to get me corpses."

"You mean snatching dead bodies?"

"Yes!"

"But that's a crime!"

"A minor felony! I'll be saving the family the expense of a funeral!"

"Gilbert, you're getting into deep water."

"Carol, are you sticking with me?"

"I love you . . . okay, I'm in."

"Good girl! Now I have to phone Angelo! I hope his father can get me two hardened criminals who aren't squishmish about handling corpses!"

Three weeks later, the basement had been transformed into the laboratory. Against the wall, reaching almost up to the ceiling, was the giant, powerful dynamoelectronic generator, into which Gilbert planned to place the fresh corpses to shock them back to life. However, after thinking things over, Gilbert decided that possibly the corpse, to become redivivus needed a strong chemical solution to give it an extra boost.

At the moment, Gilbert was showing the two men Angelo's father around the basement, as Carol, in a far corner, was standing at a table with test tubes, jars of chemicals and a Bunsen burner.

The names of the men were Ivor and Elmo, ex-convicts, who between them had served eighteen years in prison. They were big hulking brutes, just the kind of men Gilbert required.

He did not think it necessary to tell Ivor and Elmo why he needed the corpses. But when they insistently demanded to know the reason, Gilbert explained everything to them, When he did, the two men looked at each other and laughed.

"Well, it's your money!" Ivor scoffed.

"Have you handled corpses before?" Gilbert asked.

"Not exactly, but we have produced corpses!" Elmo laughed.

"Now I want you to understand exactly what I want. I want fresh corpses. I don't want dead bodies from a funeral home. I want freshly dead men and women. That means the hospital morgue. Think you can do it?"

"No problem. You have to supply us with a van and some tools," Ivor said.

"You'll have everything you'll need. I'll pay you five thousand dollars for each body, and don't forget, I want males and females."

"Not enough," Elmo grunted. "Ten thousand for each stiff."

"Okay, ten thousand. But no accident cases. I don't want mutilated bodies."

"Okay, they'll be dead, but they'll be in good condition," Ivor promised.

"I think you two should live here. You can be useful in this laboratory. There are plenty of beds upstairs."

"Do we eat out?" Elmo said.

"No, my assistant, Carol, will do the cooking."

"The setup looks okay to me, eh, Elmos?"

"Yeah, sure. Say, Mr. Fortel, how many bodies do you think you'll be needing?"

"Can't tell. It's all according the way the experiments go on the corpses.

"At ten thousand a body, I hope you have to make plenty of experiments!" Ivor laughed.

"Of course I realize there's a big 'if' in this project.

"And what's that?" Elmo asked.

"If that dynamoelectronic generator can do the trick."

Both men gazed across the room at the giant machine, very much impressed, Ivor commenting, "Say, that baby must've cost a pile of dough!"

"Eight million dollars to be exact, Ivor. Oh, by the way, do you men think you'll have any difficulty . . . acquiring those cadavers . . . breaking into the hospitals and? . . ."

"Difficulty!" Elmo snorted and laughed. "Tell him, Ivor!"

"Hell, me and Elmo did some petty burglary jobs in our younger days. Getting into those hospital morgues will be a snap!"

"You'll have the panel truck and all the tools you'll need in two days. And don't forget, fresh corpses, and preferably young ones!"

6

Gilbert and Carol were gloomily having their supper in the big dining room. Ivor and Elmo were out, getting rid of the two bodies of the failed experiment that afternoon. It was the twenty-second failure, costing Gilbert two hundred and twenty thousand dollars.

And more than forty thousand dollars in the enormous amount of electricity used.

Carol was eating, but not Gilbert. He stared grimly down at the steak and potatoes, his hand on the glass of red wine. He gulped it, and refilled his glass.

"Gilbert, you must eat!" You can't live on wine!" Carol admonished.

"I'm not hungry."

"Gilbert, how many more experiments are you going to do?"

"As many as it takes—until I succeed!"

"How many bodies are you going to have those two gangsters dump in the river with chains around their legs?"

"I'm not going to fail, I'm not going to fail!"

"Gilbert, I hate to say it, but I think it's futile for you to go on. It was a mad scheme to begin with! Raising the dead! Only God could do that—Jesus! But he had supernatural power as the Son of God. And what do you have, Gilbert? Electricity!"

"You know, Carol, I think that's the problem," Gilbert said with a slow smile on his face. "Yes, that's it! We need more power! And I want you to make those chemical solutions stronger, much stronger! Tomorrow I'm going to buy twelve great big batteries and attach them to the generator! With all that extra power I'm sure to bring back the dead!"

Just then Elmo and Ivor walked in. They looked at the steaks and inhaled deeply, rubbing their hands.

"Those steaks sure smell good!" Ivor said.

"And how!" Elmo agreed. "Miss Carol, give me the thickest steak you have! Medium rare!"

"Make mine a two-incher, and cremate it!" Ivor requested.

"Uh . . . you disposed of those bodies?" Gilbert said.

"Sure, sure," Elmo said. "They sank like a rock!"

"I want you men to get me two more bodies. But not right away. Tomorrow I'm going to buy some extra batteries. After I have them attached to the generator, and see that everything is working fine, you can fetch those bodies."

"Mr. Fortel, we have delivered twenty-two bodies to you," Ivor said.

"And so far, we haven't received a dime!" Elmo complained

"According to my calculation, you owe us two hundred and twenty thousand dollars!" Ivor declared.

"We want what's owing to us tonight—now!" Elmo demanded.

"And from now on, I suggest we have a pay-as-you go arrangement, okay, Mr. Fortel?" Ivor said with a serious grin.

"Very well. Are you willing to take a check—"

"No check!" both ex-convicts bellowed.

"Cash!" Ivor said.

"In twenties, fifties and hundreds," Elmo said.

"Okay, you'll get your money. But tonight is out of the question. I don't keep that much cash in the house. I'm afraid you'll have to wait a few days. I'll phone my stock broker tomorrow and have him sell some stock. Is that satisfactory?"

"I suppose it will have to be," Ivor said, showing his disappointment.

"And don't forget, from now on, cash for corpses, like Ivor said."

"I'll have your steaks ready in fifteen minutes," Carol said, getting up from the table. In the meantime, go wash your hands, you two."

"Why do we have to wash our hands?" Ivor asked.

"Yeah, we haven't been doing any dirty work!" Elmo joked.

"I think you should do what Carol says," Gilbert said.

"Sure, whatever you say. And how about a couple of bottles of wine?"

"Carol, take care of these . . . . gentlemen. I have to do some mathematical calculations to find out how much more power that generator needs to shock dead people back to life!"

7

"Eureka! Eureka! I have done it! I have succeeded! And there is the living proof! They are alive, alive! I have restored the dead to life! And I did it without the power of God! I did it with pure science!"

Yes, it was true. An hour ago two young dead people, a man and a women, were placed inside the dynamoelectronic generator, with fourteen powerful batteries attached to it.

And when, sixty minutes later, after thousands of bolts of electricity (and with the injections of Carol's strong chemical solution) had passed through the bodies of the corpses, the doors of the generator were opened, and out stepped the man and woman. They were a little unsteady on their legs, and they did seem a bit dazed.

But they were very much alive!

Gilbert, Carol, Ivor and Elmo stared at the young couple in stunned silence for some time as they walked about, seeming to be lost.

Two hours later, after Gilbert had given them a thorough examination, to see that they were well and in good health, the man and woman walked out of the townhouse to return to their loved ones.

To make sure the first success was no fluke, Gilbert brought back to life three more men and three more women.

Now it was no longer necessary for Ivor and Elmo to burglarize the hospitals for bodies. But Gilbert still required their services to work the generator and help around the laboratory.

The need to steal bodies was no longer necessary because Gilbert placed a full-page advertisement in all the newspapers in town and even commercials on TV, announcing to the world that the dead could be brought back to life.

In the following weeks, Gilbert brought back to life six hundred men and women, and sixty-five children. Of the corpses he had resurrected, eighty were millionaires—eighty million dollars plus millions he got from working people. Gilbert was positively on his way to becoming that billionaire that was his heart's desire.

Gilbert was so happy he even thought of proposing marriage to Carol. And she was only too willing.

As for Ivor and Elmo, Gilbert now paid them a regular salary. They were now receiving two thousand dollars a week. This was the first legitimate job they ever had, and the experience for these professional criminals was very exhilarating.

Yes, Gilbert, Carol, Ivor and Elmo were happy.

But the same could not be said for the undertakers. Their business was deader than the corpses they had formerly handled. They were going broke! They complained to the politicians, to the mayor. But what could they do? There was no law against raising people from the dead, was there?

And in the Oval Office of the White House there was gloom and consternation. Sitting at his desk, fretting and worried, was President Walter Maynard. And seated in front of the desk were two men who were worse off. They were Secretary of the Treasury Howard Simkins and Budget Director Ken Steckler. And were they in a sweat—panic-stricken and almost on the verge of hysteria.

"Mr. President, you've got to do something about this Gilbert guy! He can't go on raising dead people!" Simkins stoutly declared.

"He'll bankrupt the government!" Steckler added. "If people live forever, never dying, the government will have to keep shelling out Social Security checks forever!"

"I agree with both of you," the president said, nervously scratching his head. "This government cannot function without death. We have to bring back death!"

"But how, Mr. President, how?" Steckler asked.

President Maynard, after taking a deep breath, and seeming to come to a decision, picked up the phone and barked, "Get Phil Coleman here right away! And I mean pronto!"

"Uh . . . Mr. President, why are you seeing the director of the CIA? He can't help us avert national financial disaster, can he?" Simkins asked.

"I think you two had better leave. I want to see Coleman alone."

A half hour later, Coleman walked into the Oval Office.

"Mr. President, here I am. But why the urgent call? Has something come up? Is it anything in the Middle East? Russia? China?"

"Sit down, Phil, and it isn't anything outside the country. The problem is right here in the United States!"

"I'm listening, sir."

"The problem is about the resurrectionist guy, Gilbert . . . what's his name . . . ."

"Fortel. Yeah, he's making quite a name for himself. And is he cleaning up! Corpses are being flown into his town from all over the country—the world! His brother was a great quarterback."

"The hell with that guy's brother!" Maynard said irritably.

"Mr. President, you got something on your mind?"

Lowering his voice and leaning forward, President Walter Maynard pronounced, "Phil, I want you to destroy the whole building where this Fortel guy has that machine that brings people back to life. And I want him to go up with the building! Kill him and his assistants! Wipe them out! For the sake of the United States of America!"

And then Maynard went on to explain why Coleman had to carry out this criminal and murderous order.

When the president was done, the director of the CIA remained silent. He showed no expression on his face. Maynard looked at him anxiously. He started to worry.

"Well, Phil, how about it? Are you going to carry out my order?"

"Blow up the building with those four people in it," he remarked thoughtfully, tapping his chin with a forefinger.

"Yes. Will you do it?"

"And if I don't?"

"There isn't much of a future for this country. Retired workers can't go on receiving Social Security checks forever! They have to die! They must no go on living! Phil, it's your patriotic duty! The very existence of America as a nation is at stake! And if you refuse to do this thing, you are out, and I'll get someone who will obey a presidential order!"

Phil Coleman sat up in the chair, squared his shoulders and declared, "Okay, I'll do it."

"Good man, Phil, good man! You are a true American! Now, I want this job done just right! I want that townhouse to be blown sky high, but I don't want the buildings on each side of it to be damaged. Can you do it?"

"Yes, Mr. President, I am sure I can. I'll have my best explosives expert do it. I guarantee you a neat surgical job. The buildings on each side will not be damaged one bit."

"When will you have your men do it?"

"In three days that townhouse will be a heap of rubble."

And so it was, with Gilbert, Carol, Ivor and Elmo buried under that rubble.

And with that explosion ended the dream of immortality for the human race.